PRAISE FOR CLAIRE McGOWAN

'A knockout new talent you should read immediately.'

—Lee Child

'It really had me gripped.'

—Marian Keyes, international bestselling author of *Grown Ups*

'The definition of an utterly absorbing page turner. Richly drawn out characters, a compelling plot, and a finale that will keep you guessing.'

—John Marrs, bestselling author of *What Lies Between Us* and *The One*

'A real nail-biter of a thriller that gets darker and more twisted with every page. If you liked *What You Did*, you'll love *The Push*.'

—Erin Kelly, *Sunday Times* bestselling author of *He Said/She Said*

'Absorbing, timely, and beautifully written, *What You Did* is a superior psychological thriller from a major talent.'

—Mark Edwards, bestselling author of *The Retreat* and *Here to Stay*

'I loved this story. The flesh-and-blood characters, dry wit, and brilliant plotting are every bit as enjoyable as *Big Little Lies*.'

—Louise Candlish, bestselling author of *Our House* and *The Other Passenger*

D1350358

'A perfectly plotted murder mystery that had me hooked from the first page. Twisty domestic suspense that's perfect for fans of *Big Little Lies*.'

—Lisa Gray, bestselling author of the Jessica Shaw series

'I haven't flown through a book so quickly in a very long time. It delivers on every single level.'

—Caz Frear, bestselling author of the DC Cat Kinsella series

'What a nail-biting, just-one-more-page-I-can't-put-it-down rollercoaster of suspense!'

—Steph Broadribb, author of *Deep Down Dead*

'Smart, sassy, and satisfyingly twisty.'

—Sarah Hilary, author of the DI Marnie Rome series

'Huge fun with some very dark moments and brilliantly awful characters. Excellent, twisty plotting.'

—Harriet Tyce, author of *Blood Orange*

'A brilliantly observed and compelling thriller.'

—Anna Mazzola, author of *The Story Keeper*

'A rollercoaster read, full of thrills and one spectacular spill!'

—Liz Nugent, bestselling author of *Skin Deep*

'*What You Did* is a triumph, a gripping story of the secrets and lies that can underpin even the closest friendships. Put some time aside – this is one you'll want to read in a single sitting.'

—Kevin Wignall, bestselling author of *A Death in Sweden* and *The Traitor's Story*

'Will keep you riveted until its breathless finish.'

—*Sunday Mirror*

'A meticulous thriller full of twists and false turns.'

—*Crime Time*

'Creepy and oh-so-clever.'

—*Fabulous* magazine

'A fantastic and intense book that grips you right from the very first line.'

—*We Love This Book*

'McGowan's pacey, direct style ensures that the twists come thick and fast.'

—*The Irish Times*

'A riveting police thriller.'

—*Woman* (Pick of the Week)

'Taut plotting and assured writing.'

—*Good Housekeeping*

'You'll be desperate to know what happened and how everything will turn out.'

—*The Sun*

'An excellent murder mystery.'

—*Bella*

'Plenty of twists and turns keep you hooked.'

—*Crime Monthly*

I KNOW
YOU

ALSO BY CLAIRE McGOWAN

The Fall
What You Did
The Other Wife
The Push

Paula Maguire series

The Lost
The Dead Ground
The Silent Dead
A Savage Hunger
Blood Tide
The Killing House

Writing as Eva Woods

The Thirty List
The Ex Factor
How to be Happy
The Lives We Touch
The Man I Can't Forget

I KNOW YOU

CLAIRE McGOWAN

Text copyright © 2021 by Claire McGowan
All rights reserved.

Published by Thomas & Mercer, Seattle

www.apub.com

Amazon, the Amazon logo, and Thomas & Mercer are trademarks of Amazon.com, Inc., or its affiliates.

ISBN-13: 9781542019972
ISBN-10: 1542019974

Cover design by Heike Schüssler

Printed in the United States of America

I KNOW
YOU

Rachel

What would you do if you found a dead body? Call the police? Check for a pulse? Flag down a passer-by for help, tearful but responsible, gulping in air? You might imagine yourself with a blanket round your shoulders, cradling a mug of hot sweet tea, helpfully giving statements to uniformed officers. Being interviewed in the local paper sometime later. *Such a terrible shock. Their poor family.*

You probably wouldn't do what I did, on that bright cold morning when I emerged from the trees into the clearing, Brandy already beginning to tense and whine on her lead – dogs know, they always know. When I spotted it, at first I thought someone had dropped a coat while out on a morning run. Then I saw the white hand, turned upwards among dead leaves, the fingers curling in towards the palm, the wedding ring gleaming on the fourth finger.

I stood there for a moment. It was just after 7.30 a.m. The forest was quiet all around me, only the calls of birds and the rustle of the breeze in the trees, barely light yet, no one else nearby – or so I thought at the time. I didn't even let myself think, *This is a dead body.* I didn't call the police or raise the alarm or do any of the things you're supposed to do. Only one thought was in my head: *Get out of here. Don't let them catch you. Run.*

And so I did, Brandy yelping behind me as I tugged on her lead. I turned out of the clearing and ran back down the path and out of the woods and across the green and up the garden path to my cottage, where I fumbled the lock, opened and shut the door, and dropped the lead with shaking hands. Then I sank down on the sofa, without even taking off my walking boots. What I had forgotten most of all was how quiet a crime scene is. No breath but yours. The faint breeze that stirs over lifeless hair and clothes. The glassy, open emptiness of dead eyes. It's almost peaceful, a violent death, before they come in with heavy boots and tape and cameras. Before it becomes a story, out there in the world for people to read. Before it's something that happened to you.

But no, it wasn't real, it didn't happen. I hadn't seen it. Nothing was there. Still I didn't call the police or tell anyone, never mind go back to check if they were still alive – I didn't want to think about any of that. In fact, I did nothing at all. This might seem crazy to you, irresponsible, indefensible. But you don't know what you'd do, if it wasn't the first dead body you had found.

The ironic thing was, I had actually been happy right before I found it. Maybe happier than I had been in twenty years. I was walking in my favourite part of the woods, the cinnamon smell of leaves underfoot telling me autumn was on its way, with its promise of open fires and forgiving jumpers. I had Brandy on the lead, her small snuffling breaths the only sound, that constant strain on the collar that's to be expected with a beagle. She had smelled something already, probably, but I hadn't known that then. It was one of my best times of the day, just her and me, the trusting way she'd come to heel when I called, despite her searching nature. The faint trotting sound of her paws beside my boots.

I had felt pleasantly muzzy with sleep, looking forward to seeing Alex again that night. As I walked, I was thinking about his firm chest, the snarl of hair there I liked to tangle my fingers in, the warm smell of his neck. The way I'd palm my face to his back when he slept, holding on tight. He had stayed at mine two nights ago, and we'd woken up late, teasing each other about how slow we were to get out of bed. When I got up to shower, he'd pulled me back into bed, kissing me hard, starting things up again. He'd made me tea while I was in the bathroom, and I'd stood at the door in my dressing gown to wave him down the path (Audrey next door getting a good gawp), and he'd waved back at me as he reversed his van out.

It was going somewhere, wasn't it? When I thought of it, I'd feel a pleasant lurch in the pit of my stomach, followed by a burst of worry. Things weren't ideal, of course – and I would have thought about Anna here, I'm sure. She had been playing on my mind since our run-in the week before. She wasn't supposed to know about Alex and me – too soon after their split, and likely to muddy the waters with the divorce, he felt. But somehow she had found out, and confronted me in town. She didn't want him being with me, and was threatening to keep the house and stop him seeing his son if he didn't end it, Alex said.

Sometimes it frustrated me – the first man I'd ever felt this way about, and he was technically still married, embroiled in an acrimonious break-up. But what was perfect at our age? All I knew was I finally felt something I never had before. True desire, true, dizzying passion. My stomach turned over when he smiled at me, when he rolled up the sleeves of a shirt to show his tanned forearms. I hoarded little moments from my day to tell him, funny things the dogs had done or Marilyn's sayings, and I wanted to hear everything about his day too. What he'd had to eat, what he'd watched on TV, which trees he had chopped down at work and which were safe. What part of the Lakes he'd driven to on jobs, picnicking by the side of a tarn or on a stony

3

beach, perhaps. After years of worrying if something was wrong with me, because I always lost interest so fast in relationships, rolling my eyes as a man told me the dull details of his life, I had finally found it. Alex. I'd even let myself make plans – maybe we'd get a place together, with a room for his son, Sam, to stay in. Sam would love Brandy. Anna would settle down eventually, meet someone else. We'd be happy.

Looking back on that moment, I wish I could shake some sense into the woman in the red coat with the dog on the lead, breathing in the fresh after-rain smell of the woods. Tell her that she of all people should have known never to let down her guard. She should have realised you can't make plans. Because you never know when the safe little world you've so carefully put together will fall apart like a house of cards. And then I saw it in the leaves, the clothes, the white hand, and that was that. My life as I knew it was over.

I know it sounds strange, what I did. That instead of calling the police I came home, fed Brandy, tidied the kitchen, made porridge for my breakfast, ate it on the bench in my small back garden, soaking up the last of the October sun. Several hours passed. I hoovered, mopped the floor, though it wasn't my usual day for cleaning. I kept my body moving and my mind totally blank, as I had learned to in the past. People do strange things at times like this. Your routine keeps you running like a train on tracks, even when the engine's busted. All the same, I was sure it would come, the knock at the door. I didn't turn on the radio as I normally would, knowing at some point I'd hear the words *body found in woodland*.

I shouldn't have run away, I know. Things might not have gone so badly for me if I'd just behaved normally. But that would have required my brain to take it in, to accept I had once again been the person to find a dead body. The proverbial dog-walker, always first on the scene. I had a talent for it, it seemed.

It was around eleven when the doorbell finally went. I took my time. Rinsed my plate in the sink, tidied my hair in the small mirror I'd found in the British Heart Foundation shop. Slipped my feet into ballet pumps, my toes finding their own impressions in the leather. Outside, black-clad figures, a buzz of radios. The police. Gentler in this country, at least. No guns. The bell went again. I opened the door.

They were quite polite about it. Two officers, a man and a woman, neither a day over thirty. 'Rachel Caldwell?'

'Yes?' My heart was hammering in my chest, but I tried to keep my voice steady.

'We understand you walked your dog in the woods earlier?' Over their shoulders, I could see that a small crowd had gathered near the edge of the trees. I recognised a few of my neighbours from the nearby cottages. I knew not to lie – someone would have seen me, it's a small town, and I took Brandy on the same path each morning, both of us creatures of habit.

'Well, yes, I do most days. Is something wrong?'

'I'm afraid there's been . . . an incident. Would you mind if we came in to ask you a few questions?' That was the woman, young and pretty, with red hair and a cinnamon-sprinkle of freckles over her nose. Would I mind, she'd said. How nice to pretend I had a choice.

'I didn't see anything,' I said. They couldn't prove I'd found it – I couldn't yet think about it as a person – and it was too hard to explain why I had seen it but run away. Normal people don't do that.

Stupid of me, to lie so early on. I should have said nothing, not until they actually arrested me at least. Got a lawyer right away, watched my every word. Me of all people, I should have known that. But I didn't want to look guilty. I thought I could play dumb. Stupid, stupid. The two officers exchanged a look. The man – not much more than a boy, to my eyes – said, 'Well. If we can just come in, hopefully we can clear a few things up.'

'Well, all right.' As I stood back to let them in, Brandy came padding in to investigate, and I thought about what might happen

5

to her if they took me away. The emergency folder was in the locked bottom drawer of my desk, explaining what to do with the house and Brandy and my things, who to contact. The key was in a vase on the mantelpiece. If the worst came to the worst, I would tell someone where to find it – Marilyn, most likely. It had always been a risk, keeping the folder in the house, with the information it contained, but I couldn't bear to think of no one knowing the truth, no one on the outside fighting for me. We weren't there yet. This was just questions. I stroked Brandy and gently edged her back into the kitchen – she gave a small whine, as if she knew something was up. I shut the door on her, feeling guilty at her surprise. Then I obediently followed the officers over to the sofa, sat down at right angles to them in the armchair, hands laid lightly on my knees.

The woman officer took out her notebook and flicked through it. I found it impossible to read them, if they suspected me or this was just routine or what. 'So, we're PC Darcy Chevening and PC Sam Price. Your name is Rachel Caldwell?'

'Yes.' Legally, it was true.

'And what do you do, Rachel?' PC Price, who had spots along the line of his collar. Last time, the police officers had seemed so many years my senior. Time had moved on.

'I work at the dog shelter outside town.' Not for pay, but they didn't need to know that. 'I've been there about ten years.'

'And before that?'

'Um – I was born in London. Moved around for a few years, then here.'

'You have family in the area?'

'No. It was just me and Mum and she passed years back.' Poor Jenna. Never much of a mother to me, but all the same the fact of her death could catch me unawares at times like this, a small punch to the solar plexus.

'I'm sorry to hear that.' Perfunctory. Making notes. 'Talk us through your morning walk, Rachel.' PC Chevening again.

'Um – I left about a quarter past seven, that's when Brandy starts getting restless, and we went on our normal route. A quick turn is all, I take her later for longer.'

'Brandy is a beagle?' PC Price, glancing over at the kitchen.

'Yes.'

'They need walking a lot? And they have a good sense of smell?'

'They'll follow their noses anywhere.' As I said it I remembered the pull on the lead, her slight whine as we entered the clearing. It was our usual path, so I didn't think anything of it.

'So she would pick up on a strange scent – like, say, a body?'

There it was.

'There's a *body*?' I blinked my eyes wide. Good. That was what a normal person would say. An innocent person.

No confirmation. 'She'd have smelled something like that, yes?' PC Chevening. I kept forgetting their names and having to look at their badges. I realised my hands were clasped tight together, and tried to relax them.

'Maybe. She does run after smells a lot, all beagles do, but I kept her on the lead.'

'So you saw nothing?'

I pretended to think. 'Not that I can recall.'

'Very short walk, was it? Witnesses said you came right out again, almost running.'

Witnesses? Bloody Audrey, I bet.

'I – needed the loo. Forgot to go before we left.' No one could disprove that either. 'Why are you here – just because I was in the woods? Lots of people go in the woods.'

I heard a nervy shake in my voice as I said it. I saw them exchange another look, and various scenarios flared across my mind. Someone had seen me in the clearing. Maybe there was even a picture of me approaching *it* and running, stumbling out – or worse, video footage. People could film things on their phones nowadays. Maybe I had touched it in my shock and not remembered, left my fingerprints or hairs or some other trace. Either way, I could tell from the way they were looking at me: somehow, they knew I had found the body. And that I had lied about it.

PC Chevening put her notebook away. 'OK, Rachel. We may well want to talk to you again, OK?'

I didn't understand for a moment, lost in my worst imaginings. 'That's it?'

'For now. Thank you.'

They were going. They had suspicions, perhaps, but clearly they couldn't prove anything yet. Anyway, it wasn't a crime to find a body and not report it – was it?

As I watched them walk to their car, I saw that a large and muddy jeep was drawing up nearby. Marilyn. She got out, came towards me, and I was so pleased to see her ruddy cheeks, her untidy greying hair, brown cords held up with a safety pin and covered in dog hair, that I almost stumbled into her arms, hairs notwithstanding. Her eyes looked red and swollen. She was five years my senior, at most, but she took care of me as if it was more.

'Rachel! What on earth happened? I know you go through the woods on your walk, so I thought I'd see if you were all right. Did you get *arrested*?' Was that what people would think? I could see Audrey peering between her expensive slatted blinds, and she abruptly withdrew as I caught her eye.

'No, I wasn't arrested. Just . . . they were asking if I saw something in the woods today. There was . . . there was a body, apparently.' I said the last in a whisper.

'I know. You didn't . . . find it, did you?'

I don't know why I told her the truth. Perhaps because I still didn't understand it myself, that this had happened and I was now involved.

'I – I saw something, but I didn't really – I never touched it or anything. I just ran, I panicked.'

Marilyn drew back, biting her lip in distress. I tried not to watch crime drama on TV as it was often so wrong in the details, but a few times Marilyn had invited me over for the evening and she was a big fan. She'd probably have been quite excited to find a body.

'But Rachel! Why didn't you call the police? Or at least tell someone?'

That was the question I couldn't answer, not without revealing too much. 'I don't know. Just didn't.'

She was looking at me closely. 'You didn't see who it was?' She lowered her voice and I realised I had been talking too loudly, that Audrey might have heard me admit my lie. I drew Marilyn inside and shut the door, with a strange reluctance. Even though this was my own home, and I wasn't restrained or locked in, the old panic was rising in me, flooding my blood. *Get out of here. Run.*

'No – I don't know if it was a man or a woman, even.'

'Oh.'

'Why? Do you know?' A cold feeling was sweeping through me. 'Who was it?' I pictured a heap of clothes among leaves – jeans, feet in scuffed trainers. A small pale hand, the ring, the nails painted green – a woman then, though I hadn't registered it at the time, or else I had blocked it out. How could Marilyn know who it was, already?

'Rachel,' said Marilyn hesitantly. 'They're saying it's Anna. Anna's been murdered. They've already told Alex. He – he rang me.' Her voice broke, stoical Marilyn, who never cried when we had to put a dog down, who rarely showed emotion at all.

Anna. And I had found her, and run away. I knew then that I was in even worse trouble than I'd thought.

Casey

August 2000

David. Abby. Carson. Madison. The Safran family. I was reciting it in my head as the plane swooped into LAX. I'd never been on one before, and had overdone it on the free bar. Now I was dry-mouthed and nauseous. Nervous too. My first time leaving the UK and it was to come all this way by myself, to work as a nanny for a Hollywood producer and his wife, an actress. Madison was five. The baby was a few months or so. I didn't like kids much, but Jenna said it was a shrewd move, getting this six-month contract. It was her who'd pushed me to study child development at sixth-form college, alongside drama. She'd even brought home the application form for the American nanny agency, Little Helpers.

'Get out to the States, get your visa, then bag a part in a film. Dazzle him. He can take you places.'

They wanted an English nanny because the mother, Abby, had family from London. Probably they imagined big baby carriages and strict schedules, not me in my vest top with my copy of *More!* magazine, borderline addicted to Sunny Delight. But still. One of the many things Jenna had taught me was that people buy what you sell them, if you sell it hard enough. They were American. They wouldn't know that my version of Englishness was working class, from Watford way.

Jenna had not come to the airport with me, because she claimed the Tube made her too nervous. She'd seen me off at the station in Watford, sucking on one of her habitual fags. 'Well, that's you away then.'

'Yeah.' I waited for any words of advice, from a mother waving her only child goodbye for six months in a foreign country.

Jenna took another drag. It was August, but she was huddled in her moth-eaten leopard-print coat. Bone-thin, she was always cold. It was seven in the morning, but she'd put on her eyelashes, her hair extensions, her fake nails. Always on. 'This is your chance, Case. Find a way to stay there. Get a foothold, yeah?'

'I'll try.'

'Come here, then.' She pulled me to her in a brusque hug, and I breathed in her smell of cigarettes and Charlie Silver. My mother. I'd lugged my case across London by myself, found my way to the terminal alone. It had always been just me and Jenna – she was vague about who my dad was – and sometimes it felt more like just me.

An announcement came on over the endless sucking sound of the air on the plane. Unfamiliar American vowels. We were landing. What if no one was there to meet me? What if they didn't let me into the country? There were horror stories on the nanny geosites I'd surfed at the library, people being turned away at customs for the wrong paperwork. I felt around me for my things – Blistex lip balm, pink hoody, copies of *More!* and *Bliss* magazine, their covers plastered with the contestants from *Big Brother*, a new TV show my friends had suddenly become addicted to. I would not be able to keep up in America, and the sense of distance swept through me, leaving me suddenly desolate. But there was no way back now. I put away my brand-new Nokia, which I wasn't even sure would work in America. I brushed crumbs off myself and blinked open my gummy eyes. I was here.

◆ ◆ ◆

Trooping through customs sent my heart rate sky-high. It wasn't like home. The police had guns here! I'd never seen a gun in real life before. Even without stepping outside I could tell I was abroad – a different smell in the air, dry and hot. The loos were weird, with big wide bowls and low doors. The border agent gave me a bored look and asked some questions about my visa and job plans. I answered nervously, even though what I was saying was true. Would they arrest me? Send me home? Instead he said, 'Welcome to the US,' and waved me through. I waited for my case, a huge pink one Jenna had found in the market, worried it wouldn't turn up, but it did, and I lugged it out. Tiredness made me woolly – it was 3 a.m. back home. Was there anyone? To my relief, I saw a Latino man holding up a sign that said *Casey Adams*. I came to a halt in front of him. 'Hi! That's me. Are you Mr Safran – David?' How dumb I was. I'd soon learn that people like David didn't drive you from the airport themselves.

He gave me a look. 'José. Driver, gardener.'

'Oh – uh, OK. *Gracias.*' I'd learned some Spanish on a trip to Magaluf with college friends, but he didn't respond. He took my case from me and I started to worry I'd need to tip him. We went outside – a brief, ferocious blast of petrolly heat – and into the car, a big people-carrier that was so cold inside I saw goosebumps rising on my arms.

'Water in back of seat,' he said, starting the engine.

'Thank you.' Thirsty, I drank from the bottle. It tasted of plastic, but I was so dehydrated I was grateful anyway. I looked out through the tinted glass for my first glimpse of LA. It seemed to be all cars and flyovers and, in the smoggy distance, high-rise blocks. No palm trees. No sea view. Tiredness overwhelmed me and I sank back against the chill leather, closing my eyes.

◆ ◆ ◆

'Casey? Are you *asleep*?'

I sat up in bed, for a second unsure of where I was, where in the world, where in time, all of it. A woman stood over me, wearing tight Lycra gym clothes, holding a baby in her arms. Abby and Carson. My boss and one of the children I was supposed to take care of.

'Oh – sorry. Jet lag.' I looked at the travel clock on my bedside table; it was four o'clock in the afternoon. The middle of the night back home. The air in the room was chill and stale, although I knew it would be scorching outside.

Abby looked at me with distaste. She had been gorgeous once, but she'd done something to her face that had left it just a bit out of whack, like that of a robot. Her hair was long and streaked blonde over copper, up in a ponytail. She placed the baby on my bed, setting him down like a handbag. 'You should be over that by now.'

I had been in America for two days now, and it was hitting me hard. I'd never known tiredness like it, plus the baby slept in a room off mine and he seemed to wake up every hour during the night. 'Sorry.'

Abby turned, her ponytail slicing the air like a scythe. 'I have yoga. And Madison needs to learn her lines for the morning. Oh, and David will be home at seven for dinner.'

I hadn't realised that part of my job would involve cooking dinner – I could barely heat up Super Noodles. But apparently it did, on top of caring for the baby and Madison, keeping the house clean on days the 'maid' didn't come, running errands all over town

13

– which I was yet to do because I'd never driven on the right before – and anything else Abby wanted from me, which was a lot. Abby herself was rarely home, and when she was she was often asleep, which made her carping at me even more unfair. I knew from snooping in her bathroom that her sleep was usually chemically induced. I had yet to see anything of LA except for a supermarket Abby had driven us to, and certainly no celebrities. Brad and Jen looked out at me from the cover of the magazines I'd brought over, as if to mock me with their glamour, so near yet untouchable. Carson had already chewed several pages of one.

I dragged myself up, as Abby's footsteps rattled down the wooden corridor and stairs and the front door slammed, followed by the sound of the car, the blip of the electric gates in the distance. She was gone. Carson lay there looking up at me, a worried expression on his face as he gnawed on one fist. He was six months old, and I was frantically trying to remember what I'd learned about babies at college, wishing I had paid more attention. He didn't talk yet and wouldn't walk for a while, so at least if I put him down he stayed in the same place. Unlike Madison.

Oh God, Madison. I looked up and she was in the doorway. Her sly little face, her golden curls, her frilled pink dress – that was what she wore for a day round the house! I hated all of it. Before this, I wouldn't have thought it was possible to hate a five-year-old, but I was wrong.

'Why are you in bed?' She stared me, just like her mother had.

'I'm tired, Madison. From my big plane journey.'

'Mommy said you have to get up now.'

'I know, I will.'

'And you have to make dinner, Mommy said. In time for Daddy.'

'I know that, Madison.' I got out of bed, with some effort, and as I disturbed Carson he started to cry. The sound of it seemed to shatter inside my skull. Did all babies make a noise like that? The kind you literally couldn't be in the same room as for too long, or you'd go insane?

She raised her voice. 'Carson is crying. You scared him.'

'Yes, Madison, thank you, I can hear.' I picked him up, jiggled him, which made him cry harder. Madison gave a sigh of deep contempt, then turned on her heels and darted down the corridor, her frills and curls bouncing. I knew she would tell Abby everything I'd done, all the ways I was failing. Carson's wailing went up a notch, my top stained with his dribble. How could I cope with six months of this?

Rachel

Marilyn stayed a while, drank a coffee, saying the same things over and over, as you do when you're in shock. They had been school-friends, her and Anna, and I could see the loss punched through her. After a while I heard an engine splutter and die outside, and saw there was a white van parking up, almost blocking the small dead-end lane I live on, on the outskirts of town where it's swallowed into the woods. My heart stuttered in my chest again. I stirred, not wanting Marilyn to see who it was. Not now.

'You're so sweet to come and check on me,' I said. 'I'd better take Brandy out now. Not much of a walk earlier.' The dog, released from the kitchen, was curled up against Marilyn on the sofa, snuffling gently. 'Will you be all right?'

'Oh, don't worry about me, darling. What about you? You've had a nasty shock.'

How good she was, with her broken veins and the frizz of grey around her temples.

'I'm OK. Thank you.' She reached over to squeeze my hand, which I knew must be as cold as ice, and it meant so much, that small gesture. My own mother would never have done that, and Anna had been Marilyn's friend since primary school, and now she was dead. 'I – I'm really sorry, Marilyn. I know you were close.' I couldn't bring myself to say Anna's name.

She twisted her face in a pained smile. 'I can't take it in, really. Any of it. That it's her – I keep thinking it must be some mistake.'

'I know. Me too.' It couldn't be happening again, could it? Part of me hoped it could all be cleared up somehow. But it couldn't. Anna was dead. Alex's wife, Sam's mum. Things would never be all right again.

I waited till she drove away before I walked down my garden path. I wondered if she'd noticed the van, registered who it belonged to. When she'd gone, Alex got out, and I went to meet him, arms wrapped around myself, still freezing. I wondered if I'd ever feel warm again.

'Hey,' I said, awkward.

He blinked at me, and even in the circumstances my body began to respond, thinking: *God, he's handsome, he's so handsome.* The slice of blue eyes in his tanned face, now pale with shock, the rake of dark hair falling over his forehead. He was dressed in his work clothes, the overalls pulled down to the waist, revealing a tight blue T-shirt smeared with grass and soil. How I wanted him. How fragile this felt, our new relationship, like one of the seedlings I nurtured outside the back door. I jerked my head towards the house – we needed to go inside. There was a flurry of police activity around the entrance to the woods on the other side of the green, people in white suits unfurling tape to block it off. It wouldn't do to be seen with the husband of the victim.

Once inside, I saw him take a breath. 'Rach! Oh my God.'

'I . . .' Already he was moving towards me, arms open, and I rested my head on his shoulder, so grateful he had come, that even in his grief he'd thought to find me. *Thank you, thank you.* Something I didn't deserve, yet again. I breathed in his smell, sweat

17

and tree sap and the outdoors. My hands clutched in his T-shirt. 'I'm so sorry. God, it's – I can't believe it.'

'No. It doesn't seem real.'

'Is it really Anna? The police came – I think they're questioning everyone along here – but they didn't tell me anything.' I felt a shudder go through him.

'Her dad identified her an hour back.'

'Jesus. And it was definitely – it wasn't natural causes?'

'She was stabbed.' His voice flat and factual. 'Martin said – they tried to tidy her up, but – her throat . . . they'd cut her throat.' His voice broke. 'Jesus Christ. Who'd do a thing like that?'

'Oh.' I felt sick. It went straight to my guts before my brain had time to even process it. I had seen it before, a woman with her throat cut, the dark stain spreading out beneath the chin – I could picture it all too well. Not this time – the leaves had drifted over Anna's body and I didn't remember seeing anything but her hand, small and white, her muddy trainers sticking out. But it was the same. Oh God. 'I was in the woods earlier, with Brandy.' He would find that out soon, so better if I told him.

He pulled away to look at me. 'You didn't see her?'

I needed to keep my own story straight. 'No, I just – I spotted something in the clearing, I thought maybe a dropped coat or something and I just – I don't know. Something came over me. I ran.'

His brow furrowed. 'And what, you just came back here? You didn't call anyone?'

'No. I didn't know it was her.' Not that it made a difference. I should have called the police anyway, whether or not the pile of clothes in the clearing, the small white hand, had belonged to a woman I knew. A woman who, the last time I'd seen her, had screamed in my face and told me to stay away from her husband. Would the police know that by now? Someone would have told

18

them, surely, plenty of people had witnessed our argument. And hadn't I wished her gone, sometimes, after that, in the privacy of my head? Not like this, though. Maybe just moved away or happily remarried, whatever made her step out of the way of Alex and me. Was that why they'd come to question me, the row? But then why hadn't they asked about it?

He stroked my cheek, tender, bereft. 'Why did you do it?'

I shook my head. I couldn't explain without telling him everything, and I never wanted him to find out. 'I don't know. I panicked. I didn't even process what I'd seen. I'm so sorry, Alex. I just – believe me, I had no idea at all it was her. I didn't know it was a person, not really.'

He sighed, ran his hands over his face. His eyes, like Marilyn's, were red and bloodshot. Anna's death would devastate so many people. She had lived in this town all her life, like Alex. Whereas me – I was just an interloper, in his life and in Coldwater. 'Rach, it doesn't look good. Anna dead, and you ran away and didn't call it in.'

'I know that!' I pulled away and went to the kettle. I needed tea, something warm and soothing. 'God, if I could go back and do it differently . . . But it's too late now. I just – I'm sorry. I'm so, so sorry.' The police hadn't arrested me, at least. They couldn't prove I had seen her, could they? And I didn't touch her, so there wouldn't be prints or anything like that. I had to hold on to these small bits of hope, although I knew all too well how twisty physical evidence could be. It's nothing like as concrete as we all think, from watching TV crime shows. It's all open to interpretation, and with the right spin it can be written into a story that will condemn you. March you right to Death Row.

Having let myself think those two words, the worst ones I could imagine, my knees buckled under me, and I leaned on the counter for support. I fumbled for the kettle, the rush of the water calming me enough to let other thoughts in. Hold on to the good things. Brandy twisting around my legs, her body warm and reassuring. The time I'd met Alex, when he'd just been a local tree surgeon come to look at the half-rotted oak in my back garden, and how I'd made him tea and my hands were shaking then too, because I already knew there was something between us, some kind of heat or understanding or whatever it is when you look at a stranger and feel they can see inside you. And I'd been right, hadn't I? Until this, until now, things had been so good between us, despite . . .

'Oh my God! What about Sam?' I hadn't even considered him. So selfish. I was appalled at myself, worrying about my own skin when a little boy had lost his mother. 'Where is he? Does he know?'

'He's at school. I have to get him soon. I'll have to – tell him.' Alex leaned against the wall, and I saw how tired he looked, as if he hadn't slept at all. Shock can do that to you.

'Where was Sam earlier, though – you had him?'

Of course, I hadn't seen Alex last night because it was his time with his son, at his flat in town. So Anna had been alone at her house all night. Or had she been with someone? Her house – Alex's house, really – was on the other side of the woods, at least two miles from my side. Had she walked into the forest alone, or had someone dragged her there? It was a long way to carry something as heavy as a body. There's a reason we have the phrase *a dead weight*. Had she been killed very early today, or late last night? Her trainers were muddy – did that mean she'd gone there of her own volition, for a morning walk, then been surprised by some stranger with a knife? You hear of things like that happening.

'I had him, took him to school before we – before I heard. He was fine this morning – wanted to bring his Thomas train with him to school. I guess he never will be again.' Alex's voice was flat with pain.

I pressed my hands hard on the worktop. Right now, Sam was carrying on as normal, at school, learning fractions or building Lego or whatever it was they did there. He had no idea his mother was dead. That he would never see her again, that his young life was changed so horribly for ever. Like me back then, walking down that hot street, no idea that any second I would open a door and enter a nightmare I had never really left. I'd thought I had, but now it had returned. The worst part was, it felt inevitable. Of course it hadn't ended, not really. After all, I had never been punished for what I did, not properly, and now perhaps it was time.

The Death of a Child Star
from *People* magazine, March 2001

Madison Safran may have been only five years old when she died, but she already had an agent, a manager, and substantial earnings from film and TV. From playing a toddler on CHANGE OF LIFE to the follow-on milk baby in the popular commercials, Madison's cherubic smile and curls had made her one of Hollywood's top earners under eighteen, with several pageant wins to her name as well. Her mother, Abigail, had been a TV starlet, appearing in several shows and some 90s teen horrors before marrying the producer of one, David Safran, and retiring at the age of thirty to start a family. Four years later she was pregnant again with Carson, her second child.

Madison would not live past five, or Abigail past thirty-five. Both were killed last year in their Hollywood Hills "house of horror," Madison smothered with a pillow and Abigail stabbed with a kitchen knife, her throat slashed. David Safran was found on the hallway floor, shot in the stomach. All had other injuries too—cuts, bruises, and for Madison, a cigarette burn on her inner arm. Who had done this?

No one survived to tell the tale except their British nanny, Casey Adams, nineteen. Ms Adams claimed she had returned home from walking the baby down the street, to find the door slightly ajar and the three family members dead. With Mrs Safran's blood on her feet and tracked throughout the house, she hid in the cupboard with the baby and called 911, claiming she was afraid the killer might still be in the house. However, neighbors did not see anyone else arrive at or leave the property, and there were no signs of forced entry. Ms Adams' prints were found on the gun used to kill the father of the family, David Safran. Her trial will begin next month.

Rachel

The day of the body – day one, as it would be referred to in the police investigation – was my day off from the shelter. The next morning I got up as normal, when Brandy started her gentle whines and woofs on the dot of six. Dogs don't understand about lying in, and Alex wasn't there to keep me in bed, pulling me back against his warm, hard body. I wondered how he had broken the news to Sam. And, selfishly, I wondered what it meant for us, long term. We had known each other only a few months – could it survive something like this, me stumbling across the body of his murdered wife?

Before it all happened, when I was young, I hated getting up early. I would have slept till eleven every day if I could. But that had been beaten out of me, and I had changed, in so many ways. Now I woke up every day with the dawn and lay there in bed, usually alone, stretching my legs out to feel the width of it, feeling grateful I wasn't in a narrow metal bunk with the sounds of women screaming outside. Listening to the silence of the house, birds in the trees opposite, Brandy stirring downstairs, the odd quiet *woof* to check if I was awake and had remembered she needed breakfast. I tried so hard not to take these things for granted, but in the end, maybe it's just human nature to do exactly that. Lately, I had become used to Alex lying beside me some mornings, and I would quietly watch him for a while, the way his lashes quivered on his cheeks, how he slept with an arm thrown over his forehead. The weight of him on the other side of the bed, anchoring me down. I shouldn't have got used to it. It might never happen again now.

Forgetting myself, I had snapped on the radio as I fed the dog, only for the news bulletin to come on, starting with, '*The body of a woman has been found in woodland near Coldwater, in Cumbria. She has been named by police as Anna Devine . . .*' I turned it off. It would do me no good to follow the coverage of the case. I didn't take Brandy for a morning walk that day – I couldn't face going past the same spot where Anna had lain, and as we left the house for work, Brandy trotting on her lead, I averted my eyes from the entrance to the forest. A strip of police tape hung from a tree, and the white-suited people were still coming and going, various police vans parked nearby. They had taken her out, I assumed, if her father had identified her. What a thing, to see your daughter dead and butchered on a morgue slab. I tried to keep hold of that amid my simmering panic. This was not about me. I was just in the wrong place at the wrong time, and I'd done something stupid, but not fatally so. For Alex, and Sam, and Anna's parents, this was the worst thing imaginable.

The shelter was just a few minutes from my house, on the outskirts of the town, in the shadow of the mountain. Every day I felt lucky that I'd fetched up here, in the Lake District, where I had no connections and had only been once before. It could not have been more different from where I'd lived for years, the dry and dusty heat of the desert. Here the air was always a little damp, water all around and seeping into me. It helped me feel calm, to know that I'd never be so dry and parched again, I'd never have to worry about passing out under a merciless sun.

Approaching the shelter along the lake path, a blast of sunlight cut through the drizzle. I felt calmer as I walked towards the low and, to be honest, ugly breeze-block building with a small car park attached. I could already hear the dogs barking and yelping. Feeding time. I usually brought Brandy along, since it wasn't fair to leave her alone all day, but I felt a little bad about it. It didn't seem right that she was allowed to sit with me under my desk and leave at the end of the day, while the other dogs had to stay in their pens, behind bars. Like the guards, the way they'd sometimes seemed like our friends, but they weren't, because they had keys and we didn't.

Marilyn was behind her desk in our little office, checking paperwork. She wore the same dog-haired gilet and trousers as the day before. She looked up, and I could read the concern on her face, despite her own loss. 'Are you all right? Hello, Brandy, sweetheart.'

'Yes, fine.'

In fact, I had barely slept – paranoid about another knock at the door – but I was determined to put on a brave face. I had simply done something silly, nothing actually wrong. This was the UK, not America. Our justice system, I hoped, actually functioned. The police would see I had just panicked, that Anna's death was nothing to do with me. Maybe, if forced to, I would even tell them why I'd run. They were the police, they'd have to keep it a secret, wouldn't they?

I had never told Marilyn about me and Alex, reasoning that it was early days, our relationship still new and insecure. I would surely have told her at some point, that I was seeing – or was it just sleeping with? – the estranged husband of her old friend. But now that friend was dead.

'How are *you*?' I said, trying to remember this was not about me.

Marilyn didn't really do emotion. She winced and looked away. 'Oh, love, I don't know, it's awful, isn't it? Poor little Sam.' I heard the break in her voice. 'Such a terrible thing. She was such a lovely person – I can't think who'd want to . . . well.'

A lovely person who had screamed at me in the street. Marilyn didn't know about that, I assumed, and I wanted to keep it that way.

I put on my plastic apron and opened the door into the pens area, which always smelled strongly yeasty, like a pet shop. The dogs went wild to see me, some even throwing themselves at the bars, barking and yelping. A sound I still found upsetting, after all this time. Bars. Locks. 'Shh, shh now.' I reached through to stroke a few heads, murmur soothing words. These dogs had been through hell, some of them. Starved or beaten or left in a sack at the side of the road. We rescued a lot from the lakes too, tied up or weighted down with stones – and then there were the drowned ones, the ones we didn't find in time. Why would you do it like that? If you'd decided something had to die, that its life was nothing but cruelty and pain, wouldn't you at least give it an easy end? Trapped in a bag as it slowly fills up with water – I couldn't think of many worse ways to go. And I'd seen several.

Katrin – one of our interns, veterinary students we used as unpaid employees – was setting out feed bowls, her fair hair wrapped around her head in intricate braids. She glanced at me in a way that told me she knew the police had spoken to me. Probably everyone knew.

I forced a smile. 'Morning, Katrin.'

She nodded. She had her headphones in and I could hear the tinny blare of music. I didn't like that. I felt that if you were with someone they deserved your full attention – but perhaps that was me showing my age. Katrin was almost twenty years younger than me, after all.

'Have you done this side yet?' I bent to pick up some of the bowls she had filled from a huge sack of dried food, the meaty smell filling the air, driving the dogs wild.

'Oh. Not yet.'

'I'll do it.' As I moved off, bowls in each hand, I turned back – Katrin was holding her phone in front of her. Was she angling it at me, to take a picture perhaps? I felt sweat up and down my back, under the plastic apron. I had to remember I was innocent. I had just been questioned as a witness, not arrested or charged. I knew nothing, I'd done nothing. Maybe Katrin didn't know I'd been questioned after all, and I was just imagining it. She was a teenager, probably she didn't watch the news. Probably she was just checking Facebook or something. But was it on social media, my name or my picture, as the person who'd found the body and run? I didn't use that at all, for obvious reasons, but I knew how rumours could spread. If she put up a picture, would someone recognise me? Would the story come out – something I'd worried about for the entire time I'd lived here?

I turned my shoulder slightly to hide my face. I had learned that there was a certain amount of paranoia you just had to cope with, and I didn't allow myself to go past that. It would be no life worth living if I did.

'Rachel?' For a moment, I didn't answer. Who was Rachel? 'Rachel, love?'

That was me. Oh God. I hadn't reacted, and that chilled me, because it had been a long time since I'd made a mistake like that, failed to answer to the name I called myself. I straightened up from setting down the last few bowls, and Marilyn was standing there, a teenage boy, tall and gangling, beside her.

'Oh! Sorry, I was miles away.'

She gave me a sympathetic smile. 'Can you work with Callum today, show him the feeding protocol?'

I had seen the boy around the place without really realising it – I did my best to keep a distance from the interns. They reminded me too painfully of myself at that age, so sure that life would not hurt me. That made three of them this term, Katrin, this boy, and another one called Tom I'd also seen about, tall and cocky.

'Hello, Callum.' I tried to sound normal, gave him a smile. 'I'm Rachel.' Keep saying it and it might be true.

He ducked his head and muttered, 'Hi, yeah, I know.' Typical taciturn teenager. He was a foot taller than me, dressed in a hoody and jeans. He'd be good-looking when his skin cleared up, I thought.

'You like dogs?' I indicated the ones behind me in their pens, their hopeful eyes and wagging tails.

'Yeah.' He cleared his throat, his voice wavering, as often happens at that age. 'Yeah, I do.'

'Rachel will take good care of you,' said Marilyn. I knew it was her way of saying she still trusted me, and I loved her for it. 'I'm just going on a food run.'

The day went on, and I was almost able to lose myself in the dogs, their trusting gaze and cold noses. Accompanied by an almost silent Callum, a restful and undemanding companion, I cleaned out cages, brushed coats, detangled leads. Around half eleven Katrin went on her lunch break and didn't come back for two hours, but I wouldn't say anything, as she wasn't getting paid, after all. Neither was I, but I had plenty to live off, thanks to the compensation. I'd had the odd embarrassing conversation with Marilyn about it at the start, and I think she got the impression I was from some aristocratic family I had turned my back on, living off a trust fund. I told myself I'd earned that money, with my blood and tears, but I still felt guilty about it.

Dogs fed and pens cleaned out, I stripped off the apron and stuck my head out the back door to look over the small lawn area where we exercise the dogs and teach them basic obedience. In the distance was the shimmer of our small lake, Coldwater Tarn, coloured bright grey by the shifting light. Autumn was in the air, the lake quiet, no kayaks or paddleboarders. My walking boots dug into the marshy grass. I was all right. I was breathing. I was outside, not behind bars.

My thoughts returned to the body in the woods – Anna, it had been Anna. I had to try to understand this. Anna was dead. I imagined her body on a slab, waiting for the pathologist to confirm what had killed her. I pictured her small white hands lying beside her, or perhaps folded on her chest, which was no longer moving up and down. Anna had been a beautiful woman, but beauty is very quickly lost along with life. Death is so strange, its alchemy, its sudden and irreversible descent, like the fall of an axe. No wonder people enjoy reading about it, as ghoulish as it is – in our safe and sanitised modern world, death is one of the few mysteries left. I wondered, with a kind of detached and fatalistic curiosity, what Anna's death would mean for me.

Casey

August 2000

I had been in Los Angeles a week before I saw the city, or anything beyond the Safrans' house and garden. I felt as if I'd landed on the surface of the moon, so far away was my normal life. My college friends, Suzi and Becks, and my on-off boyfriend, Ryan, had all promised to email, but I'd no access to the Safrans' computer, and wasn't even sure if they had the internet here. We were up in what they called 'the hills', where the sun set orange every night, and on a rare clear day you could see the sea. Usually, a smoggy haze weighed over the city and you could see nothing at all. The house was wide and low, two storeys, the air churned to a conditioned coldness that felt like being touched with frozen hands. I struggled to sleep in it, with jet lag and the constant whir of the ceiling fan, outside the sirens and police helicopters that hovered sometimes for hours. Every house in the street had a sign on the lawn stating which alarm company they used.

The street curved up towards a wilderness, where you could hike a steep sandy trail to the top of a hill and look down on the city. Everywhere were signs warning of coyotes. I had only been outside to the garden, the grass so green and level it looked fake, where José kept his things in a little shed. He didn't live in like me; instead he drove from the San Gabriel Valley three times a week. I gathered this was far. I had seen one neighbour – the woman across the street, who had dyed red hair and looked at me suspiciously over large glasses, asking what I was doing with the baby. There was a pool, but it was always covered over as Abby was paranoid about the kids falling in. No one seemed to spend much time outside – Abby even drew the blinds against the sun when it was bright. The heat was merciless, beating down on your head during the few steps between the car and the door.

The car. I had said on my application I could drive, and it was true, after a fashion. Jenna had made me learn before I left school, paying for lessons from a man with chronic catarrh who patted me on the leg when I did something right. I had failed my test first time, and Jenna's wrath had been terrible. *You're wasting my money and your own time. Get it right or get out.* Next time, I got it right. But driving around Watford was not the same as driving in Los Angeles, on the other side of the road. I had blocked it from my mind before arriving, vaguely imagining I could take buses, or that there might even be a driver. José did run errands and sometimes took David places, but mostly he was busy round the house. It was down to me to drive Madison about, as Abby made clear the second week. She came into my room again and stood there until I woke up, frowning.

'Casey. Madison's at school this week.'

'Um?' I came awake slowly, muzzy-headed, my sleep patterns shot. It was 7 a.m. 'It starts at eight, so you better move your ass.'

She turned and left before I could even ask where the school was. I hustled to get up – never mind washing myself or the baby right now – and located Madison in her room. A strange thing was that she didn't seem to have any toys. Instead, she was applying make-up – actual make-up that she owned. And she was quite good

31

at it, her lips ruby-red and her eyes dark blue. It was so odd to see that on a little girl.

'You're very dressed up for school, Madison.'

She put down her lipstick and stared at me. She was only five, I had to remind myself. 'There's an audition at lunchtime. You're meant to take me.'

I was? Had I been given a schedule and forgotten, or did Abby expect me to just know these things?

'All right. Well, get dressed, we need to leave soon. Is your school nearby?'

'You don't know?'

'No one told me.'

She sighed. She was in her nightdress – a strangely grown-up one for a little girl, lace-trimmed. The whole thing creeped me out, so I retreated. Carson was sitting up in his cot, looking at me, but not crying right at that moment, so I left him for now. Downstairs, there was no sign of Abby. I began to sweat. How was I to find out where the school was, let alone take Madison there? Why hadn't I asked before? Why hadn't anyone told me? I began to look around the kitchen for an address. A flyer with the school on it, a letter on a noticeboard, in a drawer. Everything was empty, clean and perfectly aligned.

'What are you doing?' Madison had followed me downstairs, still in her nightdress. I banged a bowl on to the table. She wasn't allowed shop-bought cereal, so usually I cut up some fruit for her, but I didn't have time. I took a banana from the bowl but got distracted and started looking again for the school address.

'You're weird,' she sighed.

'Madison, I need you to help me, please. I don't know where your school is, and I'm supposed to drive you. You must know what it's called?'

'You should have asked Mommy.'

And where was Mommy? No sign of her. Yoga again, perhaps – Abby seemed to live at the gym. I was beginning to panic. From upstairs came the sound of Carson's wails – he would need to be changed and fed soon. Oh God.

'Madison, please.'

She made a face. It was an expression I'd never thought to see on the face of a child – sly, calculating. She knew the school's address, I realised, or at least how to get there, but wasn't telling me.

'Madison!' I snapped. 'Stop this.'

A door opened, somewhere in the house. Madison whipped her head around towards it, then as footsteps came down the hall, she started to cry. It was as if she had pressed a button, and I remembered she was an actress, she could do that on demand. *Oh please not Abby not Abby* . . .

'Something wrong?'

David came into the room. He was barefoot, in jeans and a T-shirt with some old band name on it, his hair rumpled. He looked not much older than me, though he was in fact twenty years my senior.

'Oh! You're here?' Usually he left for work early, and I didn't see him from one end of the day till the other.

Madison launched herself at his legs. 'Daddy! She yelled at me.'

David glanced between us. 'Did she?'

'I'm sorry.' I was on the verge of tears myself. 'I have to take her to school and I don't know where it is, plus I've never driven the car or on the right or . . . oh God, I have to get Carson.'

David detached himself from Madison, and came to me, and put his arm around me. I was shocked for a second by the heat of his body, in this frozen house, where I had not been touched since I arrived, except by Carson, who didn't count.

'Hey, it's OK. I think we can sort that out. You get the baby up and I'll drive you. Madison, why aren't you dressed?'

She looked wrong-footed. 'I didn't have breakfast, Daddy.'

'Well, you should have hurried up then. We'll stop and pick up something.'

'But Mommy says—'

'I don't see Mommy here, do you? Go.'

She went. I turned to him, and I was probably a little starry-eyed. *My hero.*

'Oh God, thank you, I didn't know what to do.'

He looked at me with an expression I couldn't read.

'Go on. We'll leave in ten. You might want to get dressed too.' Only then did I look down and realise I was still in the loose vest top I'd slept in. The strap had fallen down, and my left breast had almost entirely slipped out of it.

Jenna would have known what to do at a moment like this. Brazened it out, laughed her dirty laugh, met his eyes. Flirted, even. But I was not Jenna, and instead I shoved it back in, and scurried red-faced from the room, muttering my thanks. As I ran out, I knew he was watching me go.

Rachel

People think that a murder investigation is fast, that they arrest you and that's it, you're up in court the next day and off to prison. It's not like that at all. They won't charge you until they're absolutely sure they have the evidence, or the case can all fall apart. So they take their time. They watch you. Give you just enough rope that you can hang yourself, as the saying goes.

The day after Anna died went by as normal. Callum completed his tasks diligently, but with Marilyn gone, both Tom and Katrin gave up on any pretence at work: I thought they were maybe having a thing together. Hooking up, or whatever they called it nowadays. Out of the office window I watched them standing in the car park, talking intently. He was gripping her arms, as if trying to convince her of something; she craned her fair braided head up to him, many inches taller, rangy and lean in his Jack Wills rugby top. They were so young. When I was that age, events were about to take a turn I could never have imagined. I looked away – it wasn't my place to get involved with those two, I had enough going on. I kept thinking of Anna, the last time I'd seen her. I'd been heading out of the shop with wine and crisps in my arms, thinking about how I'd see Alex that night and if I'd bought the right brand of wine, when suddenly she was there in my peripheral vision, a flash of pink from her coat. Red-faced, furious, her fair hair flying. I had scuttled out, but she'd followed me on to the pavement.

'It's you!'

I had thought, for a heart-stopping moment, I'd been recognised for who I really was. 'What?'

'I know you. You're the one who's been fucking my husband.'

I took a step back, years of prison experience kicking in, already thinking how to run, or if necessary how to fight her off. An elbow to the jaw, perhaps, or a swift kick to the knee.

'You're Alex's wife?' That sounded wrong. Of course it was her – I had only seen her in the distance before. 'I'm sorry – I thought you'd split up?'

'We have a child, you know. There he is! Look at him.'

Reluctantly, I looked at the car she was pointing to, a child's wan face at the window. Sam. His eyes fixed on me, the woman who'd stolen his dad. I tried to de-escalate the situation.

'Anna – it's Anna, right? Let me get this straight. You haven't broken up? You're telling me you're still together? As far as I know, you split up some time ago and he's single.'

'He's still married to me, you know.'

'Well, yes, technically.'

I was trying to soothe her, my eyes darting about for a way out. She was blocking the pavement. A crowd of nosy passers-by had gathered, and a Co-op employee who looked all of seventeen had come out, in a black and green fleece.

'Look, I'm really sorry, I know it must be hurtful. But please, you should talk to Alex, not me.'

'Talk to Alex? Sure, I'll do that, because he's *so* easy to talk to. Definitely doesn't twist my words or make me sound crazy or anything like that.'

She did sound crazy, and I thought so at the time. Deranged by rejection and refusing to accept it – we'd all been there, hadn't we?

It's what Alex had said later, when I told him about it. He swore he hadn't told her about us. *I don't know how she found out. She's crazy, Rachel. She can't accept it's over.*

I was backing away. As soon as a gap came in the traffic, I would run. 'I – I'm sorry.'

'Look, I don't want you near him, OK? Stay away from my family.'

I had run then, skidding into the road, a car blaring its horn at me, my only thought to get away from there and the gawking crowd that had gathered. I wished now I could go back, and walk Anna away somewhere private, and ask her to tell me exactly what she meant.

Brooding over it, I fed the dogs again, walked a weaving bunch of them down to the lake, trying to keep their leads straight. I filled in some paperwork for prospective adopters – it's harder to get a rescue dog than it is to adopt a child in some places. Marilyn kept taking in the ones no one wanted, so she had five. Brandy was enough for me – I thought she'd feel betrayed if I came home with another dog. I didn't even want her to start with. It was too much, after everything, to care for something small and helpless again. But Marilyn's beagle Juniper – now sadly departed – had unexpected puppies and she insisted one was mine, the floppy ears and sad brown eyes irresistible. So that's how I got Brandy.

I'd never known how to thank Marilyn for taking me in at the dog shelter. She didn't know, of course, what I was running from when I applied for the job, but she sensed it was something. A dog is a good start when you can't let people in. And look how far I'd come – I had a boyfriend now, even. Or I thought I did. Alex had not been in touch, after leaving me the day before to go and pick up Sam. I could only imagine what he was going through, trying to explain it to the boy. I hadn't met Sam, not properly. We were being careful about it, trying to respect his feelings, and Anna's. They weren't divorced yet, it was still raw. But I'd had hopes that one day Sam, Alex and I would be a little family, Anna a friend even, all of us sharing childcare in some happy blended Scandinavian way. Stupid of me. To allow myself to hope again.

I got on with my work, letting my mind go blank as I measured and brushed and cleaned, replied to emails about adoption and dog care. I would be all right. This wasn't happening again. This was just an unfortunate coincidence, for me at least. I had to think about Anna, that someone had slashed the life from her. Unable to avoid it, I found myself looking on the BBC website. There was a picture of the path into the woods, which I realised must have been taken almost from outside my house. *Dead woman named as Anna Devine.* I swallowed hard. They had a picture of her, what looked like a wedding photo, Anna beaming with her fair hair twisted up. Alex must have been cropped out. There was a shot of her parents being led into the police station, an older couple in matching raincoats, their faces shattered with grief. *The body was found by a jogger around 8 a.m. yesterday, who then raised the alarm.* So she had lain there for another half an hour before anyone else came by. *Police estimate death occurred several hours before.* That was vague. What if she'd only just been killed when I passed by? What if the killer was still there, lurking in the trees, in the silence of the dawn? I shuddered.

'Rachel?'

I looked up to see Tom the intern standing over my desk. He'd never spoken to me directly before, and I hadn't realised he even knew my name.

'Yes?' Was he trying to peer over my shoulder? I glanced at my screen reflexively – nothing incriminating. I would never be so stupid as to google myself on a shared computer.

'Do you want a cup of tea? I'm making some.'

That was a first. He was one of those boys from wealthy families, all turned-up collars and floppy dark hair. He must know the police had questioned me, and be snooping for information.

'Um – no, thank you, I'm OK.' Another habit from what happened – I didn't trust other people to make my food or drinks. I watched myself, I watched them too. It's maybe the worst legacy it leaves you with. You never truly feel safe again.

I finished work at five and walked home along the lake, enjoying how my boots sank into the mud, the wet shine of the earth. *See*, a little voice said in my head, *you are here, not in a concrete yard or a boiling box with someone screaming next door. See, you are lucky. You escaped.*

I didn't feel lucky. And when I got home, the police were waiting for me.

◆ ◆ ◆

I saw the car as I walked up the lane, my heart fluttering in my chest. I was shaking. Sweat down my back. *It's happening. Again.* As I reached my garden gate, a man opened the car door and got out.

I hadn't seen him before. Dark hair, green eyes, about my age. He wore a suit and tie. Did that mean he was a detective? With him was a woman in a grey trouser suit. She was in her fifties, I guessed, with a tight helmet haircut and grim expression.

'Ms Caldwell?'

'Er – yeah. Rachel.'

His manner was pleasant, which wrong-footed me. 'I'm DS Hegarty, hello. From the Cumbria MIT. They've brought us into the case. Mind if we ask you a few questions at the station?' Still just questions. Not an arrest.

I could hardly say no, could I? 'Of course.' I had no excuse to delay, I already had everything I needed on me: bag, keys, phone. 'I'll just leave the dog, all right?'

'Of course.'

I went inside the house, but left the front door open so they could see I was coming straight out again. I took Brandy off the lead and put food and water down for her. For a moment I sank my face into her fur, so soft and warm, and gave a silent scream. Why me? Why again?

'It's OK,' I murmured to her. 'Be good, OK? I'll be back soon.' But would I? If they kept me in for long, I'd have to call Marilyn, tell her where the key was hidden in a plant pot outside. I wanted to stay where I was, slam the door in their faces and lock it and never go out again. I had a strong feeling that I might not be coming home.

I went out, a bright, helpful smile pasted on. Several people had halted along the green to watch, joggers and dog-walkers, a few I recognised. Everyone would soon know I was being questioned by the police for the second time in two days. It couldn't be helped. DS Hegarty ushered me into the back of the police car – all friendly, not an arrest – and off we went down the lane into town.

Audrey next door was in her garden, trowelling at the soil, and she gaped at me. I knew the story would be all around the village in an hour, and not long after that, people would have put two and two together and made up their minds that I was guilty. I knew how it worked.

The odd thing was how calm I felt. Here I was, reliving my worst nightmare, and I was still able to think clearly, prepare. Perhaps I assumed that lightning doesn't strike twice. I should have known that, both factually and metaphorically, that just isn't true.

There's Been A Murder!: 'Spoonful of Sugar –
Episode 24'
(podcast transcript, June 2017)

-So today we're talking about an old one – Em, do you remember this one? The Mary Poppins Murders.

-I think so – I was only five or so when it happened but I remember it being on TV. She was so pretty. The girls at school tried to plait our hair in the braid like hers, I guess we didn't know what it was she'd done.

-Convicted murderer chic! That's really sick, Carly.

-We were seven! Anyway, maybe she didn't do it. She got out on appeal after all.

-After five years. That's a long time for something you didn't do, at nineteen.

-I remember they said she might get the death penalty. I can't believe they had that in California!

-They still do. Nuts!

-Really nuts. So, let's talk about the murders. This story has everything. Child star kid – Madison. Now, this is going to sound harsh, but I didn't realise it was possible for a five-year-old to have resting bitch face, but she really does. Did. Oops.

-She did! And that blue eyeshadow is so not her colour.

-Then we have the hot mom – shades of JonBenét Ramsay, Casey Anthony – we even have a Casey in this one too.

-Is there something there? Like some creepy guy saw Madison at a pageant, got obsessed with her?

-The police never found any evidence of that. There's also the famous film-producer dad. Well, semi-famous.

-I found a picture of him with Brad Pitt, that's famous enough for me!

-And the innocent British nanny – except she was no Mary Poppins, was she? You've seen the pics.

-See, I don't think that's totally fair, Em. If you went through either of our Facebooks, how many pictures would you find where we're off our faces or have on tiny little tops? What about that Halloween you dressed up in your undies? She was nineteen, in a strange country. Plus, it's America, people get murdered all the time there.

-OK. What about the mobile phone then? She had one, a Nokia like everyone did back then, but it was missing when the police came, never turned up. She said she'd lost it the day before the murders, but doesn't that seem a bit suss to you?

-I dunno. She didn't kill them with the phone, did she? Probably just coincidence.

-So you believe her that she just came home to find the door open, and they were dead?

-Nah. My money's on the dad doing it. It's always the dad, isn't it? She was just lucky she wasn't there or she'd be dead too, and the baby.

-Aw, the poor baby. How old would he be now?

-I guess late teens? Poor kid. His whole family gone. But no, the dad couldn't have done it – he was shot from a distance, remember? Definitely didn't do it himself. The gun had his prints on of course, but it was his gun! It also had the nanny's prints.

-She explained that. She picked it up off the floor.

-Sounds well dodgy.

-Yeah, but it's America! They're all gun nuts. I think she was just in the wrong place at the wrong time, and naïve.

-What about how she acted after? She never cried, she talked to the news reporters, she even smiled for the camera? After the whole family were killed?

-She was a kid, she wanted to be an actress, plus her mum was pushing her into the limelight . . .

-Her mum! OMG we have to talk about this. The true villain of the piece!

-Jenna. The worst.

-Totally.

Rachel

Coldwater was a small Lake District town with a satellite police station, mostly kept open to process tourist complaints about lost wallets, parking disputes, and the occasional boat-related theft. I'd been to the station once before, when a dog got loose in town and I came to collect it for the shelter. I still remembered going in, a brief moment of fear, crossing the threshold, that I might never be let out again. Bending to soothe the dog, a terrified collie let out of a van on the A road, found dodging cars. I'd taken him to the shelter and he was now happily rehomed on a farm over Ambleside way. The station is quaint, a small building of old stone just off the high street, which is crowded with souvenir shops and tea rooms, huddled up beside the dark waters of our lake. I was taken into a cold room with a table and two chairs, bare floor and walls. They brought me water. Did I have a lawyer? they asked. No. Of course I didn't. 'Well, this is just a chat, Rachel. For now.' They put a tape on, an actual old cassette tape in a machine, and with the click of it into the deck I began to panic and sweat, despite the chill air, a Pavlovian response. It was happening again, somehow. And it was as if I'd always expected it. I wasn't even surprised.

I picked up the glass of water. Offering me a drink, was that a sign I wasn't a suspect, just a helpful witness? Or was it some kind of trick, like he would look at which hand I used to lift the water and convict me on the basis of that? Or collect my DNA from the rim? That was illegal, wasn't it? God. I was on such high alert I didn't know how to interpret normal human interactions. I had to calm down. I laid my shaking hands on the chipped table, trying to still them. I focused on my surroundings, something I had learned to do during long hours in holding cells. A damp stain in the shape of Africa. Small flecks in the paint as if something had once been screwed to the wall, a cabinet or bracket of some kind. A shred of what looked like balloon on the floor, and I couldn't imagine how that had got there.

'So.' DS Hegarty sat down opposite, taking his time to straighten his tie. I noticed he had no wedding ring, then got annoyed with myself for noticing. 'This is DS Margaret Hope, by the way. She's going to sit in on this with me.' This was the grim-faced woman, who so far hadn't said a word to me, but was watching me closely. 'We'll pop the tape on to record too, so we can keep track of everything.' There followed some more faffing about with the machine, and the reading of all our names. 'Now, Rachel. I'm sure you've heard that the body found yesterday is that of Anna Devine. I believe you knew Mrs Devine?'

Mrs. Because she was still married to Alex, of course. 'A little.' Did they know I was dating her husband? I had to be careful here.

'And when did you last see her?'

'Um . . . it was last week. At the Co-op in town.'

I was guessing the police would have been told about this. Half the town had witnessed it, even opening windows to listen in as Anna followed me out and screamed at me, while I stood there clutching my big bag of crisps and bottle of wine, aware of how obvious it must be that I was expecting company that evening. Her husband, in fact. *I don't want you near him! You hear? Stay away from my family!*

'What did you talk about?'

I winced. They must know already. 'Anna was . . . she didn't like that I was seeing her ex-husband.'

'Still married, in fact, weren't they?' said DS Hegarty.

So he did know. I watched the female officer taking notes, saying nothing. Her eyes slid to me from time to time, assessing.

'Technically,' I said. 'He's not living with her any more, but they haven't filed the paperwork yet. She didn't want – she was contesting it.'

'They have a child together, yes?'

'A little boy, yes. He's five.'

My heart ached when I thought of Sam. As I fled from Anna, I'd seen his face pressed against the window of her car, which was parked just outside the Co-op. He'd looked so confused. I supposed Sam would live with Alex now. And me, perhaps, in time? Would I be his stepmother, and years from now would he think of me as his mum, would he barely recall Anna? I couldn't remember much about being five. Nothing to remember. I shut down the thought – I was getting seriously ahead of myself. For all I knew, I'd never see Alex again.

'We heard there was a row between you?' said DS Hegarty.

'Not exactly. She started screaming at me, it was very embarrassing.'

'And did you respond at all?'

'No! God. I just left.'

I had been screamed at before, of course, many times, both by strangers and people who knew me. But that was long ago. You get used to it, not being hated. Even with all my experience I had found the onslaught a shock, and as soon as I could get past her I had run into the road, a car swerving and beeping. Did that make me look guilty?

'Look, they'd broken up already,' I said. 'I didn't do anything wrong, I only met Alex after they'd split. He came to cut down a tree in my garden, that's all.'

Pouring him tea. His smile. *This is the first time I've smiled in months, you know that?*

'Did you see Anna again after that?' he said.

'No.'

'And you didn't see her body in the woods.'

'No.'

That was a lie. Would he be able to tell? He laid something on the table – a photograph of something woollen, bunched into an evidence bag. 'Do you recognise that?' I peered at it. For a moment, I couldn't breathe. I looked up at him, his face carefully neutral. He must know already. He must somehow know this was my scarf, its distinctive green and pink stripes. Marilyn had made it for me on my last birthday, or at least, what she thought was my birthday, because I didn't tell people the real one. It must have fallen off. Right near Anna. Had I even been wearing this yesterday? I must have been.

I knew then there was no point in lying. Like chess, you had to give things up to save the real prizes. There was still a chance they didn't know my worst secret. 'Yes,' I said. 'It's my scarf.'

'Do you want to answer that question again – did you find Anna Devine's body?'

'Yes,' I said again. 'I did. I found her.'

Casey

AUGUST 2000

You can get used to anything. That doesn't make it good, though. After two weeks I had a sort of handle on my life in LA. I got up at five each day, doing my best to avoid the rude awakening of Abby standing over me. Usually I had been up with Carson all through the night, struggling to get the bottle into his shrieking red mouth. I felt like he hated me sometimes, but when he did finally drift off in my arms, and we lay exhausted on my bed, both just breathing, those were the times I was most at peace. He was a cute baby, with chubby legs and wrists. Little butterball, I called him, as I bathed and changed him and rocked him endlessly against my hip. His mother seemed to rarely pick him up.

Abby still got up before me most days. I would find her doing yoga in the living room, or outside, swimming laps in the pool in the pre-dawn, which was surprisingly cold with the chill of desert night air. Or she'd come back from a run, sweating and red, to find me spooning banana into Carson's mouth. Abby had not acted since having Madison, but she was going on auditions, I knew. I saw scripts lying about the house, parts marked in red. She took a lot of tense phone calls, pacing up and down on the patio, which for some reason they called a deck. Words had been a problem since I arrived – there were always at least three things on the shopping list that I didn't understand. Baloney. Eggplant. Cilantro. I had never heard of any of these things.

Shopping was another task on my list, but later, after I had woken Madison – she was hard to rouse in the morning, strange for a child her age – and dressed her and fed her breakfast. Already she had internalised the idea that certain foods were bad. She wouldn't eat cereal or toast, only cottage cheese and fruit, which I had to cut up fresh. I rarely saw David in the mornings – he went in early most days, to beat the traffic. His office was in Santa Monica, which may as well have been in another country from the way people talked about it. I didn't really understand, because it took me an hour to get most places in London anyway. An LA person would drive twenty minutes then turn around and go home because the traffic was bad, or they couldn't find parking.

Driving was the worst. Madison's school was luckily not far away, and not on a freeway, but still down a wide and fast road with six lanes. Once I had dressed and fed both children – often without having fed myself – I would put them in the car and then edge out on to the main road. On a bad day this could take five minutes, horns blaring at me the whole time, and me desperately reciting to myself *drive on the right, drive on the right*, and Madison would sigh every time I nervously braked. I drove so slowly that everyone beeped at me, and I wasn't totally sure how to read the lights. You could turn left on red here, David had told me, but I didn't entirely believe him. I dropped Madison off in the parking lot – sometimes she wouldn't get out of the car, and once I had to drag her, since I was late for Carson's paediatrician appointment, under the disapproving eyes of various mothers. It was a 'no contact' drop-off so I rarely saw any of the parents, who were mostly women in huge sunglasses behind the tinted windows of Jeeps.

Many kids were dropped off by younger women, probably nannies, and I'd thought I might make some friends that way, but we weren't allowed to linger or else a guard in a tabard came out to move us along. The guard carried a gun. At a primary school – except they called it *elementary*. Every time I used a British word Madison gave me a disgusted look and corrected me.

After this I usually went to the supermarket – grocery store – navigating the aisles, shocked at the expense of everything and the thousand varieties of sweets, biscuits, mayonnaise. Everything you could want, but little in the way of actual ingredients. I was having to learn fast how to cook, otherwise we didn't eat. Then I took Carson home. Abby had usually gone out to wherever she went all day: the gym, the mall, a coffee shop where it was rumoured casting directors got their caffeine fix. Entering the house and realising she wasn't there gave me the most enormous feeling of relief.

While Carson napped – if he did – I cleaned up, tidied, washed dishes, made beds. A maid, Marietta, came in three times a week, but the house got so dirty in between. Abby never seemed to wash a dish. I'd tried to speak to Marietta, but she raced around with her mop and cloths, always wanting to clean exactly where I was standing, so I learned to stay out of her way. Otherwise, I rarely had a minute to sit down and I often forgot to eat lunch until gone three, shaking with hunger pangs, tears close to the surface. I cried a lot in LA, while driving, which didn't help, or while mopping the floor, wiping the tears away with the back of my hand. All those unpaid skivvies in children's books – Cinderella, the Little Princess – I identified with them. I was paid a few hundred dollars a month, but had nothing to spend it on – I had yet to go anywhere except the grocery store and school, or once when I took Carson to the doctor's. The doctor had been a suave man in his thirties and I'd fantasised about him for days after.

José the gardener was there some days, but although I smiled and waved and opened the patio doors to chat to him, he never spoke much, answering me in monosyllables. I felt he resented me for some reason. Maybe because I had a room in the house and he had to drive out there all the way from where he lived, through the LA traffic. The rest of the time the house was as cool and silent as the surface of the moon.

What shook me most about LA was how far apart you felt from people. Sometimes I might hear the neighbours in their garden or in the pool, but their voices were muffled by the thick trees growing in between the houses, and I had yet to see what they looked like. Even walking up and down the street I never saw anyone. People here simply didn't stroll, even when it wasn't too hot for it. They swept past you in cars, giving you strange looks.

On my first day off I climbed right up to the Wisdom Tree, looking out over Warner Brothers and Universal, the green mountains, the dusty city. On my way down I stumbled on the steep sandy path and fell twice, finding myself almost in tears. When I finally got back to the house, my knee bleeding a little, Abby just looked at me and told me to clean myself up.

At nights, David was always watching a TV show or a film in the lounge, but not to relax. He took notes, compared them with what he called his own development slate. Often Abby sat in the same room as him, but on the computer in the corner – I had never seen anyone with a home computer before, and wondered if they'd let me on it to check my email – or she would read a script. I never saw them sit side by side, or talk about anything other than the pick-up arrangements for the day. I wasn't sure what was expected of me in the evenings, so I usually stayed in my room, until Carson woke up and it all started over again.

Madison had a schedule to rival an actress in her twenties. She had to go to school – that was the law – but she was allowed out for auditions, so I had to pick her up and drive her there, on to the lots of various studios around LA. Warner Brothers was a thrill, the famous water tower and the whiff of celebrity. I had thought I might chat to the other mums and nannies, but there was such a tense feeling of competition – the little girls eyeing each other up and criticising each other's dresses – that it felt impossible. While Madison auditioned, I would sit in a waiting room and read a book I'd found in the case in my room. The Safrans didn't have much in the way of fiction, mostly just books on film or motivational self-help texts. I'd brought my acting textbooks, but I had no idea what I was supposed to be doing to 'break in'. Here I was, living in the house of a film producer, and no closer to my dreams. If they even were my dreams, and not Jenna's. Did I even like acting, or just the fantasies of red carpets, pretty dresses? Attention?

I was so bored, so lonely, so isolated. I barely rang Jenna. I was so afraid that I might burst into tears and beg to come home, and she didn't mind because she wasn't a phone person, as she always said, and anyway, because of the time difference, I was only free when she was asleep. My friends from college had melted away – Jenna had always pushed me to be competitive, to look for an edge over them, so I hadn't made that many. *Keep your eyes on the prize*, she always said. Well, I was here, and I had forgotten what the prize was. Persuade David to give me a part in a film? How to even broach the subject?

David was the family member I saw the least, and I was sorry for it. He had come with me to Madison's school on that first Monday, showing me the way and bearing with me as I bunny-hopped the unfamiliar automatic car and panicked at the road signs. It meant a lot, small kindnesses like that, when you were as lonely and isolated as I was. Even though he was rarely about, after that day I had begun to consider him my ally.

Rachel

I sat in a custody cell listening to the boom of my heart, trying to force it down with deep breaths. It was a 'dry' cell, with no water to wash in, presumably in case of splashing away evidence. I had been formally arrested, cautioned, fingerprinted on a little digital machine. They'd swabbed me for DNA. I had been told to undress, in front of a uniformed female officer, stony-faced like DS Hope, and they had taken my clothes and left me in a sort of paper boiler suit, a well-washed sweatshirt on top. I was shivering with shock and cold. The words were echoing in my head.

I'm arresting you for the murder of Anna Devine. I'm arresting you for murder.

Those words again, the worst I could imagine. I had not been charged yet – after all, they could only prove I had been near the body, nothing else. As far as I knew, anyway.

They weren't unkind. They had offered me dinner, a choice between instant mac and cheese or some kind of beef stew. I had said no – I couldn't bring myself to eat that jail-house slop again, not unless I absolutely had to, and anyway, my stomach was a mass of knots.

They'd taken my phone, and very politely told me they were searching my house too. I worried about Brandy, but they'd thought of that, and Marilyn had taken her in with her own brood. I needed a lawyer, clearly, and one had been offered, but part of me couldn't bear it – to have someone throw away my life again, through sheer apathy and incompetence.

I had been questioned thoroughly about my movements on the morning of Anna's death, if I could prove I'd been at home the night before, that I hadn't left the cottage. Of course I couldn't, since I'd been alone. They wanted to know why I'd not reported the body – I had panicked, I said, which was true, but I didn't explain why. They had asked me too about Alex, when I'd last seen him, if he and Anna were on good terms or not. I had demurred, afraid to lie, not wanting to get him into trouble.

I don't know. Is anyone on good terms when they're getting divorced? They were OK, I think.

I was sure they knew I was lying.

I knew I should say who I was, and admit all of that. It would have been my worst nightmare prior to this. But this was a small country. Maybe I had been naïve to think it would never come out. I let myself think about it for a moment: explaining the real reason I had found the body and run. Telling the truth to the handsome detective with the slippery smile, and then to Marilyn, to Katrin and Tom and the new boy intern, to Audrey even, but most of all to Alex. Watching their faces change as they figured it out.

She's that girl? Oh my God! I can see it now!

It wasn't appealing. But the alternative was perhaps spending the next twenty years in a cell like this one, where I could stretch out both arms and touch the cream stone walls. Listening to the sounds of rattling keys and doors clanging shut and women sobbing in their sleep, screaming out with bad dreams. Then there was the unique smell of custody cells: feet and vomit and frightened sweat. I'd been here before. Peeing in front of people, having my body searched and laid bare. Eating mush three times a day, never preparing another meal myself, never petting a dog or seeing the sky. And the worst bit is the things people say about you. People who've never even met you, only seen a picture where you're smiling and drinking a vodka and Coke, wearing a short skirt, because you were nineteen years old and you never knew the world would turn its unforgiving gaze on you.

How long had I been in here? The light outside the tiny barred window looked dark, marshy. I knew how time could unspool in these little rooms, how years of your life could leak away as you waited for someone to help you. At least this was the UK. They couldn't keep me for more than a few days without a charge, could they? I wished I'd thought to learn all the rules of our legal system, just in case. Twenty-four hours, that came to mind for some reason. All the same, a long time to sit with nothing but your worst thoughts for company.

Footsteps were coming towards me. What now? Were they going to charge me with murder, put me in the system, start me on a path I could not come back from? The door opened. It was the uniformed guard, a middle-aged woman who I think they called the custody sergeant. Her forehead was shiny with sweat, and her uniform blouse had a stain on it, coffee perhaps. I stood up. Heart hammering.

She said, 'Rachel. Come with me.'

Interview in the *Los Angeles Times*, 2001

Carol Bubchek stands at her sink, looking across the street to the large detached house opposite. Its lawn is neatly mown and a discreet For Sale sign sits outside. But this is the house where, just last year, a horrific triple murder took place—and Mrs Bubchek, 61, was a key witness for the prosecution.

She points for me now, recreating the moment. "I was at the sink, I had my morning soap on, so I know what time it was. I was filling my coffee maker, and I saw her. I noticed because people don't really walk on our street, but she did. It was sorta strange." *She* being the nanny from the house opposite, Casey Adams, an English woman of nineteen. "She had the baby, and he was cranky— I could hear him through the window. Well, no wonder, poor little mite, it was a hundred degrees out! But she was walking him."

I ask if she saw whether the door of the house was left ajar or not. Adams had claimed that on her return, just a few minutes later, the door was open, though she could not remember if she'd done that herself or not. Bubchek shakes her head. "Can't see that far." She wears thick-lensed glasses on a jewelled string round her neck. I ask what happened next. "She came back, the baby was still cranky. She went inside. Then I didn't see or hear anything until the police came racing up, and that was, oh, maybe ten, fifteen minutes after."

The call to police dispatch came in at 11.08 am. Mrs Bubchek is adamant she saw Adams go back into the house sometime before eleven, as her soap was still playing. "So what was she doing all that time? It doesn't take you ten minutes to report a triple murder, does it?"

Rachel

I didn't quite understand what was happening. I wasn't being charged yet for some reason, despite my unquestionable motive for wanting Anna gone, the fact I had found her body and inexplicably told no one, lied about it when asked.

'What's going on?' I asked, as the sergeant handed me a transparent plastic bag of possessions, minus my clothes, which had gone for forensics testing. I was surprised to see my phone in there – had they already checked it and realised I only used its most basic features, texts and calls? 'You're being released on bail for twenty-eight days, under investigation.' Her face was unreadable. 'You must not interfere with the case in any way, or with other witnesses, and you must report to the station when asked.'

Clearly, there was not enough evidence to charge me. I had enough sense not to say anything more. I was also relieved that, after my experience of American justice, there was no bail charge here. I was simply free to leave, for now anyway.

Alex was standing in reception jingling his keys. He wore a blue wool jumper that matched his eyes, heavy outdoor trousers. I wanted to run to him, throw myself into his arms, howl. Instead I smiled, weakly, for the benefit of the officer.

'Hi.' My mouth was dry and it came out raspy.

He didn't say anything, just cocked his head at me to go out. I moved towards the exit of the police station, suddenly very fixated on the square of the outside I could see beyond it. Freedom to walk out, into the sun (OK, it was night-time and raining – it was the Lake District, after all). Part of me had expected to only ever feel fresh air on my face again as I was hustled from station to van to courthouse to prison. Like last time. I had no idea what time it was, but late, clearly. Most of the evening had been lost in interviews and sitting in the cold cell wondering if this was my life from now on. He was parked nearby, but even so I had the urge to cover my face as we walked. I couldn't bear to be seen like this, to have more photographs in circulation of me leaving police stations. When we were safely inside his old van, which always smelled of mud, Alex let out a deep sigh, hands on the steering wheel.

'Rachel.'

'I know, I know. This is crazy.'

'They've had me in all day, over Barrow way. The big station.'

I wondered why they'd taken him there – keeping us apart, maybe? Did they think we'd done this together?

'They asked so many questions,' he said. 'About you, about me, everywhere I went yesterday and the day before, and you too. I can't even remember exactly, it was so much.'

'But you've got an alibi, right?' He'd been with Sam the night Anna died, at his flat.

'Luckily, yes. Colette popped in a few times through the evening, so she can say I was home.'

'Colette?'

'From downstairs. You know.'

Oh yes. The young and attractive girl who lived in the flat below Alex. But I couldn't think about that now. 'Where's Sam, is he all right?'

59

'With Anna's parents. He's—' He just shook his head. Of course Sam was not all right. 'But what the hell's going on, Rach?'

'Look, I have no idea. I swear, I haven't seen Anna since that day last week.'

He'd heard all about the argument, of course, from both of us. The two women in his life.

'But you found her body. And it was your scarf, wasn't it?'

So that was how they knew. 'You told them it was mine?'

He looked surprised. 'You think I should have lied?'

'Um. No, of course not. Look, I can't explain it. I just pan-icked. It was stupid, and I shouldn't have done it, but that's it. That and the row, that's all they have on me. It's just – a coincidence. Bad luck.' And how much bad luck could one person have in their life?

He looked at me, a new reserve in his eyes that had never been there before. 'I wish I could understand.'

I couldn't tell him. Not yet. Now it had finally happened, I was desperate to hold on to the bubble, the safe, warm place where he liked me, thought I was a good person.

'What did they ask you?' I said, changing the subject. 'How did it – happen? She was stabbed?'

'She was hit over the head as well,' he said slowly. 'Or she had some kind of head injury, anyway. I don't know if I'm meant to tell you these—'

My mind was racing. 'So the stabbing wasn't what killed her?'

He winced. 'I don't know. They asked me if she'd hit her head any time in the previous few days – I said I didn't know. If I'd been to the house that day, that sort of thing.'

'But you picked Alex up from school that day, not from the house? You took him straight to your flat?'

'Of course I did.' He reached for the ignition. 'Come on, let's get out of here. We're not thinking straight.'

I had no idea what was going on. Weariness overcame me. 'We can't go to mine, the police are still there. Oh God.' I thought of them poking about in my things, touching them – that privacy such a hard-won privilege, now taken away.

He was spinning the wheel, sticking in the mud of the verges. 'We'll go to mine. It's OK, Rachel.'

Alex's place was a nondescript two-bed flat opposite the town hall on Main Street. His bedroom was bare and functional, with magnolia walls – a temporary space. Sam's was brighter, with plastic bins full of toys and posters on the wall, in defiance of the rental terms. I stopped in the doorway and stared at them. Poor Sam. He would have to be brought here soon, to live permanently – but no, of course Alex could move back into the farmhouse once the police were done with it, because it was still his, after all. He'd grown up there.

I couldn't go there any time soon, though, could I? There would be issues with contaminated evidence, forensics. Perhaps Anna had been attacked in her home – the possibilities were almost endless with a head injury: interrupting a burglar or intruder, or maybe someone she'd invited over. A friend. Or a lover – could Anna have been seeing someone too? But why then would she be so upset about Alex and me? Then maybe an accidental fall, a panicked response. Why stab her too, though? Trying to cover it up?

Already I was thinking like a criminal. I stood in the living room, rubbing my goosefleshed arms. I had nothing here, no toothbrush or clean pants or pyjamas. Part of me was waiting to wake up and find it was all one of the dreams I still had, the prison nightmares. I could never sleep in a room with the door shut. But this was real, it was happening. Alex filled the kettle, but didn't switch it on. He leaned on the kitchen counter and breathed out hard.

'I don't understand this, Rachel.'

'Neither do I! Christ, we weren't on the best of terms, Anna and me, but I'd never have done something like this. I never wanted her dead, for God's sake. Would anyone else want to kill her – was she seeing someone, do you think?'

He nodded slowly. 'I think maybe. She didn't say, but she was being kind of cagey about her plans the last week or so. She liked being angry at me over you, I guess, so if she admitted she was doing the same she'd have to stop her nonsense. Finalise the divorce.' Anna had been difficult over it, one reason they were still, technically, married. She had made threats, as people do. That she'd stop him seeing Sam, that she'd clean him out for every penny he had, she'd keep the family home, which Alex's great-grandfather had built over a hundred years ago, that sort of thing. Anna didn't work, except for some massage clients and yoga sessions in the village hall, so he was having to support her anyway.

The silence between us stretched, the noises from the street outside, this unfamiliar and uncomfortable front room with no side lamps, laundry piled on a chair and a dirty plate on the coffee table. It began to overwhelm me, the hopelessness. Why had I thought I was allowed to be happy? Or that the past was past, and my future might be bright: a loving relationship, a stepchild, perhaps a baby of my own? I wasn't too old – Anna had been about my age when she had Sam. Instead there was this. Another murder enquiry. Cold interview rooms in police stations. And I realised I could not keep pretending. Of course it had caught up to me.

'Alex,' I said, halting. *Go on, just tell him who you really are. Be honest, for once in your life.* But then his blue eyes settled on me, and I found that I couldn't. That I still wanted just one more night of him, before he knew the truth. So instead I stepped towards him, and slid my arms around his waist, and buried my face in his neck, breathing him in.

Casey

Waking up with a start was becoming a standard part of my life and I didn't like it one bit. Jenna had always encouraged me to get 'beauty sleep', lying in till eleven if I wanted. Here, if it wasn't the baby crying in the early hours it was Abby looming over me, telling me to get up. This time, however, it was Madison. She was standing in the half-gloom of my room, moaning softly to herself. I peered through one eye at the clock: it wasn't even four yet.

'Madison? Are you OK?'

Her moans grew louder. 'I didn't mean to!'

'To what?' I thought maybe she'd broken something, a glass, perhaps – Abby always went crazy if something like that happened.

'It's not my fault. It's your fault.'

'What's my fault?' I got out of bed, the floor cold under my bare feet. I couldn't get used to the way hot California days evaporated into bone-chilling nights. The sun wasn't up yet. 'Madison, you have to tell me.'

Instead, she grabbed my hand with her sticky little one and dragged me down the hallway. She had never voluntarily touched me before, so I let her. The door to Abby and David's bedroom was shut, and Carson was quiet for once in his. In Madison's bedroom I immediately smelled what the problem was. Her sheets were dark with urine, and I now saw it was on her pyjamas too. She looked so ashamed, clutching at herself, hair in disarray.

'I didn't mean to, Casey! It's not my fault, I didn't do it.'

Her cover story needed work. 'Who did, then?'

She looked shifty. 'Carson?'

'He climbed out of his cot, did he?'

She hung her head. 'I didn't mean to.'

'I know you didn't. It's OK, it happens to everyone.'

'Does it?'

'Of course.' In fact, I had no idea if that was true, or if I'd ever wet the bed myself. But I had never seen Madison act her age before, like a vulnerable child, and it touched me. 'I'll sort this out. Can you get into the bath by yourself?'

'Uh-huh. And we won't tell Mommy?'

'We won't tell Mommy.' Was that bad, keeping secrets from the child's mother? But I already knew she would throw a fit and I just couldn't deal with it. I listened out for Madison splashing in the bathroom as I stripped the bed, gagging at the wet sag of the sheets, the nose-tingling reek of urine. Then I pushed open the door to see her sitting in the bath, her head bowed in shame. I picked up her pyjamas from the floor – they had little clowns on them, with gaping smiles I found slightly sinister.

'I'll wash these right now, don't worry.'

Madison nodded sadly.

Abby might notice the machine running, but hopefully she would leave for yoga before going into the child's bedroom in the morning. Would she even remember exactly what pyjamas Madison had on?

'The water's not too hot?'

'No.'

I went over and laid my hand on her head – she flinched. I had never seen her naked before, I realised, and made sure to look away. 'It's really all right. Just a little accident, OK?'

'OK.' She still sounded so sad.

I took the wet sheets downstairs and bundled them into the machine in the laundry room, which was just off the kitchen, then turned it on. Would the noise wake Abby? I could make up some excuse. I was crossing back to the stairs when I saw a figure coming down. I was surprised by how much my heart lurched – was I really that afraid of Abby? Luckily, it was David, hair sticking up, rubbing his eyes.

'Is everything all right?' he said. 'What time is it?'

'Um, four.'

He cocked his head. 'You're doing laundry at 4 a.m.?'

This was my moment to tell the truth or lie.

'I – I spilled something on my sheets.' I didn't elaborate. Maybe he'd think I got my period. 'Sorry.'

'Oh! Well, that's all right.'

'Sorry if I woke you. Madison's up already, she's having her bath.' She didn't normally wake until much later, but David wasn't all that familiar with his children's routines.

'OK.' We paused on the stairs, me going up and him going down. 'May as well make coffee, I suppose, get a start on the day.' Right on cue, Carson made that little choking cry that meant he was gearing up to a full screech.

'I'd better get him,' I said, feeling the weariness deep in my bones. Four o'clock and I was already on the treadmill.

'All right,' he said, turning away.

For the first time it struck me as odd, hiring a teenage girl to live in your house and go to your crying baby, while you just stand there as if you've never heard the sound before.

'Casey,' he called, as I moved up the stairs.

'Um?'

'I don't know if we've said it before, but we really couldn't do this without you. Abby – she didn't do so well after Carson was born. Postnatal, you know. It's hard for her. So, thank you.'

I might have wondered why that was, why his non-working wife couldn't cope with two kids, one already at school, but I was just so pleased to have the praise.

'Thank you.' I looked at him properly and realised with a little shock that he was kind of handsome in his messy pre-dawn way, hair standing up, glasses crooked, the smell of his skin, his long legs and muscled arms. How old was he, nearly forty? I remembered the whole reason I was here – to try and break into Hollywood. It seemed a million miles away, though I drove past film studios every day. 'Busy day today?'

'Oh! Yeah, casting a new movie.'

'Cool.' I hesitated. Carson was getting louder. 'You know, sometime, if you have time, I would really love to know more about what you do. It's just so interesting!'

He looked surprised. 'Oh, well, sure, yes. OK.'

'Thanks. Better get that baby.'

I had to squeeze past him, as he kept standing where he was, and I had the impression that he was looking at my legs as I climbed the stairs. As I went into Carson's room, despite the howling red-faced baby that greeted me, I found that I was smiling.

Rachel

I left the flat early the next morning while Alex was still asleep. He'd wanted to have sex the night before, which had shocked me a little, so soon after Anna's death. I had tensed up as his hands crept from my waist to my breasts, under the baggy T-shirt of his I was sleeping in.

Eventually, after I hadn't responded to his touch, he'd said, 'What's up?'

What was *up*?

'I got arrested today. And your wife is dead.'

He withdrew his hands, sighed. 'She's not my wife.'

She had been, technically. 'You know what I mean.'

'Sorry. I'm just – my head's all over the place. I just thought we could comfort each other.'

Guilt had spread through me, plus I could hear Jenna's voice warning me that men had certain needs and if I didn't meet them he'd go elsewhere. Jenna had been dead for thirteen years, lung cancer of course, but I sometimes wondered if she would ever leave me. I'd turned over and laid my head on Alex's chest, breathing him in, the muscles of his stomach moving under me.

'I know,' I said. 'I just – I'm a ball of nerves right now.'

'Hey, it's OK.' He stroked my hair, and as we lay there I knew I would do anything to hold on to him.

Anything?

Not that. I would never have hurt Anna.

I had barely slept, the events of the last two days going round and round in my head. Anna had been murdered, people had seen us rowing in the street. I was in bed with her husband. And I'd found her body, and run away, and lied about it. I couldn't think of any explanation for what had happened that made sense, and soon the birds had started and the sky outside the bedroom window was turning grey. I got up, put on some tracksuit bottoms of Alex's, rolling up the legs, and left. Alex didn't stir, his tanned arm thrown over his face, breath coming evenly. I lingered to watch him until I realised I was being creepy.

The streets of Coldwater were mercifully empty, just a street cleaner and a few older people up and about already, but all the same I hunched down into Alex's clothes, wishing I had a hat or scarf. As I went down the lane to my cottage and saw that it was safe, the police gone, I felt myself relax a little. Audrey's house was also shuttered up, curtains drawn. I let myself in, missing the scrabble of Brandy's paws as she came to greet me. The house showed signs that someone had been searching, drawers left slightly open, ornaments askew. I'd have to clean it all to make it feel like mine again.

I realised I needed to eat something. Yesterday had not been great food-wise – a disappointing sandwich at lunchtime, too many cups of police-station coffee, and constant anxiety. What did I have in the house? Some eggs maybe. I went to the fridge, and that was when I saw it. The message on the front. The magnetic Scrabble tiles that were a Christmas present from the previous year's interns. They had been rearranged from the random jumble they were in the day before. Five of them pushed into the centre to make a word. A name.

CASEY.

Kill Me Now
(podcast transcript, March 2015)

-So can we talk about Casey Adams – the Mary Poppins killer? God, that is so dark.

-I dunno. I could see Mary popping someone's ass if they stepped out of line. You think she's guilty then?

-Who else could it be, though, Ali? That's the question.

-It is indeed. Today we'll discuss the smoking gun – literally a gun. Why were Casey Adams' fingerprints on it? She was British and British people don't know much about guns. She said she picked it up off the floor. But how would it have got there in the first place? The gardener said he didn't even know there was a gun in the house, so the dad wasn't in the habit of showing it to people.

-His prints were on it too, yeah? The dad's?

-Yeah. I mean, it was his gun.

-What about the mom's?

-No. So does that put paid to the theory she did it? Smothered the kid in her bed, shot hubby?

-I never thought Abby did it. She was so great in *In The Family* – I just can't see it. She was so pretty.

-Casey was pretty too.

-But don't you think in kind of a bitchy way – like those low-cut tops, the short skirts? Tacky.

-Yeah. So to go back to the prints, the only ones on the gun were Casey's and the dad's, David Safran's?

-Right. Could he have shot himself, that was the question. The police said no.

-One expert said no, one said maybe. Ugh, why can't these things just be clear-cut? Like come on, people, you're the scientists! Give us a straight answer!

-I know. And what about the blood smear on the kitchen cupboard – Casey's blood? She said she'd cut herself earlier in the day, but it's pretty suspicious if she just walked in and found them dead, isn't it?

-Right. And she had Abby Safran's blood all over her. Her feet, at least. Said she ran over to check on her and walked in it.

-Yeah. We'll talk more about that evidence after this message. In order to record our podcast, we need to have a good night's sleep. And the best mattress we've found for this is DreamPockets. Use the code killmenow – all one word – for a ten per-cent discount . . .

Rachel

It's no surprise that I often dream of that house. Sometimes I'm running through it, frantically searching each room for something. The laundry room where I washed Madison's sheets so many times, in the pre-dawn grey. David's study. Abby's yoga room. The TV room. They are always deserted.

In my dreams I never look in the cupboard where I hid. I don't know if I ever saw inside it until that day, and much was made of that, whether I could have randomly found it in a state of great panic, since it was so rarely opened. Instead, I rush upstairs in my dreams, feet sliding on the carpet, and through the bedrooms. My own box room, my narrow bed, the noisy air conditioner. Carson's little room – and that's when I realise that he's missing. Abby and David's room, and I only peek inside, as if I'm ashamed to go in there. It's clean and empty, the duvet pulled tight. Their en suite bathroom is empty too, as is the main one. There's no indication that two small children live here.

I understand then I'm looking for the baby, and under my fear is guilt, because this is my fault. I left him and he's missing. I don't look in Madison's room. I never saw her dead and it's as if my subconscious wants to protect me from imagining how it was. The hump under the pink frilly covers. The pillow with unicorns, the slow-turning dazzle of her night light. A faint smell of urine that no air freshener could mask entirely. I wonder how Abby never noticed it, or maybe she did and simply left me to deal with it.

Then, in the dream, I usually hear a noise. It comes from downstairs. A gun shot. And I start to run.

Of course, this isn't how it happened. I didn't hear a shot from upstairs, and Carson was never missing, he was in my arms the whole time. When the police arrived, a hard-bitten cop took him from my grasp and held him at arm's length, as if bemused at what to do with him. Carson was grizzling by then, but only because he'd missed his nap. He had been pressed tight to me in the cupboard while I braced my body against the door and bit my fist to keep from sobbing. I remember the smell of his head, a warm innocent baby smell, hot from the sun, and his soft grunts, which I silently prayed would not turn into cries.

It was always clear to me that I was hiding to protect the baby. I wasn't really scared that I was going to be killed too, though of course I told the court I was. But Carson, I couldn't bear for anything to happen to him. I loved that baby, a love that had grown inside me on all those long nights sitting awake with him, soothing his tears, changing his nappies, watching his eyes widen when he saw something for the first time, the simple wonder in him, his smile. The fact that I was never allowed to see him again was a great pain to me. I had often imagined him over the years, what he might look like, if he'd inherited David's height or Abby's eyes. His birthday, the only one of the family I remembered, was February 17th. I thought of him every year, wishing I could send him a present, like some sad spinster aunt. I was not his aunt, of course. Just someone who'd once been his nanny, who'd gone on trial for murdering his mother and father, his five-year-old sister, who'd saved him as best I could.

In the dream, I always come back to this point. I'm in the cupboard with the baby and I hear footsteps outside. Echoing across the marble hallway. Growing louder. They pause outside the door of my hiding place. I hear a click and I see the handle start to move, and I know I don't have the strength to hold it shut. That's where it ends – I always wake up.

◆ ◆ ◆

Now, I stood in my kitchen, vibrating with fear. Someone had been in here. Someone knew who I was. Someone who had broken into my house and left me this message. How long had this been there – had the police spotted it during their searches? Why now, with Anna dead? Was it possible the two things were connected – that somehow they had known I would pass that way with Brandy, as I did every morning, and that I would be the one to find the body? I didn't remember putting on that scarf on the day of the murder, and surely I would have noticed if it had fallen from my neck as I ran away? There was only one thing I could think of to explain both these things, and to be honest that was almost more scary than the idea I had somehow blacked out and done the murder myself. It seemed insane – was someone *framing* me?

It didn't make any sense. I should tell the truth. Throw myself on the mercy of the detective with the kind, tired eyes, and maybe he would understand why I had run as I did. This message on my fridge proved that somebody knew who I really was, the name I hadn't used in almost twenty years.

The sudden rush of an engine made me jump, lurch against the counter for support. I ran into the living room and looked out the window. A police car had drawn up to the green just opposite. Several uniformed officers were interviewing passers-by, while behind a cordon white-suited techs were still crawling over the grass. This investigation was in progress even as I stood here panicking and doing nothing.

I could tell the truth, yes. But look what had happened to me before, when I threw myself on the mercy of the police. No. I could not face it, not yet.

How many murders does the average person come across in their lifetime? None, right? It's why you all like to watch it on TV, because you don't know the reality. For me, it was now four. Whichever way you looked at it, those were not great odds.

Casey

September 2000

Suddenly, Abby had an audition. It was for *Blue Lines*, a long-running medical drama, and she would be playing a new nurse, tough but romantic underneath it all, who would have a flirtation with the lead doctor over half a series.

'It could be my comeback,' she kept saying, pacing nervously in the kitchen. 'It could make me.'

The trouble was, I had seen the script when she made me run lines with her, and the nurse, Nancy, was twenty-eight, described as 'effortlessly beautiful in scrubs and no make-up'. On that show, no make-up actually meant loads of make-up, plus false eyelashes to show over your scrub mask. Still, I had watched it back home with Jenna, side by side on the old sagging sofa eating low-fat popcorn, and I was impressed. Someone I knew might be on television! The only time that had happened before was when Mrs Jackson next door saw someone get run over by a lorry on the ring road and went on the local news to talk about it.

Even Madison was swept up in it.

'Do Nancy for me, Mommy!' she'd say, and Abby would compose her face, widen her eyes, say something like, 'Dammit, Dr Inglewood,

I know you're in charge here, but you're making a mistake, and I'll lose my job before I let this patient die!' And Madison and I would clap. Abby was happy, for once, and the tension in the house seemed to ease, as if the walls had moved out several feet and more air had been pumped in. David even ate dinner with us a few nights, and sat by the pool on Saturday, watching Madison splash about in the shallows. I had Carson on my lap, playing with his toes to make him laugh. I loved that sound, an all-consuming gurgle that rose up from his little stomach.

'Not going in?' David said to me, peering over his sunglasses.

I was embarrassed by my milk-bottle-white British legs, my chipped home-done toenail varnish. No way was I polished enough for LA.

'Oh. No, I'm not much of a swimmer.'

'Nice to cool down, though.' His eyes moved over my legs in the print skirt I was wearing, and I got up, pretending to show Carson the pool. As he babbled, excited by the light on the water, David winced. 'Can you quiet him down, Casey? I'm working.'

Then Abby came out and wanted to go over her lines yet again. She practised them twenty times a day. She scowled at me over her big sunglasses. 'Casey, I need you. We don't pay you to lounge about by the pool.'

'I'm watching the kids,' I said, stung. I shouldn't have answered back. She clacked over in her heels – ridiculous to wear round the house – and took the baby from me.

'It's time for his nap.' Carson was deposited in his room, though he wasn't sleepy at all, and we ran the lines ten, twenty, thirty times. I could have acted the part myself by the end. Then of course she had to decide what to wear to the audition, and I had to help her, blushing as she pulled outfit after outfit over her head. She was thin, so thin I could see all her ribs and the gap between her thighs, but her stomach was still saggy and stretch-marked, and her breasts loose inside her bra. That was what having kids did to you. In the end she settled on a short blue dress she thought was like something a nurse would wear, which I privately thought was try-hard but didn't say.

She'd mostly given up on eating, desperate to lose a final three pounds before the audition. Breakfast was half a grapefruit, lunch a few cubes of cheese, dinner an undressed salad and steamed chicken breast. I saw Madison watch her. 'Is Mommy not hungry?' Then she would copy her mother and push aside half the lunch I'd made her as well. One day I caught her in front of the mirror, pulling up her frilly dress and exposing her pants.

'Madison! We don't show our underwear to people, do we?'

'Am I fat, Casey?'

'What?' She was five years old.

'My belly looks fat.' She prodded at it with a small finger.

'Madison, you're a little girl. You're supposed to look like that.'

But at dinner, I heard her ask for 'no dressing on my salad, please', and Abby nodded, approving. Two starving women.

Me, on the contrary, I'd reacted the other way to American life. I ate everything, cramming it in whenever I could snatch a moment, often standing up in the kitchen. The junk food Abby ordered in for David – or maybe to torment herself – was like a drug to me. Salt, sugar, fat, everything engineered to be as delicious as possible. Something's already tasty? Why not add bacon? Or cream? Or bacon and cream and maple syrup too? It was all allowed, and I scoffed it down in front of the TV on lonely nights, when David worked at his office across town or in his study, and Abby went to bed at eight – pouring crisps into my mouth, cookie dough straight from the packet, long red liquorice whips, crunching Lifesavers, ice cream and biscuits and pancakes and anything I could get my hands on. I hadn't weighed myself since I came out to America, but I had to suck in my stomach to button up my shorts.

You can go one of two ways in Hollywood, they say, skeletal or obese, and I was haunted by the sight of Abby's ribs.

The day of the audition came and no one in the house had slept. After being up till two with Carson, I encountered David in the kitchen, pre-dawn. Madison had wet her sheets again, but he didn't ask any more what I was up to, just seemed to take it for granted that I did the laundry before it was light out.

'Christ, I hope she gets it,' he said, switching on the coffee machine. 'Can't take much more of this.'

'Can't you help her? I mean, you know people.'

He blinked. 'I've tried, believe me. The trouble is, you get a reputation.'

Huh? I waited for him to say more, but he didn't, and the next moment Abby swept into the kitchen in her short blue dress, all dolled up at 5 a.m. She narrowed her eyes when she saw me there.

'Oh, you're both up. Casey, I'm leaving.'

'Isn't it at twelve?' I said. The exact time of the audition had been practically engraved on my brain for weeks.

'So?' she said. 'I don't want to get caught in traffic. Make sure Madison practises her tap, OK.'

'Good luck.'

She frowned as if I didn't have the right to say that.

'Good luck, honey,' said David half-heartedly. 'You'll be great.'

Abby bit her lip. 'Yeah – thanks. I know it, right? I've learned it back to front.'

'Of course you have.'

'Right. Yes.'

And then she was gone, and I heard the sound of her car start up. David let out a long, slow exhale, and I caught his eye. We both laughed, and it was another little spark between us. They weren't much, these moments of connection, but I treasured them, storing them up like a running-away fund.

Rachel

In weak moments there were certain things I did to keep the fear at bay. I went through my escape folder and checked all the details were up to date. I unpacked and repacked my go-bag, making sure to stock up on anything that had gone off, the cereal bars or the instant pasta in the sachets. I could have camped out for a week with those, if I had to.

The other thing I did – and I wasn't proud of this – was call Jeremy.

I knew it didn't help him – I could always hear the hope in his voice as he picked up. But I needed to talk to someone who knew who I was and still thought I was good. I realised I should have taken a picture of the fridge with the letters on it as proof, before messing them up, but after so many years falling behind in technology, I had never quite got up to speed. Marilyn had once laughed at the fact my phone's photo reel was entirely empty. *Like a sociopath*, she said. She was joking, I think. If only I'd thought to buy one of those fancy new security cameras, then I would have known who was doing this. Stupid me and my low-tech life.

I listened to the phone ring, then Jeremy's thick voice answering.

'Hello?'

'Jer? It's me.'

I had trained him years ago not to say my name on the phone. 'Babe?' The tentative hope, the tremble of emotion. 'Oh my God! It's been . . .'

'I know. I'm sorry. I was just so settled here, I didn't want to rock the boat. I've been thinking of you.' That was a lie. But I had never quite been able to let my ex-husband go, even when the divorce was finalised. It was too addictive, the way he looked at me, as if I was pure and good.

'Are you all right?' he said. 'I miss you.'

I didn't need to ask if he'd met someone else, been out at all. Staying in every night running various online forums about high-profile murders wasn't good for the social life.

'Not really, no,' I said. 'Jer – something's happened.'

'Did someone identify you?' He was instantly alert – he had helped me develop my escape plan when I was first released. I think he enjoyed it, with shades of the SAS books he liked to read. Jeremy would not survive a day on the run, I knew that.

'No. Not yet. But I've been accused of something.' I outlined what had happened – the wife of the man I was seeing had been murdered, how I'd found her dead body but run away, lied to the police about it. The scarf I didn't remember wearing, found nearby. He listened in what I assumed was stunned silence.

Then he said, quietly: 'I didn't know you were seeing someone.'

'That's what you take from it? Jer, I'm facing a murder charge!'

'Sorry, sorry. It's just so weird – how could it happen *again*?' And there it was, the question everyone would ask. How could someone be accused of murder, falsely accused that way, twice? The only way that could happen was if you were really guilty, like so many people still thought about me. Although I avoided the internet as much as possible, it was hard not to see things, and Jeremy often referred to it, although I had asked him not to.

'I don't know. The only thing I can think of is – someone wanted me to find her like that.' It sounded crazy. Would he believe me? Wasn't the simplest answer that I was, indeed, a murderer? I waited.

'You mean – killed her so you would find her?'

'God, I don't know. It's all I can imagine.'

'OK. So who could it be?'

Poor Jeremy. He always believed everything I told him. At first, back then, running as hard as I could from the prison I thought I'd die in, I had fled into his arms. It had meant everything to me, to be believed, when every word I'd spoken for five years had been scrutinised for lies, twisted, used against me. But it quickly wore thin. Almost two years we lived together in a small flat in Broadstairs, before I ran again. Jeremy left me his surname, at least, which was something. A screen to hide behind. Mrs Caldwell, and my middle name, Rachel. Not Casey Adams any more.

'I've no idea who,' I said. 'Any number of people might want to see me suffer. I mean, you read the forums online.' I knew there were still several websites dedicated to proving my guilt, and discounting the appeal findings. 'One of the Safran family, even. They definitely thought I was guilty. Ruth – the aunt, maybe.' I remembered Ruth Safran screaming in my face outside the court, her spittle landing on my cheek, not being able to wipe it off. How terrible that had felt, how I'd developed a nervous tic of wiping my cheek that had never truly left me. But Ruth was in America. Wasn't she? She lived in Texas and I didn't think had ever left the US. She'd never liked me, with my short skirts and tight vests. I was just a normal British girl, but in the conservative American South that was enough to get you burned at the stake.

I could hear Jeremy thinking hard, and it was nice, to talk to someone who knew the case inside out, better than me almost.

'I can look into it,' he said, and I could hear him taking notes already. 'Who else was there?'

I racked my brains. I had been with the Safrans only a few months, not long enough to know their entire family tree. There was a grandmother, I knew, who I vaguely thought had lived in London, but she'd have to be dead by now. Abby had some siblings, but I didn't know them; she'd done her best to distance herself from her roots and reinvent herself, and I didn't blame her. I had been hoping to do the same.

'I don't know, Jeremy. They'd need to have tracked me down, and got into my house! I just don't get it.'

He thought about it for a long time, and when he spoke I heard the note in his voice, the triumphant-theory tone he used when he'd forgotten I was a real person and that real people, including a child, had been murdered.

'Babe! What about the intruder? You're the only witness, after all. They could be trying to tie up loose ends.'

I sighed. 'Right. Because we'd ever be able to prove that.'

Jeremy has always been reluctant to let go of his pet ideas. He'd spent close to five years trying to prove the 'intruder' theory in the Safran murders, travelling to the States and asking the neighbours on the street for their home-security footage. He even rented the actual house itself on Airbnb (it's still available, since they assume tourists won't know what happened there) to see how easy it would be to climb over the back fence and break in. I could have told him that the hillside plunged into an overgrown ravine, alive with spiders and snakes, and was a no-go. The front door had been ajar on my return, but no one had been seen going in that way, and it was in full view of the nosy neighbour across the street, Carol Bubchek.

'I don't know,' he said. 'Listen, I'll come up, shall I? You need someone with you.'

It was dangerous, I knew, to let him back into my life like this, to give him hope, but he was right. I had no one else, only Alex, whose wife was the one murdered. 'Please,' I said, feeling a rush of gratitude. 'Thanks, Jer.' He promised to book a train as soon as possible, and we hung up.

On the internet you can get blueprints of the 'Mary Poppins Murders' house, diagrams showing the bedrooms and where each victim was found. Madison, in her bed, pink covers pulled over her as if she were asleep. She had been smothered with a pillow, which apparently is a common way for children to be killed. Her acting and pageant awards had not been disturbed; they were all still lined up on her shelves.

In prison, I'd had plenty of time to think about Madison's last moments. Had she been frightened when it happened? She never seemed to be frightened of anything, just bored or anxious. It was easy to forget she was only five when she died. She had been wearing make-up at the time, blue eyeshadow smeared over her lids, concealing the petechiae – tiny purple spots that are a classic sign of smothering. Had the eyeshadow been put on by her killer, or was she wearing it in bed? I had told the police I didn't know – she could have done it herself, she liked putting on make-up and dressing up in her room, swanning up and down in her child-sized high heels.

There was so much speculation online about Madison – had she been hurt in any way, *interfered* with? Almost like they wanted it to be true, to make the case as sordid as possible. *Oh God, how awful*, people would say, their eyes glinting, licking their lips. There was no evidence she'd been touched in that way. Just put to bed as if to sleep. There was a cigarette burn on her inner arm, which had been done about a week before, the police thought. There was bruising on her hands, as if she had been awake and held down. People think smothering is somehow an easy death, a gentle cloud carrying you off, but imagine not being able to breathe for the two or three minutes it takes to die, and you'll get the idea. There was no foreign DNA on her body or her bedclothes, or the unicorn pillow used to kill her, just her parents' and mine. But I had been her nanny. Of course I'd left some traces in her room.

Abby was killed in the kitchen, a knife drawn across her throat and left beside her on the tiles. No prints at all on that, as if someone had held it with a sleeve pulled over their hand, or perhaps wiped it clean afterwards. Abby had fought back, she'd broken three of her long nails and had bruises to her wrists and her neck, as if someone had tried to drag her. Her long hair had been pulled out in clumps. She had not died easy. I wonder did she know her daughter was already dead upstairs? Did she think about where her baby was as she bled out on the tiles, if he was safe? There was a lot of discussion about Abby's injuries. Could a small teenage girl like me have slashed the throat of a grown woman and dragged her along the floor, a woman who went to the gym every day? Various experts disagreed, but the District Attorney was so insistent it had to be me that eventually they found someone willing to say it was just about possible, that people can find extra strength when in the grip of extreme rage or fear.

Another theory was that Abby had done it, killed herself and the others. She was the smoker of the family, most likely to have burned Madison with a cigarette, and she was known to be erratic and to have slapped the child at least once in public. But no one can drag themselves across a floor by the hair. It just isn't possible.

David was in the hallway, near the front door. Maybe he had tried to stop the intruder, my defenders suggested. That would mean he'd died first, presumably. Then the killer had gone through him to Abby and all the way upstairs to Madison in her bedroom. But why? Nothing had been stolen. Neither Madison nor Abby had been sexually assaulted. Who would kill a family for no reason?

When David was found he had his arms over his face, as if warding off his attacker. He had been shot in the stomach with his own gun, a pistol that was kept in a drawer in his office desk.

One theory had it that David killed his wife and daughter, and presumably would have done the baby too if Carson had been there, because his production company was going under and he'd put the house up for collateral. Maybe Abby had found out. Maybe he'd thought – in some terrible twisted way – that his family would be better off dead. It was sadly common, the murder-suicide. Family destruction, they called it. But David had been shot from across the room, the blood spatter analyst confirmed. He couldn't have fired into his own stomach, not at that angle. It was impossible.

So who had done it? A mysterious intruder, as Jeremy would love to believe, a one-armed man, who had somehow got inside with no one seeing? The house had alarms and CCTV, like every one on the street, but they were always switched off during the day. It was a mystery, except of course there was one other person who could have done it, who had called 911 from the hall cupboard, clutching the baby in her arms. Who had Abby's blood on her feet, whose fingerprints were on the gun that shot David. Who had fought with Abby many times. Who had joked online about smothering the kids with a pillow.

Me.

The Murder Squad, discussion forum (January 2016)

Post by tom87

OK I know we're not supposed to say that maybe Racy Casey did it – just wondering how we explain the nanny post though. Here it is in full.

85

Hi guys . . . anyone really struggling with their job? I mean I'm 19 I'm not ready to be around kids 24/7 ha. I kind of thought it would be more fun days out, not cooking and cleaning and washing sheets when they wet them (is that normal at five?) Honestly some days I could just hold a pillow over them, shut them up. Ha, not really.

Before it gets taken down by the 'admin', what do we think about this? Would a normal girl say that about a little kid?

-response by BB2000 – Hi guys. All really interesting. Does anyone know where Casey might be hanging out these days?

Rachel

I had always been too afraid to google anything about the Safran case – I knew there would be a torrent of hate towards me, and anyway I just wanted to move on with my life, pretend it had never happened. If I pretended hard enough, the nightmares sometimes eased, the ones where I was running through the house, barefoot and panting, unsure which door to push on, knowing that horrors lay behind each one. Looking for Carson.

I tried to steel myself as I sat down at the computer in the town library later that day. I purposely didn't have the internet at the cottage as I knew my willpower was weak and I would soon spiral down rabbit holes I might never climb out of. The internet never forgets, and I needed to be forgotten, and to forget myself. I looked about the library furtively – would anybody recognise me? Would they know I was a suspect in a murder case? Over in the corner, a librarian was leading rhyme time, a group of children on their mothers' knees – one dad too, looking dazed with exhaustion – clapping their fat little hands to the rhythm. I hadn't held a baby since Carson, but my body remembered the weight of him on my hip, his head drowsing on my chest, trusting me enough to fall asleep in my arms. My little butterball, I had called him. I couldn't think about that now. I logged on with the code they gave me.

First, I couldn't help but check the news, to see if I'd been identified. It just said a woman named as Anna Devine had been found dead in woodland, that police had opened a murder enquiry, and that a '38-year-old woman' had been arrested and released without charge. Would people know that was me? Then, filled with dread, I typed my name – my real name – into the search engine. CASEY ADAMS.

Immediately, hundreds of hits. Thousands. I was famous out there. A variety of pictures of me, the ones that had helped damn me to start with – vest top, Smirnoff Ice in hand, draped over several boys from my sixth-form college. There was Ryan, my sort-of boyfriend, who'd never contacted me at all once I left for the States. One of them was Jeremy, who had hung about with us though never explicitly invited to. He'd been studying computer science, which at that point still seemed a slightly obscure subject. We didn't know then how much they'd take over our lives in just a few years. He'd made much of this photo, to pretend he knew me better than he did. No harm in it, not really. Jeremy had only ever tried to help me. Based on these pictures, I was a good-time girl. But I was nineteen then. Every British girl I knew had pictures like these, dressed the same, drinking too much, flirting a little, having a laugh, wearing tight tops and short skirts. It was just that not every girl became a suspect in a multiple homicide, had her life pulled apart by the press.

Then came the photos from the crime scene – the front of the house, stretchers with body bags being carried out. Who would photograph such a thing? There I was, standing outside the 'house of horror' as the police searched it, clutching my elbows with white knuckles. No emotion, the paper had said, but really it was shock. I had even answered one or two questions from reporters, with no idea what I was saying, another thing that was used against me. Carson had been taken from me by then, carried away by police to be put into the foster care system, where he remained until Ruth arrived from Texas to take him. Ruth, who had barely even picked him up before. I had been arrested shortly after, once they'd finished searching the house and found all the nightmares it contained. I still remembered the slap of the handcuffs against my wrists, heavy and cold. My shock. *This can't be happening*. But it was.

There was a photograph from the trial too. Me hustled by a guard from the police van to the courthouse, his fingers digging into my arm. I looked terrified. Sheer horror printed over my face. And I was right to be afraid, given what was coming. I clicked on a link to Wikipedia – I even had a Wikipedia page! Jenna might even have been impressed, although I wasn't sure if she'd known what Wikipedia was. *Casey Adams was a nanny accused of murdering the family she worked for in North Hollywood, Los Angeles, in October 2000. After serving four years on Death Row she was released on appeal and returned to her native UK.* That was all – no one could have found me from that, surely. There was a lot more detail about the case, but I knew all that, of course. The bits of supposed evidence – my hair on Madison's pillow, when I put her to bed every night. My fingerprints on the front door, when I had lived there and opened the door several times a day. More damning, my prints on David's gun, although I had explained that. Without all this circumstantial evidence, would I still have been convicted? Maybe. There was no one else left alive to say what really happened, after all.

There was also my post on the nannying forum run by the Little Helpers company, which I'd made in the early, hellish days of my job. I had forgotten about that before the trial, but it too was damning. That's the trouble with the internet and why I stayed away from it after my ordeal. Any of us can say things in the heat of the moment. *I hate this kid. I'll kill you. I wish I could run away.* But we don't mean it, and don't expect our words to be set in stone, still there to condemn us some twenty years later.

Next I came across a YouTube video about me, a clip from a documentary. I didn't want to watch it, but I needed to know if they said anything about my life now, so I plugged headphones into the jack on the side of the computer, and bunny-hopped through the scroll bar, wincing each time I heard something about suffocation, or gunshot residue, fingerprints, shooting distance. I could immediately tell from the deep-throated voice-over that the documentary was on the tackier end of TV. *Women Who Kill* was the title, and I supposed I could have sued over that, since I had been cleared of murder in the end, but the whole thing was exhausting, like whack-a-mole. There would always be people who thought I was guilty.

There was a shot of the house, police tape across it, and it hit me like a punch. Next up, images of David, Abby and Madison, smiling and happy. Murder victims always look happy. They aren't going to use a bad picture, a grouchy one, are they? Me, however, they used the worst one they could find, where I had a double chin and spots, in a tiny skirt and scarf-like top, holding a bottle of alcopop in both hands. Racy Casey, that's what they called me. All the evidence against me was trotted out again, the forum post, the medicine I'd brought with me from England, the bruises on Madison's arms I had supposedly not told anyone about, her bedwetting. Pictures of her in her pageant outfits, heavily made-up. Glamorous shots of Abby in her acting days. David on a film set, headphones on. They'd even found some minor celebrities to comment on how great David and Abby Safran had been, how they and their daughter were set for stardom, Hollywood at their feet. Nothing about the constant rejections or looming bankruptcy. Very little about Carson, either, and I was glad for him. He deserved not to be forever defined by living through the murders in the so-called house of horror (very original, calling it that). The programme strongly hinted that I had done it – short skirts equalled murderer, apparently – and then at the end it just stated in a few lines of text that I'd been exonerated and released after four years on Death Row in the Central California Women's Facility, and that the murders remained officially unsolved. *Adams is believed to have returned to the UK*, it said.

So nothing that could help people track me down to the Lake District and Coldwater. Unless someone here had seen these photographs of me and recognised me? I looked around the library again. Would somebody watching this documentary connect it to Rachel Caldwell, now pushing forty, single and childless, an unpaid assistant in a dog shelter? Perhaps someone had.

I was slipping down that rabbit hole I had feared for so long. I went back to Google and typed in *Casey Adams whereabouts*. Nothing. *Casey Adams where is she now*. I tried to think what wording a post about me might use. *Does anyone know where Casey Adams is now?*

Bingo – a hit. My heart began to race as I clicked on the forum, a site about notorious serial killers. Someone had asked that exact question: *Does anyone know where Casey is now?* The name of the poster meant nothing to me, a string of numbers and letters. I scrolled quickly through the answers, but no one seemed to know my whereabouts. *Let me know if you find out*, a few had replied, followed by descriptions of the horrible things they'd like to do to me. Almost all of them assumed I was guilty. I had known, I suppose, that an exoneration on appeal meant nothing to most people, but this really hit home. But that was Casey Adams, not Rachel Caldwell. How had someone made the link between those two names? This time, I googled my new identity.

Very little. A few other people with the same name, a lot of trash about nothing, and then – the website of the dog shelter. I had never been on this site before. Marilyn updated it herself and it was charmingly shonky, with clip art of puppies and an array of different fonts. On the 'news' page, I found it. A picture of me posing awkwardly with a puppy called Flame. I remembered him well, a husky we'd rehomed from Liverpool, where it had been going out of its mind. Huskies need cold and four hours of walks a day. Central heating and indolence drive them insane, so we get a lot of them in. It was now rehomed on a farm on Skye, a happy ending. The photograph of me was illustrating a little post about not buying huskies unless you can look after them, part of our commitment to reducing the need for rehoming in the first place. At the bottom, Marilyn had typed: *Flame pictured with our right-hand woman, Rachel Caldwell*. Was this it? The piece of information that had led someone to me? I looked quite different, twenty years older, my hair darkened and short, a far cry from the vibrant girl in those earlier photographs, who attracted such hatred for her Sun-In-streaked fair hair, her low-cut tops, her alcopops, her smile. But had someone made the connection anyway?

'Excuse me.'

A voice behind me made me jump right out of my chair, my bottom actually lifting. 'Jesus!'

The librarian from the reception desk looked quizzical. She was young, with bleached blonde hair and those thick eyebrows the kids have now.

'It's just your time's almost up,' she said. 'We do have people waiting.'

I'd been surfing for an hour already. Down the rabbit hole.

'Sorry, sorry. I'll go.'

I hurriedly logged out and gathered my things, the notepad I hadn't written on, my pen and bag, and I left with an over-abundance of apologies that only deepened her frown. As my place was taken by an older man in a Liverpool top, I looked back from the door and saw the librarian watching me. Had she seen what was on my screen? Would she look at my search history, and perhaps remember that a woman had been arrested over that terrible murder in the woods, and put two and two together, and realise that the person who'd found Anna Devine's body was the same one who'd been convicted of the 'Mary Poppins Murders'? (How I hated that name. Mary would never have been as stupid as me.) Would I be recognised in the street, shouted at, spat at, unable to go to the shops or library or even work without people calling me a murderer? The same insults all over again. *Slut. Killer. Hang her, it's all she's good for. Send her to the electric chair — I'll throw the switch myself.* Then the name Rachel Caldwell would be forever linked with that of Casey Adams, and I'd have to become someone else all over again, leave this life I had so carefully built up. It could only be a matter of time. And someone out there had been trying to find me.

Casey

SEPTEMBER 2000

After the audition there was a lull of a week or so while we waited to hear if Abby had got the part. She seemed at peace, at least. They'd liked her, she said, she'd done a good job reading for Nancy the nurse. They were just making their minds up. A few days afterwards there was a huge earthquake further north in the state, in San Francisco, which alarmed me, but nobody else seemed bothered by it. We even took the kids to Disneyland, an hour away in Anaheim, and I was as excited as Madison to go there, even though I spent most of the day trying to keep them cool as we stood in endless lines. It seemed a bit like life – a lot of waiting in discomfort for a few minutes of pleasure. Madison was quickly overwhelmed by it, bursting into tears when an adult dressed as Goofy waved at her, and Carson grizzled most of the day, feverish in the searing heat. All the same, Abby declared it 'a wonderful memory' and sent me to develop the roll of pictures from the day.

More time went by, with still no word from the TV producers, and soon Abby was in a flutter again because David's sister was coming to stay, from Texas, where she lived and taught at a university. I was roped in to clean out the spare room, plumping pillows and vacuuming, even though Marietta the housekeeper had already done it. When David went to get Ruth from LAX, Abby stalked through the house, pouncing on any stray toy or hair or crumb. I was afraid to put Carson down; he was at a very drooly stage and liable to leave chewed-up food on every surface. He was picking up on the tension, too, squirming and fussing in my arms. I tickled him under the chin, and was rewarded when he laughed up at me. I snuggled him to my chest, kissing the top of his head. 'There's a good boy. My little butterball, aren't you? Aren't you?'

Abby glared at me. 'Casey, I need your help. Stop jerking around with the baby and do something, OK?'

I hefted the baby – her baby – in my arms. 'I can put him down for a nap, but he's fussy.'

'Don't be stupid. Give me him.' As soon as she took him from me he started to cry again, his little face contorted. Abby made a noise of annoyance.

'Put him in his room.'

'But he'll cry!'

'So? Close the door.'

I carried Carson upstairs. It broke my heart to shut the door on him as he cried – he was teething, and just wanted to be held – but I had no choice. Abby was his mother, after all.

Madison was in a fever-pitch of excitement about her auntie visiting, listing the presents Ruth might bring and the adventures they would have. She had practised a tap routine, singing and dancing to 'On the Good Ship Lollipop', deliberately lisping some of the words to be cute. When David left in the car, she came bouncing downstairs in her favourite pink-polyester tutu, with huge puffed sleeves, her hair teased into giant ringlets. Her face was smeared with panstick and her eyes smeared in blue eyeshadow, large spots of rouge on her face. It was pageant make-up, extra thick to stand out on stage, but this was ten in the morning in the unforgiving daylight of the kitchen.

'Did Mummy put that on?' I asked, keeping my tone neutral.

'I did some myself!' She was so excited. 'Do I look pretty, Casey?'

How to answer that? She looked terrifying. 'I think you look pretty without make-up, Madison. Shall we wash some of it off, maybe?'

She glared at me, excitement twisting into hostility in a second, and so like her mother it chilled me. 'You're just jealous, that's what Mommy says. Because you're not as pretty as me.'

'I . . .' I didn't know what to say to that. I had woken up with pre-period spots all over my chin, and part of me was hurt by her comment, even though she was only five. 'I'd rather look like this than a drag queen,' I muttered. It wasn't fair. She was a child. But really, so was I.

'What's a drag queen?'

Oh God, she'd heard. 'Nothing. I'm sorry, Madison. You do look pretty. Now, shall we finish icing the cake for Aunt Ruth?'

She wouldn't let it go. 'I'm going to ask Mommy if I look pretty.'

'No, sweetie, don't . . . She'll be angry.' That was usually enough to stop Madison. Getting me in trouble was maybe not worth the risk of getting herself in trouble too. 'Here.' I took a red Lifesaver from the bag in a high cupboard and pressed it into her hands.

Madison frowned. 'I'm not allowed candy.'

'Our secret.' A phrase you should never say to a child, especially one that isn't your own. Madison took it, then tucked it very carefully inside her pocket to eat later. She knew how to hide things, even at her age.

Not long after, I heard the car in the drive and tensed all through my arms and legs. I had never met this woman, Ruth

Safran, but the stress of her arrival had seeped into me, and I wanted everything perfect. I straightened a lemon in the fruit bowl, ran a hand through my own messy hair, which I hadn't had time to brush.

Abby came down the stairs, sweeping in a maxi dress, her hair piled up, a lot of make-up on her too. She looked beautiful, like a seventies' starlet. Carson was in her arms, held carefully away from her dress. I was wearing a short denim skirt and a vest top that I now saw Carson had dribbled on earlier. My legs needed shaving, but I'd run out of razors and didn't know where to get more, plus I had the spots and my belly felt swollen, bulging over the waistband of my skirt. Still. Abby would not have liked it if I'd outshone her.

'Where's Madison?' she said. 'I wanted everyone ready.'

'Um . . .' I had lost sight of her in my rush to tidy the kitchen. 'She was just here.'

'Madison!' Abby howled. 'Get in here right now!'

Footsteps. Madison rushed in from the garden and I saw with dismay that the illicit sweet had melted all down her dress, leaving sticky red stains. Some was on her face too.

'Mommy! Can I do my dance for Aunt Ruth?' She was oblivious to the stains.

Abby's face was like thunder. 'Oh my God, look at the state of you! Dirty little girl, you can't stay clean for five minutes?'

Madison sagged, rubbing ineffectually at her front.

'It's my fault,' I said. 'I gave her a sweet. I'm sorry.'

'Well, you've ruined it all now,' said Abby. 'You better put on a fucking smile and clean her up the second Ruth's out of sight.' She said this in a hiss through a pasted-on smile. It was one of the strangest things I'd ever seen.

Madison was almost in tears. 'I'm sorry, Mommy.'

'Don't be sorry. Smile!' Abby barked.

I pulled the child behind me, trying to hide her dress, and we all stood to attention as David opened the door.

I was surprised to see Ruth was wearing a suit, a grey jacket and skirt. It was over thirty degrees outside and she'd just come off a flight. She looked much older than David, with a pinched face and hair set in stiff curls around her head. She put on her glasses, which hung about her neck on a string, and blinked in the gloom of the house.

'Here's Aunt Ruth!' said David heartily.

'Ruth!' Abby stepped forward, face outstretched, but Ruth drew back, rejecting the kiss.

'I need to freshen up,' she said, and I could hear the Southern accent that David had worked so hard to shed. 'The way my brother drives, I saw my life flash before my eyes!'

David's face tightened. He leaned out to bring in her cases, two huge ones tied about with cables.

'Madison, say hello.' Abby covered her disappointment at the dodged embrace.

Madison stepped out from behind me. 'Hi, Aunt Ruth!'

Ruth peered at her. 'Oh dear, you've spilled something on your dress, honey. And what's that on your face? Did you get into Mommy's make-up kit?'

Madison looked confused.

Ruth turned to the baby – she was the kind of woman who made more fuss of boys. 'And this must be my precious nephew, the Safran heir!' She said things like that.

Abby said, 'Would you like to hold him?'

At that moment, Carson let out a bubble that was mostly spit and some puke.

Ruth stepped back again. 'Maybe later.' Her eyes flicked to me.

'Hi,' I said, panicking that no one would introduce me. 'I'm Casey, the nanny.'

She nodded at me, taking in my bare legs and shoulders. 'You should clean the children up before guests come.'

Really, she was a master at this. Two minutes in the house and she had managed to insult every single one of us.

◆ ◆ ◆

Ruth stayed for a week and by the end of it I couldn't believe I'd thought the house tense with just the five of us in it. She got up at five every day to pray, catching me several times with Madison's morning sheets. I made an excuse about this being my laundry time, 'before the kids wake up', but her shrewd eyes raked over me, suspicious. Before each meal we had to say grace, even if the kids were hungry and Carson was howling at the delay. She insisted on me driving her places, various out-of-the-way malls, shops right in the centre of Hollywood where there was no parking, obscure churches. When I ventured that four in the afternoon was a bad time to try and cross the city, she would widen her eyes and declare it nonsense. If I came downstairs in shorts or a vest, she would say, 'Casey, dear, I hope you don't mind a little advice. You're a young girl in a house with a man – it might be sensible to dress a little more . . . ladylike.' I ignored it, though the shame burned in me.

When I told Jenna about it on the phone, she was fuming. 'Jealous old bitch. Bet she's not much to look at, is she?'

'Not really,' I said, then making myself feel better by slagging off Ruth's hair, her weight, her clothes. All the ways women tear each other down.

On Ruth's last night in the house, Abby had organised a special goodbye meal on the pool terrace. She had been strangely quiet all week, not snapping at me or the kids as usual. She had been on her best behaviour, allowing Ruth to give her 'a little advice' as well, about everything from the right way to dress a salad to how to wear her hair – *That colour is too harsh on you, sweetie, people can tell it's dyed*. Abby had gone all out, or rather, made me go all out. I'd hauled bags from the supermarket until the paper handles ate into my palms. I'd shelled prawns and sliced fruit and arranged platters and searched high cupboards for dishes, dodging the spiders. Abby had even sent me into the untidy garage to find some folding chairs. By the end of the day I was sticky, exhausted, my arms aching, bruises on my legs. Abby wrinkled her nose at me and said I had time to shower if I was quick.

I went upstairs to change, but what to wear? I opened the wardrobe and looked at the meagre collection of clothes I'd brought over in my pink suitcase. I'd imagined buying an amazing new wardrobe out here, but I only ever went to grocery stores and had no idea where to find nice things. Rodeo Drive was obviously out, as well as being on the wrong side of town. There was no high street nearby, no H&M or Primark to pop to. I was in a foreign land. I had one nice-ish dress that Jenna had made me buy for my nanny interview, which fell just below my knees and buttoned up the front, with short sleeves. Demure. I took it out and looked at it, and then something in me reared its head. Some kind of stubbornness, after weeks of being put upon and scolded, getting by on snatched hours of sleep. Instead, I took out my shortest, tightest denim skirt, a trashy one I'd bought from a market back home, white with a frayed hem. I put on a bra that was a bit too tight after months of American eating, and a vest top I normally just slept in, with spaghetti straps that rarely stayed up. I outlined my eyes in liner and glitter shadow, made my mouth big and red and sticky. Sod Ruth. Sod Abby. I was nineteen years old and I was sick of being buried in this house.

When I came downstairs David was passing into the kitchen, a platter of seafood in his hands. He stopped to stare at me, half-frowning. I felt like a girl in a film, as I slowly descended, never breaking eye contact. My heart thundered, even as the too-tight clothes dug into me. What was I doing? I went up to him, took a prawn from the plate, and put it in my mouth, holding his gaze. I'd seen that sort of thing in films, though I felt stupid doing it.

'Don't let Abby see that,' he said lightly, and he could have meant the prawn or something else.

'I shelled these,' I said lightly, not deferentially. Not like I was talking to my boss. Then I went outside to the terrace.

Abby was there, making microscopic realignments to the table-ware. Ruth was sitting in a chair, with the only alcoholic drink she allowed herself, a diluted Martini. Despite the hot night she was wearing slacks and a silk blouse, heavy old-fashioned lipstick. She and Abby turned to stare at me. I could see they both wanted to say something about my outfit, but Abby wouldn't dare to in front of Ruth. Better to pretend it was all fine. Ruth didn't say anything either, just raised her eyebrows. 'I hope you won't catch cold, dear.'

I flopped down in a wicker chair, which would leave long welts on the backs of my bare legs. 'What time are we eating?'

Abby shot me a little look; I'd pay for this later. 'Madison has a routine for us first.'

David came out with two beers, and he handed one to me, which I saw Ruth notice. I smiled up into his face. I didn't know what I was doing – I was dizzy with myself, with disobedience. Carson was upstairs, his baby monitor on the kitchen counter. Madison was in the kitchen, I could hear her muttering to herself as she got ready.

'Are you all watching?' she called out to us as we arranged ourselves on the terrace.

David sat down, angled his chair towards the edge of the pool. 'We're watching.'

'Mommy?' called Madison.

Abby was still fiddling with the dishes on the table. David reached over and forced her into a seat, his touch not tender.

'We're ready,' he called. 'Come on, honey, we don't have all night.'

There was a pause, then Madison burst out, toes pointed, hands on hips, huge fixed smile. She launched into her routine, high kicks to show off her frilly pants, arms twirling about her small compact body, voice high and reedy as she sang about the Good Ship Lollipop. I had seen her perform before, of course, but something about it was excruciating, maybe Ruth's raised eyebrows and incredulous look. *Oh God, sit down*, I wanted to shout. I wanted to bundle her away and put her in proper clothes for a five-year-old, cotton pants and jeans and a sweatshirt with cartoons on it. Abby was watching her intently, moving along, hands twitching as she unconsciously followed the routine she had drilled her daughter in.

Finally, it was over, with a flourish. Abby clapped enthusiastically. David and I followed, half-heartedly.

'Did you like it, Auntie Ruth!' said Madison, flushed with effort.

Ruth picked up her glass and sipped. 'Honestly, Madison,' she said, 'it's not nice to show your panties off in public. Didn't your mommy ever tell you that?'

Madison looked crushed, darting glances between her aunt and her mother, whose face had gone white, then plum. 'Was it not good?'

'It was very good, sweetheart,' said David, picking up the salad tongs. 'Now, who's hungry?'

'She practised this for weeks,' said Abby, in a low growl. Like well-trained dogs, Madison and I froze at her tone. My stomach contracted and I suddenly lost my appetite.

Ruth made a grunt and reached for a plate. 'You shouldn't push her into it, Abigail,' she said. 'It's not nice for a little girl her age. There are bad men, you know, who look for girls like that.'

A moment of shocked silence.

I caught David's eye, his face as panicked as mine. Abby opened her mouth, as if to say something back, then slowly rose and went inside.

Madison had started crying. 'I'm sorry,' she sobbed. 'I didn't mean to be not nice.'

'It's all right,' I soothed, leaning over her, aware of David's eyes on me. 'You were very good. Now look, you love prawns, or shrimp, I mean – try some of these. I shelled them myself.'

Madison nodded, her face quivering and her chest heaving under her polyester dress. She smelled of sweat already, at her age. She speared a prawn on her fork, but just looked at it.

Ruth was happily tearing into a dinner roll, as if unaware of how crushing she'd been. 'It's a lot of food, isn't it?' she said. 'I hope we can eat it all. I do hate waste, what with children starving in Africa.'

I forked up some salad and put it into my mouth, but it tasted like dust. I made myself swallow. Someone should go after Abby – and it should be her husband. She wouldn't welcome interference from me, her underling, who had witnessed her shame. But David didn't move. Instead, he poured himself a large glass from the bottle of wine, and sat back to drink it. We ate in silence for a few minutes, and then I heard a faint noise, like a very small trickle. A smell I knew well from my early-morning washing sessions. Ruth caught it too, her nose wrinkled. 'What *is* that?'

Madison was red-faced, crying softly into her prawns. 'I'm sorry. I didn't mean to.'

I looked down – the crotch of her dress was damp. Oh God.

'Oh my gosh!' Ruth jumped up with a noise of disgust, as if a spider had crawled over her foot. 'There's a puddle of it! For goodness' sake.'

I was hustling Madison out of her seat, which was also puddled. 'Come on, let's go to the bathroom, sweetheart. It's all right.'

'I'm sorry,' she sobbed. 'I'm sorry!'

As I led her indoors to the chilly interior of the house, I heard Ruth say to her brother, 'It's not right at her age. It's disgusting. If I were you I'd get her professionally looked at.'

I put Madison to bed, knowing better than to knock on Abby's door. She would be in a drug-induced stupor by now. Madison was still crying, softly, desperately, into her pillow.

'It's all right,' I said, soothing her as best I could, knowing what I said was a lie. 'Aunt Ruth loved your song, she said so just now. Mommy won't be angry with you.'

It wasn't all right. Far from it. Mommy would indeed be angry. And in truth Auntie Ruth had hated Madison's performance and really didn't seem to like her.

I washed my hands thoroughly. I seemed to have done nothing but scrub urine off my hands in the last few weeks. Madison needed rubber sheets, and maybe Ruth's suggestion of seeing a doctor wasn't bad. Wetting the bed, I knew from my child development course at college, was not a good sign at Madison's age. Again, I wished I had paid more attention instead of doing my make-up in class and thinking about the hot boys in the next-door CDT class, who'd drop out within months to become mechanics or builders.

Downstairs, when I returned, David sat alone among the barely touched food. I would have to clear everything up, I supposed. It seemed to be normal now that I would do all the housework as well as childcare. I hadn't been hired to do that. Marietta would come in the morning, but she'd huff and puff about the mess, and Abby would expect it to be clean when she got up.

'Hey,' I said to David. 'She's all right,' I added, even though he hadn't asked about Madison and I wasn't sure it was true.

David just nodded. I noticed the bottle of wine was almost empty.

'Is it meant to be this hard?' he said after a while. His tone was confidential, one adult to another, which I wasn't used to.

'What? Kids?'

'Kids, marriage, the whole thing. Family. Ruth's a nightmare, she always was. I don't know why I even try.'

I sat down next to him. It was after six now. The light was fading already, the cold of the desert taking hold. 'Families are tough,' I said. 'It's just me and my mum and even that's a struggle sometimes.'

David rummaged in his pocket, and slapped something on to the table – a lighter and a packet of cigarettes. I was surprised; I had seen Abby smoking many times on the terrace, trying to keep her weight down, but not him. 'I didn't know you smoked,' I said.

'I quit. I might start again.' He lit one, sucking it in with closed eyes. 'Want one?'

I didn't smoke – I'd seen how it had aged Jenna's skin – although I'd bum the odd one back home on nights out. 'Sure,' I said nonchalantly. He passed me one and I put it in my mouth. It would have been the ideal moment to lean over, get him to light it between my lips, but instead I held out my hand for the lighter and did it myself. I felt somehow ashamed of my behaviour, my skimpy clothes and cheap make-up.

He looked at me. 'I know so little about you, Casey, yet here you are, raising my kids, cleaning up our messes. Literally. You know everything about us.'

'Not everything,' I said lightly. 'Can I have a bit?' I lifted my wine glass. Technically, I was too young to drink in this mad country, but he filled my glass, emptying the bottle.

He went on. 'I mean, look at you, you're young, you're beautiful, you have your life in front of you. Why be a nanny? Stay away from it as long as possible, is my advice. Don't have kids till you're forty.'

All I had heard in that was *beautiful, he thinks I'm beautiful*.

'You want me to quit?' I swirled my wine, feeling sophisticated.

'God no. We need you. Just – think of yourself as well. Don't stay here too long.'

This was my chance. 'I'll be honest,' I said. 'I was really excited to come to LA. I've always dreamed of being an actress. My mum pushed me into it, too. She was in a soap in the eighties and she wanted more for me. Maybe you know it – it was called *Brackley Street*?' He shook his head. 'No. I guess it wouldn't have shown over here.'

Poor Jenna with her out-of-date publicity headshots and failed auditions, although she got occasional requests to appear on a panel show or be a talking head in a reunion show or to attend a TV convention. She took it all. Living in poverty, waiting for scraps, instead of giving it up and finding a proper job.

David barked a laugh. 'I should have known. So you came out here to make it big? Nannying just a step to something better?'

'No, I . . .'

'It's fine, Casey. I don't blame you at all. Makes sense of why you're here. You knew I was a film producer?'

I knew to play this down. 'Not really. I was a bit clueless, to be honest, how it all works, but it's so fascinating to me, what you do.' I rested my chin on my hands. The wine was stealing through my veins, loosening my limbs.

'It's not so much.' He was drunk, about to tip over into melancholy.

'You said you'd take me to your work one day.'

'Oh. Did you want to go?'

'Definitely! I'd love it.'

'Tomorrow? Oh, what about the kids?'

'Madison has school and Carson naps around eleven. We could . . . let him sleep somewhere.' I was suggesting leaving his baby alone, but David just nodded. He ran a hand over his face.

'I should go to bed. Early start. Christ, it's hard work.'

I knew he didn't mean his job. I leaned in a bit closer.

'I'm here to help you, you know. They sometimes call this job a mother's help, but . . . I'm a father's help too.' My hand rested on the table near his. I wasn't brave enough to touch him, not yet. But the invite was there. What was I doing? I didn't like David, not in that way. I was just lonely. And Abby was so awful to me.

'Thank you, Casey.' He stood up. 'You're more of a help than you know. Now leave all this, please, and go to bed. Carson will be up in an hour, I'm sure.'

I went to bed, obscurely disappointed, but with a small tick of excitement deep in my stomach. Something was going to happen. I knew it. At nineteen, I still thought something was better than nothing. How wrong I was about that.

Rachel

I should have gone to see Jeremy, by rights. I was the one who needed his help, and he lived miles away, in a coastal town in Kent. But that was the way it had always been with us – I called, and he came. All the way to California the first time, and he stayed there for months while I was in prison, finding a lawyer for the appeal and raising the money and eventually getting me out. I owed Jeremy a lot. But owing is no basis for love, as we found out in the eighteen long months we tried to live together as husband and wife, in his one-bed flat overlooking the English Channel. Until I realised I had traded one kind of prison for another.

The police were on the green again as I left the house the next morning, and I saw DS Hegarty talking to some of the white-suit people. 'Ms Caldwell. Going somewhere?'

'Um, no. Meeting a friend at the station.'

He looked me over. 'That's good. Someone to be with you at such a difficult time.' The meaning was clear – they were watching me, and another arrest was extremely likely. They just didn't have enough evidence yet. I thought again of telling him about the letters on my fridge – but that would mean admitting who I was. And what could make me look more guilty?

I took the bus into Oxenholme and met Jeremy off the train, my heart softening and sinking as I saw him bumble towards me, arms full of plastic bags and manila folders, in the same old parka as fifteen years before. My ex-husband. The only man who knew the truth of me, or at least, the only one alive. Even he didn't know it all.

'Hey you.'

I held my arms out for a hug, fell into his squashy softness, noting his laboured breathing and sweaty face. Jeremy was not in good shape, and no wonder since he spent about eighteen hours a day glued to a screen of some kind. He was filled with theories and speculation about Anna's murder, as if he kept forgetting that this was my life, and the death of a real person I had known, or that I might once again go to prison for something I didn't do.

'I've been thinking, I really should start a podcast,' Jeremy said as he opened the door of the taxi I'd decided to splash out on, files slipping from his arms on to the road. I stooped to pick one up and recognised a police photo of Abby. Dead. I tried not to look as I passed it back. 'These kids that do them, they don't even bother checking the facts. I mean, I could do that. I actually know things.'

I didn't like to say you needed more than facts to hold an audience.

'Mm,' I said. 'So how are things?' I was very aware of the taxi driver in the front, a quiet man in a turban. I hoped Jeremy would have the sense not to say too much during the drive.

'Oh, ticking along,' he said. 'We got the Tulsa police to release the tapes on that case I was researching.'

Jeremy ran a website and forum for true-crime enthusiasts, including documents and artefacts from old cases. The Murder Squad was the name, as if they were serving police officers, not just randoms in their living rooms. They prided themselves on being armchair detectives, finding people like me guilty, but really they were ghouls, raking over dead children, murdered women, the more horrific the crime the better. I couldn't bear to look at it – it upset me too much. In every 'irrefutable fact' I saw just another angle, another way to explain what happened. Like the forum post I wrote back when I was struggling with the kids, especially a difficult five-year-old whose own mother couldn't handle her. Anyway, is there a correct amount of time to wait between finding your entire household dead and calling the police? I'd spent a lot of that time hiding in the cupboard with Carson. Saving the baby's life was all I could think about at the time. But to these people online, these complete strangers, it was all just proof of my guilt.

Jeremy, to be fair, had always been on my side, and would boot people off his site if they tried to say I did kill the Safrans. I thought he capitalised on it a little too much sometimes, our relationship, a whiff of real scandal, having been married to a convicted (then unconvicted) mass murderer. But he was good to me, and I couldn't afford to turn away anyone who cared about me. I had so few.

Jeremy was still banging on about this other case, something about bloodied tissues, as the taxi arrived at my cottage, and he staggered out with all his files and bags. I unlocked the door, Brandy emitting a soft whuff from the kitchen but not running to greet me, seeing me with a strange man. I had picked her up from Marilyn's the evening before, too embarrassed to come in for the tea she'd offered. She must know I'd been arrested over the murder of her friend, and even if I hadn't been charged, surely she would have wondered. If I had actually done it.

'Jer. Please. I really need your help, I'm losing my mind here.'

'Of course. I'm sorry. So this woman Anna, you knew her?'

'Not really. She was married to my – this man I've been seeing. They were split up, but not divorced yet.'

'Oh.'

I busied myself with the kettle to avoid looking at his face. He knew, of course, that I saw people from time to time, and we'd been divorced for more than ten years, but he didn't like to hear about it all the same. I wished he would meet someone. He was seeing a woman from the Murder Squad forum for a while, but they had fallen out over their interpretations of a piece of evidence in the Madeleine McCann case, and their relationship never really recovered.

I said, 'Trouble is, people saw her yell at me in the street last week. And the rest. Me dating her husband, running away from the scene. They haven't charged me yet, though – that's a good sign, right? That they let me go?'

Jeremy flopped on to my sofa. Brandy, who saw this as her place, retreated in a huff to her crate. 'Dunno. What they do, see, is they watch you. Build a case. If they charge too soon the whole thing can fall apart. Remember the Soham inquiry? They knew he was acting well suss, putting himself into the investigation, far too helpful, but they'd no proof. So they just watched him, for weeks.'

Was this supposed to be comforting? 'But I didn't do it, Jeremy! So we have to figure out who did.'

'Right, right. You think someone's found you then? From the past?'

'It looks that way, doesn't it? You never . . . ?'

'No! God, no, I'm very careful. I would never tell anyone your new name.'

Still, he might have slipped up over the years, said something to the wrong person. I'd never been given a new legal identity, simply started using my married name and my middle one. It's not illegal to call yourself something different.

'You don't have anything with my name or address written down? An address book or something?'

He scoffed. 'Of course not. Who has address books nowadays?'

'Right. There's nothing you can think of?'

Mildly affronted, he ticked it off on his fingers. 'I only have your number in my phone, saved as initials, and I only ever text you, then delete it right after. I never print out anything and I don't actually *know* your address, remember.'

That was true. I had never given it to him, sticking to digital communication only. As far as I knew, he had never been north of Watford Gap before this.

'I'm sorry. I'm just trying to think of every possibility.'

'I understand,' he said soothingly. 'But someone has found you, by the looks of it. So we have to work out who that could be, then prove that they – what? – murdered this Anna woman to frame you?'

A short silence. 'It sounds crazy when you say it like that,' I said sheepishly. 'Why would anyone commit murder just to get back at me?' I thought of the depths of hate that would require, and a shiver ran through me.

'Crazy things happen,' he said. 'We know that. And you didn't do it, so someone else did.'

I almost loved Jeremy for that, and not for the first time I wished I could have been happy with just that, with the small things I had dreamed of during my years in prison. A man who believed me, a door I could open, blue sky over my head. By asking for more, leaving his protection and starting this new life, had I opened myself up to yet more doom?

Jeremy was staying with me, of course. The B&Bs round here cost a fortune and got booked up months ahead, all artisan biscuits and rainfall showers. He was cheerful about sleeping on my sagging sofa: 'You know me, could sleep on a log if I had to!' So that little bit of awkwardness was passed. I didn't want to even entertain the idea of sharing a bed.

I hadn't told Alex that Jeremy was coming, or even that he existed. Keeping secrets was so ingrained in me now, a habit natural as breathing. Alex had not been in touch since I left his flat early the day before. I told myself that was right, that he needed to take care of Sam, but all the same my hand kept straying to my phone, only to see the screen blank. I was angry at myself, waiting for someone to get in touch, wanting something I couldn't have. I had tried for so long not to want anything.

I'd made a lasagne for dinner. It wasn't anything special, but Jeremy was touchingly enthusiastic about it. He lived off ready meals most of the time, eaten with one hand on his mouse, always clicking and scrolling. I'd often wondered what drove people like him, the true-crime enthusiasts, the murder ghouls. Was it the thrill of the unsolved, of never quite knowing? It was because of people like them that my past would always hang over me, unless the Mary Poppins Murders case – and even that name was so callous – was solved one day, and I knew it never would be.

We ate sitting at the table, and I even lit a candle to clear the cooking smell, then wondered was that a mistake. Candles are romantic, after all, and he might get the wrong idea. I poured red wine and it was all very civilised. You would never have known I was possibly facing the second murder charge of my life.

Jeremy was scrawling with one hand on a big pad of paper. I had never seen him eat a meal without doing something else at the same time.

'So it's someone who got into this house and put your name on the fridge. Maybe with a key?' He looked about him, frowned. 'It's not that secure, Case, anyone could get through that lock if they knew the first thing about picks.' A slip – my old name. I looked at him across the table until he realised what he'd said. 'Oh

113

God, sorry. But it's just us. You leave your windows open too?'
The windows here were old and wide – a person could easily climb
through them.

'Yeah, if it's hot. For Brandy.' Brandy was in the kitchen, in a
huff. Jeremy had tried his best with her, but he was asthmatic and
not a dog person. One of the many reasons I'd left him.

'So someone could get in that way,' he said. 'Do you still leave
a key outside too?'

I sighed. 'Yeah, in the pot.' I'd started doing this after I was
released from prison – some kind of residual horror at the idea of
not being able to open my own door. I saw now it was stupid. I
wasn't that careful at work either, I left my bag on chairs in the
office all the time. 'Did you have any luck tracing people? I was
thinking of Ruth. You know, the sister.'

I hadn't seen Ruth since the trial, hard-faced, red-eyed, refusing to
look at me. Maybe she had cared about her brother and his children,
in the end. I'd never forget the way she described my clothes and my
behaviour – I think she actually used the word *wanton*. It was a bewil-
dering feeling, to be hated so much by someone I hardly knew. The
Abby and Madison she described – happy, beloved, content – bore
no resemblance to the people I had known.

'Yes!' Jeremy exclaimed. He wiped a hand over his mouth,
smearing tomato sauce. 'I have something here . . . wait.' He got up
and rooted in his rucksack, the same fraying rucksack he'd turned
up in America with almost twenty years ago, when I had never
been so glad to see someone in my life. He brought back a folder
of notes. 'Right. Ruth Janet Safran, born 1954, that was her, yes?
Texas?'

'It must be, yes.'

'She died. Two years ago.' Jeremy sat back, pleased with himself.
'Oh.'

Ruth with her beady eyes, tissue balled in her hand on the witness stand. *Wanton.*

I shouldn't have cared – she had hated me and helped condemn me to death – but some part of me mourned her. Was it because I would never be able to tell her the truth now, prove my innocence? Did some part of her know I'd never have hurt a child? Why else had she lied so much in her testimony? Hand on the Bible that she pretended to live by, selling me down the river, the jury frowning at me as this respectable Christian woman detailed all my faults. And now she was dead.

'So not her then,' I said dully.

'Can't be. She had cancer.' Jeremy slapped the file with a sort of jolly energy.

'She's dead, Jer. It's not a good thing.'

His face fell. 'Oh. No. But it means we can eliminate her as a suspect.'

'But then who did it? She was the only person I could imagine doing something like this. That means – what? It's someone I haven't even thought of? Some stranger? How am I supposed to fight this?'

'Come on, we'll solve it.' He laid his hand over mine, sweaty and heavy. I pulled away. I wasn't so sure.

The evening quickly wore out. I was too worried to talk about other things, so I let him ramble on about various topics. Jeremy's mother in her nursing home, where she'd led the residents in a rebellion to get better biscuits, and his ongoing battles with his neighbours over his many internet cables sucking the power from the building. His nominal job building websites, which didn't involve going outside or seeing other people. Jeremy was by nature a bit obsessive. He wouldn't notice he'd been wearing the same T-shirt for five days, or that he hadn't stood up from his desk in twelve hours. When we were together I had tried to get him drinking water and exercising, but now I was gone the habits clearly hadn't stuck. His stomach hung down under his Marvel T-shirt, and his hair and nails needed trimming. But his earnest, sweaty face was dear to me all the same. If only I'd been able to love him back.

'Right.' I stood up, wearily, stacking dishes. 'We're not getting anywhere, are we? I can't think of anyone else.'

We had a paltry list on the pad – José, Marietta, some unnamed intruder who may or may not have existed. Jeremy tapped it with his chewed pen. 'We need to track them down. There's a guy in the Netherlands. He can find anyone. Seriously, the police go to him all the time. A really cool dude. I have some clout with him. Jochem Groeneveld.' Typical Jeremy, name-dropping someone nobody had heard of outside the true-crime forums.

'All right. Thank you.'

Jeremy yawned. 'But also, have you thought about this? If it's not someone from your past, from America, maybe it's someone from your new life. Who knows you here?'

I hadn't wanted to think about that. 'I don't really know anyone. I only go to work, and now and again to the pub or something. There's Audrey next door. Huh. She might do it, because Brandy digs up her begonias.'

'At work, you were saying there's lots of kids there, right?'

'The interns. Yeah. But they're only young. They probably don't even remember the case. And I already tried an internet trawl. I couldn't find that I'd been – what's the word for when your details are online?'

'Doxed.' Jeremy was very up on the latest internet lingo. 'I can look. You might not know all the forums. There's some on the dark web, even.'

That idea made me shiver. 'OK. I'll get you some sheets.'

I was just moving to the stairs when the doorbell rang. I froze. Was it the police, again? It was after midnight.

Jeremy frowned. 'Bit late for a visitor?'

My head was spinning. I began speaking very fast, walking to the door.

'Listen. There's a folder in the bottom drawer of my desk. It says what to do if I – if I don't come back. With Brandy and the house. Please can you see to it? You don't have to take her, obviously. Just – don't let her be alone. Please?'

He was looking at me in dismay. 'Case, it's not come to that.'

'Don't call me that!' I took a deep breath. The bell went again. 'Sorry. I'm sorry.' I opened the door – the porch light was out, so for a moment I could only see the dark shape of a man, and my whole body was trembling, sure that this was it, they had come for me . . .

'Rachel?' Alex stepped forward, out of the gloom. 'Are you OK?'

'Oh, it's you! You scared me.'

'You didn't answer my message. I thought I'd just come by, see if you're all right.'

He hadn't contacted me in two days, and now he was worried about me? 'I'm all right.' I wasn't, though. 'I'm just . . . oh God, Alex, this is all so weird. I don't know what's going on.'

He was looking past me, as Jeremy made himself at home on the sofa. He had a way of spreading. 'I didn't realise you had company.' His face and voice had hardened.

'Oh! No, this is Jeremy. He's helping me with the case. He's a bit of an armchair crime expert.'

Jeremy was up and barrelling over, hand outstretched. He laid the other on my shoulder. Was it deliberate, marking his territory, or just unconscious? 'Hello. Jeremy.'

Alex didn't shake it, and didn't say his own name. 'And how do you know Rachel?'

It was just for a second, but I saw Jeremy hesitate on the name. *Who's Rachel?*

'Well, she's my wife!' He said it jokingly, probably to try and cover up the tension, but I saw the look that crossed Alex's face.

'Ex-wife!' I said hastily. 'We were married for a bit years ago – we're good friends now.'

'I see.' Alex's tone was frosty. 'I don't think you ever mentioned that.'

Of course I hadn't – I'd told him nothing about my past. 'Do you want to come in? We were just going to bed.' Oh God. I couldn't explain what I meant by that without digging a deeper hole.

'I'll leave you to it.' I had never seen Alex so cold, and I had to remember that his wife had been stabbed, the mother of his son, and his girlfriend – was I even that? – had been implicated in the murder. And now he had turned up here to find me with another man – an ex-husband I hadn't told him about.

I was pleading now. 'I'm just – I thought Jeremy could help, maybe. Figure out who hurt Anna, who did this.' I couldn't explain that I thought someone was framing me – and it was so tenuous. Someone had been in my house, yes, someone who knew me, but that didn't mean they'd killed Anna, or left my scarf nearby. And how would I ever prove it if they had?

He had stepped away from me. I didn't know how to rescue this.

'Can I see you tomorrow?' I said, desperate.

'I don't know, Rachel. Anna's dead – Sam, I've been trying to take care of him all day, but he doesn't understand – and her parents, they're in bits. And you were arrested! You actually found her body and you didn't call it in! How do you think that looks? But all the same I've come to see you, I wanted to be with you – and you're here with some other man? A husband I've never even heard of. I mean, Jesus. What am I supposed to do with that?'

'I . . .' He waited for a moment, but I could say nothing to defend any of this, and after a second or two he turned away, disappearing into the night.

Post by liljackie

Is anyone going to talk about the drugging? That the kids were found to have some sort of British medicine in their systems? It's like liquid paracetamol, but it makes the kids sleep. You can only get it there, so she must have brought it with her. And the aunt said the baby was really sleepy when she was there, plus the little girl had been late for school a few times because she wouldn't wake up. My theory is that Casey gave Madison too much of this medicine and she stopped breathing, so she had to stage the "intruder" set-up to cover it up when the parents found out what she'd done, and she panicked and killed them too. Except she did it so badly there weren't even signs of a break-in!

Rachel

In prison I'd had to learn to control my reactions. You can't cry in a place like that, not in public anyway. You have to keep your face neutral, not make eye contact. And when you start to panic, you have to force yourself to breathe and keep going. Because no one is coming to help you, and once you're medicated, strapped down to a bed, there's no way back. I'd done four years on Death Row without a single drug.

Now, as I stood outside Alex's flat summoning the courage to ring the bell, I needed those techniques again. *Fill yourself with breath, let it out. Fill and out. Fill and out.* I couldn't believe how nervous I was, me who had promised myself I wouldn't get attached to anything ever again. All I knew was I had to make Alex talk to me, convince him I wasn't cheating on him; and so, after a sleepless night, I had got up and walked to his street first thing in the morning. Was it even cheating if we hadn't talked about exclusivity? For all I knew, he'd been seeing other people anyway. This Colette girl, for example. No. It was real, wasn't it? The way he looked at me, like I was precious, like he couldn't tear his eyes from mine? That had been real. Before all this.

I waited until someone came out of the main door of his building, barely giving me a second glance, for which I was grateful. I was already paranoid, sure that people in town must know I'd been arrested and it was only a matter of time before my real identity came out. I went up the stairs to his flat, rapped on the door and waited a while, starting to wonder if he was even home. Then the door opened. A small child was standing there in Thomas the Tank Engine pyjamas. Sam. He just stared at me. I had seen him at a distance a few times – in Anna's car when we rowed at the Co-op, and once with Alex at a café in town, but I'd very quietly slipped out again so he wouldn't be forced to introduce me. Sam was a good-looking child, with Alex's eyes and Anna's fair hair.

'Hi!' My voice was too hearty. 'Is your daddy here?'

'Yeah.'

'Can I see him, please?'

Sam continued to look at me for a moment, then turned and ran back into the flat, shouting, 'Daddddeee there's a ladeeee.' That was me. A lady, a stranger. A few moments later, Alex appeared, wiping his hands on a tea towel. He was also in pyjama bottoms and a white T-shirt, hair peeking up from its v. I wanted to press my face there.

'Hey. I'm sorry to just turn up. I wanted to explain about Jeremy. He's my ex, truly, we've been over and done with for years.'

Alex's face was closed. 'You never even told me you were married before. And he's staying at your house.'

'To help clear my name. He's really good at that kind of thing.' I took a deep breath. This was it. Was I really going to tell someone who I was, after all this time? Break my cardinal rule? I had to. It was the only way to explain my behaviour. 'He did it for me before, when no one else would.'

Alex frowned. 'Before?'

My hands were shaking. 'There's a lot I should have told you, Alex. Not just that I was married but . . . other things. Please, can I come in?'

It was cold in the hallway, dismal with dust and other people's post abandoned in a pile on a window ledge. Alex stood aside, and I went in. He led me into the kitchen/living room. The remains of scrambled eggs stood on the hob and Sam's toys were scattered on a rug by the small TV. Sam was on his knees, watching me.

Alex said, 'Sam, bud, will you go and play in your room?'

'Who is that lady?'

I forced a smile. 'I'm Rachel. A friend of your dad's.'

'Oh.' He raised a Thomas train to his mouth and put it in. He was only five, and his mother was gone. He'd never see her again. Someone had cut her throat, dumped her in the bushes, and I was the chief suspect. I couldn't connect with this child, not now.

'I'll come and get you ready in a minute.' Alex rested his hand on Sam's head, and something in me contracted. Maybe I could never have this, a child, a home, normal things that normal people had.

'How's he doing?' I said, when Sam left, looking curiously back at me.

Alex draped the tea towel on the rail by the cooker. 'I've told him the minimum. I don't think he really understands, to be honest. When you rang the bell just now he said, "Is that Mummy?"'

'I'm sorry. Really, I'm so so sorry.'

'So what did you need to tell me?' Alex said. 'Here, sit down.' He cleared some dishes from the table, some magazines and papers. 'Oh. Do you want a drink or something?'

'Tea would be nice.' I needed whatever comfort I could get. I watched him make it, opening the cupboards and taking down teabags, finding mugs.

When it came I picked up the hot cup and blew on it, absorbing the warmth through my cold hands. I felt like I was about to jump off a cliff.

'Alex, I don't know how to tell you. I'm not who I said I was. My name isn't Rachel. And there's a reason I ran away when I first found . . . Anna, there in the woods. It's a really good reason.'

'OK.' He didn't sit down but leaned against the sink, arms folded. I cast a last look at him: pyjama bottoms, strong forearms, too-long dark hair, ice-blue eyes. I might never hold him again after this.

I took a swallow of tea, so hot it burned my mouth.

'My name's Casey, not Rachel – or at least, it was. Casey Adams. And when I was nineteen I was convicted of murder.'

Casey

September 2000

The day after the disastrous dinner with Ruth, I overslept, waking in a panic bolt upright. It was eight already. Eight! I hadn't slept past six in the entire time I was here. Why hadn't Carson woken me? When I went to his cot, he was asleep, his fists balled up by his face. A wave of tenderness went over me. He was so sweet when he wasn't howling. I gently shook him.

'Carson? Do you need a change?'

He didn't stir – that was weird.

Downstairs, I found David at the table, drinking coffee, bleary-eyed. I had dressed more conservatively today, in jeans and a gypsy-style top. Ruth's words had got to me, despite myself.

'Where is everyone?' I said.

'Abby took Madison to school. And Ruth left earlier.'

'She left?' I was supposed to drive her to the airport that afternoon, which I had been dreading.

'She got an earlier flight. Called a cab.' He shrugged and I didn't press further. I imagined they had parted on bad terms. He looked at me then. 'So. Are you coming to work with me?'

Part of me had assumed this was just a drunken late-night promise, not meant. 'Can I?'

'If you want.' This was it – my big break. My chance to actually see something of the industry that fuelled this town.

'Carson's asleep still. He doesn't normally sleep this long.'

David looked at his watch. 'My PA can watch him while I show you about. Get him ready and we'll go soon.'

I ran upstairs, taking them two at a time. Throwing caution to the wind, I called Jenna from my mobile. I had no idea how much it would cost, and got the country code wrong a few times. It was four o'clock at home.

Jenna picked up. 'Yeah?' I could hear from the woody slide of her voice she was already drinking.

'Mum, it's me.'

'Why are you ringing at this time? And don't call me Mum, please, it's so ageing.'

'Sorry. I was just – it's happening. I can go to the office with him, he says. The production company.'

'Right!' Suddenly she was alert. 'What are you wearing?'

'Jeans and a top. It's very casual here.'

'Huh. I always wear a dress and full make-up to every audition, plus eyelashes and my hair.' Her extensions, she meant. She always called it 'putting my hair on'.

'It's not like that here, Mum. Sorry, Jenna.'

'Whatever, men always like to see a pretty girl's legs.'

'But it's not an audition.'

I heard the chink of the ice cubes in her glass. 'Everything's an audition, Case.' She was right about that, come to think of it. Her lessons on presentation and acting might have helped me at the trial, had I paid any attention. I should have blubbered more. Prayed in public. Gone back in time and never said anything negative about my nannying charges. But I didn't know any of that

125

then. I changed into a summer dress, and put on make-up while trying to make it look like I hadn't. Black-rimmed eyes, Heather-Shimmered lips, my cheeks shiny like a Barbie doll's. When I came downstairs, holding Carson carefully away from me, David was standing with the car keys.

'That's a pretty dress.'

'Thank you.' Jenna had been right – men did notice these things.

Carson was still drowsy and silent, sucking his thumb, wanting to sleep again. As I put him in his car seat and settled into the front, I thought that we were almost like a couple, with Carson as our baby. I smiled at David and noticed him glance at my bare thighs as he put the car in drive. It was another beautiful day. The car slid out on to the freeway, moving nicely along now that we'd missed the worst of the rush hour.

'Music?' David switched on his stereo and jazz poured out.

The leather was hot against my legs, from where the car had sat in the driveway. Cold air filtered over me, lifting the tiny hairs on the surface of my skin.

'So what are you working on at the moment?' I was pleased with the question, sure that I sounded knowledgeable.

'Well, keep this under wraps for now,' he said, 'but we're getting the rights to that YA series, you know the one about the witches?'

'Oh! I've read that.'

It was a huge series and I'd even picked up the next book in the airport, then put it down because the hardback cost too much. If David was making the film of that, he must really be hitting the big time. Maybe I could even be involved.

He smiled over. 'I'll have to get your thoughts on it, then.' He turned his gaze back to the road. 'You know, there's a character you'd be great for!'

I could hardly believe it. 'Miranda?' The main character, Miranda, was seventeen in the books, easily within my playing age. A star-making role, and one they might actually cast an unknown in. Best of all, Miranda was British, and had moved to America to live with her mysterious relatives at the start of the series.

'Sure. Why not?'

I smiled back. I was genuinely happy in that moment. Full of anticipation of good things ahead. I remember the moment well, as there weren't many good ones afterwards.

Rachel

Alex took my early-morning bombshell with a strange calm.

'I see,' he said after I had told him all about Casey Adams. 'I guessed there was something you weren't telling me.'

'Do you remember the case?'

'Um . . . vaguely, I think. I wouldn't have recognised you.'

I had changed a lot. My face had thinned out, my hair was different, no longer long or streaked blonde. These days, I never wore anything short or tight or revealing. Trying to be safe, but also because you can't go through something like that and come out the same person.

'You know I didn't do it,' I said. 'I was exonerated.'

'Right.'

This was so odd, his flat calm. 'Don't you – you don't have anything you want to ask?'

'I don't know, Rachel. Sorry – Casey. I don't know if I can call you that. I'm sure you've been asked everything there is to ask. You have no idea who killed them?'

'I used to think someone must have got into the house, some stranger, but . . . some people say it must have been Abby. You know, she was very unhappy.'

'But it couldn't have been her, I thought?' He saw my look of confusion. 'I'm starting to remember a bit.'

'Yeah. They said she was probably killed before D-David.' Even now, I couldn't say his name without tripping up. 'Listen, I've driven myself mad trying to solve it. I had five years in prison to think about it. All I know is, I didn't do it. And now, with Anna . . .' When I said her name, his face convulsed. I realised what I was telling him was that, even though I was innocent, Anna was possibly dead because of me. My past. 'I'm so sorry, Alex. I can't think what's happened. But someone has tracked me down. And me finding her body – well, I don't know if it's a coincidence. It seems too crazy.'

He nodded slowly. 'The little girl who died . . . she was five? Sam's age?'

'Yes. I cared for her. She was – she wasn't the easiest child. Things weren't right in that family. But I did my best for her.'

Had I, though? The evening she wet herself on the terrace, hadn't that been my cue to step in? And what had I done? Nothing, thinking only of myself and how to get out of that house and on with my life. Never realising I'd be abandoning those kids to their fate. So yes, I was guilty too. Maybe that's what the police had picked up on, all those years ago. The fact that, even if I hadn't held the pillow or the knife, I was still not entirely innocent.

'So who's doing this?' Alex frowned. 'If you really think some-one killed Anna to frame you? They'd be in America, surely, anyone to do with the case.'

'That's what I'm trying to find out. Jeremy's here to help me.'

'Oh, Jeremy.' He sighed as if he'd forgotten about my ex-husband. 'I don't know, Rachel. What am I meant to believe? You didn't tell me you were married, or that you spent years in a federal prison!'

'It's not the kind of thing you can just say!' I cried, putting my face in my hands. 'I wanted something normal, for once in my life. I wanted you.'

He softened at the break in my voice. 'I know. But a lot's happened. Anna's *dead*. I mean, we had our differences, but – she was such a part of my life. And now all this. You have to give me a minute to process it, all right?'

'OK. I can go – I just – needed you to know what's going on. I'm as baffled as you are. And Anna – I didn't know her, but she was your wife, Sam's mum, you need to mourn her. I can disappear, for a while, if you need me to. But I have to know we're not over, not for good.' I heard my voice crack. 'I have to know there's something to fight for.'

Otherwise, why bother to clear my name at all? If I couldn't have a normal life, fall in love, find some happiness, I may as well be in prison. If I couldn't have him, what was the point of it all?

'We're not over,' he said reluctantly, and I nodded, then got up and made myself walk out.

I'd hoped he might reach out for me, or touch me, but maybe that was too much to ask. All the same, I was happier as I headed home through the fresh morning, light skiffs of rain landing on my upturned face. When I got home I found Jeremy still snoring on the sofa and Brandy wagging her tail in a slightly aggrieved manner. It was seven – well past walk time. 'Come on, then.' I grabbed her lead, glad to get back to something like normal. All the same, I would not be taking that same woodland path, probably ever again.

◆　◆　◆

Now it was afternoon, and the remnants of a huge fry-up lay all over my table. Jeremy had got up and gone to the shop, the very Co-op where Anna had so publicly confronted me. No doubt

Audrey had seen this new strange man at my house and was feeding all the juicy details to the neighbourhood gossips right this second. He was very quiet, and I knew he was upset about Alex, but didn't want to broach the subject.

In a different time, I might have gone to Amsterdam to meet this Jochem, the internet wizard, but since the police had given me bail conditions, Jeremy arranged for us to Skype him instead. He'd set up his laptop on the coffee table and got me some kind of 'dongle' for Wi-Fi. Now Jeremy was tapping on his laptop, adjusting the sound levels.

'The network round here is Stone Age,' he grumbled. 'It's practically at dial-up speeds.'

'It's fine,' I said. 'I don't want to go online anyway.'

'You'll need to set up email as well, so Jochem can get in touch. I mean, how do you manage without email? It's 2019! Oh, here he is.' The screen had darkened and the words *Jochem calling* appeared. Jeremy clicked. 'Hi, Jochem! Can you hear me?'

The sounds of scuffling and a dark screen. 'Turn your camera on, Jochem! That's it . . . no . . . you've gone again.' If this was the modern world, I wasn't fussed. Eventually, Jochem Groeneveld appeared, and I could see Jeremy and myself in a small box at the bottom of the screen. Was I really so pale and wan? I fidgeted with my hair, which looked twice its normal size, and not in a good way. Jochem was in fact a bit wizard-like, with a long grey beard under dark hair and glasses. Despite the grey, I thought he was no more than fifty.

'Hello, Jeremy?' His Dutch accent made it sound more like *Yeremy*.

'Hi! I'm here with Ca— er, with my friend.' I waved awkwardly at the screen.

'It is indeed an honour to meet you. Do you prefer to be called Rachel?' So he knew my new identity.

'Um – yes, please.' I shot a look at Jeremy. 'I need to stay in the habit of it.'

'Good, good. So you wanted my help? There has been another murder?'

'Yes, my – well, my boyfriend's ex-wife has been killed and I'm a suspect.' I saw Jeremy wince slightly at the word *boyfriend*. 'I didn't do it, of course. I think maybe I'm being framed.' I explained quickly about the scarf and my old name spelt out on my fridge. 'So you see, someone must know who I am.'

He nodded slowly, contemplatively. 'I did a deep sweep online and could not find anything public stating your new identity or your address. Which is not to say no one knows it, of course. You have a list of suspects?'

'Sort of. I thought maybe the aunt of the family, she never liked me – Ruth Safran. But apparently she's dead. Marietta the maid, her surname was Estepan. The gardener, José . . .' Oh God, what was his last name? Why could I remember the Anglo names and not his? I was ashamed. 'I'm sorry, I'm blanking on his name.'

'Not to worry, it will be in the trial transcript.'

'You can get that?'

He laughed softly. 'But of course, this is easy to get. Tapes of your interviews and videos of the trial, all of that is very easy to get too.'

'Oh.' I had never thought of that. Those hellish hours, nine-teen-year-old me grilled over and over in a small, airless room, exhausted and dirty and grieving, giving answers that led me straight to Death Row.

'I can send you them. This is easy to do.'

'Thank you.' But did I want to read the transcripts, relive those terrible days? 'I can't think of anyone else, unless it's some stranger who still believes I did it. Then it could be anyone.'

'Yes, I have seen the posts online. There are those who call for your death.' He said it very calmly, but I flinched, even though I knew this was true.

'I just can't really imagine anyone going to these lengths, killing an innocent woman just to frame me.'

Jochem thought about it. 'You have considered that maybe you're looking at it the wrong way round? This dead woman – Anna Devine, yes? I have looked at the news stories. She is the one who was killed, so it makes more sense to ask who would have killed her, perhaps. Not who would want to hurt you.'

'But – it's been made to look like I did it.'

'Perhaps someone is panicking. Trying to cover it up, what they did, and they know who you are. They think: a convicted killer in our midst, people will easily believe she did it. It's – what do you say – a set-up? That is correct?'

'Yes.' My mind was racing. 'You're saying look at who might have wanted Anna dead?' Who apart from me, that was. I was the one to most obviously gain, to step into the life she had vacated, have Alex all to myself, and maybe Sam too.

'Exactly.' He beamed at me through the computer screen, pleased to have solved my problem. 'The police – if they believe it was you – they may not work as hard to find someone else. There are many cuts to services in your country, is this not true?'

'Well, yeah. I suppose. They seem pretty sharp, though.' I thought of DS Hegarty's bright green eyes. They hadn't charged me yet, though, so they obviously hadn't made their minds up.

'Well, that is all I can suggest,' said Jochem. 'Is there anything else I can help with?'

'You're good at finding people, I hear?'

'I am the best at this, yes.' Again, very matter-of-fact. 'Even the police all over the world, they use me. If the person has left any trace online, even in databases, I can find them.'

'You're a hacker?'

For the first time, he looked offended. 'I do not use this term. I am a finder, that is all. And only people who need to be found. I do not find those who need to disappear. I am white-hat not black-hat.' I had no idea what this meant, but Jeremy was nodding knowledgeably.

'Jochem – could you have found me? If someone had asked?'

He smiled. 'Of course, Rachel.'

'But – how?' I had been so careful.

'One moment.' He tapped away for a few seconds.

I looked at Jeremy, who was grinning. He loved all this. As only someone untouched by actual violent crime could.

'Yes, here we are,' said Jochem. 'You had a bank account in your old name, and you then changed the name on it, using a marriage certificate, in 2006. Then I look for this name and your middle name, and I find you working at the dog shelter in Coldwater.'

I was jolted. 'That . . . that's right. But isn't that all confidential?'

'It is very easy to get, for someone like me. They do not use the right protections on their systems, the banks and other organisations.'

'Maybe you can't tell me this, but – have you ever been asked to find me?'

'I have not, Rachel. But there are others like me. Maybe not so good, but – you see I found this in seconds.'

Oh God. So I was right – someone from the past could easily have tracked me down. But who? Who on earth would go to such lengths?

freecaseyadams.com, Website (October 2003)

Hi, this is a message from Jeremy, the website creator. Casey's a friend of mine from school and

I want to help her in this terrible situation. She's a young girl in a foreign country with a corrupt justice system, and she's been convicted just for being in the wrong place at the wrong time. I mean, look at her face – it's so clear she's innocent, gentle, kind. Imagine her stuck in the hell-hole of an American prison. She's even facing the death penalty! But look at the facts. That child was being abused long before her death – her teacher said she came in with bruises. And this started before Casey ever went to work for the family. It seems pretty clear to me the mum did it. Check out the forums to read more about Abigail Safran's history of mental health problems and violence.

Rachel

I decided to go back to work the next day, after I left Jeremy at the bus stop for the train station. He had offered to stay for as long as I needed, but I needed to be alone. I was in some strange limbo, neither charged nor cleared, but legally, that meant I was innocent. So I should behave normally, I reasoned.

Things were still awkward as we said goodbye. I sensed he wanted to hold on to the hug for longer, but I detached myself. 'Take care of yourself, OK? Eat a vegetable now and again.'

'I will,' he said sadly, and stood waving till I'd moved out of sight. I walked to the dog shelter on my usual route. The lakeside path was damp underfoot, autumn settling in. Still, I could see the bobbing heads of a few hardy wild swimmers out in the water. I didn't fancy it myself, not being able to feel the bottom beneath my feet, or see what was below me in the gloomy water. These days, I didn't like surprises any more, but Marilyn was keen on swimming there – she talked about it like a spiritual experience, an immersion. I wished I could take joy in things like that.

As I tramped down the muddy path with Brandy trotting along beside me, my spirits rose a little. The sun was glinting off the lake and the mountains in the distance soared into a fresh blue sky. Soon the tourists would leave, we would withdraw inside and light our fires, huddle down. I had built a life here, however small it was. I wouldn't let someone take that from me, not without a fight. And this was Britain, not America. Our justice system functioned, didn't it? They wouldn't convict me of something I didn't do.

One of the interns was out in the yard when I got there, filling up water bowls. Callum, that was his name.

'Hello,' I said.

He jumped. Perhaps I had just startled him, or maybe he knew I'd been arrested. Maybe he was afraid of me. He was a tall and gangly kid, still spotty with adolescence, and swathed in layers of hoody and beanie hat and tracksuit bottoms.

'Hi,' he said.

'How are you getting on?' Would I normally make the effort with these kids, or was I trying extra hard to be nice? To show him I wasn't a killer?

'Oh – yeah, fine. I like the dogs.' His accent was from somewhere around London, I thought.

'You're studying to be a vet?'

'Yeah. It's hard.'

'They say that's the toughest course to get into, don't they? Worse than medicine.'

'I guess.'

A conversational wizard, this boy.

'Well, have a good day, Callum. It is Callum?'

'Er – yeah.'

'I'm Rachel.'

He dipped his head down, the water plinking into the bowls making a sound I'd always loved. 'I know.' Of course he knew who I was, I was probably the talk of the town. There was no way someone hadn't connected the dots and realised it was me who'd been arrested. I passed Katrin at the reception desk, her hair in two little bunches like I would have worn in the late nineties, and felt her eyes on me. That comfortable anonymity I had so treasured, it was all beginning to peel away, and I didn't like it. As I moved past, with an awkward smile, I could see her phone was in her hand, and the old paranoia rose in me. But kids are always on their phones nowadays, it didn't mean anything.

Inside, Marilyn was at her desk, talking on the phone.

'I'm afraid that's just our policy,' she said. 'A full background check and home visit. We can't release these dogs to suffer any more, many of them have been through so much. Well, I don't know if it would be easier to adopt a baby from China than get a dog. Yes, breeders will sell you one, but those dogs are often very damaged!' She sighed deeply and put down the phone. 'They hung up. People, eh? Give me animals any day.' Then she realised it was me standing there. 'Rachel! I didn't expect . . .'

'Why not?' I went to put my bag and coat by my desk, then saw someone's things were already there, a parka and a leather satchel. The screen was active, open to my Documents folder. Brandy, not noticing anything awry, had already run to her basket in the corner and was chewing on her squeaky mouse. 'What's this?' I said, gesturing to my desk.

Marilyn bit her lip. 'I asked Tom to cover for you. I assumed you wouldn't be in.'

'I haven't been charged with anything, Marilyn. I'm just answering questions is all. They let me go.'

'I know, but . . .' She wouldn't meet my eyes. A horrible feeling slid down into my stomach.

'I didn't kill Anna, Marilyn. You do believe me?'

'Oh, Rachel, of course I do, but . . .'

'But?'

Marilyn let out a deep sigh. She tapped into her keyboard, then spun her monitor around, so I could see what was on it.

'That's you, isn't it? You're Casey Adams.'

Casey

October 2000

Abby didn't get the role of Nancy the nurse. I knew it as soon as she drove up that day, the angry way the tyres crunched on the drive, and I felt myself tense. I was out the back with the kids, Carson asleep in his pram under a parasol, Madison splashing in the pool under my watchful eye.

Being Madison, she wore a pink swimsuit with frills and sequins, but she seemed happy for once, playing and singing to herself, sometimes shouting, 'Look, Casey!'

'I'm looking,' I'd call back, one eye on my paperback, the first book I'd been able to read all summer. It was a Marian Keyes, cheerful and funny, and it reminded me of home. No one in America got my jokes, and I found myself missing the guys at college, Suzi and Becks, Ryan, and even Jeremy, always panting and sweating. *Casey! I found this article on the internet!* In 2000 I barely went on the internet. I'd checked my email at David's office the day before, but there was nothing from any of them in my brand-new Hotmail folder. The visit had been a little strange. Nothing had happened, as such, he'd just shown me round the small, cramped offices near the beach, with hardly anyone else there, except for one receptionist with blue hair who seemed surprised to see us. The lack of glamour, the abandoned props and dusty posters of low-budget nineties films were a bit disappointing, but I felt hopeful all the same. Next time a part came up for someone my age, maybe he'd let me audition. Or even just cast me. That happened, didn't it, unknowns propelled to stardom?

It was October now, every house already decorated with pumpkins and spider webs, the shops full of trick-or-treat sweets, and I was almost looking forward to Halloween in LA, planning how to dress the kids up. I had let my guard down, and would soon pay for it.

The sound of Abby's car. Madison heard it too, and her head whipped around, her face guilty, as if she was doing something wrong by playing in the pool. I heard the door slam and Abby's flip-flops slapping across the tiles. She threw open the patio doors, which they called something else.

'You left the front door open, Casey!'

'What?' Surely I wouldn't do that?

'It was, like, ajar. You can't do that! We could get robbed!'

I wanted to point out that we'd hardly get robbed in the middle of the day, with me at home, on a street so quiet it felt deserted, but I could see she was spoiling for a fight. Anyway, I was sure I had closed it. I remembered pushing it to earlier as I struggled inside with Carson in one arm and a brown bag of shopping in the other. I glanced at Madison and saw the guilt on her face. She liked to look out of the front windows to see if her dad was on his way home – perhaps she had graduated to opening the door?

I decided to take the blame anyway. 'I'm really sorry, Abby, I'll be more careful. It won't happen in future.'

'See that it doesn't.' Her gaze swung, landing on her daughter. 'What the hell are you wearing?'

Madison was trembling. 'I'm sorry, Mommy.'

I didn't understand what was wrong. 'She's allowed in the pool, isn't she? I've been watching the whole time.'

'Not in that suit! That's a competition swimsuit, it can't get wet! Look!' And sure enough a handful of sequins were floating about the shallow end, catching the sun in sharp, shattering fragments. 'That suit cost a hundred dollars!'

Madison started to cry. Abby strode over and lifted her out, soaking wet. She must have been strong, despite her tiny frame, because Madison at five was no lightweight. Her fingers dug into the child's arms and legs, which must have hurt. But what could I do? I listened to Madison's howls as she was dragged up the stairs, then suddenly cut off as a door slammed deep in the house. I tried not to think about what might be happening in Madison's bedroom now, how Abby would be yanking off that expensive swimsuit, then perhaps slapping the backs of Madison's legs, as my mother used to do to me if I was naughty. Leaving her to stand there, dripping and naked, humiliated.

Carson had woken up now, and was fussing. I lifted him out of his pram, pressing my lips to his forehead to check he wasn't too warm. He settled in against me, his eyes drooping again as he drifted back to sleep. At least I could protect him.

'Shh, shh, it's OK. I won't let her get to you, I promise.'

Abby wrenched the door open again, making me jump. She was barefoot now, so I hadn't heard her approach. 'I'm taking the cost of that suit out of your wages, just so you know.'

'But . . .' A hundred dollars was almost a week's salary. 'Abby, I didn't know it was special. She came downstairs wearing it, and she was so happy, she wanted to look pretty . . .'

'You should be calling me Mrs Safran,' she said, her tone crushing. There was a flat quality to her eyes, a glassiness, as if she wasn't really seeing me. 'Give me my baby.'

For a moment I imagined taking Carson, who I had changed and fed every day for months now, and running with him, down the street to the dusty, scorching highway and out of the city. It was madness. It was a felony – kidnapping. So I passed him over, and as she took him in her arms he began to cry again. As I followed her back into the house, I saw David had arrived home, slamming the front door. Abby swept past him, howling child gripped in her arms. From upstairs came the sound of Madison, also crying. David looked at me. 'What now?'

I just rolled my eyes. 'Don't ask.'

He ran a hand over his face and I wondered what he was doing home at this hour. 'I can't take much more of this. Christ, will it ever get easier?'

I didn't have an answer for him.

◆　◆　◆

That wasn't even the strangest moment that day. Later that evening, after hiding in my room all through dinner, eating some very stale peanuts left over from the plane, I crept downstairs in the hope of some real food. Abby was sitting in the kitchen, at the island, staring into space.

'Oh!' I said. 'Sorry, I . . .'

She shook herself, as if coming back to consciousness. 'I didn't get that role. The nurse.' Her voice was flat.

I had already guessed as much. 'I'm sorry.'

'The odds are stacked against me,' she said, carefully stirring her black coffee. 'I'm thirty-five, a mom. They don't want that. I tried to shed the mom bod, but they could tell. They can always tell.'

'Couldn't David help – he must know producers casting for films? Or his new film?'

'What new film?'

142

God, she was really out of touch with his life. 'His company have the rights to that YA series, you know, the one with the witches. Maybe there's a role in that for you? I, er, I read about it somewhere.' I didn't want her to think David and I were talking behind her back, although, of course, we were.

Abby laughed. It was strange, because her face didn't move above the mouth. 'David has the rights? Yeah, *David*. The big-shot producer.' She heaved herself off the stool, moving as if her body hurt. 'Don't believe everything you read, Casey. This town runs on hype. Once you stop believing in yourself, you're toast. People can smell it on you. Desperation.' She moved towards the stairs. 'There's noodles in the fridge, you can have them.' This was one of the odd little kindnesses among her rages and mood swings. It was so strange.

I heated up the noodles in the microwave, which I had finally learned how to use, and ate them in silence at the kitchen island, listening to the noises of LA outside. Police choppers, coyotes howling, endless traffic flowing, and, underneath it all, the seeping silence of the desert.

Rachel

Marilyn was standing over me, tentatively rubbing my back. I was sitting in my desk chair – now someone else's – with my head between my knees. I had almost fainted when I saw what was on her screen. It was a picture from two days ago, snapped by some paparazzo, of me coming out of Alex's flat, looking shifty in his ill-fitting clothes. How had I not seen the photographer? It was alongside a picture of me back then, in my skirt and vest top. 'Racy Casey questioned over murder', read the headline. *Exoneree Casey Adams, formerly accused of murdering her employers and their child in Los Angeles in 2000, has resurfaced in the picturesque Lake District. We can reveal that she is once again a suspect in a murder enquiry, having been questioned over the death of Anna Devine this week. Local sources have confirmed that Adams, now 38, is going by the name Rachel Caldwell. Sources close to her say, 'We are totally shocked. She always seemed so quiet, keeping herself to herself.'* (Exactly what they always say about serial killers.) *'I can't believe I've been living near a convicted murderer all this time. I remember the case well – that poor little kiddie. She must have changed how she looks, to pull the wool over our eyes.'* Who was this source? I suspected Audrey, from the references to living nearby. Of course she'd make it all about her. She was probably already worrying about the effect on the value of her house. She'd be dining out on this for years. The article ended with *Rachel Caldwell was released without charge in the matter of Anna Devine's murder*, but who would read that far without passing judgement?

Feebly, I said, 'I'm not convicted. I was, but then I was . . . unconvicted.' People never knew how to describe that. One trial said I was guilty, another had cleared me – how did you know which to believe? Once again, I felt the futility of it. Here was a perfect story, me linked to two murder cases. Of course I must be guilty. The appeal had been a mistake. My breath came quick with panic. What if they extradited me back to America and put me through a third trial? You couldn't do that in America, could you? No. God, no, what was going on? If this story had already broken, it wouldn't be long before the reporters were back, here and at my cottage. I had to get away.

I looked up at Marilyn. 'I – I'm sorry I didn't tell you. I had to, to avoid . . .' I gestured at the newspaper web page. They must have been thrilled with it. 'But I didn't do it. Either time. Marilyn, you do believe me? You can't think I would do something like that.'

'Of course,' she said, half-hearted. 'It's just so strange. And your name isn't even Rachel.'

'It's legal to change your name,' I snapped. 'Wouldn't you have done the same?'

'I don't know.' Marilyn's face said that she'd never have been involved in a murder enquiry, not even once. As they say, once is unfortunate. Twice looks like carelessness.

But what had I done to cause this? I thought I'd taken every precaution to hide my true identity, but had I let my guard down? Had I been careless at some point along the way? What had brought this down upon my head, like some inescapable fate?

Marilyn was gentle, but something had gone in her manner with me. Her eyes were cloudy. She didn't know what to believe.

'I don't think, in the circumstances, we can have you back here during the enquiry. We've already had two people call up to cancel their adoptions.'

'What, in case I've corrupted the dogs somehow?' My voice was high and wavering. 'That's ridiculous.'

'Well, yes, the great British public.' She shrugged. 'It's the interns too. I have a duty of care.'

I nodded. I didn't want to give up this piece of my life, but I knew I couldn't be here.

From the car park, the noise of an engine made my head snap round. The rising of voices. Katrin came in from reception, half-running, wide-eyed.

'There's, like, millions of people out there! What's going on?'

They had found me.

I caught Marilyn's eye. My adrenaline had already kicked in, ready to run, to fight. Not that either had helped me last time.

'I'll see to Brandy. Go out the back,' she said, and I ran.

Article in the *Daily Mail* – October 2005
'Mary Poppins killer' released

Casey Adams, 24, dubbed the 'Mary Poppins killer' after the family she worked for were found slain in their multi-million-dollar home in the Hollywood Hills, was released on appeal today. Supporters of Adams, who will return to the UK this week, claim it's a victory for justice. 'There was never any evidence against her,' said Jeremy Caldwell (25), who runs the website freecaseyadams.com. 'She was just lucky not to be a victim of the killer herself, and that was used against her, the fact she survived.' Adams has always claimed the family were murdered by an unknown intruder, while she hid in the hall cupboard with the youngest child, Carson (eight months). However, police determined that Ms Adams' prints were on the gun used to kill the father of the family, David Safran (39). She claimed she had picked it up after finding it discarded beside Mr Safran's body, before realising the killer might still be in the house and taking shelter. Also killed were Abigail Safran (35) and Madison Safran (5).

Mr Safran's sister, Ruth, said it was a travesty of justice and she hoped that Adams would be held to account for her actions in future. Dubbed 'Racy Casey', the then 19-year-old nanny was often pictured wearing low-cut tops and hot pants. Adams will fly in to the UK this week.

Rachel

The news was out. I sat on a bench by the river with my phone in my hands, and clicked through endless reports. I had been so good at staying off the internet for years, and now it had sucked me in. The newspapers had it all. A picture of the dog shelter, the Happy Paws sign clearly visible. My full name, the lane I lived on in Coldwater. It had only five houses on it, so they may as well have given my full address. They knew about my marriage to Jeremy, fleeing America terrified they might lock me up again, desperate, broke, alone, not welcome home with Jenna, who by that stage had sold the flat and moved in with Steve the ex-milkman in Hove. 'Steve, he reads the *Sun*, you see, he doesn't want you here. I'll come and see you soon instead.' She never did.

There were pictures of Brandy, even, and I felt afraid for her. She was so trusting, she'd go up to anyone. I'd heard of dogs being poisoned with spiked meat before. When I ran from the shelter she'd followed me with her tail thumping, and I'd had to shut the door on her and flee out the back. I could already hear a babble of voices in the car park – the reporters were there.

There was even a photograph of me from several weeks before the murder, holding Carson, with Madison by my side. She was wearing Minnie Mouse ears. It was the day we went to Disneyland.

But how did the press get hold of it? I'd never seen it before. Someone had stolen it from the house, maybe. I remembered it had been on a roll of film that Abby sent me to get developed, largely because she liked some of the pictures of herself near the start. David had taken the photo, I remembered, on Main Street while waiting for the parade – there were dozens of other people in the shot, strangers, who would perhaps have seen this photo in the paper or on TV and said, *Look, it's me!* – a brief taste of fame, standing close to a murderer.

As I looked at the photograph for the first time in nearly twenty years, I remembered how it felt that day. The punishing heat of midday. Carson red and cranky, Madison exhausted from putting on a show for her parents, twirling all day in her princess dress, pure polyester, now overheated and whiney. Disneyland is supposed to be fun for families, but I'd never understood why. Soaring heat, queues for everything, hungry, tired kids missing their naps, dads more used to being at the office put on childcare duty – it's a recipe for disaster. But all you see when you look at that picture is smiles. Either a kind nanny who loved the children and would never have hurt them. Or a cold-blooded murderer, who'd smile now but kill them all later, maybe still smiling as she pressed the pillow down. *A man may smile and smile and be a villain.* The line surfaced, I didn't know where from. Shakespeare, maybe? One of the few books in the dusty prison library.

The articles were only reporting the facts, of course, that I had been convicted and then cleared of the Safran family murders, that I'd changed my name on my return to the UK, that I'd moved to Coldwater and started a new life. That I had been arrested and questioned over another murder, that of Anna Devine. That I had been dating the estranged husband of the victim – I hadn't thought anyone knew about that. I shivered. It was cold out, a fine drizzle settling over my coat and hair. I wondered if Alex had seen the news, the scrutiny I had exposed him to, a man still in mourning. A horrible thought – was he the one who'd outed me? He was one of the few people who knew. But surely not – he wouldn't do that to Sam, to himself. A familiar burn in my stomach, no less painful for being so. I had lost him. I'd told him who I really was and ruined everything. Never mind that I was innocent, that I'd been exonerated – the fact remained that I had been accused of murdering a child the same age as Sam. I understood, in a way, why he hadn't called. There was no way back from this.

So what was I going to do? I couldn't just accept my fate and I couldn't sit on this damp bench all day. I needed to do what Jochem had said: turn my attention to the murder victim, Anna. What was her life like? Who would have wanted to kill her, cut her throat and dump her body in a forest half-hidden under a drift of autumn leaves? Aside from the most obvious suspect, of course: me.

I stood up – it was cold, and I couldn't stay here. I had forgotten, with all this on my mind, that home wasn't safe any more either, my little cottage haven. As I rounded the lane I noticed, distractedly, that there were more cars than usual, parked even on the grass verge opposite our houses. Audrey would not be happy about that. Then I saw a small knot of people round my gate, and realised – oh no. I had been stupid. Of course the reporters had come here too.

I froze. They hadn't seen me yet, so I could still turn and run. But where? I couldn't go to Alex's – I couldn't draw them to his door. Besides, some deep streak of stubbornness rose up in me, the same that had stopped me from breaking down when, at just nineteen, I had been sentenced to death by lethal injection. I hadn't done this. I would not accept the blame. I had every right to go to my own home. Several passers-by had already stopped to gawk, and I even recognised some of them – the guy with the man-bun who ran the kayak rental in summer, the woman from the pet shop where I bought Brandy's treats. It was a small town. People knew each other.

I walked down the lane, never breaking my stride or taking my eyes away from my front door with its cheerful green paint. Ten steps, twenty – that's all it would take, and I'd be safe. They couldn't hurt me.

'Rachel!'

'Casey!'

They were shouting both my names.

'Have you anything to say, Casey?'

'How does it feel to be accused of so many murders?'

'Did you do it, Rachel?'

Focusing on my front door while fumbling in my bag for my keys, I had a hazy impression of people with microphones and cameras. Camera flashes went off as I kept walking, taking me back twenty years. *Casey! Why did you do it?*

'Rachel!'

Just get in. Get in. I knew that once I was inside, they couldn't follow me.

'Casey!'

The keys were in my hand, hard and cold. One reporter got too close, stumbling in his haste – so close I could smell his coffee breath – and I gave a sob and lunged forward, scrabbling for the lock.

Please open. Please!

The lock turned and I almost fell in. I slammed the door behind me, hard. The noise level dropped, though I could still hear them calling, and then they began knocking and ringing the doorbell. They had taken their pictures, filmed me for the evening news and the morning papers. Me with my head down, not answering their questions. Would people watch it and decide I was guilty? Not just of Anna's murder, but of David's and Abby's and Madison's? *No smoke without fire*, they'd say. *She's a killer. I always knew it.*

I stumbled to the window, pulled the curtains. As I did, I saw something – a car nosing its way through the crowd, down my lane. I recognised the car – it was DS Hegarty's, and there he was behind the wheel. I stepped back from the window, quivering all over. *Run. Out the back. Just go.* But no. This was a small place, they would find me soon. It seemed almost inevitable he'd come – of course they'd question me again, now they knew this wasn't the first murder I'd been involved in. And Anna had even been killed in the same way as Abby Safran. Soon, everyone would know I'd been picked up by the police again, if they didn't already. But there was nothing to be done about it. I waited by the door for him to come, unable to escape my fate.

Casey

OCTOBER 2000

After David took me out to his production company, things were different between us. He started coming down for breakfast earlier and helping me with Madison's sheets, then once we'd cleaned up we made coffee and chopped fruit together in companionable silence. Now the kids were sleeping longer we had hours, sometimes, before Abby padded downstairs like a wraith. After a few days she wasn't even surprised to see us there together.

'Breakfast?' I would offer, like the good dogsbody I was.

'Oh. No.' And she'd fill her workout flask with some stinking juice and be on her way to the gym. After being rejected for the role of Nancy she'd lost even more weight. In fact, I hadn't seen her eat solid food in weeks. She would be at the gym all morning, so often it was just David and me in the house. He was going to the office later and later, or sometimes not at all, and he helped me get the kids ready. Sometimes we dropped Madison off at school together, Carson asleep in the car seat, then we'd stop to get coffee. The first few times I took the baby in with me, but since he never stirred I started leaving him in the car, conked out. We could see the car from the window and I told myself it was fine. Certainly David never seemed bothered.

We talked about everything. Our childhoods, how he'd shaken off his Christian right-wing family in Texas, how I'd struggled to find any boundaries at all with Jenna, her failed career, her painful hopes pinned on me. His work, how he'd grown to love films as a small boy in a dusty neighbourhood cinema, the projects he dreamed of making, how frustrated he was directing Hallmark stuff when he deserved to win an Oscar. I stirred my enormous Frappuccino until the cream melted and the ice turned to slush.

Then I went reluctantly home to tidy the house and prepare dinner. David actually helped me now, picking up groceries and running the hoover on the days when Marietta didn't come, and it made such a difference. I had time to myself, to sit by the pool and finally get a tan, to read my acting texts or start jogging round the neighbourhood, though usually the heat meant I didn't get far. The only sticking point of the day was when Abby eventually came home. Often, she went straight back out again, to acting classes, supposed castings, meetings with producers. She was like a ghost now, and the house felt like mine and David's, the children ours.

I should have known such a state of affairs couldn't last. This wasn't my home, and Madison and Carson weren't my children. David was not my husband and, if I was honest, I didn't want him to be. I was just so happy that someone was finally paying me attention, that the horrible starving time was over. It's terrible, the things we'll put up with just to feel seen.

◆ ◆ ◆

I was dropping Madison off at school one day, Carson sleeping in the back, when her teacher came out to meet me. Miss Oliver was her name, not much older than me, with long, straightened blonde hair and a Southern accent. I wondered if she'd also come to LA to make it in the movie business. I couldn't imagine why you'd live here otherwise – it was a city that seemed barely fit for humans.

'Hey, Casey. Do you have a minute?'

'Sure.' I put on a polite smile. 'Is something wrong?'

Madison had gone ahead into the school, head bowed. I noticed how she walked like an older person, weighed down by life, not skipping like the other kids.

'It's just . . . I'm a little concerned about Madison,' said Miss Oliver. 'I should speak to her parents, really, but there's never any answer at the number we have.' The school had Abby's cell number – was she not picking up? I wasn't really surprised, but it was supposed to be for emergencies.

'Here, I'll give you mine.' I found an old flyer in the footwell of the car and scribbled my number on it. 'Is it about missing school for auditions? I know it's a lot, but we always try to make up . . .'

'It's not that. She's doing well academically, and well, we're a school in Hollywood, we understand about auditions. It's just – I noticed bruises.' She said the last bit in a rush.

I didn't understand at first. 'All kids fall, don't they?'

'Yes, but . . . there are patterns that we're taught to look for. Bruises that couldn't come from falling over, in certain places.'

I tried to think when I'd last washed Madison or helped her dress. She had become shy recently, didn't want me in the bathroom, so I'd help her into the tub then go outside, leaving the door ajar.

'She has bruises?'

'On her arms.' Miss Oliver touched her own. 'And . . . the inside of her thighs.'

'Oh.' I couldn't make sense of this. 'What are you thinking?'

She held up her hands. 'Look, I don't know. And it's not at the stage yet where I'd take any action. But there are signs we watch

155

for – bruises, acting up, like those tantrums Madison has, bed-wetting . . .'

I froze. Madison was wetting the bed almost every night at the moment. 'Signs of what?'

The pretty young teacher didn't want to say it, I could tell. 'Well – of abuse.'

I gaped at her, suddenly aware of the early-morning heat rising up off the tarmacked playground, or whatever they called them in America. I was Casey's nanny. Wouldn't I know if someone was hurting her? I thought suddenly of Abby, hauling the child out of the pool, her fingers digging into the flesh until the knuckles turned white. And despite the heat of the day, I felt cold all over.

Rachel

This time they took me to a different station, the big one over in Barrow, where the MIT were based. I gathered this stood for Major Investigation Team. The station in Barrow was a lot bigger, with more rigorous security, uniformed officers scurrying down the corridors, phones ringing constantly and voices murmuring. I tried to focus on the details of my surroundings, but it was hard not to be swamped in panic. Nothing had changed, I told myself. It wasn't illegal to go by a different name, or to conceal a past conviction that had been overturned. I was innocent. All the same, it was hard to hang on to that as I was escorted in for interview. I wasn't in cuffs, but I had been rearrested, and the threat was clear. 'What's going on?' I pleaded with DS Hegarty. 'Have you found something new – can you tell me? Is it true Anna had a head injury too?'

With a slight roll of his green eyes, he directed me to the interview suite.

'You've been involved in a murder enquiry before, Rachel, yes? Because you don't seem to have any idea how it all works.'

◆ ◆ ◆

It was much fancier in this station. The carpet smelled new, a strong chemical reek, and there was a video camera recording my every move, making me even more nervous. 'So let me get this straight,' DS Hegarty said, after the formalities were done. 'Your real name is Casey Adams, and you were convicted of three murders in America in 2000.'

'Do you remember the case?' I asked, earning another set of raised eyebrows from DS Margaret Hope. My heart had sunk when I realised she was in this interview too. Disapproval radiated off her. Likely she was one of the people who thought I was a child-killer.

'A little. The parents and the little girl were killed?'

'Yes. I called the police, but they arrested me. Sent me to Death Row.'

He nodded. 'But you were cleared on appeal?'

'Well, yes, because I was innocent. The evidence was all circumstantial. I came back to the house and they were – like that. I thought the killer was still in the house, so I hid in the cupboard with the baby. Carson.' It was strange to say his name out loud after all this time.

'And you and the baby were unharmed?'

'Yes, we were both fine. I was in prison in California for five years, then I got out and came home.'

He was nodding slowly. 'I think I remember. They gave you a new name?'

'No, I just got married, started using my middle name. I'm not married now, obviously.' Stupid. He didn't care if I was married or not.

He was still staring at me. It's an odd thing, to have served time in prison, but then been cleared of all charges. It clings to you, the taint of it. An *exoneree* is the technical name for what I am. 'You didn't think to tell us this, Rachel – should we call you Casey now?'

'No, no, please keep calling me Rachel. It's taken me years to train myself to it.' Luckily, Casey was not a common name – Jenna had been banking on that when she gave it to me. So I rarely heard it in public and turned around, before I remembered who I was now. 'And of course I didn't tell you – can you blame me?'

DS Hope sniffed. 'It's very unusual, isn't it,' she said, speaking for the first time, 'to be involved in not one but two murder investigations?' She had a Manchester accent.

Here we go, I thought – just what I was afraid they would say, jumping to conclusions. But I had an answer for it.

'Well, that's the thing,' I said. 'You understand now why I didn't call in the body, that I ran. And there's more – I think I'm being framed.' Then I told them about the letters on my fridge, spelling the name *Casey*. 'No one around here knows my real name. And my scarf – someone must have taken it from my house. You see? It's too obvious to have been me. I would have noticed if I'd dropped it, wouldn't I? Especially me – I'm not exactly naïve when it comes to police investigations.' That was my trump card: that I wasn't stupid enough to have done this. I could not allow myself to be stupid any more. I had paid too dearly for it when I was nineteen.

DS Hegarty was still nodding, as if trying to process everything I'd said. DS Hope was making notes.

'If this is true, and someone is framing you, who could it be?' he said. 'Do you have a list of possible suspects?'

I'd expected this question, but the trouble was my list was so sparse. Ruth Safran would have been top of any such one, but she was dead. José – I had given the LA police his name towards the end, desperately trying to save myself. How was I to know what would happen to him as a result? He was one possibility, although surely he was either in America too, or back in Colombia. Then there were any number of nutjobs who were sure I'd done it, killed a beautiful child in cold blood. Apparently, that was worse than killing a plain one. They frightened me most, because how could I defend myself against total strangers? It could be anyone doing this, a person I had walked past on the street or sat beside on the bus or bought soap from at the market.

'I . . .' I shrugged. 'I've done my best to make sure nobody knows I'm Casey Adams. But someone has found me. Think about it – they're convinced that I got away with murder the first time, so now they want me to go down for Anna's killing. I know it sounds far-fetched but – it's the only explanation I can think of.'

DS Hegarty's moss-green eyes studied me, and I got the feeling he wasn't missing a trick, that all my secrets were laid bare to him. Little did he know that I'd wrapped myself in many layers of lies, so anyone who did unpeel me would have more and more to contend with. It was the only safe way.

'Please,' I said again. 'Will you tell me what's going on with the investigation?'

DS Hope cleared her throat. 'Ms Caldwell, usually suspects are kept updated by their legal representation, which I understand you have declined, as is your right.'

'Yeah, no, I don't want a lawyer. I don't trust them. Not after last time.'

She sighed. 'We can tell you a certain amount. Anna Devine had her throat slashed, as you will no doubt have read in the papers.' I winced. 'She also had a head injury. It's difficult to ascertain the order of these injuries, or which led to her death, if not both. We have not yet located the knife used in the attack. We're pursuing a number of lines of enquiry.'

'But this, you can't use it against me, right? I mean, I was cleared.'

'Yes. You were.' Her tone strongly implied I shouldn't have been.

'Why don't you take us through your movements the day before the murder?' said Hegarty.

I looked between their impassive faces. I had said it all so many times already, yes I had been alone all night, no I had no witness to that except for Brandy, yes I had found the body, but hadn't reported it because of my deep-seated fear of being once again accused of a murder. Which had happened anyway. I knew this was how they worked – put you through your story a hundred times, looking for cracks. But this time I had nothing to hide, especially now my secret was out. So instead of saying all that, I took a deep breath and once again went over the story of my actions right before a murder. Luckily, this was something I'd had a lot of practice at.

'Notorious' discussion forum, Comment on Casey Adams thread (September 2018)

Poster armchairdetective73

For me there's just so much that doesn't add up. Like the cigarette burn on the little kiddie's arm— Casey said she wasn't a smoker, but if you look at those pictures of her in England, the ones with the short skirt and alcopops, you can see her holding a cigarette in some of them. So that's a lie. And the neighbor, Carol Bubchek, said she'd seen her outside the house, smoking, a few times in the days before the murder. If she lied about that, what else did she lie about? And why'd she leave the house in the first place, on such a hot day? To try and make an alibi, by leaving the door open? But the police don't find any other prints on the door or shoe marks in the garden. Just Casey's, the family's, the gardener but he had an alibi. This neighbor also says no one comes to the house during that hour, or even up the street. No cars, definitely no one on foot—people do not walk about in Los Angeles, so it would look suspicious if they did. Anyway Carol Bubchek has a security camera and there's nobody on it, you can see for yourself online. Just Casey sort of pacing with the baby up and down the street. As if she's waiting for something. She even looks at her watch at one point. Why? Is she working out how long she has to stay away for? She wants us to believe someone gets in, kills the entire family, including the dad, who's a tall guy, 200 pounds or so? A stranger who's not familiar with the house layout? Kills them all and doesn't take anything, not even some cash that's sitting out on the side? Gets away, covered in blood spatter probably from stabbing Abby, and no one notices a thing, in this neighborhood full of paranoid rich people? I'm sorry but none of that is remotely believable. It's the kind of thing someone not from LA, or America, might say. Someone with no experience of the police. A young English woman, for example.

-Reply by justiceformadison

I always thought she did it too. Look how cold she is right after it happened. You see the pictures of her standing around the door of the house, the police tape, the ambulance parked outside, the

162

bodies brought out—poor little Madison, her tiny little body bag. And Casey's there and she's not even crying, not even losing it. She's totally calm, her arms folded, and we're supposed to believe a teenager would act like that if she found the entire family dead, blood all over the place? Plus has no one mentioned that she had gunshot residue on her hands? She said she picked it up, without thinking, in case one of the kids got hold of it, but would anyone be that dumb? And don't you only get that if you actually fire the gun? I mean she's not dumb, is she? She managed to get out of prison after killing three people. IMO she's very clever, very cunning, kind of a psychopath, really. Look at her eyes when she's standing outside, and the police are in the house finding them all dead. Nothing, no emotion at all. She doesn't feel a thing.

-reply by BB2000

Does anyone have an idea where Casey Adams might be these days? She went back to the UK, right?

Rachel

After hours of questioning at the police station in Barrow, I was allowed a break. I asked if I could go outside for some fresh air – I was becoming paranoid about losing that again, and needed to get as much into my lungs as I could.

DS Hope looked boot-faced but didn't say no. 'All right,' said DS Hegarty. 'Come with me.'

He led me through the building, down winding, windowless corridors, past small, cramped offices, and out a fire door at the back into a car park. It was raining again, swept with a salt-tinged wind off the sea, and I shivered – I had left my coat inside. All the same, I was determined to stay out. I lifted my face to the darkening sky. Then I realised Hegarty had not left.

'Have to stay with me at all times, huh?'

He shrugged. 'I like the air too. Sometimes I pretend to go for a smoke just to get out of the stuffiness. I haven't smoked in ten years.' Neither had I, of course, after it became such a contentious issue for me, the odd fag I had sneaked and thought would have no consequences.

'Have you always lived here?'

He froze slightly at the question. I had often tried to talk to the prison guards in America, to make them see me as more human, but also just to keep myself from going insane. Even a guard was a person.

'I grew up here. Went to London for a bit to work with the Met – it's tough down there. Came back about six months ago.'

'Have you always wanted to be a policeman?'

Another pause. 'Runs in the family – Dad was one, and I've a cousin down in London who's a detective too.'

I wondered what ran in my family. Lies. Delusion. An inability to stay in touch. I didn't even know if I had any cousins. I'd no idea who my father was, and Jenna had cut herself off from her parents and brother so thoroughly I had never even met them.

'Why did you move back?' I said.

I was really just chatting to keep my mind from looping back over my fears, but he answered me seriously. 'My dad's been poorly. His lungs – well, he's on his way out. Came back to help Mum with him.'

'Oh. I'm sorry to hear that.' Jenna had also died of lung cancer, and I had not been with her at the end, because her new husband hadn't told me it was coming.

He shrugged his shoulders. Under other circumstances, I might have fancied him, or at least liked him – I did like him, in fact. It made the whole thing somehow worse.

'It's interesting being back,' he said. 'People say it must be quiet, after all the murders in London, the gang stuff these past years, but there's plenty here too. Rich tourists snapping on their family breaks, the wife stabbing the husband with the knives in the Airbnb kitchen. Local teens overdosing. Not to mention all the family feuds over who owns which tree, farmers who drink too much and go mad with guns or farm tools. A lot of accidents that maybe aren't accidents.' An awkward pause. Maybe he shouldn't be talking to me like this.

'And your dad?'

'Well, it's like he's just leaking away, really. Every day. Like . . . a bowl with a crack in it, and all I can do is watch.'

He stopped then, as if realising he'd said too much.

'I bet you didn't expect anything as complicated as this case,' I risked.

He cleared his throat, as if signalling an end to this conversation. 'Yes, well. I don't mind complicated. It takes your mind off things.' He moved back to the door. 'We should resume, Rachel, if you don't mind.'

'All right,' I said reluctantly. 'Will I – can I go home tonight?' I knew they had to charge me if they wanted to keep me past a certain time.

His face gave nothing away. 'We have no plans to keep you in at the moment.'

'Thank you.'

'Oh.' He turned back. 'I'm concerned you may not be safe at your home, Rachel. With the press camped outside and the message on your fridge. I'm afraid we don't have a budget to put you up, but I can recommend a number of vacant rental properties nearby.'

'I'd have to pay for it myself?'

'Well, yes. But no one would know where you are.'

I had thought that about the Lake District in general, but someone had found me all the same. I wondered if, assuming I got out of this, I'd ever feel safe again.

Casey

OCTOBER 2000

'This isn't costing me, is it?' I could hear Jenna lighting a fag all the way across the Atlantic, where it was four in the afternoon. Ever since David had given me that one on the terrace, I'd smoked the odd fag myself, even buying a packet in the grocery store, where I had been IDed and felt thoroughly guilty. I sneaked them between errands, or outside the house when Abby was gone. I'd never do it in front of the kids, but it seemed to help my anxiety, plus maybe it would get off some of my American weight.

'No. I called you, didn't I?'

'All right. So, any progress? After he took you to the office?'

'Well . . . I don't know. He'll keep me in mind for roles, he said.' Had David actually said that? 'He's got this big new film series under option and there's a part I could be right for.' I didn't know how to describe the eerie silence of his office, the receptionist who'd looked so shocked to see us, the rows of empty cubicles. It didn't seem like a busy working office, but then what did I know?

'Make sure you make the most of it. Smile, show some leg. If the wife's a right bitch, like you said, he'll like to have a pretty young girl about the place.'

That was what I was afraid of. The way he looked at me sometimes, my breasts, my thighs. That I might have given him the wrong idea about what I wanted. 'That's not why I rang.'

'Oh? You shouldn't be wasting your money on calls, Casey. You need headshots, and LA's all about the glamour. You need to have your nails and hair done, and maybe your teeth, you'll have to save up for that.'

I looked down at my hands, red from scrubbing sheets and raggedy where I'd picked at the cuticles. I was ashamed to tell her how far away I was from any kind of Hollywood glamour.

'I'm worried about the kids, Mum.' She didn't like me calling her Mum, thinking it aged her to have an adult daughter.

'What?'

'The little girl, Madison. She's . . . she has bruises.'

After school I had suggested we went in the pool again, and although Madison was not at all keen (was that strange? A five-year-old who didn't want to swim?), I coaxed her into it, and sure enough, there were the smudged marks of fingers on her inner arms, as if someone had grabbed her and dragged her along. Her thighs too looked red, chafed almost. I didn't know what it meant, but a fear was swelling in my stomach and I couldn't think what to do. So I rang my mother. Not that she was much help.

'All kids have bruises. Clumsy little twats, aren't they?'

'But – she wets the bed, every day. That's not normal, is it? At her age? And they sleep a lot, both of them. Even the baby.'

I couldn't articulate why this was a worry. Shouldn't I have been happy that Carson was no longer waking me up every hour? Maybe he was just getting older, or settling down now he had someone actually taking care of him.

'How old is she again?' Jenna had blocked out all information about the Safran children. To her, my nannying post was merely a step on the way to stardom.

'Five.'

'You rang me all the way from the States to tell me a five-year-old kid wets herself? Grow up, Case. That's what kids do. You were in nappies till you were four, practically.'

'But her teacher seemed . . .'

'Oh, teachers, what do they know? Not a mum herself, I'll bet?'

Miss Oliver was too young to have kids, surely. 'I don't think so, but . . .'

'She's fine. Anyway, she's not your concern. You just feed her and ferry her about, and as soon as you can, get out the door and make your fortune. Bring your old mum over to live with you!' I was silent. This was her dream – she imagined me as a stepping stone to her own career revival. Playing beautiful older women. On my arm at award ceremonies. She really thought it was possible.

'I have to go,' I said, disappointed but not surprised.

'Right. Don't call at this time, OK? It's office hours, you're tying up the line.' She still thought her agent might ring out of the blue and offer her a role, like in a fairy tale. Finally, she would be a star, the magical solution to all her problems. I pictured her there, in our living room that smelled of tobacco, her nails and hair always perfect, starving herself to a skeletal thinness just like Abby, caking her ageing face in make-up to try and hold back time. Poor Jenna.

I hung up, realising I was on my own. I couldn't just do nothing. I wanted to tell David about the bruises. But if Madison were being hurt – if someone was doing things to her – then David and Abby were the most likely culprits.

◆ ◆ ◆

I tried Marietta next. The housekeeper came in three times a week, preparing meals and cleaning up and doing laundry. I already did most of this, of course, but she never acknowledged that. An older woman from El Salvador, she slapped about the house in flat sandals and wore pedal pushers and loose tops, like mothers did. She looked about Jenna's age, but the two were poles apart. Marietta always had the TV on while she worked, watching something, and later that day I went into the kitchen to find her very slowly shelling peas, eyes glued to some kind of courtroom TV show, real people bringing complaints against each other in front of a real judge.

'Hey.'

She jumped slightly, realised it was only me, then slid her eyes back to the TV.

'Good afternoon.'

'Marietta, I want to ask you something. It's a bit delicate. I mean, um . . . it's a tricky subject.' I wasn't sure how good her English was. Would she know the word *tricky*? She said nothing. 'Madison has some bruises on her arms and I'm worried about her. I just wondered if maybe you'd noticed anything. If you knew how she could have got them. You have kids, right?' Perhaps that was the right note to strike. I was just an ignorant teenager, but she was a mother. Finally, she looked at me.

'You have seen these bruises?'

'Yes, they're definitely there. On the inside of her arms.'

Marietta sighed. 'Children are always getting bruises.'

'But her legs – she has this red rash, all over.' I gestured vaguely.

'From the *pipi*.'

'Maybe. But that's weird too, right? She shouldn't be wetting the bed at her age?'

Marietta thought about it for a long time, her fingers working away to pop out the peas, which burst forth like little green bullets. 'You should talk to Mrs Safran, not to me,' she said finally.

'I know, but . . . I'm afraid.' I lowered my voice. 'What if Mrs Safran is the one doing it?'

Marietta's eyes flicked to mine. She must have known it was possible, seeing how Abby behaved towards Madison. She sighed. 'I will talk to her. Say there are bruises and maybe some child is hurting Madison at school, OK? We will see.'

'Oh, thank you!'

The huge rush of relief showed me I had been more worried about this than I knew. But I was nineteen, a guest in America. I didn't want to rock the boat. And so I passed it on to Marietta to deal with, never thinking how this might affect her or what the consequences might be.

Rachel

I knew so little about Anna. She'd had a pink coat, she'd married Alex, given birth to Sam. She'd worked as a massage therapist – might some client have gotten too close? Asking Alex about her life was obviously impossible – I hadn't heard from him in two days – and if her killer was someone she'd met after she and Alex split, then he probably wouldn't know anyway. The police had let me go late the night before, again without charge, and I'd returned home to my empty cottage. It was so late there were no reporters left, though I could see people had been in my front garden, trampling the grass. A few envelopes and calling cards had been pushed through my letter box, offers for me to tell my story. Early that morning Audrey had marched up my path, an expression like thunder on her face, and rapped on my door.

'Rachel!' she shouted in. 'What's going on? There were *dozens* of reporters here yesterday, they ruined my lawn borders!'

I ignored her until she went away, but already I was worried they'd come back, so I had slipped out while it was still dark, hoping to avoid them. I'd not had time to put the cottage back to rights after the search, and Brandy was still with Marilyn. I told myself she was better off there. I had things to do. If I was going to work out what was going on, before I got arrested again and probably charged this time, I had to find out more about Anna, discover who might have killed her. So really there was only one thing I could do – break into her house.

Not actually *break* in, of course. Did it count if you let yourself in with a key? Even if it didn't, it was at best highly suspicious, and for all I knew the police were tailing me all the time. But how else to find out if I was crazy, or if someone really had killed Anna to get to me? I had never been to the house before, of course, but I knew where it was, and Alex had once mentioned Anna left a key near the door, as I did. People were more trusting in Coldwater – or they had been, before this brutal murder.

I walked all the way up there, going the long way instead of cutting through the woods – I still couldn't bear to take that path. It had stopped raining, but I pulled my hood over my head just in case someone saw me. I passed a few people on my walk, no one I recognised. A beady-eyed old man with a walking stick said hello, but I just grunted and kept my gaze down. Stupid. That was probably more suspicious than smiling and answering.

Soon, sweating in my big coat, I reached the house, a ramshackle nineteenth-century farmhouse. It had been Anna's home, although Alex's family owned it and she would have tried to take it from him in the divorce. She'd kept chickens and I could hear their soft cheeps in the distance; I wondered who would feed them now. The place was big for a single woman and a child. And lonely. I thought about her setting off early that morning, pulling on her trainers and heading into the clear bright dawn. Was she in the habit of early solo walks? I had no idea. Maybe she hadn't even showered yet or put on a bra, little knowing she would never come back, that her body would be undressed by a stranger's hands in a mortuary, her flesh laid bare. The patch of leg hair she'd missed on a shin, perhaps. The scars of Sam's birth. The mole on her shoulder she'd been meaning to get checked out.

The farmhouse appeared to be in darkness. It had a dilapidated air, the bricks crumbling in places, a lingering farmyard smell. I wouldn't have wanted to live here, so out in the middle of nowhere. That was a point. Sam had been with Alex on the night of Anna's murder, in the flat in town. Anyone could have been out here with Anna and no one would know. Did she have a lover, as Alex had suspected? Someone who had killed her and dumped her body in the woods? But how would a stranger know exactly where to leave her body so that I would find it, or how to frame me? How would they know I was Casey Adams? I couldn't make sense of it.

I felt along the top of the door and there it was, sure enough, a key with a little green fob. I tried it and the door opened smoothly. There wasn't an alarm, was there? Not around here, where people barely locked their doors? I heard nothing as I walked inside, wiping dirt from my shoes on to the mat. Houses have a strange silence with no one in them. The hum of the fridge seems louder, and here the occasional rumble from the Aga. The place was untidy, shoes piled up at the door, letters in a stack on the hall table, and the surfaces dusty with fingerprint powder, dirty dishes on the table and around the sink. Signs of the police search, muddy boot prints and furniture left askew, and I wondered if they'd found anything here, any of Anna's secrets. Years in prison had taught me to keep things in order, or be punished for it, but I resisted tidying or even touching anything here. As it was, I'd surely be leaving something just by being here, a dropped hair or fibre. I had learned from the trial that you didn't always leave DNA traces just by touching things. There was a woman's coat hanging by the door, a distinctive cerise colour – Anna's coat. I remembered her wearing it when she confronted me that day outside the Co-op. *I don't want you near him! You hear? Stay away from my family!* This was her house, filled with her things, with her skin cells, her essence. I shouldn't be here.

174

I didn't know what I was looking for. Something, anything, that might explain why Anna was found murdered a mile from her house. And what was she doing in the forest in the first place? She wasn't wearing her coat when I found her, or I'd have recognised it, I was sure. Was that strange, on a cold morning, or did she have another? I wished I had paid more attention to the body lying in the clearing, because of course the police wouldn't tell me anything, and if I asked them it would be even more suspicious.

There was a calendar beside the fridge, a freebie from a local garage. Marked on it with a loopy hand was Alex's name, over and over. Days when he had Sam, probably. Also other people's names and times – massage clients, I supposed. Alex had told me she sometimes drove to them, a folding table crammed in her car, as I'd seen on that day at the Co-op, but had she also invited people into this house? That was dangerous, surely.

I checked the day of the murder, and was surprised to see Alex's name on there as well. But of course, that was why Sam was with him and why Anna was alone in the house that night, or why she was possibly free to have someone over. Since Anna had been killed first thing in the morning, or very late at night, I looked at the day before too. Two names, an Alison Harper at 11 a.m. and a Don at 3 p.m. No surname for him, and I felt frustration rise in me. Had the police looked into this, or did they think they already had their killer, so no need to look further? I peered closer – also on the calendar square for that day, right at the bottom, was a small asterisk in blue pen. Did that mean anything? Could have been her period, but would she have marked that on a family calendar? I hadn't known her well enough to say. Then I caught sight of the name of the garage that had produced the calendar, a generic series of lake views – Don Samson Motors. Could it really be that simple? Was he a massage client, or had she just taken her car in for a tune-up?

With my sleeve over my hand, I opened a few drawers but found nothing of interest, just piles of odd screws and spare light bulbs, books of matches. I looked at those in case there was another convenient clue, but they were all just from local businesses or bought in the supermarket. Nothing else. The fridge was full of wine and kids' smoothies, microwave meals and the remains of takeaways, going off now. Clearly Anna hadn't liked cooking much. The kitchen had a large stone fireplace in it, and I noticed a corner of this was taped off with police markers. What did that mean – had they found something there?

I shut the fridge with my elbow and moved into the bedroom. Anna's and Alex's bedroom, it had been, and I was surprised to see men's things still in there, one side of the wardrobe full of suits and jeans. Alex's, presumably. It made me uncomfortable, the sense that their marriage was not as over, as I'd imagined, that I'd been sleeping with a man who was still heavily involved with his wife. On one bedside table was hand cream, tissues, a sleep mask, a paperback novel I'd read myself and enjoyed. A bookmark near the end – she would never finish it now. On the other, a lamp, a book about Churchill. Likely the police had also taken some items away to test – I could see some dusty spaces – and I had no idea what else might have been here.

It felt strange being in there, looking at her shoes in the wardrobe, the beads and earrings hung from a jewellery stand on the dresser, a framed photo of her and Alex with Sam on a beach somewhere. They all looked so happy. Again, wouldn't she have moved that if she had another man over? I didn't know. I was no expert at relationships. I'd spent less than two years with Jeremy, and even though in name he'd been my husband, in reality we were more like flatmates. Feeling guilty, I checked the bedroom drawers. Nothing, apart from some sexy lingerie. It looked unworn, some of it, tags still on. Interesting. Perhaps there really had been someone else, then, a secret new lover.

I found nothing of note in Sam's bedroom, just some more toys and books, his little-boy clothes folded in drawers. The bed was unmade – sloppiness again. The bathroom was not as clean as it could have been, toys piled on the wide windowsill. Peppa Pig bubble bath. I then came upon a small room with a massage table in it, draped with a sheet. So Anna had worked from home after all. Had she seen a client who took things too far, misinterpreted her touch?

I poked about the room, which also contained a desk with a square of dust where a laptop might have been. The police likely had it. I sifted through the mess of papers on the desk, finding nothing except a copy of the local free newspaper from just before the murder, when Anna must have woken up with no idea that this would be her last day alive. How much more fragile life is than we know.

I was realising with frustration that the police had already taken anything of interest from the house, and I was about to give up when I heard the noise. The front door slammed. Footsteps on the tiled hallway. Someone had come into the house. I froze like a thief. They were coming closer, down the hallway.

'Hello?' It was Alex! 'Is someone here?'

He would have found the door unlocked. Would he know it was me?

The sensible thing to do would have been to own up and show myself. But I had not been doing the sensible thing for quite some time now, and I couldn't bear to be caught in his dead wife's house, after all I'd already done to damage our relationship. So instead I ducked under the sheet on Anna's massage table, hiding beneath its folds, and I held my breath.

Casey

OCTOBER 2000

Madison was so sleepy the next morning I had to practically drag her out of bed. At least she hadn't wet the bed this time, but I was careful to make no reference to it – this was the advice from the nanny forums I'd looked at on the living-room computer, which David had said I could use. Best not to make a fuss, and maybe they'd stop on their own.

'Come on, Madison, time for school!'

Sulky, she rubbed at her eyes while I took clothes from her drawers, seeking out anything she had that was remotely age-appropriate.

'I don't want to go to school,' she mumbled.

'Why not? You love school, with all your friends.'

'I don't have any friends.' It was so sad to hear a five-year-old say that, and I tried to think why. Was it her odd behaviour, or all the lessons she'd missed for auditions, or maybe her strange pageant clothes and the fact that she liked to wear the make-up of a fifty-year-old woman? Did she wet herself at school as well? Miss Oliver would have told me, wouldn't she?

I tried to change the subject. I know now I should have listened, asked her what she meant, taught her how to be more popular, but I was still immature myself and it embarrassed me. Loneliness carried its own smell and it repelled me. I was afraid of it.

'I'm sure that's not true,' I said. 'Now, put your socks on, I have to get your brother up.'

Carson had also slept through the night again and didn't want to wake up, so I was feeling well rested that morning and therefore more cheerful than usual. Maybe I'd cracked it, both Madison and Carson sleeping well, and I could actually get some time to myself. Go to the beach, maybe, given I'd never actually seen it. Do something about breaking into acting – take a class, even, like Abby did.

Downstairs there was no sign of either parent, but Abby's blender from her morning smoothie sat unwashed by the sink. I'd leave it for Marietta, since it wasn't my job to clean up. If Abby didn't like it, she could check the terms of her contract with the agency. I was confident, finally, that they wouldn't want me to leave, no matter what I did. They needed me, like David kept saying.

I shoved some fruit down Madison, Carson whingeing into his baby porridge, then after quickly wiping their faces I got them into the car. I had this journey down pat now, and even enjoyed it sometimes, cruising along as if driving right into the dark gold-tinged mountains around the city. I'd go to them one day. I was due some holiday. I let myself have a brief fantasy, Carson in the back, smiling sweetly and quietly, David at my side, sunglasses on, following the line of the coast. Then I felt bad about that. Maybe we'd take Madison too, if she could learn not to wet herself every day. Definitely not Abby. Abby was never present in my fantasies, and I didn't like to dwell on what might have happened to her in my imaginary universe. Some gentle disease maybe, that carried her off, and on her deathbed she gave me her blessing, left her family in my capable hands. Or she decided to join a cult or become a nun.

Of course, it was only a fantasy, a way of filling the long, dreary days. David was almost forty and, although in good shape for his age, not exactly the hunk of my dreams, and I wouldn't actually relish being a surrogate mother to these two. Not Madison, anyway, poor kid. But Carson – perhaps. Carson was my sweet little boy. He was being so good in the car, his eyes open and looking about him, but not making a peep, that I decided to stop for coffee after I'd dropped Madison off, Miss Oliver watching me from across the yard, reminding me I'd heard nothing further from Marietta. I'd ask her today. In the coffee shop, cool and chilled, I ordered a huge iced coffee, full of caffeine and sugar, and I drank it down with Carson on my lap, his cheek resting against my chest, arms dangling at either side of his body. Poor kid was worn out.

A woman with a fractious toddler came in, throwing a tantrum about getting her own Frappuccino. 'I want my own, Mommy!'

'You can't have a whole one, it's too big, sweetheart. Have a sip of Mommy's.'

Cue hysterical screaming and the repeated kicking of the counter. The mother met my eyes, and I tried to convey sympathy with a smile.

'You seem to have no trouble with yours, anyway,' she said.

I didn't quite get what she meant, not right away. 'He's no bother,' I said.

'Enjoy that age while it lasts.' She flashed a smile. 'How old is your little boy?'

That was my cue to say I was just the nanny, but as I sat there with his warm, trusting body drooped on me, I found myself saying, 'Almost eight months. He sleeps so well.'

'Lucky.' Sighing, she took hold of her toddler's arm and steered her out to the patio. 'He's precious, enjoy him.'

Just a throw-away moment, but I felt a faint glow of happiness that someone thought I could be Carson's mother. I didn't know the prosecution would somehow dig that woman up, and at my trial she would testify that I'd told her Carson was mine. She was backed up by the cashier at the coffee shop, who had remembered the conversation. She knew it wasn't true that I was Carson's mother, because Abby was in there all the time, and since a British teenager was much more likely to be a nanny than a mother round here. The little things we do that damn us.

◆　◆　◆

Back at the house, I was surprised to see the blender still unwashed and the greasy breakfast dishes. The washing machine was also silent, a stack of dirty baby clothes in front of it where I'd left them.

'Marietta?' I called out.

No answer. The house seemed empty. I carried Carson through it, my flip-flops echoing on the patio, where Abby sat with a script and half a grapefruit, all she would eat until four in the afternoon.

'Oh!' I said. 'Is Marietta not here today?'

Abby was wearing huge sunglasses and black Lycra. She turned the page, coolly.

'No. Or any day.'

'What?'

'I fired her. She overstepped her boundaries.' Abby turned her blank, reflective gaze on me. 'Let that be a lesson to you, Casey. I don't tolerate people breaking my confidence. What happens in this house stays in this house.'

I knew immediately I had done this. Marietta had brought it up with Abby, Madison's bruises, and she had been fired for it.

'But – what will she do?'

I knew so little about Marietta, I realised. Had she family, a husband to support her?

Abby shrugged. 'Her visa's tied to her job, so I guess she'll be sent back to wherever she came from, or she'll disappear.'

And that was indeed what happened. My defence could not trace Marietta for my trial, and there was no one to back me up. When Madison's teacher, Miss Oliver, testified that she'd told me about the bruises, there was no one to say that I'd done anything about it. And Abby could not be questioned, of course, because she was dead, her throat cut and bleeding out over the kitchen floor I'd mopped so many times.

Rachel

I crouched under the table in an uncomfortable squat, peering out through a fold in the sheet. Would Alex come into this room? If he found me, how could I explain myself? I'd thought I was doing so well, moving on from the trauma of America, but here I was, behaving like a crazy person. Like a criminal, in fact.

I held my breath, listening to his footsteps fade away towards the kitchen, but just as I released a long gasp I heard him coming closer again, loud footsteps on the bare tiles. The door squeaked open and he was in the room with me. *Don't breathe, Casey, don't breathe*. I had gone back to calling myself Casey in my inner voice, as if I'd known all along that Rachel was not the real me. Rachel was a nice woman who wore anoraks and worked in a dog shelter and grew herbs, but she was just a shell I'd built around myself. Casey Adams, as lean and scrappy as a street dog, was still in there. The one who'd do anything to survive.

Alex went over to the desk, and I heard him rooting about in the papers just as I had, as if looking for something. I shifted a little under the table and he stopped and glanced round for a moment. My heart almost stopped. But then he went out of the room again, and I heard his footsteps retreating. Then the front door opened and shut and his key turned in the lock. It took me a few moments just to get my breath back, desperately thankful I hadn't been caught, but then another worry surfaced. If Alex had locked the door behind him, was I stuck in here?

I crept along the corridor in case he was still outside the farmhouse, but then I saw his van disappearing, far too fast, out of the drive and down the lane. As I'd thought, I was locked in. I'd put the key back on the door frame after I opened the door, not thinking I'd need it. Had Alex found it strange, that it wasn't locked, or had he assumed the police did it? But now what? I was stuck inside the house of the woman I was suspected of killing. I would be caught here, and this time they would certainly charge me and try me as a murderer and I would be found guilty and go to prison for life, and there would be no second chances. Oh God. I was trapped.

I sank down on to the cold floor, feeling despair flood over me. Someone was maybe trying to frame me for a murder I didn't commit, but how could I fight them when I didn't even know who they were? So much of the evidence pointed to me, and I'd found nothing to help me defend myself here in Anna's house.

Come on, honey. Get it together. Help yourself.

I summoned Rhonda's voice from deep inside. Rhonda, who'd got me through my time on Death Row. She'd have been shaking her head at me, the silly little English girl stupid enough to get accused of yet another murder. How ashamed she would be of me, wasting the chance of freedom that she'd been denied. It did the trick. I pulled myself together and stood up. There had to be a window I could climb out of. Sure enough, a few minutes later I crawled out of one of the big sash windows in the living room, and landed in a flower bed outside. I pulled the window down behind me, wiping it off as best I could with my sleeve, remembering how my fingerprints had been used against me before. Thinking like a criminal again. But I remembered what Rhonda had taught me: if they treat you like a criminal, the only way to survive is to behave like one. Be sneaky, be strong, fight dirty. *Get out of there, Casey.* So I did. And although I hadn't found out much, I had the names of Anna's final two clients, surely some of the last people to see her alive. It was something, at least.

Casey

OCTOBER 2000

After Abby fired Marietta, it was just assumed that I would do all
the work in the house. But Abby had become even more unmoored,
and when I realised she didn't even notice if I left dirty dishes on
the table all day, I began to slide too. It was a lot, looking after
two small children, and David was hardly about or only there at
strange hours, leaving mid-afternoon for the office and coming
back after midnight. From time to time I asked after his latest
project, the witch series that he supposedly had the rights to, and
he'd make vague comments about the 'development pipeline'. One
day I overheard him arguing on the terrace with José, something
about unpaid wages. After this, José left in a slam of doors and a
squeal of brakes, and I never saw him back there again. The grass
grew parched and straggly, the pool filled up with leaves and no
one cleaned it.

I should have seen all these things as signs, worrying red flags
that meant I needed to do something, and quick. But I was tired,
and overworked, and I was nineteen, little more than a kid myself.
I needed rest, and time away from that house.

Carson at least was sleeping better now, going down at eight and waking up at seven, his nappy sodden and chafed. Should I wake him up to change it? I wondered. He seemed so peaceful. I had asked about it on the nanny forums, but we were all clueless young girls, and no one knew what to do. Let him sleep, seemed to be the consensus.

So things were sliding. Groceries not bought, takeaways ordered and decanted quickly into saucepans to look like I'd cooked. Nobody cleaned, so dust built up on the furniture and there were bits of food dropped on the kitchen floor. The laundry piled up and we all wore clothes for three, four, five days. Neither David nor Abby appeared to notice. She was out a lot still, at the gym or supposedly at auditions. She didn't tell me where she went any more and I got the impression that she and David weren't speaking at all. The children, and the house, had become my sole responsibility.

I began to plan my escape – my contract was up in four months, but I was starting to think I couldn't last that long. The nanny agency, Little Helpers, was no help. No one ever answered the helpline, and when finally I got someone they just asked if I had immediate concerns about the children's welfare. I didn't know what to say to that. Madison was acting strangely, yes, and she had bruises I was sure I hadn't caused (but was I totally sure? I did have to pick her up sometimes and she was heavy, I might have dug my fingers in too hard), but those could be normal childhood things. Carson was all right. He slept well, he ate, he smiled at me slowly, melting my heart. He was sedate. A quiet and good baby. I didn't know enough to worry about that yet.

One night I found out the reason why the children were suddenly much easier to manage. Madison had come home from school with a fever, complaining she was cold, though her head was hot to the touch. She didn't want a snack or any dinner, so I helped her into bed. It was one of the times I felt closest to her, she was so weak and helpless. I laid out her pyjamas, realising I needed to wash her favourite pink ones, and lifted her into bed, smoothing the covers.

'Now, be sure and drink your water, and you'll feel better tomorrow.'

She lay back, closed her eyes. 'Casey? Will you tell me a story about England?'

I had so much to do – Carson to bathe, laundry to put on, since we were all out of clean underwear, dinner to start, or order at the very least. But she was so sick and she never asked for things.

'Of course,' I said. 'Let me just see if I have something to make you better.'

I went to my own room, glancing in at Carson on the way, where he lay calmly in his cot, staring at his feet. I took my pink suitcase down from the wardrobe, thinking how much I had changed from the girl who'd packed it back in England, crossed the Atlantic full of hope and anticipation. I knew there was a bottle of liquid paracetamol in the side pocket – the nanny forums had recommended bringing one with me. However, when I took it out, the bottle was almost empty. I frowned at it for a moment. I'd bought it at the chemist's in the airport and I'd never opened it. But somebody had.

When I went back in, Madison was already asleep, her chest rising and falling. I laid a light hand on her head – still hot. I lifted out Carson and carried him downstairs, without a peep from him. Somehow I didn't want to leave him alone. With him on my lap, floppy and acquiescent, I sat at the computer in the TV room and googled *does paracetamol make kids sleepy*. I learned that yes, it was sometimes given to make them tired, and more docile. *Helps with bedtime*, someone said. *They sleep through the night better*. But then I found a more official site that said this wasn't recommended – it was paracetamol, after all, and could cause liver toxicity. It should only be given very rarely, for serious fever.

I'd been living with the Safrans for barely two months, and neither child had been sick, in the warm climate of LA. The bottle should not have been empty, even with two children. Troubled, I stood up, walking back and forth with the baby against my chest, patting his back. His little arms around my neck, his head lolling on me. Trusting. Carson trusted me to keep him safe. The trouble was, I didn't know how to do that. I was too young, too naïve. What could I do? The agency would be no help. I'd have to talk to David. He was at least sane – or so I thought. He'd understand.

I let myself entertain that brief fantasy again, David and I on the beach, a patterned rug on the sand. Myself in shorts, splashing sparkling water to the sky, Carson toddling towards me from his father's arms. I catch him, lift him to the sun. He laughs. He's mine. He says, *Mummy*. Where was Madison in all this? I didn't think. It was only a fantasy, after all. I was just getting attached to the baby.

I sat down with a sleeping Carson in front of the big TV, and waited for David or Abby to come home. As long as he was in my arms, I could keep him safe. Couldn't I?

Rachel

Back then, in 2000, I had ignored every instinct that said something was terribly wrong in that house, that I should run and never look back. Was I doing that again now, staying in Coldwater waiting to be accused of murder, when I should have fled on the day I found Anna's body? Was there still a life for me here, love with Alex, friendship with Marilyn and the others, my job at the shelter? Maybe it wasn't worth the gamble of staying. This came even more home to me when I made it back from Anna's house, and there was a police car on my doorstep. I wondered if I'd ever get over it, or if my nerves would go to pieces every time, telling me to run, never come back. Did they know I'd been to Anna's house? It was the young uniformed officer from the other day, PC Price. 'I'm here to help you move?' So they didn't know, not yet. Or else they did and were waiting for me to make even more mistakes, walk right into their trap.

A while later, I looked out the windows of the dingy rented flat that DS Hegarty had helped me to find, barred as they were, and realised I was already in a kind of prison. Although I could move about this flat, and make myself tea from the scaled-up kettle, or watch daytime TV on the antiquated set, I couldn't step outside without the risk of encountering reporters or passers-by with camera phones. DS Hegarty hadn't said as much, but I imagined they were monitoring my phone calls too, and probably had someone outside watching me. I couldn't do anything except sit and wait for my fate, getting up occasionally from the old foam sofa to look out the window or boil the kettle. I felt untethered, unable to sit down or settle. Luckily, I had been allowed to keep my phone, and I stared forlornly at it, waiting for a message from Alex, which didn't come. The only messages I'd had so far were from journalists asking for an interview. How they'd got my number I had no idea.

With nothing else to do, I turned to the task in hand. Alison Harper. Don Samson. Not knowing how else to find people, I went to Google. There were a lot of Alison Harpers in the area, most of them on Facebook, and I had to join the site in order to contact them. My profile didn't have a picture and I kept each message vague, saying I was investigating Anna's death and wanted to ask them some questions. Maybe they'd think I was a private detective or even a police officer. I'd called myself Jenna Adams, and wondered what my mother would think about that, her name living on. Not that it was her real name – she'd changed it as soon as she could escape from her rural childhood in Devon. Fake names ran in the family.

While on Facebook I had a good look through Anna's friends list, what I could see of it anyway. Alex was there, a black-and-white picture I'd never seen before of him laughing on top of a tractor, handsome in an open-necked shirt. Was it strange for Anna to still be Facebook friends with her ex? I had no idea of the etiquette. I clicked through both of their pictures, but hardly anything was public except for one lovely shot of them with Sam, on a picnic blanket on a beach somewhere, the same one framed in Anna's bedroom. Anna was in shorts and a jumper, her long legs thrown out, her fair hair windswept. She'd had a long, slightly pinched face, beautiful all the same. Alex was holding Sam in front of him, tickling him. He was topless, tanned, lean. I was lonely for that body, and not sure I'd ever get to touch it again. Sam appeared to be screaming with laughter in the picture, Alex smiling, Anna laughing too. So why had they broken up? It was definitely over before I came along. Wasn't it?

The identity of Don Samson, car mechanic, was easier to trace on Google. Mechanics were quite likely to have back problems and need a massage, weren't they? No one else with that name locally. Don wasn't on Facebook, sensible man, so I decided I'd go and see him. I opened the door of the flat, looked up and down the depressing linoed corridor. No sign of any police. And they hadn't said I couldn't go out. I wasn't actually a prisoner, although I might feel like one.

Outside the flat, a car was parked – some nondescript red one. I never knew the makes of cars. There was a man inside, alone, drinking a cup of takeaway coffee. Was that the police, watching me? Just in case, I turned and slipped out of the street the other way, while he was looking ahead.

I trudged out of town on to the main road, quickly getting tired. The ground was slippery underfoot, and the pavement ran out after a while so the cars whizzed close to my head. I was wishing I hadn't bothered when I saw the sign for Don Samson Motors. The smell of petrol was somehow comforting as I approached.

Don was listening to Classic FM on a little radio, and was alone, whistling to himself while he wiped a spanner on an oily rag.

'Er, hi,' I said.

He looked surprised to see me.

'Are you Don?'

'Aye.'

He was from Yorkshire, I thought. I put his age at about seventy, grizzled and wiry, tattoos on his arm under his rolled-up overalls. Perhaps he'd been in the army or navy once. I explained who I was, that I was looking into Anna's death and knew he'd been her client the day before she died.

'You're not with the police.' That must have been obvious from the way I'd turned up, damp and dishevelled from the walk.

'Well, no.'

He pointed the spanner at me. 'You're that lass they arrested, aren't you?'

Stupid to think I wouldn't be recognised in a place like this.

'I didn't do it, but I need to find out who did. Did the police speak to you?'

'Called round a few days back, but they've not been back to ask me owt.'

Probably because they were so focused on me. I waited. Don Samson would either help me or he'd call the police. After a moment he put down the rag and spanner.

'Cup of tea?' he said.

◆ ◆ ◆

Don's tea had a faint petrol tang to it, but I didn't mind. We sat in the little glass-fronted office that looked out on his workshop, various cars in states of disembowelment.

'I liked her,' he said, taking a gulp of tea. 'Anna. She was a nice lady. Didn't embarrass me for getting massages.'

'Had you hurt yourself?'

193

'Aye. Pulled something stretching under a Beemer – not as young as I used to be, see.'

'And you went to her house for the massages.'

'Aye. Not room in mine for the table, like.'

'And . . . I'm sorry, I don't really know what to ask. Did you see anything strange that day, at the house? You must have been one of the last people to see her.'

He thought about it. 'She was excited, I reckon. Maybe not as focused as usual, but she did a good job all the same, very professional. Asked could we finish up a bit early since she had someone coming over.'

My heart started to race. 'She didn't say who?'

'I didn't ask, lass. I mind my business.'

If that was a little barb at me, I let it go. 'You got the impression it was a man, maybe?'

'Could be.'

'Nothing else?'

'No, lass. I don't like a lot of chatter when I'm having my back rubbed. She gave me some exercises, arranged the next time, I paid her, that were that.'

'OK.'

It was disappointing. I was no further along and had no way of finding out who she'd been expecting.

'Thank you,' I said.

'One thing.' Don's brow was furrowed, as if he was thinking hard. 'She went to answer the door once. In the middle of seeing to me. I know she didn't like to do that, told the postman just to leave parcels and that outside if she were busy.'

'Did you hear anything?'

'Well, I'm flat on my front, love, can't hear that much. But it was her little boy. Someone dropped him off, I suppose. Bless 'im, they can't stay quiet, can they, little kids, so I heard him shouting in the hall, running up and down like.'

Sam? Sam was at the farmhouse the day before Anna was murdered? Wasn't he with Alex then?

'And – sorry, Don – you don't know who brought him?'

'No idea.'

My mind was racing. I definitely hadn't seen Alex that night, because he was with Sam. Had Don got the wrong end of the stick and Alex was actually picking Sam *up* from the house then? But I thought Alex usually got him straight from school, to avoid seeing Anna. Don's massage had been at four, I remembered from the calendar. I needed to ask Alex about the timings, but how could I do that without revealing my secret investigations?

I put down my mug, which was branded with the logo of his business, and sighed. 'Thank you so much for talking to me.'

Don gave a gruff nod. 'Everyone deserves a fair trial, that's what I always say.'

'They don't always get it, I'm afraid.'

'No. Well. Good luck to you, lass. The truth will out.'

But would it? I had sat on a lie for twenty years already, and no one else had any idea of the true extent of what had actually taken place in the Safrans' house that day. And I still wasn't ready to tell.

Casey

October 2000

A lot of people have wondered over the years why I didn't leave my job if things were so intolerable at the Safrans' house. Of course, there were many reasons. You know that saying about the frog in hot water? I was that frog. Yes, Abby was unstable, and David was up all night in his office with a bottle of whisky, and Madison and probably Carson too were being drugged, I assumed by their mother, but I had nowhere else to go and I wasn't ready to fly back to England with nothing to show for it. I'd boasted so much about my new Hollywood life, and Jenna had boasted even more – she was convinced that I'd be on the red carpet within a year. If I left my job at the Safrans', I'd have to leave America too, and I'd lose my placement bonus, a significant amount I was relying on to get me to drama school and on to my starry career. And I still held out hope that David might find a film role for me. Another reason was that I was nineteen and not used to standing up for myself. I did what I was told. I listened to my mother and the nanny agency, and to David, who constantly told me the family would fall apart without me, and I believed him.

The other reason was the oldest, sneakiest reason of all time – love. Not David, but Carson. I loved the baby I'd been taking care of for months now. I loved it most of all when he fell asleep on me and latched his little arms around my neck. I couldn't leave him to whatever catastrophe was unfolding in that house. I was even fond of Madison, for all her difficulties. It wasn't her fault, after all. Abby had made her the way she was.

Anyway, I didn't realise how bad things were until that final day, when everything came to a head. It's human nature. We tell ourselves it can't be as bad as it seems in our darkest hours, lying awake at 3 a.m. It will get better, we say. We're imagining it. So yes, it was love and ambition and hope that got me in the end. I had plenty of time afterwards, in prison, to think over the events of that last week, to get the sequence right in my head, and yet I'm still not entirely sure. Memory is like that. It protects us from the worst.

Marietta was fired several weeks before the murders, as far as I recall. José and David had the row maybe ten days before. I remember being frantic, struggling to get the kids up and to school, feed them. Abby was rarely around. David was awake at all hours, and I'd meet him in the kitchen as I warmed Carson's bottle or put Madison's sheets on to wash yet again. His brief period of helpfulness had waned, and I was back to doing it all myself.

One night – I think it was the Friday, perhaps, and the murders happened on the following Monday – he came in as I stood at the stove boiling water, a crying Carson on my hip. I was utterly exhausted, too young for all this responsibility. It was around two in the morning, outside a pitch-black LA night, the howls of coyotes in the canyon, the whir of police helicopters overhead. Carson was barely awake, struggling against his drowsiness – not natural, as I now know – and the pain in his teething gums. His little face was red and shiny.

David padded in, bleary-eyed, a whisky glass in his hand. He was wearing the same jeans and T-shirt I'd seen him in two days before, and I wondered if he'd changed or showered. He didn't seem to have gone to work in days. 'Why's the baby up?'

I said nothing. Increasingly, I just went through the motions of my routine.

David winced as the baby's wails went up a notch. 'I thought he was sleeping right through now.'

'He was. I think he's teething.' Which was all I needed.

You have to get out of here, said a voice in my head, one that I should have listened to.

'There's always something, isn't there?' he said. 'With kids.'

I just looked at him. It was on the tip of my tongue to ask why he and Abby had had kids when they didn't seem to want them.

'Here.' He held out his arms, and I gratefully surrendered the heavy, howling baby to him, as I busied myself with the bottle. David spoke to Carson. 'What's wrong with you? God, does he ever shut up?'

That jolted me. 'He's just in pain.' Carson was actually quite a good baby, as far as I could see.

'I mean, you're doing your best,' he continued over the din, jiggling Carson hard against him. 'But it's a lot, isn't it? For someone your age. Two kids, not even yours.'

'I love them,' I said, and mostly meant it. 'Look, I'll take him back.' I eased Carson on to my hip, feeling some strange relief to have him in my arms. David hardly seemed to notice I'd taken him.

'But it's not what you'd want, ideally. A young girl like you.'

I didn't understand at the time what David was saying. Of course I didn't – who could have imagined it? As it was, I was grateful for the sympathy.

'It has been hard. Abby, she seems . . .' I trailed off. It wasn't wise to criticise his wife, I knew that. But David latched on to it.

'I know. I know. It's unbearable – you see what I . . . I mean, where even is she half the time? I don't know.'

'Auditions.' I tested the milk on my wrist, as I'd been taught. It was OK. Carson flailed in my arms. 'Shush, shush now. It's almost ready.'

'Auditions? Huh. She's pushing forty, that's the dead zone for actresses . . . If she's lucky she can start doing character parts in another five, ten years, but is she even good enough for that? I don't know. I really don't. But try to tell her that, to give up the goddamn yoga and aerobics and I don't know what else, and stay here being a proper mom to her own kids . . . it's like talking to a wall.'

'I know. It's hard.' Of course, David wasn't much of a parent to his children either, but I didn't expect it, not back then. My internalised misogyny was strong. 'She's very . . . unsettled.'

'She's crazy, Casey. You should see the pills in the bathroom cabinet. Wow.' I didn't want to say I had seen them already.

'Does she need some kind of help?' I said. 'I mean, a doctor or something?'

'She won't go,' he growled. 'Says she's fine. Sometimes I think the only way is to end it all.'

I assumed he meant divorce and my heart began to beat with something close to fear: what did that mean for me and my job? And my chance of playing Miranda?

'Oh no,' I said, 'it's not come to that.'

'Tell me what else it would take?'

He was looking right at me and I didn't want to meet his gaze. I wasn't ready to have this conversation or look directly at what we'd been dancing around. The way he stared at me as I moved round the house.

'I have to feed Carson.'

David followed me upstairs. The house was as quiet as a tomb, despite Madison and Abby being asleep up there. He stood in the doorway of the baby's room as I settled into the armchair there, feeling as self-conscious as if I were about to breastfeed.

'Poor baby,' I whispered to Carson, as he found the teat of the bottle. 'Poor, poor baby.' He quietened, his hand reaching for the milk, one twined in my hair. David watched us, and I was afraid to look up at him.

'You're so good with him. So natural.'

'He's a good boy,' I said.

'But the crying, waking up all night long? And Madison – God, you see what she's like. Sometimes I wonder if it would be kinder. The mother they have.'

I wasn't paying attention. I should have been. I didn't ask what would be kinder, because of course I had no idea what was going on in David's mind, the dark abyss of it. Instead I said, 'How's it going with the witch series?'

'Oh. Well, you know how it is. These things take time.'

But I didn't have time. I had to go home in four months.

He stood watching me a while longer, then eventually turned and I heard his footsteps going down the stairs. I breathed a sigh of relief. I knew we had brushed against something, some truth I didn't want to acknowledge.

The next morning – or rather, four hours later – I was up packing Madison's lunch, cutting fruit for breakfast. Carson was in his high chair, playing with some slices of banana, quiet again, and Madison slumped at the table, not eating hers. I was surprised when Abby came into the kitchen, dressed not in workout clothes but in a summer dress and sandals. She'd even blow-dried her hair and wore it loose, reminding me how beautiful she really was.

'Good morning,' I said, trying to hide my surprise.

She didn't answer, but took some of the kiwi I was cutting and put it into her mouth.

'Are you going somewhere?' I asked tentatively.

200

'I'm going to get the role that's made for me. Esmerelda.'

That was a witch in the YA series David said his company had the rights to. Esmeralda was a mother, but still young and beautiful and with a good storyline. I was confused. If Abby wanted the part, surely she wouldn't have to try out for her own husband's company.

'I thought David said . . .'

She barked a laugh. 'Oh, David doesn't have the rights to the series. Didn't you hear?'

'Hear what?'

'He never had them to start with. The money didn't go through for the option fee and Sony snapped it up instead.'

'What?' For weeks now David had been talking as if it was a done deal.

She smiled. She had seeds in her teeth. 'He doesn't have the rights. So let's see him shut me out of it now!'

'So you're going . . .'

'I have a meeting with Sony, yes. Luckily, I still have some clout left in this industry!'

Spitefully, I didn't tell her about the seeds. I was so disappointed. My head was spinning. Leaving Carson in his chair, I went to David's office and knocked loudly on the door. When there was no answer I tried the handle and found it unlocked. I hadn't seen inside his office for weeks, and the lack of cleaning was evident. A bin overflowing with Coke cans, fast-food wrappers, even cigarette butts, and the stale smell of the room confirmed that he'd been smoking in there. The desk was ringed in drink marks and covered in a layer of dust and crumbs. The computer was also dusty, as if it hadn't been used in weeks. Screenplays were piled everywhere, held together by little metal clips, alongside reams of paperwork, contracts. What was going on? How did his company not have enough money to pay for an option? I'd read enough movie news to know that this wasn't usually all that much, not until a project got the green light. I stepped forward slightly, seeing that one of his desk drawers was open. In it two things – an almost empty bottle of whisky. And a gun. David had a gun. I would later find out it was a 9mm Glock, but at the time I had no idea what type it was, just that it was there, and it was terrifying. I stood in the doorway feeling the fear grow inside me, blooming like some dark desert flower.

Rachel

So I'd learned something from Don Samson, although not what I'd expected. I had to think of a way to ask Alex why he'd dropped Sam off with Anna on the night before she was murdered, assuming I ever saw him again. He hadn't answered my last two messages and I was trying not to send a third, but really I knew my pride was leaking from me, along with everything else.

I was back in town now, and I stopped in the quiet evening street, the shops around me shuttered, rain moving in over the lake, and mulled it over. I'd sent Facebook messages to all the Alison Harpers I could find, but it was starting to feel like a bit of a long shot. However, as I was trudging home, rain all down my back and into my boots, I checked my phone and was surprised to find a message from one of the Alisons, the one with a professional profile pic of her smiling, arms folded, as if in a brochure. *Yes, it was me who met with Anna Devine, but I'm not a massage client. Can I ask what this is regarding? Are you with the police?*

I clicked on her profile. Why did she meet Anna if not for a massage? I soon found out – this Alison Harper was a divorce lawyer, based in Barrow in Furness. That made sense, didn't it? Anna and Alex were splitting up, so of course she would want to consult a lawyer. But Alex had told me she was in denial about it, that she didn't want a divorce, and that was borne out by my own experience of her confronting me in the street. I tried to remember exactly what she'd said to me that day, as much as I had taken in through my fog of shock that it was happening at all. *I don't want you near him. Stay away from my family.* That seemed unequivocal – she wanted Alex back.

It was getting late now, the night drawing in already, the days an hour shorter than even two weeks before. I had nowhere else to go, so I'd have to return to the dreary flat, face whatever was waiting there for me. It had been a long and stressful day, and I was half-dead on my feet from hunger and shock. Rousing myself from my funk as I reached my side of town, I clicked on the website link from Alison Harper's Facebook page, and found the phone number. I'd do this the old-fashioned way and make an appointment. A little dishonest, perhaps, since I wasn't married and therefore didn't need a divorce, but what else could I do?

◆　◆　◆

Alison Harper's firm was based in the centre of Barrow, on a busy main street with shops and offices, cafés, all of life bustling around me. As I walked down it the next morning, I realised I had started to log things away, feelings and impressions, in case I went to prison again. The smell of brewing coffee. The freedom to walk into a shop and browse a rack of blouses, riffle my hand through the silky fabric. The breeze on my face, even. British prisons were nicer, weren't they? You got TVs and they didn't let the inmates kill each other. And a life sentence here, what was that – ten years maybe, if you kept your head down? I'd be less than fifty. Still time left.

No. It was no good bargaining with myself, calculating the years in my head. I would not survive if I went to prison again for another crime I didn't commit. I had to figure this out. I buzzed and went up the stairs to Alison Harper's office, to a neat reception area with a Nespresso machine. Alison, when she came out to greet me, was about my age, in an M&S trouser suit and with shiny highlighted hair. I noted her maroon gel nails and felt I could trust someone like this, who paid attention to the little things.

'Rachel, is it? Do come in.'

I had called myself Rachel Smith. I couldn't call myself Jenna in case she remembered that from my Facebook message – it was hardly a common name. I had so many fake identities, shrouding myself in lies.

Nervously, I followed her down a small corridor, declining her offers of coffee or water. Her office was small but tasteful, with awards and legal books on the shelves, a sofa with some scatter cushions. A table with tissues. Of course, people must cry all the time in here. They came to her at their lowest ebb, when life no longer made sense, and I was doing the same, but for different reasons.

Alison sat opposite me, notebook and pen in hand. 'So, Rachel, why don't you tell me what brought you here today.'

Oh God. 'Um . . . Alison, I'm sorry. I'm actually kind of here under false pretences. I mean, I don't want a divorce or anything. I'm not even married.'

She looked confused. 'You don't have to be married to use a family lawyer.'

'No, but – it was me who sent you that Facebook message. About Anna Devine? I'm sorry, I just – I really needed to talk to you and didn't know how. I'll pay for your time, of course.'

She sat back, looking mildly irritated but not yet furious with me. 'I don't understand. Are you with the police?'

'No.'

'But you're looking into Anna's death?'

May as well tell the truth. 'Well, the thing is, I'm the chief suspect. The one who found her body. But I didn't do it. I swear, I didn't touch her. So I need to find out who did.'

She was no pushover, Alison. Her carefully lined eyes widened, and she just looked at me for several long seconds without speaking – try it, it's harder than you think – then she placed her notebook on the table. 'You're – what's your real name?'

My real name was not my real name, but I couldn't go into all that now. 'Rachel Caldwell. I'm – I was dating Anna Devine's husband, Alex. They'd split up, as far as I knew.'

'Right. Yes.'

'I'm so sorry to trick you. I'm just desperate to find out who really killed her.' Someone to offer up to the police instead of me. 'That's why she met with you that day – you weren't there for a massage. She was a client of yours?' Alison nodded. 'And she saw you the day before she died.' Another stiff nod.

'I can't talk to you about her case. Confidentiality.'

'Of course. But – that doesn't apply if someone is dead, does it?' I had checked.

She frowned. 'Not exactly. There's still a moral duty – and you're not a police officer, so why should I talk to you?'

'Because I didn't do it, and that means someone else did.' I had a hunch, suddenly, from the way she was looking at me. 'Did Anna mention me?'

'Not by name.'

'Well, all I can say is, they were already split up when I met him. Do you know Alex at all?'

'I . . .' She stopped herself. 'I really can't talk about this.' And yet she hadn't thrown me out yet. I took that to be a good sign.

'When you saw Anna that day, how was she? Happy?'

'She wasn't happy, no. Her marriage had fallen apart, her husband was seeing someone else.' Alison's tone was crisp.

I refused to say sorry for that, it wasn't my fault. Was it? No. I couldn't start doubting everything.

'And – she came to you about divorcing him?'

She tensed up. 'I've told you I can't . . .'

'Right, right, just tell me anything you can.'

'She came to see me about . . . the situation, yes. Preliminary discussions.'

'He told me she wouldn't agree to it, the divorce.'

Alison raised her eyebrows. 'Oh. Well, that isn't the case, I can tell you. That's a matter of public record. Anna came to see me to start the process.'

Strange. Had I just misunderstood, or had she finally changed her mind? 'All right. So she was going to file?'

'That was my understanding.' Alison looked at her watch. 'Look, I shouldn't be talking to you. Apart from anything else, you're the prime suspect in my client's murder.'

'I know. But all I can say is – I really didn't do it. I know you've no reason to believe me, but I didn't, truly I didn't. And someone else did. Is there anything you can tell me, anything at all that might help stop an innocent person going to prison?' As a lawyer, I imagined she would care about justice being done. 'For Anna,' I risked. 'I just want to find out what really happened to her.'

Alison bit her lip, then she stood up. 'I'm sorry, there's nothing more I can say. But to say she opposed a divorce, that's . . . not entirely accurate. So. I'll have to report this to the police, that you came here.'

'That's fair. Thank you, Alison. You've been really kind to talk to me.'

I left, exiting on to the busy street, my head full of our conversation. Why had Alex told me Anna wouldn't agree to a divorce? Had she perhaps changed her mind, if she really was seeing some mystery man? How could I ever find out for sure?

Casey

NOVEMBER 2000

Bright flashes. Everywhere I looked. My brain couldn't take it in, the dazzle, the glare. All the TV cameras and press photographers, the jostle of different faces, constantly hearing my name.

'Casey! Casey!'

'Did you do it, Casey?'

'Why did you kill them, Casey?'

I tried to concentrate on my other senses, since my ears and eyes were overwhelmed. Touch – the female guard gripping my shoulder like a vice, as if I could run away with handcuffs biting into my wrists. They were heavy, and my forearms already ached. Taste – sour fear in my throat, my tongue dry from the hot van ride from prison. And smell – the heat of an LA day, petrol from the TV vans surrounding the courthouse, and my own terrified sweat. They were all dead – David, Abby, Madison. I had been accused of their murders, a triple murder, including a child. And California had the death penalty.

My legs buckled under me and the guard grunted in annoyance, dragging me upright. Then she pressed down on my head and pushed me through the crowd of reporters. Even in my panic, struggling to get each petrol-soaked breath into my lungs, I could see the irony. It was exactly what Jenna had told me to visualise as I was growing up: *One day you'll have a crowd of press all calling your name.* Except I wasn't on the red carpet. I was being taken to court for an arraignment, after three days of non-stop questioning by police. It was just a formality. Then I'd go back to prison to await my trial, and if found guilty, I might get the death penalty. I might die for this.

◆　◆　◆

The holding cells were deep in the courthouse, so at least the noise of the crowd faded to a dull hum. I sat on a crackly blue mattress and felt the heat of the van's stuffy metal interior evaporate from my body, leaving me shivering. I was wearing the familiar orange jumpsuit I'd seen on TV, that people back home sometimes bought as a Halloween costume. Halloween had been and gone, just after the murders, a fact made much of in the press, that such horrific killings had taken place in a city full of skeletons and fake blood and ghouls. But this was real.

The jumpsuit was too big for me, so I'd rolled up the arms and legs, and underneath I wore plain white cotton underwear, a bra that didn't fit, with no wire in it. Someone else's clothes, washed many times, reeking of industrial laundry detergent. It's strange how helpless it makes you feel, not wearing a stitch that is actually yours. The suit smelled of someone else's sweat, and the 'sneakers' for my feet were also too big. I could still wear child's sizes. My female guard had signed me over to a male one. He was large and slow. All the guards were slow, as if their brains were fried by the heat. He was chewing gum and ambled over to the bars of the cell to look in on me.

'Well, well, quite the crowd for you outside, little lady.'

My teeth were chattering. 'I'm innocent.'

He laughed softly. 'If I had a nickel for every time I heard that . . .'

'But I am! I'm, I'm only nineteen!'

I knew that wouldn't count, that some states sentenced children to death, younger than me. I was an adult in the eyes of the law, even if I wore kids' shoes and ate Lucky Charms for breakfast.

The guard passed me a paper cup of water through a hatch in the bars, then shuffled back to his chair and raised his newspaper. On the front was a picture of Madison in one of her pageant costumes, made up and smiling. I started to shake, so hard the water splashed over my jumpsuit. Madison was dead. She would never smile or laugh or wet the bed again. She had lived only five years of her life. That was an abomination.

I sat on the bunk until the shaking stopped. I tried to tell myself a trial was exactly that, a way to find out the truth. They would look at me, small, young, British – they loved us Brits over here – and they would see straight away that I couldn't possibly have murdered a child. I had saved Carson! I had protected his soft body, squirming against mine, as I hid in the walk-in cupboard and held my breath and prayed he wouldn't cry. I had called the police. I had saved us both. And now here I was.

I wondered where Carson was now. Would they give him to Ruth, his aunt? I couldn't imagine her cuddling anyone, or remembering which soft toy was his favourite, or singing him Spice Girls songs to get him to sleep. Poor Carson. Poor Madison. Poor David. Poor Abby, and poor me! I just had to hope the jury would see the truth.

I wondered if Jenna had come, if she was on a flight right now. She had said so little on the garbled phone call I'd been allowed after my arrest, breathless with hysteria.

They think I did it, Mum! I don't know what to do! I need a lawyer!

Had she actually said she was coming? I knew she had some money saved up, planning to retire to the seaside one day and open a café, but would she spend that on me, on a last-minute flight across the Atlantic? I needed a good lawyer and, in America, that cost a fortune. The flight alone would be expensive, but I needed my mother here, as inadequate as she was. She was all I had. What if I walked into that courtroom and saw not a single friendly face, just people who had decided already that I looked the type who could smother a child? A child I'd cared for. Washed her urine-soaked pyjamas. Cut her apple into the shape of a fan. If only Carson could speak, he'd tell them what he'd seen. I kept reliving the moment, over and over. I was in shock. Trauma. Just three days ago, three days I had spent mostly in the windowless basement of a police station, telling them again and again I was innocent. Reliving that final day.

'Adams, come on.'

I snapped back to the present. The guard was jangling his keys. I sipped the rest of the warm water and tried to focus. *Say you didn't do it*, I repeated to myself. *Just say you know nothing and you'll be all right.*

Rachel

Juddering home on the bus from town, still puzzling over Alison Harper's information, my phone pinged. I had an email in my newly set-up account. I hated that, the way I'd been drawn into this world I had successfully avoided for so many years, responding to noises like Pavlov's dogs. A world where you could never truly make a fresh start. Already there was a mountain of spam in my inbox, and I wondered how that worked, how the internet had figured out that I'd stirred into life.

Hello, Rachel, wrote Jochem cheerfully. *I have found out what happened to José and Marietta from your case. I am afraid to say they have both also passed away these past few years.*

Oh. Well, that wasn't so surprising. They had both been at least in their fifties at the time of the murders. Still, it was another dead end, and I felt a sad twinge that two more people were gone without me ever making peace with them, atoning for what I'd done to them without meaning it.

He went on: *However, I have noticed the same poster looking for you on different forums. Always they use the name BB2000. I do not know what this means but this is a person who has been trying to find your location for several years now. I would advise you to be careful, Rachel.* I had seen this person posting too. If they were looking for me on more than one forum, they must be serious about finding me. But who could it be?

Jochem had signed off, *Best intentions, J.*

Best intentions. I liked that. It was what I'd had, back then, when I tried to care for those poor children. It's what I'd had in Coldwater, starting my life over, rescuing neglected and abused dogs, and yet no matter what I did, I always seemed to end up back where I started – fighting to clear my name.

I emailed back, thanking Jochem and asking if there was any way he could find out who had sold the story of my real identity to the press. Someone must have, and if I knew anything about the British press, whoever it was would have been well paid for outing me. Was it the same person who'd left my name on the fridge, or someone else, trying to make some quick money? Who did I know who really needed cash? Everyone, really.

It was amazing he'd already found so much out, when the police had totally failed to trace Marietta back then. Jochem truly was a wizard of the dark arts of the internet. How could I ever thank him? If only I'd had him on my side during my trial, I might never have been convicted. I stared out the window at the passing scenery, the green curves of the hills and flashes of blue water, which for once left me cold, my hands twitching with nervous energy.

We were passing through the next town over from Coldwater, little more than a village really, a place called Holmdale. As the bus paused for a moment at the stop, I glanced out at the main street, and froze. Someone I knew had just come out of a chippy there, a styrofoam carton in hand. Someone who should not have been here at all, who should have been hundreds of miles away.

Jeremy.

Casey

The lawyer looked at me over the table. He had old-fashioned glasses, with clear rims, and coffee breath. He was sixty, maybe. Even his name was old-fashioned: Garrett Cooper the Third. So American. I could tell he had no idea how to even approach me, in my too-big clothes, shivering with shock and the cold of the police station. He'd been sent by the nanny agency that hired me, Little Helpers. They were understandably terrified of the bad publicity. One of their employees accused of murdering the entire family she worked for – it didn't exactly look good.

'I don't understand,' I said again.

I felt so stupid, like my brain wasn't working. I couldn't remember the last time I'd eaten or been to the loo. My stomach felt like it was dissolving in acid fear and hunger.

'I don't know how else to say it, Miss Adams,' the lawyer said. 'This is a death-penalty state, and it's certainly on the table for a crime of this magnitude.'

'But . . . it's California!'

I knew the death penalty existed in America – Jenna and I had watched *Dead Man Walking* – but weren't those Southern states, bigoted, racist?

'Nevertheless, it has the death penalty, and executions have been taking place since the seventies, after a brief hiatus.'

'But – what do you get the death penalty for?'

He reeled off a few examples. 'Multiple murders. Exceptionally wicked murders. The murder of a child – that will likely come under the guidance.'

All right. The world made no sense, and I just had to try to understand it.

Focus, Casey. You'll wake up from this soon.

'But I didn't do it. I had no blood on me, did I? Except my feet?'

They'd told me, and I had seen for myself, that Abby's throat had been cut. I couldn't have done that without getting blood on my skimpy vest top and skirt, could I?

'They'll find a way to spin that. You changed your clothes, maybe.'

'But I didn't!'

'It was all over your feet – walked throughout the house.'

'I stepped in it!'

The horror of it hit me again, and I began to shake. I reached down to brush at my ankles in their nasty prison socks, although I had showered several times since walking in Abby's blood. I wondered would it ever leave me. Her *blood*. She was dead. David. Madison. All dead. I would never see or talk to them again. The shock of it was moving slowly through me, numbing me. Dead. All except Carson. I had saved Carson. That was the only thing I had to hold on to, a ray of light in the darkness.

He sighed. 'You have to understand, Casey, the evidence is against you. No one else went into the house. There's no other prints, or hairs, or DNA – only yours.'

'I lived in the house – of course my DNA was there. Anyway, you mean no one *saw* them go in. They might have – the front door was open when I came back.'

'So you claim. But we can't prove that. And the public mood, with a dead child . . . well. And you're not from here. It looks bad.'

I gaped at him. I suppose this was my privilege, a young white girl, never expecting to be judged by appearances. I didn't know it was happening right at the moment, my photo circulating on the internet and on TV news and in the papers. A nickname was even being coined: *Racy Casey*. One that would haunt me.

'They don't give women the death penalty, surely?'

Garrett Cooper pinched his nose, as if dealing with me was giving him a migraine. I would later learn that California in fact has the most women on Death Row of any American state.

'They most certainly do,' he said. 'A woman was executed a few months back in Arkansas. It happens. But listen, actual execution is rare. What you need to worry about is spending the rest of your life on Death Row. It's not a nice place, Casey. It's not even near here in this state, it's out in the desert. You want that? To die in a hot steel box?'

'Of course I don't want that!' I sat back in the plastic chair, bewildered and shaking, cold and sweaty and hungry. I hadn't slept in days. I was shell-shocked by loss and confusion and fear. 'I don't know what else to say. I'm telling the truth. I took the baby out, I came back and they were dead.'

'But you were in the house for at least ten minutes before you called the police from the closet. The neighbour saw you go into the house; she took note of the time because her soap opera was on.'

Mrs Bubchek, with her dyed red hair and suspicious glances, the kind of woman with nothing of value but who always thinks she'll be robbed. I wasn't surprised she would try to burrow her way into the case. She'd called to me from her lawn a few times when I was out with Carson, asking who I was and what I was doing on the street. A police officer's dream, the local busybody.

'That's – how do they even know she had the right time? Her clock might have been wrong, or I, maybe I took a while to walk about the house, I was in shock! I was terrified! They were dead! I'd never even seen someone dead before. And Madison . . .' Here my voice broke, and thickened. You can hear it on the interview tapes, if you want. They were leaked a few years after it happened, and have appeared on various podcasts. 'I was so scared. I cared for her. I looked after her every day for three months.'

'There are witnesses to you losing your temper with her.'

I thought back. That time at her school, when she wouldn't get out of the car so I had to drag her, or maybe a neighbour had overheard me scolding her in the house or the garden.

I gritted my teeth. 'Everyone does that sometimes! I was taking care of two kids and doing all the housework. I was stressed out, I hardly got any sleep. And Abby . . .'

He pounced on that. 'That's another thing. She'd complained about you to various friends. There was tension.'

I could just imagine it, Abby and her mom or actress friends, moaning about their help over iced coffees. Or maybe Ruth had said something; she clearly hadn't liked me.

I buried my head in my hands. 'What do I do? Tell me what to do. This is a nightmare. I mean, sometimes Abby and I, yeah there was tension, but for God's sake, I'd never have killed her! I'd never hurt Madison! And I don't know how to shoot a gun! I'm British!' I kept stating these facts: *I'm British, I'm nineteen, I'm a girl*, as if they somehow absolved me of guilt. Stupid. 'What can I do? Aren't you supposed to help me?'

He considered it for a moment. 'Talk to the cops. Cooperate. Sometimes the DA'll cut a plea deal, and you'll get less time, they'll take the death sentence off the table.'

Was he actually advising me to plead guilty? This was insane. I had stepped through a mirror into a crazy world. 'You mean . . . tell them I did it?'

'With the evidence against you, it's your best outcome, Casey. That's my honest legal advice.' He leaned in then, and patted my hand in a gross, avuncular way. 'It's what I would say to my own daughter, I promise you.'

'But I didn't *do* it.'

This was what I kept saying, what I kept coming back to, the only thing I could say. And yet no one believed me.

Rachel

He tried to hide from me. As I fought my way to the front of the bus, yelling at the driver to wait please, I saw panic cross Jeremy's face, and he ducked back into the chippy. But it was only a small place – he had nowhere to go. I ran across the road, a car honking and swerving, and confronted him. 'Jeremy! Get out here.'

He slunk out on to the pavement, eyes down, chips in hand, the greasy smell hitting my nose. 'Oh.'

'What are you doing here? I thought you left!' I'd dropped him at the bus stop for the train station, assuming he had a ticket back to London.

A beetroot flush had spread over Jeremy's face. 'I – babe, I was worried about you. You said yourself, someone's trying to frame you. A woman got killed – what if you're next?'

I couldn't make sense of it. 'But why didn't you tell me? Where've you been staying?'

'Airbnb. Someone's house. Case – I wanted to do some digging.'

'About what?'

He hesitated. 'This guy Alex. How well do you really know him?'

So that was it. I stared at him. 'We're divorced, Jeremy. You've got no say over who I date.'

'His wife's been murdered – who do you think's the most likely person to have killed her? There's a reason they always look at the husband, Casey!'

He was calling me that again. Maybe he was the one who'd leaked my identity. All these years, I had trusted Jeremy with my secrets, but perhaps I had been wrong to. Perhaps his goodwill had only lasted until I met someone else.

'That's ridiculous. He was with Sam all night! And why would he kill his son's mum, even if they weren't getting on brilliantly?'

'You believe him, do you? You trust what he tells you?'

'Oh, for God's sake. You're just jealous.'

He flushed even deeper. 'Casey. It's not the first time.'

A cold seam ran through me. 'Not the first time what?'

'Alex. He's been arrested for murder before.'

I felt myself start to shake. 'You're lying.'

'Look it up. It was years ago – a girl was strangled and he was the main suspect. Never told you that, did he?'

Casey

NOVEMBER 2000

'I keep telling you, I didn't *do* it.'

Still this was my endless refrain, but it wasn't getting me anywhere. I had been in this jail for weeks already. The next step would be a grand jury trial, which I wouldn't appear at. I had pleaded to be allowed to speak for myself, but my lawyer said that wasn't a good idea. I gathered this meant that the prosecution's case was strong.

If I couldn't prove my innocence, they said, I was facing the death penalty. I had assumed at first they meant the electric chair, but the older male cop put me straight on that. In this state it would be lethal injection. He took a malicious pleasure in describing it to me in great detail.

'What happens is, Blondie, you're strapped down to a table. And there's a machine that slides a needle into your vein, just here' – a light tap on my arm. 'First injection paralyses you, so you won't be able to move or even breathe, and you'll just lie there and think of those folks you murdered, that innocent little kid. Then the second injection kills you, just a vein full of poison moving all over your body, and the last thing you'll see is the ceiling of that execution room . . .'

'But I didn't do it,' I sobbed. It was all I could say.

Outside, an election was going on, history was being made, but my world had shrunk to this stuffy interview room and my cell that smelled of feet, and which I shared with three other women, one of whom screamed in her sleep all night long. Still I kept being questioned, by the police, by lawyers for the DA's office.

'Someone did it, Ms Adams. Just tell us who it was then, if it wasn't you.'

'But I don't know! They must have left while I was hiding in the cupboard. The closet, I mean.'

Even these tiny variations in language seemed to be a problem. They didn't quite get what I meant by *cupboard*, or how I could hide in one, even though it was surely obvious. There had been many questions about whether I'd heard any noise in the house when I first went in, but I couldn't remember. All I recalled was that first shocked moment of walking into the lobby, the smell of the place – hot blood, a buzz of flies already. Then a short time later, realising I had to hide, with the baby, or we were going to die.

'It must have been so hard with those kids,' said the woman cop, who was always nicer to me. 'The baby crying all the time and the little girl, she had some behaviour issues, yeah?'

'Well – sometimes, but she couldn't help it.'

'It must have been so tough, Casey,' she said kindly. 'You must have been at breaking point, huh?'

I wasn't stupid. I knew she was trying to trick me into a confession. But it was so nice just to have someone even pretend to understand, to sympathise. Even my own lawyers didn't care about me. They were clearly only concerned with protecting the nanny company from a lawsuit. Ruth Safran had one in the works already, apparently.

'No one was seen going into the house, Casey. How'd you explain that?'

It was the older male cop again, the one who stared at me with exasperated eyes and snapped his chewing gum.

'I don't know,' I said. 'Maybe they got out the back.'

'Down the canyon?' He was sceptical.

'I don't *know*. But someone must have done it, because I didn't.'

'Who, then? Who would want to hurt a little girl and a lovely lady like Abigail Safran?'

Of course they thought she was lovely. All they saw were her smiling photos, her publicity pictures, Madison's audition tapes. Pictures never show the truth.

'I have no idea. Apart from delivery people, the only people who came to the house were me, Marietta and José. And Marietta got fired weeks ago.'

I sensed a shift in the room, a flick of their eyes to what looked like a wall, but I knew from TV was probably a two-way mirror. José? They were looking into him?

A chink of light seemed to open up in my darkness. An oubliette, that was the word that came to mind, from a class trip to Warwick Castle. They left you there to be forgotten, that was your punishment. To live as if you were dead. The male cop leaned forward in his seat, his manner suddenly nicer. 'Tell me about José, Casey.'

'Um, I don't know him that well. He came to clean the pool and do the garden. Three times a week, but he hadn't come for a while either.' Because David hadn't paid him. I wondered if they knew about that.

'And was that one of his days, Monday?'

'Not usually, but sometimes if he wasn't finished he might stop by again.' I hadn't really noticed him, I suppose. People came and went sometimes, dropping off packages, doing Abby's hair or giving her massages or fixing things around the house. But none of them had keys. The murderer must have had a key, the police insisted. Unless I'd left the door open when I took Carson out. I wished I could remember that moment of stepping out the door. The rush of heat to my head. Flip-flops slapping on hot tarmac. But I hadn't known how important it would be, to remember every detail of those few minutes.

'So José could have been there that day.'

'He could have. But like I said, he hadn't been for a while.'

It was true, I told myself. For all I knew he'd come back that day. No one would have thought to tell me.

He nodded, and I sensed him warming to me a little. 'See? This is helpful. That's all you need to do, Casey – be helpful. This man José, where is he from? Is he documented?'

'I have no idea. He's from Colombia, I think.'

José had told me this once, reluctantly, when I tried to make conversation as he cleaned the pool filter. I was so lonely I kept badgering him, but he didn't want to talk. I found out much later he had wanted his daughter to nanny for the Safrans, since she had a degree in childcare and four years' experience, but they had preferred an unqualified British girl. A white girl.

'He's kind of – not that friendly,' I said. 'Doesn't talk much.'

I felt guilty saying these things, but now that the mean cop was being so much nicer it was like water in the desert.

'Did he ever have a dispute with Mrs Safran or her husband?'

'Er . . .' All I was saying was the truth. It was OK to say the truth, wasn't it? And let them figure out what had happened. 'He said they hadn't paid him last month. I heard him and D–David rowing about it, and José said he was going to tell Ab— Mrs Safran.'

'And did he?'

'I don't know. I only overheard them because it was so loud.' And because I had opened the bathroom window and stuck my head out to eavesdrop.

'Interesting. So he might have had a grudge against the family.'

'I don't know. I don't know.'

I was bewildered, I hadn't slept in days. I hadn't washed and could smell the sour stink of my own body. I was losing track of what I had told them and what I had just thought in my head, or what they said I'd told them when I hadn't. They just kept questioning me, relentless. *But Casey, you said before the door was closed when you came home.* Did I? No, I was sure it had been ajar when I went back to it. I remembered my spike of fear that I had left it open, that Madison might have run out on the road. She had opened the door once or twice before – maybe she'd done it this time too, and that meant anyone could have come in, in theory.

The male cop slapped the table lightly. 'We'll certainly look into this José guy. See if he has a record in his own country. Maybe send him back there.' He winked at me. It seems insane, but it actually happened. This man who was questioning me over a multiple murder, he winked at me over the subject of deportation. I wondered had it ever crossed his mind that I was an immigrant too.

◆ ◆ ◆

I was lying on my bunk later that day when the door buzzed. I had found I was able to spend hours this way, looking at the damp stains on the ceiling, just breathing in and out. If I thought only about that, my breath and the ceiling, the sagging mattress beneath me, I could manage not to think about the terrible situation I was in, Madison, Abby and David dead, and me accused of their murders.

At the sound of the buzzer I jumped up, almost hitting my head on the low ceiling. It was the female guard I hated, broad about the hips and fond of hitting out with a baton, which was what they called a truncheon. I'd always thought that was a funny word, but the reality was not funny at all, when it jabbed you in the soft space under the ribs, leaving hollows that ached for days.

'What?' I said.

'Detectives want to see you.' I blinked and she barked at me. 'I don't have all day! Jesus, who do you think you are, Paris Hilton?'

I had only the haziest idea who Paris Hilton was, but I scrambled down the rusty ladder. I was in the orange jumpsuit we all wore, deeply unflattering to my skin. Except for that brief trip to court, I hadn't seen the sky in what I calculated was three weeks.

She grabbed my arm above the elbow, which I knew would leave deep finger-marks, and I tried to go floppy and unresisting. Be like water. Water could not be marked. She dragged me along to the interview room, where I'd been a constant presence for weeks now.

I could smell the male detective's BO as I went in. He glared at me. 'There she is.'

'Um – hi.'

What was it this time? Were they about to tell me I was free to go?

'Let me ask you something,' he growled. 'You think you're smart?'

I was confused. 'Well – I don't know. A normal amount, I guess.'

He slammed his hand on the table, hard, making me jump. 'You think it's smart to lie to the police?'

'I haven't lied.'

'Oh yeah? How d'you think it looks when you say it's the gardener, and we go arrest him and he has a cast-iron alibi?'

'He does?'

I was pleased at first. At least José could escape from the whirlpool that was dragging me under.

'Like you don't know. Mondays he works for another client, three miles away – very famous actor, you'd know him if I said the name. Mowed the lawn all day, actor's wife never took her eyes off him. Couldn't have been him, and now we look like a bunch of anti-Mexicans, arresting the guy.'

I later found out it was a particularly brutal arrest, that José's teenage son had been punched in the face by a cop and ended up in hospital. At the time I just said, 'He's not Mexican. And I never said it was him – I was just giving suggestions, trying to help.'

226

'Suggestions.' He turned to the female detective with a nasty chuckle in his throat. 'You think we're in the business of suggestions? This is a murder enquiry. A little kid is dead.'

'I know that!' I flashed. 'I'm the one who looked after her, not you. You think I don't care? I'm trying to help, but you won't listen!'

He leaned on the table and stared into my eyes, so I could smell his bad breath. 'You better start coming up with some better answers, Mary Poppins. Cos you're looking at the lethal injection, as things stand.'

I almost laughed with hysteria, it was so absurd. I was a teenage girl from Watford, and this was like something out of *The Green Mile*. I ignored the tick of panic in my stomach. This would all be sorted out soon, and this detective would have to make a formal apology, and maybe they'd even have to pay me compensation for the lost time, the distress I was in.

'Look, I don't know. Did you try to find Marietta, the maid? She might know something.'

He narrowed his eyes at me. 'You think we didn't think of that? Takes time.'

Tartly, I said, 'I don't know what you think of. You don't seem to take in anything I tell you.' It was a mistake to sass him, me a young girl, a foreign girl. Men like him joined the police so that if someone sassed them, they could arrest them.

'Smart-ass, hey? Well, we'll see about that. Those cameras don't show anyone else driving up, so you can kiss goodbye to the rest of your life.'

He banged on the door, and the guard came immediately. From her smirk, I could tell she'd been listening outside. As she came in to grab my arm again, I realised that none of them wanted to help me clear my name. For some reason they had decided already that a naïve British girl was capable of murder. Of pressing a pillow over a child's face, slashing a woman across the throat, and shooting a man twice her size in cold blood.

Rachel

I was paranoid walking through the streets of Coldwater, feeling so many eyes on me. I would have to leave this town, no matter what happened. I couldn't bear that sense of being watched. *It's her. Racy Casey. The one who* . . . All I wanted now was to never be recognised again, to be totally anonymous. And to think, all this happened because I'd dreamed of being famous once, a household name. Well, I was now.

Soon, I found myself back at the town library. It was an older librarian this time, a man with an impressive grey beard down to his mid-chest. He didn't seem to recognise me, and I was glad – perhaps there were still people out there who didn't watch rolling news or go online, who would not have seen my picture or know there was a former convicted murderer on their streets.

'Hi,' I muttered, approaching the desk.

'Sorry?' he boomed. 'Can you speak up?'

Louder, I said, 'I want to look up some old news stories. Is everything online now?'

'Oh no, not by a long chalk. We have all the local and national papers, though, going back a hundred years – microfiche, or some of them are bound.'

'Great.' I wished he wouldn't talk so loudly; weren't librarians supposed to be quiet? 'And if I didn't know what year, but say I wanted to search for a particular name?'

'Aha! Then you'd want the digitised archives. We have a subscription to all the UK newspapers, and Irish.' Enthusiastically extolling the wonders of the archive, he set me up on a computer in a quiet side room, the shelves lined in large bound copies of the local paper, the *Lakeside Courier*. If there was something to find out about Alex, it would be in here somewhere, surely. Trouble was, I had no idea what I was looking for. Jeremy hadn't given me many details, and I'd refused to ask, turning on my heel and leaving him there in Holmdale, walking the rest of the way back to Coldwater. I wasn't sure I would ever speak to him again.

The archive was easy to use – you just set your date parameters, and typed in a search term to the blank bar. Feeling intensely disloyal, and glancing nervously at the door to make sure no one came in, I entered a name: Alex Devine. Immediately, results came up. Hundreds of them. It was a common name – would it even be the same person? Heart in my mouth, I clicked.

An hour or so later, I came back to myself. My wrist ached from scrolling and my eyes burned. No one had told me the internet was so addictive – I felt I could not look away, no matter what I found, how awful it was. And it was awful. One article summed it up best, from April 1994. Long before my own troubles began.

LOCAL BOY ACQUITTED IN STACEY DONNER MURDER

Alex Devine (18) was today acquitted of the murder of Stacey Donner (16) in August last year. Alex, a schoolmate of Stacey's, has always denied involvement, though he was seen leaving a party in the woods with her. He insisted she was drunk, and he had walked her to the gate of her parents' house, leaving her there. Stacey never returned home, and was found strangled and sexually assaulted three days later, her body left in undergrowth in Coldwater Wood. Lawyers for Devine, who had minor convictions for drug use and theft, claimed he had been scapegoated while the real culprit went undetected. After three days of deliberation, jurors returned a verdict of Not Guilty. 'Justice has been done,' said the boy's father, local farmer John Devine. A spokesperson for the Donner family said they were 'devastated' by the verdict.

At first I had thought it was some other Alex Devine. But no, the age was right – he was born in the late seventies, a little older than me – and there was even a grainy black-and-white photograph of Alex on the courtroom steps, flanked by various people I assumed were his lawyers and parents. His father, a stocky man with a clear resemblance to Alex, stood with a hand on his shoulder. Consoling, or controlling?

There was a picture of Stacey, too, a teenage girl with the overly layered type of nineties hair we'd all had then, in her school uniform. Smiling, pretty. She had been found with her jeans and pants dragged off round her ankles, the reports said. Her top still on. She had fought hard – her nails were broken, her arms and hands bruised – but someone had been stronger, had overpowered her. Choked the life out of her.

I drew in a deep, shaky breath. All this time, I had been hiding my past from Alex, and I had no idea he, too, had been accused of murder as a teenager. The difference was that Alex had not been found guilty. Did that mean he was like me, the unfortunate innocent person who was the last to see a murder victim alive, or who found their body – or did it mean something worse?

My phone buzzed, earning me a severe glance from another librarian stacking books nearby. It was a text from a number I didn't recognise.

I think we might be able to help each other, it said. *I'm the person Anna was seeing. Can we meet?*

Casey

APRIL 2001

'Ms Adams, I will have to ask you to look at the photographs.'

The prosecutor stared down at me as I cowered on the stand.

I was almost in tears. 'I can't.'

'You'll be in contempt of court if you don't.'

I was almost hysterical. The trial had taken the best part of six months to begin, which they told me was fast, but it didn't feel fast to me, stuck in that overcrowded county jail. Garrett Cooper had warned me I'd be shown the crime-scene photographs if I took the stand. He had strongly advised me not to, but I couldn't just sit there and let them all talk about me while I stayed silent. He also told me to appear sad, but not overwhelmed. If I lost it on the stand, he said, it would make me look guilty. But who could be confronted by photographs of dead people, people you had known so well, let alone a dead child you'd cared for, and not lose it?

Abby was first. Her body was splayed out on the kitchen floor, eyes open and staring up, a wide gash across her throat, the lips of the wound gaping. A large puddle of blood, which appeared dull red in the picture, had spread out around her head. Garrett Cooper had, rather half-heartedly, claimed I didn't have the strength to make that slash across the throat, but how could you prove something like that? In the photographs I saw how several of her long nails were broken, as she'd fought for her life.

Next came David, and as I looked at photograph after photograph I felt my breath come louder in my chest. He had been shot, messily, in the stomach. He had taken a while to die, dragging himself across the floor of the hallway, which was smeared and streaked with his blood. His eyes were open and his face looked angry, an unnatural stiff white shade. His fingers reaching out, clawing on the floor, as if trying to move himself. He had turned over half on his side, so at least most of the mess of his body was hidden.

Then came Madison. I had not seen her body before, since I hadn't gone upstairs, and I let out a whimper as the photographs were held in front of me by an impassive court official. Madison's face was blue. Her eyes were bloodshot, another tell-tale sign of suffocation. Her bed with the pink frilly sheets was so familiar. Her hair was spread out around her. She almost looked like a doll.

'Please,' I said. I was choked with tears. 'I can't – I don't want to see it.'

The prosecutor turned to the jury with a smirk. 'Hard to look at the fruits of your work, isn't it?'

'I didn't do it,' I wept quietly. 'I didn't kill them.'

'Ms Adams, I have to ask you to stop crying so we can continue.' The judge was a stern old man, close to retirement. What could he know about being a girl of nineteen, trapped in a world that no longer made sense? 'Ms Adams! You're disturbing the court.'

I gulped in deep breaths, but my chest was tight, and I couldn't get any air. They were dead. Madison would never dance or chatter or tantrum again. Abby with all her dreams of rediscovering fame. And David. David . . .

I completely lost it then and didn't care what the cameras or reporters thought of me, or that the judge had ordered me to stop crying, as if I could just turn it off like a switch. Over the desperate gasps of my tears, I heard him order a recess. The guards moved towards me, cuffing me to them, yanking me up. I'd be taken to a small, airless room where – if I was lucky – I might be given a sip of stale water, while listening to the sounds of the courthouse outside, the free people watching my life go up in flames, as they laughed and chatted and made phone calls.

As they passed me on their way out, I saw the prosecution lawyers give each other a discreet high-five. Things were going well for them. Whatever I did, whether I managed to stay composed or broke down weeping, it made me look guilty. There was no way out.

In the overheated break room, I fought to get a hold of myself. *Come on. Use everything they give you.* Those awful photographs, those were evidence, and I hadn't been allowed to see much of that. Was there something in them that could help me – a clue that only I would be able to interpret? *Think, Casey, think.*

Sitting there, my wrists sweaty and chafed, my entire body sour and damp, I tried to reconstruct what I'd seen that day, detail by detail. Do you remember those Spot the Difference quizzes you used to get in magazines? I was very good at those. There must be something I could do to save myself. But as I sat there, I found I couldn't think of a single thing.

Rachel

Who knew my phone number? Marilyn, Jeremy, Alex, a few people I trusted, or had done at least. How on earth had this person got it? Anna's lover. *I'm the person Anna was seeing. Can we meet?*

The mysterious man! He did exist after all, assuming it was a man. I read the text over and over. No name was given. Possibly the last person to see her alive. Did he spend the night with her? Were the police pursuing this possibility, one step ahead of me? If this man had slept over at Anna's house the night she died, what time had he left? Why had she gone to the woods that morning, and when exactly? Was she alone, or had she arranged to meet someone?

Gripping my phone so tight I left prints on the screen, I knew it was a mistake to follow this up. I knew that every rogue action I took made me look more guilty. I, of all people, was aware how important appearances were in a murder enquiry. But I couldn't help it, I had to know. And that was why I texted back. *Meet me by the memorial. Ten minutes.*

I pulled my hoody over my head and left the library, hoping no one would recognise me, notorious murderer Racy Casey, out on the streets of this quiet tourist town.

In a few minutes I'd reached the centre of town, where a war memorial was set in a square of benches. It was almost five now, so the place had emptied out. The shopkeepers were putting down their shutters. A few people shuffling about, the elderly or dispossessed, kids with nowhere else to go. No one who looked like Anna's possible lover. I was racking my brain to understand how this new information fitted in with everything else. If Anna actually was seeing someone, why did she have such a go at me in the street that time? Why had she been so jealous of me and Alex?

I was mulling this over, standing by the names of the fallen with my hands in my hoody pockets, when I saw him. A man in a suit and a sensible raincoat, tie loosened. He was handsome, with close-cropped hair and a chiselled face. I thought he was mixed race, perhaps, and a good bit younger than Anna, who had been older than me. Somehow I knew right away it was him.

'Rachel?' he said nervously.

'Yes.'

'Oh. Hi. Sorry about all the cloak-and-dagger stuff.'

I shrugged. 'That's my life now. How did you get my number?'

'Marilyn from the shelter, she said I should talk to you. I didn't know who else to ask – Anna mentioned once you worked there.'

So Marilyn hadn't entirely condemned me. She was still trying to help – that meant something.

'So – you and Anna were . . .'

'Um, yeah. The thing is, I'm, well . . .' He waved his hand awkwardly and I saw the wedding ring.

'Ohhhh.' That was why he hadn't come forward.

'Yeah. It's – it wasn't ideal. But I liked her. I really liked her. It was horrible to find out . . . you know.'

'I'm sorry.' I wasn't sure of the etiquette here. Presumably he wouldn't have reached out to me if he thought I was guilty. 'I didn't do it, you know. I only really met her once.'

'At the Co-op. Yeah, she told me.'

'She did?' A blast of cold air ran through me and I shivered. 'Shall we walk around a bit?' There was less chance of being spotted that way. A small town at closing time is a desolate place.

The Costa on the high street was open till half six, and the tired-looking barista made us lattes. Anna's lover paid for mine, which was kind of him, and when she asked his name for the order (though the place was empty), he darted a furtive glance at me.

'Um . . . Ciaran.'

'Is that your real name?' I asked, as we walked off towards the lake, the hot cup warming me a little.

He grimaced. 'It is, yeah. I couldn't think of anything else.'

'I'm not really Rachel. Do you know about that? Who I am?'

'Eh – yes.'

I sighed. This was how leaks worked. First one person found out, then it spread, and before you knew it you had to run again, burn your life to the ground and start over. 'Ciaran, you'd better just tell me everything you know, and I'll do the same. OK?'

'OK,' he said nervously. 'I've never been wrapped up in something like this, you know. A crime.'

'Well, I have, and let me tell you, it has a way of sticking. So it's in both our interests to find out who did it.'

It could have been him, of course, but why then would he reach out to me? Surely it would be easiest to let me take the rap, the obvious suspect.

He nodded reluctantly. 'The police, they still think it was you?'

We had reached the lake now, a small path winding down the side of it, sadly littered with bottles and plastic bags. The kids around here had so little to do. A cold wind rippled the dark surface of the water.

'I don't know – they haven't charged me, obviously. I think someone's framing me. I didn't do it. You know that, right?

Otherwise, you wouldn't have messaged me.' Or be alone with me on this deserted path, I thought to myself.

He didn't say anything for a minute. 'Look, I don't know for sure, I'll just be honest. How could I? I hardly even knew Anna that well. I mean – it couldn't go anywhere. It was just – both of us needed something else, I suppose. Outside our marriages. I know it sounds sordid, like, but it wasn't. I cared about her.'

How strange that this man and I were the opposite sides of a square made up of us and Anna and Alex. Their shattered marriage our opportunity for love.

'When it happened, I saw it on the news like everyone else,' he said. 'That a woman was found dead in the woods. I sent her a few messages, asking had she seen it. I never thought it might be . . . well, anyway, they released her name later that day. Couldn't tell anyone, of course. Had to hide it from my – my wife.'

What a way to find out. I watched his profile, the pain evident beneath his self-control. Could I trust him, though? He was a total stranger.

'The police never spoke to you?'

'No. I kept waiting for a call from them – I was meant to see her that night. The one she died. My, em – my wife was away for work.' He sounded so ashamed saying that, *my wife*, and I wondered about this unknown woman, also involved in this tangled case without even realising it.

'You sent her text messages? Anna?'

Those would have been on her phone if so, surely, and the police would have found them by now.

'No – we talked through a kind of secure app thing. It doesn't stay on the phone.'

I'd heard about things like this, apps that deleted messages right away. For people who didn't want to leave a trace. Maybe, then, the police didn't even know she'd been seeing someone.

I realised what he'd said – he was supposed to be with her the night she died. 'But you didn't see her in the end?'

'Well, no. She cancelled last minute.'

'So . . . I'm sorry, Ciaran, just to be clear, you didn't see Anna at all that night?'

'No. She had the kid and, obviously, I couldn't be there if he was.'

That didn't make any sense. 'Wasn't Sam with his dad that night, though?'

'He was meant to be, but Alex cancelled.' As he said the name, I heard bitterness in his voice. 'It happened a lot. She'd have to change plans at the last minute, because his dad flaked out. And I can't get away all that much.' He looked at me. 'Anna assumed he was seeing you those nights, I have to say.'

'No . . . well, not that night. He told me he had Sam, so we didn't see each other. You didn't contact the police to tell them this?'

'No,' he said, shamefaced. 'I was afraid. Thought they might suspect me, and my wife would find out – and I've no alibi, since she was away. I just stayed home, had an oven pizza.'

How could I say he was wrong not to contact the police? I knew from bitter experience that being innocent was no protection. 'So – Alex told me he had Sam, and Anna told you she did. Question is, who was lying?'

'Well. Obviously, I'm going to say Alex.'

'But you didn't know Anna all that well, right? She could have had other secrets.'

'How long have *you* known Alex?' he countered.

'Only a few months,' I admitted.

'You trust him?'

'I . . . I did.' But he hadn't told me about Stacey Donner. That he too had once been a murder suspect. 'I'm sorry, Ciaran, but when Anna came for me that day at the shop, I got the impression she wanted Alex back. That she was warning me away from him.'

He frowned. He had a faint moustache of latte foam on his lip and I felt a pang suddenly. He was a nice man, attractive, and I hoped Anna had been happy with him, in the little time she'd had. I imagined his marriage wasn't that successful, if he was having an affair. How much sadness there was, hidden in everyone's life.

'No, that can't be right. She definitely didn't want him back. Things were pretty bitter between them.'

But that was often the way with divorcing couples; it didn't mean there wasn't love left. Quite the opposite, in fact.

'She told you about the fight with me?'

'Yeah. She was kind of ashamed, to be honest. I think she was just having a bad day, with the custody battle, and she saw you there and lost her temper.'

'The custody battle?'

'You didn't know? Alex was trying to get full custody of Sam. Crazy, really, with all the hours he works, but some men will do that, just to spite the wife.'

This made no sense. Alex had told me he wanted to split Sam's time, do their best to keep things normal for him. *Anna's crazy*, he said, *she won't let me go, she's jealous.* That had chimed with my experience of her shouting at me in the street.

'Did she tell you why she shouted at me – what had annoyed her so much?'

'Oh. Well, because she – well, she knew who you were, and she didn't like it.'

I stared at him. 'What? She knew I was Casey?' No one had known. How the hell could Anna have found out, of all people?

'She thought so. She'd been shown this picture of you – Casey Adams – and thought maybe it was you. I thought it was kind of crazy, to be honest, but she insisted, and she told Alex, though he didn't believe her of course. Said she was just jealous.'

'She told *Alex*?' Alex had already known I was Casey? He hadn't said anything when I went round to his flat to tell him everything.

'Yeah, but he didn't believe her. Neither did I. But she was right, I guess.'

My mind was crumbling, every bit of information sending me in different directions. I looked at my watch – I'd been out too long, and it was getting dark already. I was here alone by a lake with a man I had never met before. Would I ever learn?

'Ciaran, listen, I think you should talk to the police. The main detective. DS Hegarty. He's nice, he wants to figure this out. They haven't charged me yet, despite all the evidence. They probably know she was seeing someone. They're smart. I just . . .' I took a deep breath, looking into the dark depths of the lake. Imagined it closing over my head, carrying me away, the shock of the cold, of surrender. 'I have to sort this out. I can't go back there.'

'Where?'

'Prison.'

'Oh yes.' He looked uncomfortable.

'Rule yourself out, at least. Tell him Anna had Sam on the night she was murdered.'

Meaning, if it was true, that Alex had no alibi. Where had he been, if not in his flat looking after Sam?

Ciaran was nodding. 'It's just scary. My wife . . .'

'Well, believe me, I know all about that. But they'll find out in the end, and you'll just look guilty.' We were back at the head of the path now, and I could see cars going past and the odd pedestrian. I was safe. 'Thank you for contacting me. It was brave.'

He nodded. 'I just – she deserves justice, is all. And I don't think either of us has been told the full story.'

'Ciaran – how did she feel about Alex?'

He paused a moment. 'Honestly? I think she was afraid of him. She never said, but just – little things.'

'All right. Thank you. Take care.'

As I headed back to the flat, breaking into a light jog, I suddenly wondered. What if I'd misinterpreted what Anna had said to me that day outside the shop? *I don't want you near him*, she'd shouted. But it suddenly occurred to me there were two people she could have meant. Sam had been in the car, had she glanced over at him as she said it? Knowing who I was, Racy Casey, what I had supposedly done in America, did she actually mean she wanted me to stay away from her *son*? After all, Sam was the same age as Madison had been, when someone suffocated the life out of her.

Casey

June 2001

Prison was so much louder than I could have imagined. A constant echoing cacophony of metal doors, keys in locks, rattled bars, and women shouting and screaming. They knew a new inmate was arriving. Fresh meat. And they knew what I'd supposedly done.

'Baby killer!' someone hissed, as I was led down a corridor, and a fresh gob of spit landed just near the white laceless sneakers they'd given me. I cowered, and the female guard who was dragging me along sighed.

'Gonna have to toughen up, Blondie.'

I was in a nightmare, except I couldn't wake up. Going to court, awaiting trial, that had been bad enough, but I'd been so sure that justice would be done and I'd walk free. Why wouldn't I? The evidence was flimsy at best, and I would never hurt a child, especially not one in my care. I was practically a child myself. But I hadn't counted on Garrett Cooper the Third and his useless legal team. They weren't actually working for me, not really, but to protect the nanny organisation. They'd told me to plead guilty for a lesser sentence, and when I refused, they let me go it alone in court. The company didn't care. It was better for them if I seemed like a lone psychopath, clever enough to bypass their rigorous vetting process. I hadn't counted on a corrupt justice system either, an ambitious DA, a governor who wanted to seem tough on crime.

Just a few hours before, I had stood before the judge. The jury had taken only two hours to find me guilty of three counts of first-degree murder. And then I had been sentenced not just to jail, but to death.

'You shall be put to death by lethal injection,' said the judge. 'Casey Rachel Adams, may God have mercy on your soul.'

I still didn't believe it. I was on Death Row.

Just one prison in California held all the women who were sentenced to death. It was out in the middle of the desert. I had seen glimpses from the van as we drove here, hot white sand and blank sky. I'd felt oddly out of my body, despite the extreme heat and my need to pee and the chafing of the cuffs on my wrists. They were so heavy, I could hardly hold up my hands.

Inside, the place was scorching, foetid with the smell of too many women and old boiled food. They had taken my prints and my picture, vaguely mentioned I would be given clean clothes and a towel, though none had yet materialised. I would be here for the rest of my life, either until I died here, in this windowless box, or until they did the job for me with poison in my veins.

No. Hold on to something. I didn't do it. They would have to see that, wouldn't they? I'd launch an appeal. I'd be all right.

The guard tugged on my arm, and I was dragged to the right. 'Home sweet home, Blondie.'

I didn't know why they'd all started calling me that. I wasn't even blonde, it was just fading Sun-In streaks, my real mousy-brown colour already showing through.

My new cell was about two metres wide, like the compartment on a sleeper train. A rickety sink and a lidless metal toilet. That was it.

The guard saw my face and laughed. 'Better get used to it. This isn't your castle in England now, Princess.'

'I grew up in a council flat,' I muttered, even though she wouldn't know what that was, and it earned me a sharp tug on the handcuffs, breaking the skin even more and making me gasp. All the same, I was glad I'd said it, because it showed me I hadn't gone under yet. I was still fighting.

The guard uncuffed me and directed me to the bed. I sat on it, because there was nowhere else to go. There were no windows, of course, and no TV or anything like the British papers had led me to believe you got in prison. *It's a disgrace!* they would say. *Like a holiday camp!* Here, there was just the bed, the sink and loo – which stank – and me. I felt a rising panic. What was I going to do in here for the rest of my life, day after day? A hot empty box, with only my own thoughts for company.

'So – what do I do?' I ventured. The guard swung back.

'Do? You stay put. In a few months you might get work detail, but right now there's more prisoners than jobs.'

'But can I – is there a library, or a TV or anything?' If I could at least read, that would be something. Find some law books, get started on my appeal.

She sneered. 'All those things have to be earned. And you're not off to the best start, are you, with your English sass-mouth?'

Enjoying the power she had over me, she went out, slamming the barred door and turning the key.

I was locked in, without a breath of air or a slice of sky. I had not a single thing on me, no pockets, no bag. Not a picture or a single personal item, not so much as a pen. No soap or toothbrush, not even a towel, just the already sweaty clothes I had on me, dank from the long van trip. I had nothing. I was no one. I was totally alone, and all that my future held was the execution chamber.

As I sank down on my bunk, feeling every metal spring through the thin mattress, I heard my own voice in my head: *Jesus Christ, Casey. You're really in trouble here.*

Rachel

So Anna had somehow known, or at least suspected, my true identity. She had told Alex, though he perhaps had not believed her.
And someone else had made the calculated decision to sell this
information to the press. They had looked into my past and discovered it had been carefully erased, that Rachel Caldwell had no
history, no family, no work experience. And who was it? Someone
perhaps whose business it was to dig into my life a little, who knew
me better than anyone locally. Who had been Anna's friend. Who
always needed money for the shelter, who might have decided
it was worth sacrificing one human being, a possible murderer,
in order to save dozens of dogs. In other words, Marilyn. Kind,
frowzy Marilyn, with her rumpled clothes and red cheeks. The
closest thing I had to a friend around here. Could she really have
done this? How would she have got hold of that picture of me at
Disneyland with the Safran kids? I didn't want to believe it, but
on the other hand, I was a convicted murderer and I had managed
to keep it secret until now. People hide deep pockets of secrecy, of
darkness, and we don't like to admit it.

She'd asked me to stay away from the shelter now that my
true identity had been exposed, but I couldn't just sit there in that
horrible flat. It was dark now, the town emptied out except for a

few hardy smokers outside the pubs. Rain sweeping in from the dark water of the lake. It took me just a few minutes to walk to Marilyn's, a rambling Victorian house on the lake shore, inherited from her parents and now probably worth a few million or so. Her dogs, sensing my approach, started barking as I swung open her gate and went up the gravel drive. As I rang the bell, the noise reached a crescendo. I could hear Marilyn inside, shushing them. 'Come on now, quieten down.' I recognised Brandy's yelp among them and felt a pang. I hadn't seen her in days now – it was as if I'd already lost her.

Marilyn opened the door, silhouetted against her hall light, dogs weaving about her legs. She was wearing her Happy Paws Animal Shelter T-shirt, liberally stained with various spatters, her greying hair coming down from a ponytail.

'Oh! Do be quiet, everyone, it's just Rachel, she's a friend.'

But was I? I shoved my hands deep in my pockets. It couldn't be her doing all this. Could it? Marilyn, who couldn't pass a dog without patting it, who'd never turn an animal away? But someone had leaked my name to the press. Someone had broken into my house, spooked me with my old name, taken my scarf and planted it. Killed Anna. Was it the same person behind it all?

'How long have you known?' I said. 'Who I was?'

Horror filled her eyes. Marilyn was no liar. Reluctantly, she said, 'You'd better come in.'

That was something, then. She knew I had once been in prison for murder, and she would still let me in her house. It was getting cold out, and I could see Brandy padding into the hallway, black nose twitching. I nodded and stepped inside, falling on the dog, stroking her silky ears. 'Hello, sweetheart, are you OK?' Of course she was fine. This was the best place for her, a garden to roam in, other dogs to play with. But I missed her so.

'She's been quite happy,' said Marilyn. I stood up.

'So. Are you going to answer me? You knew, didn't you?'

She sighed. 'I suppose I've always known. When you first took the job, you seemed a little familiar, and then, later on, there was a documentary about the case. You know I like to watch true crime.'

Of course. Marilyn, gentle soul that she was, loved such documentaries, the gorier the better. 'You recognised me from it?' The thing I had always been afraid of. I had thought my appearance changed enough, the case so long ago in the past, that no one would make the connection.

'I thought she looked familiar, the – Casey. I was curious, so I looked back into your CRB check . . .'

And found out that Rachel Caldwell only went back as far as 2006. I'd told her I'd been ill before that, that I'd been in a car accident and needed several years to recover. My conviction for murder hadn't come up on the check, because it had been quashed. I was innocent, except in the eyes of most of the world, of course. 'Oh.'

'But I swear, I didn't tell the papers, Rachel! I believe in second chances, and you know I hate the gutter press. I'd never have leaked it to them.'

'Not even for fifty grand?' I remembered being offered that for my story years ago – perhaps the rates were even higher now.

She blanched. 'As much as that? No, no, I never would.'

But someone had. 'You told Anna, though, right?'

Marilyn looked miserable. 'I'm sorry. I just felt I had to, really. Once I knew about you and Alex, at least.'

I had never told Marilyn I was seeing Alex. Never told anyone, in fact. And I hadn't realised Anna knew until that day at the shop. Marilyn's good friend, Anna Devine. Of course Marilyn would tell Anna that her husband's new girlfriend was in fact Casey Adams, the British nanny accused of murdering an entire family. Including a child the same age as Sam.

'How did you find out? About me and Alex?'

'I drove past your house one morning – I'd been out on a rescue, a farm dog, and I thought you might want a lift. He was coming out. His van, you know.'

'Oh.'

'I— I'm so sorry, Rachel. I just showed Anna some pictures on my phone, asked if she remembered the case. I thought perhaps she might see it too, the resemblance between Casey and you.'

'But – why? You knew about me and Alex – you didn't want us to be together?'

Marilyn seemed close to tears. 'They were a family, Rachel. Sam, he needs both his parents. If there was a chance for them to work things out . . .'

'You thought Anna would tell Alex who I was, and that would be the end of it?' I said. And she had done, according to Ciaran. Had Alex in fact known for some time that I was Casey Adams?

God, I needed to talk to him. But he wouldn't answer my messages. I took a deep, juddering breath. 'I wish you'd told me Anna knew who I was, Marilyn. This is serious – I think someone's framing me. Someone tried to make it look as if I killed her. But I didn't!'

She nodded, but wouldn't meet my eyes. 'You need to go, Rachel. I can't help you. I'm sorry, and I hope – well, I hope they find whoever killed Anna. For both our sakes.'

I turned and left, with a last look at Brandy, knowing I'd never go back to work at Happy Paws, that the sanctuary I'd found was lost to me. Even if this blew over, everyone round here knew I was Casey Adams. Racy Casey. I'd have to start over somewhere else, with a new name and another identity. How would I find work without revealing who I was? Something that didn't require checks, I supposed.

On my way home, even on the isolated lake path, I kept my head down, anxiety flaring every time I passed someone. Marilyn was one of the few people I'd trusted even a little. Now, I could no longer do that. On my journey through town I recognised various people. The instructor from the activity camp. The yoga teacher, the librarian who kept books aside for me (never thrillers, I'd had enough of that for a lifetime). The little connections I'd made here. Did they all know who I was? Even if I managed to stay out of prison this time, I knew that my life in Coldwater was gone, up in smoke.

Casey

MARCH 2002

Before my arrest, my only knowledge of prison had come from soap operas and drama, where inevitably a character would end up stabbed in the shower by episode two. For the first few months I'd been terrified, trembling every time I queued for the bathroom, letting people cut in front of me if they wanted. Our showers were only twice a week, with the harshest, cheapest soap that left my skin dry and red.

Death Row prisoners were considered too dangerous to mingle with the others, so we spent most of the day in our cells. We took our exercise in a small dirt yard with a basketball hoop and no ball, alone with a guard, and in the distance I could see the larger yard where the regular prisoners exercised. I heard their voices, laughter even, and I wanted so much to be among them. One day, their sentences would come to an end and the door would open and they could walk out. Whereas I would never leave this place alive. There are so many degrees of hell, you have no idea.

There were eight of us on Death Row when I arrived, and I'd been terrified of meeting these other monsters, these murderous women whose crimes had been bad enough to warrant execution, but they weren't anything like I'd imagined. It took a long time to even meet everyone, we were so seldom allowed to mingle, except for church or education, or the occasional time more than one of us was allowed in the yard.

There was Paola, from Chile, who'd shot a cop ten years ago, while on the run with her meth-dealing boyfriend. She was only in her forties but worn out, a silent woman with greying hair who rarely spoke.

Julie was the only other white woman. She'd killed her boyfriend with a machete, after years of abuse and coercion. She'd chopped his body up and put it in the drainage system at their caravan park.

Then there was Amber, our undisputed queen, a black woman from New York with flickering, dangerous eyes. I was afraid of Amber. She had killed two of her girlfriends, getting away with it the first time on a self-defence charge, but then later she'd stabbed another woman fifty times in a jealous rage. I always prayed that Amber wouldn't be in the yard when I went out there, or the small recreation room we were sometimes allowed to be in when they were cleaning our cells or tossing them for drugs. We were probably the safest prison population there was, since we rarely had any visitors who could smuggle us things. Most of our families had long ago given up on us.

Rhonda came after I'd been there nine months. I was keeping a diary, when I could get paper, because I was afraid of losing all track of time – that I'd look up and be sixty and every single day would have been like this. Although maybe in some ways that would have been easier. Every morning I woke up with my sentence heavy on me, like weights on my chest. I would die in here, so what did it matter if it was sooner rather than later? What kind of life would it be in this place? Not worthy of the word, surely. So really, Rhonda came at the exact time I needed her. It's not an exaggeration to say she saved my life – she literally did.

Suicide is ever present in prisons, especially when a prisoner has been told they will die here. It's thought that it deprives the state of their vengeance, if someone takes their own life. That your life is no longer yours, even to end. You have to sit and wait in a claustrophobic box, smelling your own sweat for decades, and you can't know what year or month or second they will choose to end that life for you, as is their right. It's appalling, when you think about it, which I had only vaguely before, when that film *Dead Man Walking* came out. That was me. Dead Woman Walking. I wished I'd paid attention in school, to know these things.

The eight of us on Death Row had become used to each other, like cats forced to share a small flat. Most of us were flattened down by our misery, and in Paola's case half dead from enforced drugs detox, and barely had the energy to start a fight. Rhonda was different – she had been through all of this, and come out the other side, the place where you decide you aren't going to die after all, not until they drag you into that chamber kicking and screaming.

She had previously been held in another prison while her case shuttled back and forward between appeals courts, but a new right-wing judge had decided she deserved the death penalty after all, and she was moved here. It made little difference, since she would die in prison either way. I first saw her while in the exercise yard, staring up at my patch of sky, trying to fix it in my memories, the white lid of the Californian desert, the hot air irritating my eyes and nose. While in the yard, you could see out through the fence to the main gate of the prison, spot any new people arriving. Not many people arrived at Death Row, so when I heard a truck and voices, I sauntered over there, trying to look nonchalant. My guard was playing a game on his phone, which they weren't supposed to have on duty but nearly all did.

A woman, tall and black, was being led into the prison in cuffs, the same orange jumpsuit we all wore. Her hair was in long braids and I wondered how she'd managed that, since we weren't allowed to have ours done in here. My own hair was ratty and dull. For a second her eyes caught mine and I jumped back, as if burned. This woman was still alive inside. She had not given up, though she'd been sentenced to death. She was still here, not roaming through a fantasy world or numbed by drugs either legal or illegal, like the rest of us. My heart was hammering.

I didn't see her again for a few days, but I was aware, sitting in my cell, of how the energy had shifted in our small block. New sounds, an extra set of footsteps, another person breathing and moving about. It was exciting, actually. So little ever changed around here. A few days later, I was taken into the yard and found Rhonda already there, standing quietly under the basketball ring with her arms folded. I looked back at the guard, who just shrugged – sometimes they wanted us to see each other, to make sure there'd be no clashes later on. The way you introduce a new pet into a house. I was suddenly shy – it was so long since I'd met anyone new, and in this capacity as convicted killer. I shuffled over, giving her space.

'Hello.'

She looked at me steadily. 'You're the British girl.' She had a soft Boston accent, the first time I'd heard one of those in real life.

'Casey.'

'The one who killed the family. The nanny.'

'I . . . I didn't kill them. I know everyone says that in here but – I really didn't.' I gave a stupid little laugh. 'I don't know why I still bother telling people that. No one ever believes me.'

She said, 'I've been in prison for years now. I'm sure at least, what, ten per cent of convicts are innocent. More for black people.'

I was so surprised at her voice, how educated and clear it was. Everyone else I'd met in prison seemed, well, lower class, brought here by a terrible confluence of drugs and poverty and abusive men.

She saw my surprise and laughed. 'You never met a black college professor before?'

'Of course I have,' I said heatedly. 'I've just never met a professor in prison.'

She inclined her head, and I saw she was pleased with my response. 'Not many of us around, that's for sure.'

I glanced over at the guard, sure that I'd be pulled away at any second. This was the best conversation I'd had with anyone in all my time here. 'So you believe me, that I didn't do it?'

'If you say so, honey.'

How I valued that 'honey'. Tears filled my eyes at it, the simple kindness.

'Thank you. Even if no one else ever will – it means a lot that just one person does. And you, what about you?'

I shouldn't have asked the question. Her whole demeanour changed. 'Didn't anyone tell you not to ask that question in prison?'

I backed away a little. I should have known not to trust someone on Death Row, just because they called me honey.

'I'm sorry. Really, I am. It's just – everyone already knows what I supposedly did. It's like I'm famous.'

She softened a little. 'They used to know about me too. I'm not so famous these days, of course, now it's taken so long to get here.'

The gate buzzed, another guard coming to get Rhonda. We were on a one-to-one ratio here, at least at the start, before the prison was privatised and the cuts began to bite. She stirred herself, and I couldn't help it; a wave of desperation swept me. How could I have blown my only social encounter in so long?

'I'm really so sorry!' I cried. 'Please. Let's start over?'

She laughed. 'What do you think this is, a sorority? Honey, what are you, twenty?'

'Twenty-one next month.' I would celebrate my birthday in prison in a foreign country. No keys for me, ironically.

'Casey, that's your name?'

'Yes.'

'Rhonda. Rhonda Castle, you want to look me up when you get the chance.'

Passing me, she gently squeezed my arm, which wasn't really allowed, but it was so quick the guard probably didn't see, or didn't care enough to remonstrate. Just a little touch, but it sustained me all through the following week, until I saw her again. By then, of course, I had found out what she did. Unlike the others, Rhonda never bothered to say she was innocent. She was a murderer all right, and she never even tried to deny it.

Next time I saw her was about a week later, in the canteen, on a rare occasion we didn't have food in our cells, due to staff shortages. To keep us apart from the other prisoners, we ate lunch at 10 a.m. She was sitting with Paola, who was a twitching wreck, nails scraping at phantom itches under her skin. Seeing Paola had made me resolve never to try drugs, no matter how good oblivion seemed in this place. Of course I'd done a little weed as an idiot schoolgirl – a fact that had been dragged up at my trial, like everything else – but the hard stuff, heroin and crack, they scared me. Rhonda was the same. Despite years in prison, she had maintained standards, like keeping her hair and nails neat, always wearing pressed clothes, and speaking in educated full sentences.

We didn't have the internet in prison, not in 2002, but I'd looked Rhonda up on a sort of newspaper microfiche thing, much like we had in the library at college. My heart had been racing with a combination of fear and curiosity. What had she done? Something really bad, to be in here. Or maybe she was innocent, like me. I found her after some while of clicking – WOMAN DROWNS CHILDREN. Well, that was short and to the point. Feeling sick, I read on. Rhonda, who'd been a professor of Black Literature at a university in San José, and was thirty-seven at the time it took place, in 1998, had one day driven her car into a lake, with her three children in the back. The children were aged one, five and seven. A dog-walker had seen the car go in and managed to pull Rhonda out in time, but not the kids. That poor man. What a thing to witness. As soon as Rhonda woke up in hospital, she was arrested, then a while later she was convicted of triple homicide and sentenced to death.

Her own children! I knew it happened sometimes, but I recoiled from it all the same, so when I saw her in the canteen I didn't know how to act. I would have preferred to avoid her, like I would a girl at school who'd got too clingy, but there was nowhere to go in this place, no one else to talk to. I sat down, banging my tray nervously. Paola, who was mashing her potatoes in furrows, didn't look up. Rhonda's keen eyes took me in.

'Paola, dear, might you leave us, if you've finished.' And she did. Rhonda had been here a week and already ruled the place. 'So. You looked me up.'

'I – yes.'

'I murdered my children.'

'Did you? I mean – it wasn't an accident?'

'No. It wasn't an accident. I just wasn't supposed to be rescued.'

A murder-suicide. Very common when mothers killed their children, I knew. I had learned a lot about such things in prison. My lawyer had at one stage half-heartedly considered a defence where we blamed Abby for killing David and Madison, but the evidence all seemed to rule it out.

'OK,' I said cautiously. 'And – you knew you were doing it?'

Rhonda shrugged. 'I knew, but I couldn't stop myself. You ever feel a darkness inside you, Casey, and you can't help it rising up and taking you over?'

Had I ever felt that? Once, maybe. 'I don't know.'

'Well, it happens. And I have to live with that until they want me dead.' She shrugged again, capturing the insanity of it, that they'd dragged her back to life so they could have the privilege of killing her. Nowadays we'd probably say Rhonda had postnatal depression after the birth of her last child – same as Abby – or even psychosis, that her husband was coercive and threatening to divorce her and take the kids, that she'd been traumatised by a violent rape when she was fifteen. But in the nineties, she was just a black woman who'd done the unthinkable, the worst of the worst, beyond evil, and she had to die for it.

That day, in the canteen, she nodded to my untouched tray. 'Eat up, honey. You need to take care of yourself if you're getting out of here.'

I frowned. 'I'm not getting out of here.' I was almost angry at her for suggesting it, when I'd finally started to accept my fate.

'There's an appeal process, isn't there?' she said. 'You haven't had yours yet? And you said you didn't do it, right? So there's hope. There's always hope.'

Hope. I knew from school it had been the only thing left in Pandora's box when all the evils of the world flew out. So far I had not been able to find any. Instead, any optimism I'd had had been stripped from me, until I realised that my situation could in fact be that bad, much worse than I could ever have imagined. But Rhonda saying the word stirred something in me. It lit a kind of fire, and that kept me going until hope did reappear, in the most unlikely form.

Rachel

Less than half an hour after talking to Marilyn I was back outside Alex's flat. My heart was sinking – I had to admit it, there was no way back from this. Our relationship, all the hope I'd had in it, had ended the moment I stumbled over his wife's body in the woods. The same woods where Stacey Donner's dead body had been found in 1993 – I'd looked it up, the sites were less than a mile apart. Did the police know about this older case, that Alex had been tried for Stacey's murder? They must do. I had to talk to him. I waited till a middle-aged woman came out of the flats – she gave me a double take that showed she recognised me – and went up the stairs and knocked on Alex's door.

Here was something else I had taken for granted about my new life. That whenever Alex saw me he would smile, his eyes boring into me in a way that made me lose all control of myself. No smile today. When he opened the door all I got was a frown, a clouding of the blue eyes I loved so much. I could hear the TV on in the background, the evening news.

'Hi,' I said, voice sticking in my throat.

'We really shouldn't be talking, you know. Did the police not tell you that?'

'But we have to, Alex! I know what happened, when you were younger. Stacey.'

Saying her name felt wrong. The names of the dead should be spoken with care, with reverence. Especially those whose lives were brutally snatched away from them.

He flinched. 'I didn't do it. I was acquitted.'

'I know, but we're in the same boat, don't you see? We were both accused of something we didn't do, as teenagers. Maybe it's *you* being framed, not me. I don't know! But we have to at least talk!'

He stood back and let me in. In the kitchen, he leaned against the sink. I noticed how dirty it was, toys and dishes everywhere. I wondered where Sam was – in bed already, maybe.

He said, 'So? Talk.' Alex was like a different person with me now. I thought of the last time I'd seen him before all this, the day before Anna died. How he'd cupped my face to kiss me, stared into my eyes. 'You want me to explain myself, is that it? Why I didn't tell you?'

'No, Alex – I just think we need to at least be honest with each other. The day before Anna's murder, you left mine at ten, right?' A late start for him.

'I think so.' He looked away, as if he didn't want to remember that happy bubble, how we couldn't keep our hands off each other and he'd lifted me up to kiss me against the wall of the living room, my legs around his waist.

'And then you went to work?'

'Over Windermere way, yes. Coppicing.' I didn't know what that was exactly, but I nodded.

'And . . . you got Sam from school in the afternoon?'

'Yes, I told you, I had him that night.'

'I know, I know, but when did you get him exactly?'

He paused, as if trying to remember. 'I suppose it was about four. They finish earlier, but there's after-school club. We went back

260

to the flat, I made him baked beans, he watched TV, and he went to sleep about half seven. You want to know what *Peppa Pig* episode we watched, is that it?'

Don Samson's massage had been at four, I'd seen on the calendar. And I felt sure Anna would not have given a massage while Sam was in the house. He was too young to be left by himself for an hour, so he must really have been with Alex at that point. So, what – Alex had actually picked Sam up from school as he said, but then for some reason gone to Anna's farmhouse instead? He'd changed his mind about having Sam that night? That would explain the raised voices Don had heard, Anna's air of irritation when she came back in, why she cancelled on Ciaran. It would also mean Alex was lying to me for some reason. That he really had seen his ex-wife that night.

'You didn't talk to her that night at all?'

I didn't want to come out and say I knew he'd been at the house. What if Don was mistaken? He'd seemed sharp, but he was getting on a bit, and you couldn't always hear clearly when flat on your front.

'I messaged her to say I had him, that's all.' He shrugged. 'We'd split up, Rachel. I wasn't in the habit of calling her to chat.'

'Did she have plans that night?'

'How would I know?'

This wasn't going well. I thought sadly of our previous conversations, spiralling and affectionate, where I felt like a plant gradually unfurling after years in cold storage.

'I was just wondering if she was seeing someone else, if someone was at the house that night . . . you know.'

He let out a frustrated sigh. 'You think she would have told me?'

'No. Of course not.'

Despite this, his attitude to me seemed to have softened with what I'd said. He stepped forward, took my hand. Even with everything that was going on, I felt myself respond to his touch. The

261

rough skin on his hands, their strength and size. I found myself thinking of Stacey Donner.

Gently, he said, 'I'm sorry. This is very hard, and I can't – well, people will talk if I'm seen with you. And the police – they must be watching you, right? I just need to get through this. Make sure Sam is all right.'

'But you don't think I killed Anna?' I heard myself pleading.

He pushed a lock of hair back from my face. 'Of course not. We just have to wait for this to blow over. Once they catch the guy.'

'You think it was a guy?'

'I mean, probably. It usually is, isn't it?' He looked at his watch. 'I'm sorry, but I have to put Sam to bed. He's down with Colette.'

I felt a sudden desire to talk to Sam, to ask him some questions, but surely a five-year-old wouldn't remember whether his father or mother had looked after him on a night days ago. And there was another question I needed answered, too, before he made me leave.

'Wait, Alex – why didn't you tell me? When I told you what had happened to me, going to prison. Why didn't you say the same thing happened to you? With Stacey?' If anyone could have understood him, it was me.

He sighed again. 'Oh, I don't know, Rachel. I try not to think about it. It was a bad time in my life, all right? I tried to do the right thing and walk her home – we were friends from school, and she was hammered, but she wouldn't let me take her to the door in case her parents saw. Next morning I'm in bed hungover and the police are at the door. Everyone at the party said I was the last one seen with her. Then it's like – this nightmare you somehow can't wake up from. Trying to prove you didn't do it when there's no evidence either way. I was terrified – I was barely eighteen, and I thought I'd go to prison for life.'

'I know,' I said quietly. 'If anyone knows, it's me.'

'So. Everyone round here knows about it, and I'm sure a good few still think I did it. Her family moved away.'

'You didn't want to leave too?'

He shrugged. 'Why should I? My family have been here for generations. Our home's here; I wasn't giving that up. Anyway, it's just gossip. It can't hurt me.'

I wished I could take that view. My mind was working overtime. 'You don't think – maybe someone thinks you did it back then, and wants to pin Anna's murder on you? To frame you? I know it sounds mad.'

He looked at me curiously. 'Why would someone do a thing like that? And anyway, the evidence doesn't point to me, does it?'

He was right. The evidence so far all pointed to me.

◆ ◆ ◆

I walked down the stairs of Alex's flat, feeling jittery and afraid. Even if I was sure Alex had lied to me – and I wasn't – I would never be able to prove he'd been at Anna's house that night. Would I tell the police on him, assuming they didn't already know what Don had told me? A murder enquiry is certainly a sobering way to evaluate how much you care about someone.

Rounding the staircase to the middle landing, I almost fell over Sam, playing with some cars on the steps, making little whirring racetrack noises. He looked up – he was wearing an *Octonauts* T-shirt and jeans, his cheeks flushed.

'Oh! Hello,' I said.

He stared at me. I wondered if he remembered who I was, or knew I'd fought with his mother that day in the street. 'Hi,' he said warily.

'Are you driving your cars?'

He nodded. Stupid question.

'I'm a friend of your daddy's.'

'I know.'

'Sam – I'm really sorry about your mummy.'

Was that the right thing to say, or was it better not to remind him? He bowed his head, putting a car in his mouth and sucking it. Shame swept over me – was I really trying to pump a small child, a bereaved child, for information to save my own sorry skin?

'OK, Sam. See you. Let me just climb over you.'

I was several steps down before he said, 'Does she know I'm here?'

'Hm?' I turned back. He was watching me intently, head cocked to the side. He had Alex's eyes, Anna's fair hair.

'Mummy. She put me to bed but then she wasn't there.'

Careful, careful.

'I'm sorry, Sam. When was this?' Stupid question. He was too young to know one day from another. 'Was it here or – at the other house?'

'Yes, home,' he said impatiently. 'Mummy was cross with Daddy. Now I don't know where she is.'

Oh, God. So he was saying, what – Alex had brought him to Anna, just as Don said, and Anna had put him to bed there? And something had happened to her while Sam slept? But how then had he got back to Alex's – and why had Alex lied about it? I wished there was some way to be sure what day we were talking about.

A door opened on to the landing then, and I jumped. It was a young woman, mid-twenties maybe, in jeans and bare feet, with long, reddish hair.

'Sam, there you are! I was looking for you.'

This was Alex's neighbour, Colette. He'd mentioned her a few more times than I was comfortable with. She worked for the tourist board, I thought. She spotted me, her face darkening. 'Oh.'

'I'm just going.' I held up my hand. 'Bye, Sam.'

And I left, heart hammering and mind racing, trying to work out what it all meant.

Casey

JUNE 2002

'Adams. You have a visitor.'

I roused myself from my bunk, where I tended to lie in a kind of stupor during visiting hours. No one ever came to see me on Death Row. Jenna kept saying she couldn't afford to fly, and my lawyers had long stopped visiting. They considered they'd done their job by advising me to plead guilty, and since I'd ignored them, I could now rot for the rest of my life, or until the state killed me. I was supposed to have an automatic appeal, but the date kept moving, and with no new evidence, it seemed clear it would just confirm the guilty verdict.

Meanwhile, life went on beyond those prison walls. The Twin Towers had fallen, a war had begun, and it all felt as far away from me as another planet. My world had shrunk to this building, these unhappy women, my cell where cold food was pushed in on a plastic tray. I was on my own now, which I had thought would be better, but some days I didn't see another human face from one end to the other, the guards simply opening the hatch in my door and shoving things in, walking away. I talked to Rhonda when I could, but our meetings were snatched moments of kindness in the blank despair of my life.

'Who is it?' I said.

The guard slammed my door with irritation.

'How the hell should I know? Get your ass down there now before I write you up.'

I stood and held my hands behind my back so she could cuff me, as was regulation. I was used to the loss of circulation now.

I hadn't been in the visiting area for over a year, since no one ever came to see me, and I looked around it with fresh eyes. It felt good to be anywhere other than my cell or the tiny exercise yard. In the early days I'd made efforts to keep fit, running in circles, preparing myself for the time when I'd be cleared and could resume my life again. But lately it was as if I'd given up. What was the point? I hadn't gained any weight, though, because I barely ate. I hated the sickening slop they called food. My hair, once so glossy, had started to fall out. I knew from the little plastic mirror in the cell, which was welded down so I couldn't break it and cut my wrists, that I looked like someone else. My skin was yellow, my teeth loose from poor nutrition. I looked like someone who'd lost all hope.

It took me a moment to place the man at the table they led me to. That surprised me too, that I wasn't behind glass talking into a phone – apparently you didn't always have to do it that way, it was just another lie from films and TV. Was he someone from my legal team who I didn't know? A young man about my age, but large, tall and broad and slightly overweight, with messy brown hair and glasses. He wore a T-shirt with cartoon characters on and he was sweating like crazy. It was always too hot in the prison, but I was used to it now. He stood up when I came over.

'Casey! Oh my God, it's you. I'm sorry, they said I couldn't hug you.' He had a British accent.

'That's OK.' I sat down. I still had no idea who he was. He was familiar but somehow I couldn't quite place him. 'I'm sorry, you are . . . ?'

His face fell. 'It's Jeremy! From college? Jeremy Caldwell?'

Of course, Jeremy who hung around my crew, who ran the college newspaper and had done a feature on me heading off to America, as if a job as a nanny was something to be proud of. Always on the periphery of my vision, though I'd known him since I was eleven.

'God! I'm sorry. I just – I didn't expect to see you.' It was surreal, in fact, as if someone from another life had walked into a dream – or a nightmare. 'What are you doing here?' I was suddenly very aware of how awful I looked, seeing someone from my old world.

'I told them I was a journalist to get in,' he said, looking around him furtively. 'Well, I am a journalist. Got a trainee job on the local paper, so I had my NUJ card and all.'

'You were in California?' I couldn't understand what had brought him here.

'No, no, I've come to see you. I've been following your case right from the start. I wrote to you.'

I shook my head dully. Why was he here? I had left that student life behind, the one where I was a popular pretty girl going places. It was the only way to survive what I'd become.

'I don't get letters,' I said. 'I'm supposed to but – there's some court case going on.'

There was a wrangling in process with the governor's office over the rights of Death Row prisoners – that is, whether we had any or not. The guards were not above confiscating letters and packages, out of greed or just spite.

'Oh,' said Jeremy. 'Well, as soon as I heard you'd been found guilty, I set up a website to prove your innocence. It has a lot of traffic – people want to hear the other side of your story.'

Again, it took a few moments, the way light has to fight its way down to the darkness at the bottom of the ocean.

'You mean – you think I didn't do it?'

I didn't know if I'd ever met anyone who thought that. My lawyers clearly didn't, and even Jenna rarely answered the phone to me now. My own mother had abandoned me here in this place.

'Of course I do.'

He laid his hand on the table, and for a second, before the guard saw, he touched mine with his little finger. It was clammy, but all the same it was pretty much the first kind touch I'd had in two years. I nearly jumped out of my skin. He snatched his hand away, staring at me hard instead, as if touching me with his gaze.

'I know you could never do a thing like that,' he said. 'You love kids, don't you? And you're gentle, you're kind. Anyway, there's no real evidence.'

'They said no one else could have done it. And all the other stuff, the stupid forum posts, the prints on the gun . . .'

He waved a hand. 'Circumstantial, all of it. You gave explanations. No, it should never have been enough to convict you. There was no motive, for a start. No blood on your clothes.'

I was gulping this in like water. 'You really believe that?'

'Of course.' His eyes were the faithful brown of a puppy dog. 'Case, I promise I'll do everything I can to clear your name. I'm working on it right now, talking to private investigators, checking all the so-called evidence again. I'll talk to the neighbours, I'll get into the house – I swear it.'

'But – how? Are you allowed to be in the States?'

'For three months. That's long enough, if I work at it.'

'Your job, though?'

He beamed. 'Actually, I've quit. This is more important.'

I was amazed. This man I barely remembered from my college days, he had dropped everything for me, a convicted murderer.

'How will you live?'

'Oh, the website brings in some money, advertising and stuff. And I've arranged to cover the case for a few papers back home.'

Jeremy, for all his other-worldliness, was good at practical things like that. I think because he felt no shame asking for things.

'But – why?' I was bewildered. The guard looked at the clock and I knew she'd take me back any minute now. 'Why would you do this for me?'

He hesitated, and I saw in his open, guileless face exactly why. Jeremy was in love with me. And suddenly I recalled other incidents – mix CDs he'd made for me, snakebites he'd bought me and never taken money for, since bartenders always assumed he was at least twenty-five. Jeremy Caldwell was in love with me. Oh God. 'It's really a shame you didn't get my letters,' he said, blushing. 'I sent quite a few.'

'I'm sorry. I'll ask them about it.' The guard tapped her watch at me and I stood up reluctantly. 'I have to go. Thank you, Jeremy! Thank you so much. I'll put you on my call list and then we can talk. They have to allow that.'

He watched me go, his eyes hungry, despite my orange suit and ratty hair and dead skin. This man loved me; he'd do anything to help me. As I walked back into the prison, I had the thought – *You don't love him back, Casey, you never could*. And then another – *But he's the only one who's going to help you now*. You learn a lot about yourself in a no-hope situation. Namely, the lengths you will go to in order to survive.

The guard took off my cuffs, rough as usual.

'It's funny,' I said. 'That man there, he's a journalist, and he said he wrote me lots of letters. But I never get any post.'

'Post?' she mimicked. 'What's post?'

'Mail, then. Is there any chance the letters went missing?'

'How the hell'd I know?'

269

'Because I think it's against the law to intercept mail. Even in prison. I mean, I could always check in the law library.'

She said nothing, slamming the door again. But the next day a pile of envelopes appeared on my bunk, addressed in Jeremy's spidery mad-man writing. And I feasted on the letters inside, like a starving woman. Not the words, which were banal and mostly descriptions of the injustices in my case, memories I didn't share of times we'd spent together back in England, and stories from his Dungeons & Dragons group. Not the words, but the sense that someone cared whether I lived or died, whether I ever got out of this scorpion hole in the desert or whether I curled up and shrivelled to a husk.

Rachel

It was raining again as I trekked back to my rented flat. Coldwater was a small place, so it was just a few streets away from Alex's, but it might as well have been thousands of miles, I felt so far from him. I was exhausted to the soles of my feet – a long and ultimately fruitless day of investigating. Jeremy had lied about going home. Alex had possibly lied to me about being at Anna's house that night – assuming that was what Sam meant. Poor kid. How would he ever be able to make sense of this?

The noise began slowly, swelling from the distance. At first I did not even realise it was for me – after all, it wasn't unusual to hear rushing cars at night, bored kids driving too fast. The engines grew louder, and I froze as I saw two police cars turn down my street. Outside the door of my new flat, the same red car was parked – as I'd thought, that must have been an unmarked police one. Several officers were gathered around it, but that wasn't all. The engines swelled and dipped as the cars came to a halt. Both ends of the street were blocked. As if I might run, as if I was dangerous. They had come for me. I didn't move at all as the car doors clunked open, and DS Margaret Hope got out. Her face was grim as the streetlight swept over it, her grey mac swirling about her in the wind. 'Rachel Caldwell, I'm arresting you on suspicion of the murder of Anna

Devine. You do not have to say anything . . .' I didn't hear the rest of the caution. I realised I had backed away until I was pressed against the wet pebble-dashed wall of a nearby building. This was it. They had me now.

◆ ◆ ◆

No DS Hegarty this time. It was Margaret Hope again, and another detective I didn't recognise, an older Asian man with a lean, suspicious face. DC Bakshi, I thought he'd said. The two of them faced me over the interview room in Barrow station. 'To confirm, Rachel, you have declined legal representation.'

'I – yes.' Was that stupid? Had my stubbornness condemned me again? It was certainly a lonely place, this side of the table.

DS Hope folded her hands in front of her. 'Can you confirm your movements today, Rachel? You've been away from your flat for some time.'

'I – I went to speak to a few people.' What a day it had been. Alison, Jeremy, Ciaran, Marilyn, Alex. All different pieces of the same puzzle, and I still couldn't make sense of it.

'You've been harassing witnesses in fact, is that right?'

Alison Harper must have called the police, as she'd threatened to. I didn't blame her.

'Look, I'm sorry. I can't sit at home doing nothing, I have to try and solve this.'

She frowned. 'And you don't trust us to do that? Our actual jobs?'

'You keep arresting me! I didn't do anything.'

She raised her eyebrows. 'Do I need to remind you of the evidence against you? Your motive, your lack of alibi, the fact you lied about finding the body?'

'I'm only trying to find who murdered Anna,' I muttered, looking round the room and noticing how close the walls seemed. My brain was screaming at me to run now, head for the hills, but I couldn't. I was under arrest, and could not leave this place until they said so or the clock ran out. 'We're on the same team.'

'Well, we'll see about that,' she said. 'We don't generally encourage amateur sleuthing, whatever *Midsomer Murders* would have you believe.' DC Bakshi gave a small, appreciative chuckle. She went on. 'You've been conducting your own side investigations. You met with witnesses Don Samson and Alison Harper – and you knew about them because you broke into Anna Devine's house and searched it.'

How did they know about that? For a second I couldn't think what to say. 'Someone saw me?'

She sniffed. 'We're not required to give you that information.'

'I didn't break in as such. There was a key.'

She raised her eyebrows at that and made another note. 'Well, thanks for clarifying, Rachel. You realise you've contaminated a possible crime scene, and put your DNA all over it.'

'You already searched it all, though, yes? Did the forensics?'

She gave a tiny sigh. 'Can you explain your behaviour for us, Rachel? Because I certainly can't.'

'Well. I think so.' I hadn't told them about Alex possibly bringing Sam to the farmhouse that night. Part of me still hoped Don had made a mistake. He was old, his ears must be shot from years of using noisy machinery. I couldn't just sell him down the river – anyway, maybe they already knew. 'Look, I didn't do this. But it's being made to look like I did – the scarf, even where the body was left, on my usual morning route. And I told you about the letters on my fridge. Even the fact of my identity coming out in the press – it's someone who knows me from before, it must be. That picture at

273

Disneyland. I've never even seen the original before. It could only have come from the Safran house.'

'This comes back to your thesis that someone is framing you.'

'Yes. I know how it sounds.'

Another raise of the eyebrows. She glanced at the other officer, who cleared his throat and said, 'Rachel. Do you own any knives? Sharp ones?'

I blinked. 'Well, I mean – doesn't everyone? I have one sharp one.'

'Do you cook much?'

'Not if it's just me.'

I became quite good at cooking in LA, catering for entire dinner parties, but it had been ruined for me, like so much else. Cooking for Alex in recent months, I had begun to enjoy it again – romantic dinners for two – but on the nights when he didn't come over I rarely bothered, just made a salad or some pasta, sometimes eating straight from the saucepan.

'When was the last time you used your sharp knife?'

This seemed like a strange question. Who could remember a thing like that? And more to the point, why was he asking?

'I . . . well, I made a lasagne at the weekend. Sunday.'

The day before Anna's death, assuming she had died the following night. Alex had come over, and afterwards we'd lain awake for hours, talking in the dark, my skin tingling every time his fingers brushed it.

'And you washed up after that?'

What the hell was going on?

'Of course.'

Alex hadn't offered, so I'd done it the next morning when he left. Smiling to myself as the radio played love songs, remembering the night before. Not knowing what was coming my way.

'So you had a knife about the place, you washed it at the week-end, left it on the draining board, yes? When was the last time you saw it?'

'I have no idea. I guess Monday. But I can't be sure.'

I kept the kitchen fairly neat, so I would have put the knife away sometime that day or Tuesday, I was sure. But who could remember doing something so automatic?

'What brand is it, do you know?'

'I . . .' I shrugged. 'Honestly, I don't know. Could you answer a question like that?'

He slid over a photograph. It was a knife inside a plastic bag, tagged. Evidence. There were red stains on the tip, and I tried not to think about that.

'Do you recognise this?' he said.

I'd said I had no idea what brand my knife was, even though I looked at it several times a week, held it in my hand as I chopped onions or carrots or meat. But once I saw the picture, I remembered. It was a Sheffield steel one, which I'd bought when I ran from Jeremy, determined to start my own life. The wooden handle, the shining blade. All very familiar. This was the knife in the picture. My kitchen knife.

I raised my eyes to him, helpless.

Quite pleasantly, he said, 'We found this in the undergrowth near where Anna Devine's body was dumped. Your knife, is it?'

Casey

November 2003

It was crazy how much I'd started to look forward to Jeremy's visits. There was nothing else to structure my life around, just the same featureless cream walls and the hour a day of glimpsing the sky, often grey and flat, not even a cloud to raise some interest. That and the post I was now allowed to receive – full of nutcases, some of whom seemed thrilled by what I'd done, and even a few proposals of marriage. *I've seen you on TV and you look so sweet, I know you couldn't do something like that. When you get out you can come and live here, I have a double bed and I'll take care of you.* Then of course there were some who sent death threats, earnestly describing what they would do to me for the crime of murdering a child (rape, mutilation, all of that, these good Christian people).

At first, I had flung them away from me, horrified, and scrubbed my hands clean, weeping. Now I read them with a kind of detached interest, sometimes correcting spelling or grammar mistakes. These people had never met me and yet they wanted to kill me. The state also planned to kill me, but that felt so far away I could hardly worry about it. My main concern was my appeal, what I could do differently this time. No one had been executed in

California for years, so it didn't seem like a big risk. I didn't know that wheels were in motion and a Republican governor had been elected, a popular actor whose films Jenna had enjoyed, full of muscles and sweat. She liked a real man, did Jenna. She wouldn't have thought much of Jeremy.

In college I had hardly thought about Jeremy Caldwell, and I struggled to dredge up memories of him. He'd been there when we went to see *Austin Powers 2*, hadn't he? He'd bought me a jumbo Coke since I was broke, as always. When there was a prom and we'd all gone as a group, I vaguely remembered him broaching the subject: *Of course we could always go together, I mean, if you wanted to, ha ha.* I'd brushed off the idea – *Ugh, can you imagine, so American* – and he'd laughed, but I remembered a look of disappointment on his earnest face.

I had known he liked me, but I didn't let myself think about it, how much it might hurt him when I flirted with other boys, danced to Britney Spears, in my peasant tops and low-slung jeans, my thongs on display. When my reprobate boyfriend Ryan and I broke up – which we did once a week, then reunited with passionate snogging – had we done it in front of Jeremy? Of course we had. He was always just there, and now I had lost everyone, including my own mother, and here he still was. He'd had to go back and forward to the UK over the past year, since he didn't have a visa, but he always returned to me.

When I came into the visitors' room, even stripped of my make-up and hair straighteners and tight clothes, in the unflattering orange jumpsuit, he always looked thrilled to see me, leaping to his feet, a big smile breaking over his sweaty red face.

'Casey! Are you all right? Can I get you anything?'

We weren't allowed to accept items from visitors, of course, but they could put money in our accounts to buy little things, a comb or some noodles to supplement our bland, mushy food.

277

They could also buy us things from the vending machines in here. I craved chocolate, stuffing the sweetness into my mouth, a moment's relief, but I was worried I'd get fat, and that this would mean I'd truly given up, that no one would ever find me attractive again. That there was no life outside of this place, no hope. I sat down opposite him.

'Any news?'

'Have you heard of something called the Innocence Project?' He was almost bursting with excitement.

'No, what's that?'

'They help people who've been wrongfully convicted. Honestly, Case, there's literally thousands of people in this country in prison on dodgy evidence. They have alibis, even, or the DNA evidence clears them, but the court never heard it. They all do deals, the cops and the defence lawyers. It's so crooked.'

'You spoke to them?'

'They knew about you already! They think you have a good case – those lawyers for the Little Helpers, they told you to plead guilty?'

'Yeah. They said that way I'd do twenty years, maybe, get out while I was still young.'

At nineteen, the prospect of twenty years had seemed horrific, not the merciful kindness they presented it as. So I'd pleaded not guilty, and now I was on Death Row.

'So you weren't properly represented, you've got a case there, and also there were key witnesses they never called, like the housekeeper.'

'Marietta? They never found her.'

'They didn't even look, Case! I've almost tracked her down, I think. She moved to her daughter's in San Diego. Also, the gardener, José, he was a hostile witness, so he shouldn't have been allowed on the stand.'

José. Well, I had accused him of murder, unwittingly of course. I didn't really blame him for being hostile.

An unfamiliar ache had begun in my chest, and it took me a moment to identify it: hope. I quickly stifled it. Hope was dangerous in here. The only way to survive was by accepting reality.

'My appeal's set for early next year, but it might not happen. They keep moving it.'

'But this is a good thing, Case. Gives us time to mount a proper defence, get all this evidence presented. A mistrial, even, maybe, given the bad advice you got.'

'But – Jeremy, I don't have any money.' American lawyers were expensive, I knew.

Jenna had made it clear there was nothing she could do for me, and I had no one else. The pitiful amount I'd saved from my nanny job would not have covered an hour of a lawyer's time.

'There's no charge!' He actually slapped the table in excitement, causing the guard to look over, fingering his gun. 'They raise funds to defend people, and they think you, well, you'd make kind of a good poster child.'

I didn't quite understand this at the time, in my naivety, but later I saw why. I was white, young, pretty, scared and British – the American public were more likely to follow my case, and care that I'd been wrongfully sent to Death Row. More than they'd care about, say, the hundreds of black men in the same position. At the time, I could only think about myself. That maybe someone was going to help me, and this nightmare might end.

◆ ◆ ◆

As my appeal date grew nearer, I was in agony. What if the Innocence Project people didn't get to my case in time and I was reconvicted? It would be so much harder to get another appeal then. We'd need new evidence, and I knew better than anyone there was no more to be had. I was pacing my cell, watching the mail every day, looking up like a hopeful dog when they announced visitors.

One day, it was my turn. The guard was in an even fouler mood than ever, her skin red, her breath wheezy. 'Adams. Visitors.'

Visitors, plural. My heart began to hammer.

'Who is it?'

I knew better than to ask that, and she just shot me a look. As she put my cuffs on, she was rough, muttering to herself when they wouldn't catch. I could smell her sweat and the cheap body spray she used, the drug-store shampoo. I felt a wave of sympathy for her, in this crappy job with its ever present threat of violence. She hadn't convicted me or sent me here.

'Are you OK?' I asked. A harsh yank on the cuffs. 'It could be allergies, you know, if you're struggling to breathe. I had them really bad when I first came to California. Something about the pollen.'

She paused. 'Hush your mouth now, Adams.' But it was gentler, and as she led me along, her hand rested lightly on my arm, not tugging me.

I passed Rhonda's cell on my way, and had time to flash her a big smile. She nodded happily – she knew who I hoped my visitors were.

In the visiting room, two young people. My mood sank a little when I saw how very young they were, not much older than me, surely. In fact they were law students, Andrea and George, both white and clean-cut and preppy.

'Casey! So nice to meet you.'

I sat down, wrong-footed by their warmth. In here I was used to being treated as a child-killer.

'You're from the project?' I could barely say the word *innocence*, it was so loaded for me.

'That's right. We're here to work on your case, ahead of your appeal in a few months.'

It was so soon. I clenched my fists.

'I'd rather know now if there's no chance.'

They exchanged a look. 'Casey . . . you were convicted on very flimsy evidence. Character witnesses, really. Impugning your behaviour and demeanour.' They meant my clothes, my drinking, the fact I'd behaved like a normal teenager and didn't know it would one day be used against me. 'There's very little actual physical evidence.'

'My prints on the gun. DNA.'

'Yes. But you lived in the house – and your explanation of picking the gun up is very plausible.'

That was Andrea, who was earnest and a little pudgy, with a kind freckled face and flat loafers. George was tall, slightly gangling, his tie worn loose. It had horses on it, I saw. I wondered if they were romantically involved, noticing how she blushed when he slid a file to her and their hands touched.

'But I said all that at the trial,' I said. 'Why would they listen this time and not then?'

'Well, for a start, some key witnesses were excluded from the trial. It seems your lawyers made a deal with the prosecution for an easy conviction and less prison time. But you wouldn't take it?'

'No. Because I didn't do it. They were trying to threaten me with the death penalty if I didn't, but why would I plead guilty to something I just didn't do?'

They nodded earnestly. 'Totally.'

'The system is so broken.'

'So that's something we can use – inadequate legal counsel. And we can put a new spin on the other evidence – Madison's bruises and her odd behaviour, the teacher's testimony, the fact some of the witnesses were hostile to you.'

'José,' I said, leaden. What a mistake I'd made there.

'Right. And of course, Ruth Safran.'

I let out a long sigh. 'I never understood it. She just didn't like me, right from day one.'

'Totally. So we can use that as well – bias, a failure to call adequate defence witnesses, the fact you were alone in a strange country – your mother didn't even come to the trial, did she?'

Another fact that had counted against me. *Casey's own mother won't support her! She must be guilty!*

'She doesn't have much money and it's a long way to fly. She's nervous,' I lied. I wondered if Jenna knew that her silence had helped to seal my fate. 'And the rest – the stupid forum comments, the bottle of medicine?'

'Circumstantial,' said Andrea, wrinkling her button nose. 'Speculation at best – it doesn't meet the evidentiary threshold, is what we'll submit. Same with the neighbour's statement about seeing no one else go in the house. Eyewitness testimony is notoriously unreliable.'

I was twisting my hands, trying to hold back the terrible wave of hope inside me. 'So – who will we say did it, if not me?'

They exchanged another look, one that made me sure they were sleeping together. (I was right about this; they are married now, with two adorable children. They sent me Christmas cards for a while.)

'We don't have to prove that, Casey. Just that there isn't enough evidence to convict you specifically. That you didn't get a fair trial.'

I looked between them, their clean, shining faces. Not broken down by life. They were inside prison walls now, but soon they would get up and go out, walk into the sunshine, perhaps stop at a diner for a milkshake and fries. Hold hands under the table, even. While I would stay here, perhaps till I died, if this didn't go to plan. I would never be touched by a man again, feel his hands

282

on my body. Never hold my own baby, heavy on my hip, where Carson used to sit.

'But – even if I get off, won't people always think I did it?'

'That does happen, yes,' said George earnestly. 'But you'd be free, Casey. You could go home. That's what we have to focus on.'

'You mean they'd literally open the door of the courthouse and let me go.' I could hardly believe it.

'Right. I mean, after some processing. Forms and stuff.'

'So this is the plan,' I said. 'Re-present the evidence?'

'Exactly. Poke holes in all the inconsistencies of the case, the collusion between your so-called lawyers and the prosecution. They just wanted to indemnify the nanny agency, so they weren't acting in your interests. And the evidence is paper-thin. We're confident that some new expert witnesses can present it in a different way. People who know about eyewitness deficiencies, patterns of abuse in children – which we can show started long before you ever got to America – and also behavioural and cultural experts, who can testify that the way you, uh, acted, was very consistent with a British person your age.'

They meant my so-called coldness outside the house, when I'd been photographed standing rigid, my arms folded. Not crying or wailing. But you have to understand I was stunned, and terrified. All I knew was that Abby and David were dead – I hadn't gone upstairs. I was afraid for Madison, terribly afraid, hoping desperately she was somehow all right, knowing she wasn't. 'And the pictures from before – me drinking and stuff?'

George blushed slightly. 'Trial by media – another way you didn't get a fair hearing. We'll be talking about British culture versus American too, that the drinking age is lower there, that people go out partying more. All that.'

I sat back. 'You seem to have a really strong plan.' It sounded too good to be true.

'We hope so! We'll keep in touch as we prep, and of course, on the day, we'll be there with you in the courthouse.'

That sounded nice. A courtroom was the loneliest place in the world, especially when you looked out and saw no one on your side. Just hostile, angry eyes, sure that you had murdered a small child.

There was no more to say after that, so the guard came back, but instead of taking me to my cell she led me to the exercise yard, where Rhonda and Paola were sitting on a picnic bench. This wasn't normally allowed, and I looked at the guard in surprise.

'Go on,' she said, nudging me. A reward for caring about her, maybe. Today was a good day. Uncuffed, I went bounding over.

'Rhonda! It was the Innocence Project lawyers! They think I've got a really good shot, and . . .' I saw her face, the grey shade of it. Dread. Her hands were shaking. 'What's the matter?'

Paola was having a lucid day today. 'She get a letter. A date.'

I didn't understand. 'You mean for an appeal?'

Rhonda shook her head. She seemed to have aged ten years since I saw her earlier. 'No, honey. An execution date. It's time.'

'No. That can't be it.' It hadn't happened in so long, I couldn't believe it. 'There'll be a stay, there's always a stay. Or an appeal . . .'

Rhonda's head swung to and fro. 'It's my time, honey. I knew it. I felt it.'

'No. No!' I elbowed Paola aside, took both Rhonda's hands in mine, the rules be damned. 'Listen, there must be something we can do, talk to these lawyers I have, even, or . . .'

Gently, she took her hands away.

'But honey,' she said, 'I did it. I'm not innocent. I killed my babies. And now the state's going to kill me. We're on *Death Row*, Casey. Where did you think this was?'

Rachel

Think, come on. Think. I was back in a holding cell, on a short break between the endless rounds of questioning. Over and over. When did I last see Anna. Could anyone prove I hadn't left the house the night she was murdered. When did I last see my knife. *Rachel, we know what happened. You were jealous of Anna, and wanted her gone so you could be with her husband unopposed. You lured her into the woods, where you stabbed her and left her to die. Now isn't that the truth?*

'No,' was all I could say. 'No, I didn't.'

It was just like before. How could you prove you hadn't done a thing, with no witnesses except for a dog? I was sure they would charge me any minute – this knife, that was powerful evidence. A literal smoking gun.

How could this be happening? I didn't kill Anna. Of course I didn't. I hadn't even seen her since that Co-op incident.

Is that true?

Of course it was true. I didn't need to start doubting my own mind, on top of everything else. Back then, they had done their best to make me think I was crazy. *But did you touch the knife that day? Are you sure? Fingerprints don't last that long, you know* (that was a lie, but how was I to know?). *Exactly what was your relationship with the deceased, David Safran? We have proof of your affair, you know. You may as well confess. Did you do it and block it out, maybe? That would sure be understandable.*

I was older now, and I knew it was rare to have total blackouts, the kind where you could kill someone and not remember. It did happen, but it was unlikely.

Think.

Occam's razor: the simplest explanation is most likely the right one. That was a thing Jeremy used to say a lot, until it began to irritate me and, eventually, I had to leave him – for that and a million other reasons.

So, I hadn't killed Anna, but she had probably been stabbed using a knife from my kitchen – at least, she had been stabbed and my knife had been found by her body. Therefore, someone else had taken the knife and put it there. But why had the police only just found it? I knew they had searched the woods thoroughly after the body was found.

How was that possible, that someone had got hold of my knife? Unlike most people in the village, I locked my door every time I went out – I had more to hide than them. There was a dog flap for Brandy, though. It would be possible for a small person, maybe, to climb through that, assuming they could get over my back wall and into the garden without Audrey seeing. She was harder to get past than a prison guard. There was the key in the flowerpot too, which someone might have found. Or else they had picked the knife up while in my house, but I never had anyone over. Just Alex – and I was sure I'd seen the knife since the last time he'd been over. *Think.* And how did the police know it was my knife? Someone must have tipped them off – they wouldn't tell me when I asked how they knew, when I couldn't lie that it was mine, this knife they had apparently found near the body. Anna's body.

Then I realised who it could have been. Someone who had stayed at my house, with plenty of access to my kitchen, and who had lied to me about his whereabouts. Who was still in love with me, as he had been twenty years ago, when he got me released and took me home, like some bird in a gilded cage. Maybe he still wanted me all to himself, safely behind bars, where I couldn't be with any other man.

Had *Jeremy* done this?

◆　◆　◆

Footsteps, the turn of a key in a lock. Sounds I had been attuned to for so many years, Pavlovian. My entire body contracted in fear. What now? It was the custody sergeant, here to take me back to the interview room. I followed him through the silent, carpeted corridors, my heart sinking at the thought of yet more questions. I had no better answers for them. Margaret Hope was alone in the room, leaning with both arms on the table. The sergeant retreated, leaving me there with her, the door ajar. My eyes darted about in panic. This wasn't allowed, was it? Everything had been so above board up to now.

'What?' I said, terrified.

She just looked at me. 'Very smart, aren't you, Casey?'

I'd asked them before to keep calling me Rachel. 'What do you mean?'

'Good at getting away with things. Like those murders in America. All that evidence, and you still somehow blag your way off Death Row. Amazing.'

She wasn't supposed to be saying these things to me, was she? I looked around for a camera, some kind of recording device. 'I didn't do it.'

'You know, when you're a police officer for as long as I've been, you get a sense for these things. I remember thinking back then, that girl's guilty as sin, lying through her little white teeth.'

'No. No, it's not true.'

'I don't know what kind of person could do that, press a pillow over the face of a little kiddie. Lie about it in cold blood.'

'But I didn't! I never hurt Madison!' My voice was rising. Someone would hear, surely. But the sergeant was just outside, and letting this happen.

'And now there's another kiddie motherless. Because you cut his mum's throat.'

'I didn't! God, what is this?'

She stepped back. 'Seems you've got yet another chance. Like a cat, you are. Nine lives. But they'll run out sooner or later, you'll see.'

I didn't understand. 'I'm not being charged?'

'It seems not. I pushed for it but – well. No one wants to take the fall for putting you through yet another wrongful charge. Assuming they aren't both entirely justified, of course.'

'But . . . the knife . . .'

She sighed. 'Not Anna Devine's blood. Not even human, it seems.'

What the hell? 'What do you mean? Please tell me.'

'Chicken, they think. It's funny, isn't it? You keep sliding free every time. Just know this, Casey – if there's anything else to find, I will find it. And I won't stop till you're behind bars, where you belong.'

I was stunned. Both by this conversation, and the fact they were apparently letting me go again. How could it be chicken blood? Anna had kept chickens, of course. But how had the blood got on my knife, and my knife into the woods? I just didn't understand.

DS Hope straightened her suit and pushed the door wide. Her tone changed. 'You're being let go for now, Rachel. The sergeant will read you the list of bail conditions. Any breach of those, any attempt to interfere with witnesses, you'll be straight back into custody before you can draw breath.' As she stalked out, behind her harsh words I heard something else – I had one more chance to work out what was going on. But only one.

Casey

JANUARY 2004

Despite Rhonda's fatalism, I was determined something must be done to help her. I badgered the guards, who stonewalled me, or, when really pushed, threatened to stop my own lawyer visits. I wrote to the Innocence Project people, who diplomatically told me they only dealt with cases of alleged miscarriage of justice. I reached out to charities for postnatal depression, thinking there might be some support available. Surely Rhonda had not been in her right mind when she did it. The Rhonda I knew was kind and intelligent. To have drowned her three children, and attempted to die with them, that was the sign of serious derangement. I do believe that, in another time and place, in a less racist country, Rhonda might never have gone to prison. A secure hospital, maybe, to help her. She needed help, and instead they were going to kill her.

Her execution date had been set for two weeks away. As it ticked round, I didn't really believe it would happen. There was always a last-minute reprieve, wasn't there? The governor would call, or her appeal would go through, and there'd be a stay. Yes, she'd still be stuck here for life, but she would be breathing, thinking, feeling. It was unimaginable that everything Rhonda had ever done or felt or seen was going to die with her. Just snuffed out like that, and not even an accident, but deliberately. Calculated. There was no victim to even witness this so-called justice – the person who mourned her children most was Rhonda.

She herself refused to engage in any of this, appeals or letters or pleading. 'You still have a chance, honey. Let me help you. You have to stay alive and get out of here.' And she taught me, in those final weeks, everything she'd learned about how to survive prison. How to work the system. Get the best food. Stand up for yourself in a fight. How to kill someone, if absolutely necessary. I hadn't wanted any of it. 'Jesus, Rhonda, no! It's not going to come to that!'

She was implacable. 'A girl in my last prison got shanked in the shower, the day before her release. Some people are jealous, they don't want to see you walk out.'

'But I'm not getting out!'

'You don't know that. If you're alive, there's still a chance. That's what you have to do. Stay alive, no matter what.'

On the morning her execution was scheduled, I woke up sensing a new atmosphere. When everything is the same every day, you notice tiny details. The guard had done her hair, coloured some greys over, and she brought me breakfast in my cell, a small packet of cornflakes such as you get on planes or ferries, toast long gone cold, coffee in a plastic cup. There was no point in asking for tea, I'd learned.

'No eggs?' Bland as they were, it was something hot inside you to start the day – or rather, lukewarm.

'Not today.' She seemed excited, cheerful. Not her usual self. I smelled a different perfume too.

'Oh. Because . . .'

'Execution Day!' she said, and she actually smiled. She was happy. 'You wanna see the crowds outside, Blondie. Whole lotta publicity on our little prison.'

I learned later, when I had access to the internet and the strength to read about it without feeling sick, that in fact there were people rooting for Rhonda that day. There were death-penalty abolitionists, who thought no one should be executed, no matter what they'd done. And a postnatal depression charity actually had taken up her cause, but they were small and broke and no one really listened. This was before postnatal psychosis was understood as a condition. In my cell at the time I knew nothing of the news reports and raging debates on morning talk shows, but I could hear the roar of the gathering crowds, the whir of news helicopters overhead. I could see why the guard was excited – the mood was different. In a place where nothing ever changed, the air was electric, new voices echoing, unfamiliar footsteps up and down the hallways. The clanging of gates.

But I didn't feel excited, I felt terrified. Living on Death Row had still been an abstract experience for me, because it was rare for anyone to actually be executed. It was just like another prison, only quieter, smaller. Today I realised that all those words I'd heard spoken in court – *you shall be put to death* – had real consequences. This was a death house, and we were all just waiting our turn. In an hour, Rhonda, my good and kind friend, would be strapped to a gurney and have her arm filled with poison. It was going to happen. But still I had hope, stupid, blind hope.

'Will they not call it off?' I asked the guard. 'I mean, that happens, right? A last-minute reprieve?'

She shot me a look. 'Not this time.'

'But – why?'

'Why you think? Governor wants to make an example, they ain't done a woman in years. And she killed her babies, Blondie. Who does that?'

'A sick person. Who needs help.' I was stepping out of line here, and she glared at me again.

'You forget where you are or something? *Who* you are?'

In her eyes I had also killed a child. I was shivering, freezing cold despite the hot desert pall we lived under. I rubbed my arms, noticing how pale they were, how spindly. I was weak from years inside. I was twenty-two already, and I would die in a prison cell, or else follow Rhonda to the execution chamber. Unless a miracle happened.

I was still hoping for it, a last-minute reprieve, as Rhonda was led past my cell. Four guards were escorting one woman. I think they paraded her like this on purpose, to remind us we were next. That our lives were an illusion we could lose any second. That we too were dead women walking. As she passed, I ran to my bars, though I'd been warned not to.

'Rhonda!'

She was dressed differently, in a white jumpsuit, her hair carefully braided. I knew she had done that for her pride. She seemed calm.

'Stay back, honey,' she said.

Sure enough, the guards had their hands on their guns.

'Adams, step away from the bars!'

I couldn't. I stretched out my hand to her, trying to touch her, just for one second. I couldn't reach.

'Rhonda! I can't – they can't do this!' I was weeping, incoherent. Like the child I still was.

'Honey, they can do anything. Be strong. You get out.' She lowered her voice. 'Remember what I taught you. When there's no hope left, you fight. To your last drop of blood.'

Then she was yanked away and my last sight of her was her back, clad in white, the way her legs moved forward. The way she was breathing, thinking, feeling, until she was gone.

I sat back on my bunk, shivering violently, trying not to be sick. I knew I would pay later for going up to the bars, but I didn't

292

care. This was barbaric. Just feet away from us, Rhonda was being murdered in the execution chamber. I couldn't hear anything, just the usual hum of the ventilation and the vague murmur of people outside. I cried for a few minutes, and then I heard a roar. Cheers.

I looked at the clock, which I could see by squinting down the hallway: 9.43 a.m. Rhonda was dead. They were cheering her death. Over the choke of my own sobs, I could hear something else. The chink of metal dishes against bars. The women were commemorating her, our friend Rhonda, and so although I wanted to lie down and never get up, I picked up my bowl, dragged myself back to the bars and did it too. *Bang, bang, bang.* A requiem. A protest. Proof that we were still alive. And as I banged and called and the prison guards yelled at us, I swore to myself I wouldn't let them kill me like they had Rhonda. Somehow, I would save myself. *When there's no hope left, you fight. To your last drop of blood.*

Rachel

I barely slept that night, in the dingy surroundings of the flat, hoping and dreading to hear from Alex, but there was nothing. Did he wonder where I was? Did he care about me at all? Did he know I'd been arrested again – or that I'd been digging and knew he had lied about not seeing Anna before she was murdered? Could I even trust Don Samson's recollection of events? I passed a fitful night. The saggy and lumpy bed reminded me of all the comforts I'd learned to take for granted since leaving prison. In my cottage I had an expensive mattress, a bedside lamp, heating I could control. Hot showers daily, baths. I could eat what I wanted, and not at 4 a.m., when the prison officers decided it was time for breakfast. I couldn't give it all up, not again. I had to keep going.

I woke at three, after a few hours spent dozing, then looked at my phone, bathing my tired face in white light, and found another email from Jochem.

> *Hello, Rachel. I thought you would like to know I have traced the IP address of someone who was googling you, the day before the story broke in the papers, and also googling 'how to sell a story to a newspaper'. It is the IP of Happy Paws Animal Shelter.*

I read his message several times to be sure I understood. Whoever had sold me out to the press worked at the shelter.

There was more, too. *Although you did not ask for this, I was also curious to know what happened to the infant, Carson Safran, after the death of his family.*

That was a kind way to put it, the death. Not 'after their brutal murders, which you were convicted of'. I scrolled on, suddenly breathless. I hadn't thought to ask him to find Carson. Perhaps because I was afraid to even think of him out there in the world, lost to me for ever.

> *The child was taken in by his aunt, Ruth Safran, and moved to Texas. However, he only stayed with her there for six years. I believe there was some kind of Family Services intervention.*

Wow. Had Ruth been judged unfit to care for Carson? I mean, I could have told them that, but I was still surprised. I wondered what she'd done to him, that cold-hearted woman, a little boy who'd lost his entire family. He would have needed rocking to sleep, and games and cuddles, all the things I could have done for him, if only I'd been allowed to keep him. But that was stupid. Even if I hadn't been convicted of the murders, they'd never have let him stay with his foreign teenage nanny. He'd have gone to Ruth no matter what.

I read on. *I have also found out that Carson went to live with the mother's side of the family – the relatives of Abigail.* Jochem's email then said: *Her mother had a younger sister, Abigail's aunt, who despite never having met her great-nephew was judged the nearest family relation. She was a teacher and very experienced with young children, and had never married herself. She went to Texas to pick up Carson thirteen years ago, and took him to live in London, in the borough of Wandsworth.*

I was stunned. Carson had been in *England* this whole time? I remembered now that Abby had an English mother. That's why they hired me in the first place, because of the British connection. She had been an actress in the sixties, quite big in the Ealing comedies; she went on to Hollywood but found the dream was rotten on the inside. She had died of skin cancer when Abby was in college, and Abby had talked about her a lot. There were framed pictures of her around the house, a wide-eyed innocent with cat's-eye liner and a blonde beehive. Beautiful, in a very different way to how Abby was beautiful.

I was astonished by this news. My little butterball, growing up so close? I might have walked past him in the street. The regret, the wasted years, seemed to land on me then and I gasped slightly. Then I had another thought. No one could want revenge on me more than Carson. After all, he had been told by the justice system, and no doubt by his poisonous aunt, that I had murdered his entire family. And he'd been here, in the UK, for years.

I read the final lines of Jochem's message, though my hands were shaking. *I believe that Carson's name was changed, to avoid the publicity of the case, as I cannot find any records for the name Carson Safran anywhere in the UK.*

Carson could be called anything now. I tried to remember had I ever heard Abby's maiden name; couldn't recall. I couldn't help thinking about the years I'd missed with him. I imagined him at six, moving to a new country, probably scared, traumatised by whatever Ruth had done to him. Then at ten, maybe playing football, running and laughing, skinny with excess energy, maybe even with an English accent now. Carson as a teenager, perhaps sullen and angry, but sweet underneath it, surely. He had been such a placid baby.

I couldn't keep everything straight in my head. I kept coming back to the one thing I knew for sure: someone at the shelter had sold my story to the press. I believed Marilyn when she said that she would never do such a thing. So someone else then. One of the interns? It had to be. I ran through them in my head. Katrin, who I'd caught trying to take a picture of me? Or one of the boys, Tom and Callum: the confident, tall one, or the shyer one who was so good with the dogs? Had one of them recognised me too, realised I was Casey Adams and sold my story to the press, outed me? Just for money? I wondered how old the boys were. Nineteen, twenty?

Carson's age. My heart stilled for a second. Carson was in England and he was the same age. It didn't seem possible. Could one of those boys – the boys I had walked past for weeks and barely looked at, those hulking boys so much younger than me – could one of them be Carson? The sweet baby I'd held in my arms, whose life I had saved? Had he come to find me? But that wasn't a good thing. Raised by his aunt, he probably thought I'd murdered his family, his parents and his sister. Why else had he come, if not for revenge? But which boy was Carson? Tom or Callum? I had to find out.

Getting out of bed, I got dressed in jeans and a jumper, put on tennis shoes and my coat. Gently, I eased the door of the flat open and looked up and down the corridor. No one. I went to the front door, with its depressing reinforced glass, and peered out to the street. There was no sign of anyone in a car watching me, but I knew they would be there somewhere. I went back inside, down the stairs to the basement of the building. Down there was a kind of laundry room, warm and smelling of damp and detergent. There was also a window, and I sucked my stomach in tight, grateful for the stress-induced weight loss of the last week, and squeezed through it, banging my knee on the frame. I landed awkwardly on top of a bin outside, getting a wet mark on my jeans. I closed the window most of the way, hoping no one would notice, and snuck down the alley between the houses. Out front, I could see the unmarked police car, the officer inside looking at his phone and eating a pasty. It was fine. I'd be in and out in an hour, tops. Then I cut through the town and down towards the shelter.

The night streets felt eerie, deserted. The odd light behind windows, people with warm homes to hunker down in. I no longer had a home. My cottage was surrounded by the press, rifled through by the police, and Brandy was gone from me, likely absorbed into Marilyn's barking pack. What was left for me here in Coldwater? Nothing. Once I had cleared my name, I would run away again, start over.

Within fifteen minutes, already soaked in a fine mist of rain, I was at Happy Paws. I still had my keys. Marilyn had not thought to ask for them – poor, trusting Marilyn. She had no idea what people are capable of when their back's against the wall.

Inside the shelter was dark, only faint lights from the dog pens and the hum of computers idling for the night. Hearing me, the dogs started up a chorus of barks and howls. Warning of an intruder. If only the Safrans had owned a dog, might everything be very different? Probably not.

I unlocked the door to their area, and went from pen to pen, calming them. 'Hush, hush now. Ruby, be quiet. Jack, it's me, you silly. It's Rachel.' Eventually they calmed, recognising my scent, and the only sound was the odd huff of breath or the scrabble of claws on concrete. I moved back into the office. Once, I'd felt at home here, the peeling advice posters on the wall, the clunky radiators and drips of coffee all over the little kitchen. Shabby, comfortable. I fired up the computer, pleased that my log-in still worked. Marilyn would never have thought to bar me from the system. I knew the intern applications were saved in a folder on the shared drive, so I quickly clicked in and searched for the right ones, to find out the boys' surnames.

Tom Bastion, that was the tall one. David Safran had been tall too, and dark-haired like this boy. Could he be Carson? His accent was posh, Home Counties. He didn't sound American, but Carson had come here as a child and likely didn't either now. I ran through his CV in the hope of finding clues. Born in Surrey, in May 2000. Carson had been born in February, but that could easily be a lie. Educated at some private school, where he was rugby captain. At university he also played rugby and cricket. Not how I'd imagined Carson turning out, but what did I know? Just because I'd cared for him as a baby, before he would even remember, that didn't mean I knew what kind of man he'd grow into.

I sat at the desk, trying to puzzle it out. I'd seen Tom watching me a few times, hovering by my desk, even angling his phone towards me, I thought. If he was Carson, he must have found out my fake identity in time to apply for the internship, tracking me down to this place where I was hidden away. But how? Had he chosen to study veterinary science to end up here? Was that too far-fetched?

I clicked on the other CV. There was less detail for Callum Stevenson. His first job at sixteen was working in a pet shop. So he'd always liked animals – Marilyn would have taken note of that when filling the internships. A-levels at a comprehensive, the glowing grades you need to become a vet. Some other work at university, positions on various student committees, part-time jobs. This kid had to work for a living, and yet he'd done well. Was *he* Carson, not Tom? The name stuck with me for some reason. Stevenson. It was common enough. Had I heard it before somewhere? Maybe I could look them both up on Facebook and—

I jumped as a noise reached my ears. In the next room, the dogs were stirring again. Whines, a few barks. Someone was coming.

One of the interns maybe, and they'd find me looking at their information.

'Hello?' I called cautiously. I got up from my chair. Footsteps at the front of the building, coming through the reception area. Had I locked the door behind me? No, I hadn't. Stupid.

My heart was in my throat as the footsteps came closer. I saw a dark shape through the frosted glass of the door. But it wasn't either boy. It was someone I'd never have expected to see here.

'Casey.'

They called me by my name. They knew me.

Casey

JUNE 2007

In prison I couldn't sleep because of the constant screaming and crying, the sheer racket of the place, and the constant terror, jolting awake in the night realising this was real, I was on Death Row. Now, released from prison two years ago, after the miracle of my appeal trial, and back safe and sound in the UK, I couldn't sleep because my husband was snoring.

Husband. I couldn't get used to that. When my trial had ended, and they'd said those unbelievable, astonishing words – *Ms Adams, you are free to go* – Jeremy had been the only one there, waiting for me. Apart from the Innocence Project lawyers, of course, who had been amazing and hugged me tight, but they had a load of other cases, all the thousands of other innocent people still in prison. But there was Jeremy, waiting among the scrum of reporters screaming my name, the protesters with their *Murderer* signs, Ruth Safran, who looked at me as if she wanted to kill me. For a second, the crowd had pushed me right up against her, and she spat at me – she actually spat, this mannered Southern woman. It landed on my face, slid down my cheek. I flinched. My arms weren't free to wipe it away. I was still being held by a guard, this time for my own protection, probably. Then there he was: kind, sweaty, bumbling Jeremy, who had wrought this miracle for me.

'You're free!' He seized me in a big, damp hug. 'Casey, you did it! You're out!'

I was struggling to breathe. I had hardly let myself believe this would happen, and yet I was free. My brain was trying to catch up. I wouldn't go back to my cell? What would happen to my things, the books I had collected, my toothbrush and hard-protected toiletries? I had worked for two weeks to buy that shampoo, a generic brand no better than Fairy Liquid. I hadn't said goodbye to the women, Paola and the rest, who were still stuck behind bars. I almost gasped as I thought of them, a kind of strange survivor's guilt.

'I can go?'

I had been escorted out of the courtroom, but already it was different. No handcuffs. I was wearing my sweaty court dress, the only non-skimpy outfit I had. The same one I'd worn for my nanny interview, ironically.

Jeremy had his arm around me, so I could smell his body.

'It's OK,' he said. 'You're overwhelmed. Come on, I have a hotel booked for us.'

And that was it. I walked out of the court, through the lobby, and into the fresh air. I was gasping, the vast expanse of the sky above and freedom all around me. Jeremy was there to whisk me away from the media scrum.

He never pushed things. We had one hotel room, because he wasn't well off, but it was a twin. I almost couldn't believe it when we got there and the door shut behind us. No guards, no cameras. Part of me wished, selfishly, I could be totally alone to take in the moment. He was busting with excitement.

'What do you want to do? We could go out for dinner, watch a film . . .'

I looked longingly at the bathroom door. 'I want a bath. I want to wash with no one watching me.'

He seemed slightly crestfallen. 'All right. And dinner after?'

'Honestly, I couldn't face it. The stares. Do they do room service?'

A slight pause. He had imagined taking me out, feting me. Glorying in his triumph, how he had saved my life. I found out later he had even bought me a dress, though in the wrong size, a tight bodycon thing I would perhaps have worn back in England, but not now. In fact, I would never wear revealing clothes again, after the way they'd been used against me.

I locked the bathroom door after me, feeling a bit ungrateful, and breathed a deep, shuddering sigh of relief. A lock on *this* side of the door. Alone on my own terms. I turned on the taps, marvelled at how the hot water gushed out. And no one was watching. I stripped off my sweaty dress and tights, right down to my prison undies, which I threw into the bin. I would buy some more – I could do that now, walk into a shop and get anything I needed.

I filled the bath with a whole tiny bottle of bubbles and sank in, letting out a moan as the warm water surrounded me. It was like getting my body back, when it had not been my own for so long. I ran a hand over my ribs, so pronounced, my skin so pale and saggy.

A knock on the door. 'Are you OK? I heard a noise.'

I rolled my eyes slightly. It would be the first of many times, though I didn't know that yet.

'I'm fine.'

I could hear Jeremy breathing outside, hovering. 'If you need anything, just say. What do you want to eat?'

I could have whatever I wanted. I thought back to what I had most missed. 'Pizza, please. Really hot and crispy.'

In my bath, I breathed in and out. I took further stock of my prison body, noting the dryness of my hands and feet, the weak give of my nails, undernourished. My hair was a frizzy, half-mousy-brown, half-blonde disaster. My eyebrows were a monobrow, and I hadn't shaved any part of my body in years – razors obviously were very much not allowed, in case we slashed our wrists. It was only for the state to kill us, when they so chose.

I began to shake under the water. I had come so close to death. I was alive, I was free. They had said in court I didn't do this thing – I didn't hold a pillow over Madison's face, or cut Abby's throat with a knife, or shoot David in the stomach. I was free, I had been ruled innocent. But I thought of those protesters outside the court, and I knew that, in the eyes of some people, I would always be guilty.

◆ ◆ ◆

The next day, Jeremy and I had flown back to Britain. Landing in a drizzly Heathrow, dry-mouthed and sleepless from the economy flight, my eyes had filled with tears. I was home. I would never set foot in America again, I swore. Indeed, it would be some years before I felt able to go abroad at all.

We took the Tube to London Bridge and then a train out to Kent, where Jeremy lived by the sea. Everything was overwhelming to me, even the pressure of the air on my skin, the wind and the cold of England after years in the desert. I had assumed that people would stare at me, but they didn't notice me at all. They were too busy going about their business, rushing to work. I was just a sallow-faced, tired young woman in a big hoody. I didn't even have any luggage, just some free toiletries I'd taken from the hotel and my dress in a plastic bag. I wondered what had happened to my things from the Safran house, my books and clothes. The prison had held on to my passport, so I was able to leave right away when they gave it back.

I was home. My ordeal was over. I'd had multiple requests for interviews already, offering large sums of money. Jenna had passed them on to me, and seemed disappointed when I said no, even to the offer of fifty grand. I had promised myself I would never talk about what had happened. I wanted to burrow away like a mole. I wanted to be no one now.

I was surprised there were no reporters at Heathrow – Jeremy told me, pleased with himself, that he'd changed our flights at the last minute, with the help of the airline, and I was grateful for that. The press would be waiting for a later flight, and I would already be gone. I was so pleased I reached out and took his hand, and saw his eyes soften.

Oh dear. I would have to face up to this sooner or later, his love for me. Perhaps I could love him too. After all, he was the one who had got me off Death Row. He was the only one who seemed to care. Jenna had not come to meet me at the airport, saying it would only create publicity, and nor had she invited me to her new home in Hove.

'They know where I live,' she'd said, when I rang her from the American hotel. 'Best to let it die down a bit.'

'And I can come and stay then?' I'd said into the hotel phone.

She hesitated. 'I'll talk to Steve. He just wants a quiet life, after the things he's seen.' Her husband Steve's experiences as a milkman had apparently been hair-raising, but I would never find out, since I would never meet him. Jenna would be dead within two years and I had no further contact with Steve after he didn't tell me when her funeral was. My own mother, buried without me.

Jeremy was snoring so loudly now, two years later. He slept on his back, mouth open, arms flung out, so I found myself cramped at the side of the bed. I nudged his head so it fell to the side, and he gave a gurgling sound, then went back to snoring. Sighing, I got out of bed.

I had been back in the UK for almost two years now, but I was still not used to freedom. I would shoot awake, heart racing, and it would take a while to remember I was not in prison, I had not missed the wake-up call. I was safe. But my brain did not understand this.

In my bare feet and the heavy pyjamas I slept in, to discourage touching, I went into the living room of Jeremy's little flat, overlooking the seafront in a dilapidated former resort. The screech of seagulls and crash of waves all night long. The orange of streetlights illuminated the living room/kitchen, which, thanks to me, was now tidy and clean, with cushions and lamps and candles. I'd never had my own space to decorate, and I'd gone a bit mad in Ikea, throwing things into the trolley while Jeremy smiled nervously. He was almost out of cash back then, I knew.

I should have got a job, but how could I go to an interview as Casey Adams? Racy Casey? A brief look on the internet after my release had filled me with horror – so many people thought I was guilty still. So many websites dissecting every detail of the murders, trying to prove it was me. I needed to change my name. And there was an easy way to do that, a free way in fact, unlike deed poll. Jeremy had awkwardly suggested the idea over my welcome-home dinner in a Frankie and Benny's, me still half dead with tiredness and shock.

'So – I mean, only if you want to, of course,' he said. 'I thought we could, maybe, if you like, get married.'

It took me a while to pick through all the clauses. I was drinking a cocktail, something sugary sweet, after no alcohol for years.

'You want to *marry* me?' I was genuinely shocked. I'd realised he had feelings for me, but we barely knew each other. Marriage, already?

He seized my hand, almost knocking over a bottle of ketchup.

'Of course! Casey, I love you – I always have. I'd do anything for you. And this way, you can start over. Change your surname, use your middle name maybe, and no one will know. You can go back to college, even, if you want.'

I wanted my own money. 'No. I need a job.' I would get some compensation for my wrongful incarceration, but it didn't come through for some time.

'Well, then – won't this be the easiest way? And I really do love you. I'll look after you.'

It was those four words that swung it. The idea of being looked after, by someone with no agenda (although he did have one, of course). I looked across the plastic tablecloth at his earnest brown eyes, his tender smile. OK, so I didn't fancy him, but maybe I could learn to. And did that really matter, when compared to feeling safe? And above all, the chance to be a different person?

I should have said no, learned to stand on my own two feet, left that faded town and gone far away. Instead, exhausted, frightened, still in shock, I said, 'OK. If you want to, Jer.'

Which was not the most romantic way to respond to a proposal. Two weeks later we were married in a registry office, me in a cheap white dress from Monsoon. Jenna had not come, saying she couldn't get away at such short notice. Jeremy's father was dead and his mother was in a nursing home with MS, so it was just us and two witnesses from the council building. As he slipped the cheap ring on to my finger, I couldn't help thinking of that moment back at the Safrans' house, when I had been handcuffed by the officers who answered my 911 call. *You're never getting out of this one.*

Now, in the pale light of morning, I rummaged in the bookcase, careful to be quiet, and took out a road map of the UK. I spread it wide on the dining table, with a noise like flapping wings. Where would I go? Anywhere but here, this poky seaside flat with rising damp and the sound of seagulls keening all night long, burrowing into my nightmares, so I imagined myself back in prison, the women wailing and crying.

Jeremy would agree, in his sad way, giving me everything I wanted, even an easy divorce. He must have known we weren't happy – we had only slept together a handful of times in the past two years, and for months I had paced the flat, round and round like a dog on a chain. The fact I didn't love him and didn't want him to touch me set against his love for me, his clumsy attempts to care. He couldn't cook or clean or look after himself, but he tried. He didn't seem to notice as I quietly shrank away inside, finding out that the life I'd fought so hard to get back did not after all have much left to it.

And now my mother was dead. I'd found out from Steve the day before. She was dead and already buried, since he 'didn't want a fuss'. I didn't get to say goodbye to my own mother or to forgive her for abandoning me in an American jail, or for pushing me out of the nest in the first place, telling me I could fly high, when in fact I couldn't. Not that she had ever asked for forgiveness, or even admitted she'd done wrong. The most she would ever say was it had been *very hard for me too, Case*, as if being locked up on Death Row was a minor inconvenience.

Her death had made me realise that my life with Jeremy, much as he loved me, was still a prison. Just with a more comfortable bed. The map lay before me, wide with possibilities. I focused on the green areas, the blue bodies of water, lakes and rivers and the sea. I would avoid the cities, where there was more chance of being recognised, and I would not leave Britain, since I still had a fear of foreign jails. Where then? Scotland – a bit cold, maybe. The south coast was expensive and too close to Jeremy. My hovering finger alighted on the Lake District, its curves of green and turquoise. I had been there on a school trip once. We'd smuggled vodka and boys into our youth-hostel room, and Lacey Chamberlain threw up in her kayak the next day. I remembered the Lake District as pretty, rugged, remote. Peaceful. All that water to absorb bad memories. I made up my mind, pleased to have a plan. I would go and visit Jenna's grave and leave flowers, careful to avoid my stepfather, and then I would travel north. Towards a new life, where hopefully nobody would ever stop me on the street and say, *Wait a minute, I know you.*

Rachel

I put my hands on the desk to steady myself and tried to keep my voice calm.

'Alex? What are you doing here?'

'I saw you were coming here.' He was looking about the room, restless. I noticed he was wearing all black, jeans and a jumper. So he wouldn't be spotted?

'You followed me?'

'If you want to put it that way.'

'Why?'

He sighed. In the low light of the office, I could see how tired he looked, as if he hadn't slept since Anna died. 'I've known for a few weeks who you were, you know. After Anna told me, I did a bit of investigating of my own, watched some of the old footage from the trial. And I knew you were her. You have the same mannerisms. The way you push your hair out of your face.'

To my horror, he touched a lock of my hair and smoothed it back. I leaned away, my back against the wall. There had been a time when I longed for him to touch me. Now every sense was screaming *no*!

Why was he here? Why had he followed me? My prison instincts had kicked in already. I was scanning the room for something to use as a weapon. A metal dog chain on Marilyn's desk, but it was thin and wouldn't be much use against a strong man like Alex. Over to the side was a fire extinguisher. Maybe. My body was tense, waiting to see what he would do. But this was Alex. I loved him, didn't I? Why was I so afraid?

'You did believe her, then. So that's what Anna meant. At the Co-op. About not wanting me around "him" – she meant Sam, not you.'

'She didn't want Racy Casey anywhere near her son, and who can blame her? That little girl you suffocated, she was Sam's age.'

I felt overwhelmed by it, all the years of hostility. Would no one ever believe me, so long after I'd been declared innocent and walked free?

'I didn't kill Madison,' I snapped. 'I cared for her.'

'So who did it then, Casey? I'll have to start calling you that, I guess. Who killed the Safrans if it wasn't you?' Alex moved in even closer. I couldn't see a way to get past him.

'I don't know! I've never known.'

'Come on, you can tell me. We get each other, don't we? Sometimes we do things that we don't mean to, but people don't understand. That doesn't mean we deserve to rot away in jail.'

I stared at him. 'Stacey Donner?'

He smiled – a smile that used to make me melt. Now I was terrified.

'Look, I was a kid. She led me on,' he said. 'All over me all night, then I walk her home and suddenly she changes her mind, and I'm supposed to just stop? I didn't mean to – it was an accident. She shouldn't have fought so hard, I wasn't planning to hurt her. Not at first.'

A small pulse was beating in my throat. 'So you did kill her.'

He shrugged. 'Accidentally. I was a teenager, for God's sake.'

'And Anna? You were with her that night. You did go to the house – you lied to me.'

A sigh. 'Sam spilled the beans, didn't he? Colette heard you. I told him not to mention it, but he doesn't understand, poor kid. Never thought you'd talk to him, to be honest. Unlucky, that.'

So that was why Alex had followed me here. He knew I was on to him. I was very aware of my heart, how it raced in my chest. 'Colette, she made up the alibi for you?'

He shrugged. 'Very keen to help me out, poor bereaved single dad that I am. Nice girl.' He rested his hands on my shoulders. My breath was coming fast, I tried to control it.

'You told the police I was at Anna's house the other day – you saw me?'

Again, a soft laugh. 'That really was dumb of you. Honestly, some of your behaviour – let's just say it's been a real gift to me.'

I flinched. The idea that he'd been watching all this time, seeing me stumble about, tangling myself further in his web.

He moved back, sat on my desk. 'So, you know my story. How about you tell me the truth about yours? Let's be honest with each other, Casey. At last.'

I felt nineteen again, terrified, lost. 'I didn't do it.'

He sighed. 'That's not true, though, is it? I read all about it. No one else went into the house or came out. Someone would have seen an intruder – or all the security cameras on that street, they would have captured it, right? And there was no back way in, it was too overgrown.' He'd looked into it, then. He knew all the arguments against me. 'So it was you or it was one of the parents,' he went on. 'And the police said neither of them could have killed themselves. So what was it, a suicide pact they just happened to act out in the ten minutes you stepped outside with the baby?' He was sneering at me now.

'I don't know. I don't *know*.' It was what I'd always said, for twenty years. That I did not know what had happened to David and Abby and Madison. That they'd been dead when I stepped back into the house that day, bewildered as anyone, walking into a nightmare I couldn't get out of. Innocent, hapless, unfortunate.

But that was a lie, and I felt it leave me as I realised I was finally going to admit it, the tension leaking out of my body. It was time to stop pretending. Because I did know what happened to them that day. I had always known.

Casey

OCTOBER 2000

The house was unbearable. So much tension I could hardly breathe. In the night I'd lain awake listening to David and Abby arguing downstairs. His voice a low rumble, hers manic. They were so loud Carson had woken up and I'd taken him into my bed, then we'd been joined by Madison, crying a little. Between the two of them, I'd been up for most of the night.

I gathered that David wasn't happy that Abby had gone for the audition at Sony. 'Give me a break, you're far too old for the part. You'll be lucky if you ever work again. And you're fat, Abby, way too fat for the screen.'

Too fat, that was the phrase he used, when she had starved herself away to nothing. Abby screamed back that he was useless, washed up, that she'd checked the bank accounts and knew all the money was gone, his company bankrupt. Was that true? So he'd lied to me – he wasn't making the YA film at all, as Abby had said?

'You'll never make a film ever again! You're a failure, David!'

A glass smashed and I wondered what would happen now. Would they get a divorce? I guessed David would move out and

Abby would need even more help with the kids. But could I stay here, if David was gone? Just me and Abby? We'd kill each other.

I gave up on sleep around six and got up with the baby. Madison had finally dropped off, so I carried her back to her own bed, glad of the peace. I arranged her pink pillow under her head, smoothed her golden hair over it. Poor little girl, none of this was her fault.

Downstairs was littered with broken glass. A chair had been pushed over. I tidied it all up while Carson sat in his high chair, playing with slices of kiwi fruit. There was no sign of either parent, though I could feel they were in the house, their leaden presence. I had no idea what to do, so I just kept on with my chores. Feed the baby, change him. Wipe the counters, throw away the broken things. I nicked my finger on a shard of glass and held it to my mouth, filled with the metallic taste of my own blood. I must have left some on the cupboard door, where it was later found. But they read it wrong, came up with the wrong story.

As the clock inched to eight I knew I should wake Madison for school, but she'd hardly slept at all, so I called them and told them she was sick. That recording would later be played in court, seen as further proof of my guilt. I waited. Now, when I think of those few hours of morning calm, my stomach churning with unease, I would give everything to go back, to wake Madison, take Carson from his chair, pile them both into the car and drive far, far away, not stop until they were safe. But I didn't.

Abby came downstairs around half ten. She looked terrible, her face stretched and swollen with crying, hair ratty and greasy. I felt bad about that for a long time after, how she would have hated being brought in dead like that, having her picture taken with dirty hair and no make-up, no false nails or eyelashes.

'I suppose you heard all that last night?' she said to me.

I was standing with a dishcloth in my hand. 'Um . . . the kids were up, yeah.'

'He wants a divorce. Well, he's not getting one. Unless he wants to give me everything.'

I said nothing. Her eyes landed on me, dark and sharp.

'You know, it gets put in the court documents, Casey. The co-respondent, they call it. The person he cheated with. Means I get it all. House, kids, the lot.'

I couldn't think what to say. It wasn't true – no one would believe her, would they? I was keeping very still, as if a predator was in the room with me. I had to get the kids out of there, and I was thinking of ways to take them on a day trip or something, just take them away. Then the terrace door slammed and David appeared. He had slept out by the pool, clearly, clothes rumpled and breath sour.

'Don't talk to her,' he said to Abby, his tone poisonous.

'Why not? She's a part of this, isn't she? I'll be telling the court as much.'

'You stupid bitch. What court would give you anything? You're crazy.'

Very slowly, trying not to get between them, I inched across the kitchen towards Carson. He knew something was up from the raised voices, his eyes moving between his parents. I lifted him out, feeling his warm, solid body, and laid his head against me. His little heart was racing. I would keep him safe.

'I'm going to take him for a walk,' I said quietly.

Both their heads swung round, but they barely noticed me. I should have gone up and woken Madison, taken her too. But I thought, stupidly, that this morning might be the last chance she got to sleep thinking she had two happy parents. Before her life changed for ever. That decision led to her death.

I slipped my feet into my old dirty flip-flops, put on Carson's sun hat and opened the door, rushing to get away. I might have left the front door open, I don't know. Or maybe someone got that far, almost escaped, but didn't make it. Maybe Madison woke up and opened it, then later was taken to her bed by force, smothered there, fully aware of what was happening to her. I'll never know for sure.

I stepped out into the sunlit street, almost staggering under the heat of the day, Carson heavy against my hip – too late to go back for his buggy, or stroller, as I should have learned to say – and walked down the street with him. It was 10.43 a.m.

Rachel

OK, think, think Casey. Same thing I had told myself that day in the Safrans' house. *If you don't think fast, you're going to die.*

Alex was on his feet now, pacing around the shelter's office, sometimes stopping to pick up random things and put them down, the dog lead I had eyed earlier, Marilyn's stapler with her name on it in Tippex, a dog-shaped donation box.

'I just don't know why you didn't tell me right away,' he said. 'I said to Anna, you're crazy, there's no way that's her, she'd have told me if she'd been to prison. But then I saw it was true after all. I could have told you my story too, then, if you'd just been honest. I thought we had a thing, you know?'

I pressed down on my hands to stop them trembling.

'We did,' I said. 'We do. I just – how could I tell you that? I thought you'd run a mile.'

'You think I don't understand about being judged? Wild Alex Devine, the kid who got into all that trouble? Come on.'

'I'm sorry. I should have trusted you.' I made my voice soothing, as if I was talking to one of the dogs. 'Tell me what happened. I know you took Sam to Anna's that night. I know you weren't at yours the whole time, like you said. You went there about what, half four?'

He swung around, his face full of contempt.

'Well, look at Nancy Drew here. I did go to hers, yes. Mine, really, though she seemed to think she could keep the farmhouse, along with Sam and all my money. A last-minute job came up, so I had to leave him there. It would just have been a few hours, but she was so bloody unreasonable. She was having her toy boy round to fuck her, I guess, and I scuppered her plans. After all the fuss she made about me seeing you! Bloody hypocrite. When I got back, I'd have taken Sam to mine and left her in peace, but no, she couldn't let it go. Wanted to have it out, there and then. She wanted to use you to swing her divorce case.'

'Me?'

'If I'm dating a murderer, how can she trust her precious son around me? So she gets full custody of Sam *and* she keeps the house, my family home! It was too much, Casey!'

Spittle flew from his lips and I wondered how this could possibly be the same man I'd fallen so in love with, weak at the knees from his touch.

'So you and Anna, what, you had a fight?'

He ran his hands through his hair. 'She was off her head. Threatening to expose you if I didn't agree to her terms. I got so mad. Trying to clean me out! Take away my son! My house! Why are all women like that?'

It was as if I'd always known. 'You killed her.'

'She did it to herself!' he snapped. 'Shouting and throwing things. Took me ages to clean it all up. Sam woke up, but I sent him back to bed, told him it was just a dream. I just – saw red. Grabbed her and . . . I let go – she fell over. Hit her head on the fireplace.'

That explained Anna's head wound. 'She was still alive then?'

'She was breathing, but . . . she wasn't conscious. I couldn't risk it – not with my record. I'd have lost everything. I just – finished it.'

319

I nodded, trying to stay calm. 'You used a different knife, though? Not mine, it wasn't her blood.'

He jerked away, as if he didn't want to face the truth. 'I just – I panicked, all right. I had to keep her quiet.'

'And then you decided to frame me.'

He didn't answer.

'How did you get my scarf?'

He almost smiled. 'I knew where your key was, remember. From when I did the tree.'

'And my knife – that was later?'

'You were getting a bit close, I had to do something to put the police back on to you.'

I tried to digest this. Not Jeremy at all. Alex had done this, left the scarf and then the knife to incriminate me. 'So what – you took Anna to the woods, dumped her there? You knew I'd take Brandy that way in the morning.'

It was clever, I suppose. He'd thought of everything.

He was impatient. 'Look, it doesn't matter, all these details. I just had to do something. Can't you see? You were the obvious suspect. Because you're Casey Adams. You're a murderer. A convicted murderer living right here in Coldwater.'

'I'm an exoneree!' I snapped, in exasperation. 'I didn't do it.' But that didn't matter. Because as long as an obvious murderer was right there, perhaps the police wouldn't look too closely at the estranged husband, who'd maybe killed a girl before, the most likely suspect if I hadn't been there, shiny and distracting with my dark past.

Alex laughed. He actually laughed. 'You're really not going to tell me the truth? OK then.'

I stared at him. I was still absorbing the idea he had killed his wife and framed me for it. 'So you just . . . you sacrificed me.'

'I'd have gone to prison otherwise. What about Sam? I had to think of him.' Amazing. He somehow expected me to understand. I felt the rage crystallise inside, like a flaming coal in my chest. I thought of Rhonda's wise words, passed on to me in the months before her execution, which I refused to believe would happen but she knew would. *Fight. To your last drop of blood.*

In the pen holder on my desk was a pair of scissors we used to open packs of dog food. They were large and sharp. My eyes rested on them, until they were all I could see.

I heard my voice coming from outside myself.

'Well, Alex. You really had it all worked out, didn't you?'

'I tried. You do understand? I had no choice.'

Did he really think I'd forgive him? His body was sagging now, with relief. The crazy thing was, I did understand in a way. Because I too had done something terrible on the spur of the moment and had to think fast to cover it up. I too had created a cover story that looked plausible. But that didn't mean I forgave him. After all, I had never forgiven myself.

I waited till his eyes flicked away for a second, then grabbed for the scissors, holding them close. I walked the few steps to Alex. I put my hand on his arm first, and he must have thought I was going to hug him, kiss him even, forgive him for what he'd done, because for a second I saw relief bloom in his eyes. Then it faded into shock as he clawed at the scissors sticking out of his neck, right over the carotid artery.

Casey

OCTOBER 2000

'Shhh, Carson. Shh, baby.'

It was too hot for him. I was always forgetting you couldn't be outside in Los Angeles so much of the time. The heat, the pollution, made people stay inside, living as if underground. The porches were decorated with gaping pumpkins and spider webs, surreal in the blazing sun. The street was entirely deserted, not a car, not a child playing football, not a person tending their garden. That was all done by low-paid Latino gardeners. Not even they were out in the sun today. It was just me and the baby against my chest, warm and heavy. I had my phone in the pocket of my shorts, but who could I call for help? I had tried everyone I could think of, and no one had come through for me. There was nothing else to do. I would have to take the baby home and face what was going on there.

And then what? How much did Abby know? How David and I had started taking Carson places, just the three of us? I liked to pretend we were a family sometimes, but it wasn't what I wanted, not really. How he stood so close to me in the kitchen, brushed his body against mine. How he held my gaze, searching my eyes for some promise I'd never made. And I knew it, too, but I had ignored it, because I was so lonely, and the comfort of his gaze and the hungry look in his eyes when I bent over were all I had to keep me company. Because he told me all the time that he couldn't live without me, and though I knew from Jenna's lessons that men never meant this, part of me still fantasised about running away with him and Carson, buying a beach cottage up the coast. A new life, where I didn't have to be Casey the nanny or even Casey the aspiring actress. Where I could just be myself.

I shouldn't have gone out. It was too hot to go for a walk, even just a short way down the street, even before noon. I was already exhausted, the heat almost crushing me into the pavement – sidewalk – sending me off balance. Carson was lethargic too, grizzling in my arms, his skin warm. At least I'd thought to bring his hat, but I'd forgotten one for myself.

'All right,' I sighed, hefting him on my hip. 'Time to go home.'

I walked back up the street, the five or six houses I'd passed on my walk out. There was nobody around, no cars on the road. A ghost street. I went up the front drive of the Safrans' house, past the burglar alarm sign and the stiff green lawn that had once been tended by José, but was now growing straggly.

When I noticed the front door was slightly ajar, a thrill of fear hit my stomach. Had I left the door open? Abby would kill me.

I hurried forward to push open the door, Carson under my other arm. Later, the police would find my fingerprints on the door, which meant nothing, of course – I lived there. Everyone else's fingerprints, too: Abby's and David's, even some small smudged ones of Madison's.

Inside the house was blessedly cool. I looked around me, checking frantically to see if we'd been burgled. Nothing seemed stolen. The TV was there on the side as usual.

'Hello?'

I remember how my voice echoed in the marble hallway. I walked the few steps into the kitchen. Did I know something was wrong? Did hairs lift on my neck, some ancient instinct telling me to run now, get out? I don't know. I was still holding the baby when my foot nudged against something on the floor.

Then I saw it: a bare foot, a leg, a body on the kitchen floor. It was Abby, her hair over her face. I thought at first she had collapsed, fainted – not surprising if you starve yourself all the time. I stooped, Carson on my hip.

'Abby?'

She was lying in a red pool, spreading out over the tiles, and my first thought was, *She's going to go mad about the mess*. Then I realised she was dead. A large knife beside her. Her eyes looked wide and shocked, her hands held up as if she had fought someone, her nails broken. I couldn't take it in for a long moment, like a scene in a horror film. She was dead. Murdered. Abby was dead and I had stepped in her blood; it was all over my flip-flops.

Get the gun. The little voice in my head, quiet and calm, told me exactly what to do. I could picture it so clearly, in David's drawer, where I'd seen it before. The drawer was supposed to be locked, but maybe I could find the key. I ran out of the kitchen, kicking off my flip-flops, which sounded like gunfire on the tiles. I could see splashes of blood on my bare feet. Carson made a noise against my chest. I wondered if he knew he'd just seen his dead mother, if that would haunt him for ever. I wouldn't put him down, although he was heavy.

Holding my breath, I crept towards David's office. The door was not locked and I went in. So much mess and dust, a terrible smell of rotting food and cigarettes – why had I ever thought he was successful? The bottom drawer was unlocked too. I suppose he had given up on a lot of things by then. I took out the gun. It was heavy, black with no shine. I had no idea how to use it.

'Casey?'

A voice behind me.

It was David in the doorway. Blood all over his T-shirt. He looked tired, so tired.

'Casey. You're back.'

Rachel

'You stabbed me! You—'

Alex's voice was lost in a gurgle of blood, and very soon he fell to his knees, then on to his back.

'This is your own fault, Alex,' I said, bending over him. His blood was sharp in my nose. It had all come back to me, Rhonda's advice. So many women were murdered in prison. She had always believed I would get out, if I could only stay alive long enough. *When you're in a tight corner, just find something sharp and swing it fast. Hit them in the right place, they're never getting up again.* I had done it. Adrenaline raced through my veins, and in that moment I could have lifted the desk over my head. My rational brain was gone in a kind of vengeance lust. Alex was going to die choking on his own blood, as he had killed Anna. He'd got what he deserved.

But he was stronger than I knew. He was pulling himself up on the leg of the chair, knocking things off the desk, a cascade of crashing and falling office equipment. The dogs were barking now, snarling at the noise, the smell of blood.

'You bitch!' he burbled.

He was coming for me. I did the only thing I could think of. I ran. Out past the dark dog pens, hearing them yelp and throw themselves against the bars, a clanging noise that was just like the day they killed Rhonda, and then I fumbled with the back door lock and I was out into the night, a chorus of howls behind me.

Casey

OCTOBER 2000

I tried to sound calm, but I was shaking so much I could barely hold the gun. With my other hand I clutched Carson tight.

'Abby,' I said, 'she . . .'

A little vomit surged into my mouth and I had to swallow it down. It burned my throat. I should have called the police first. Why had I looked for David's gun? I would wonder that often, over the years I had to sit in prison. My first instinct had been to defend myself. The fact that the gun was unlocked and loaded, that was just blind fate. A compression of circumstances that led to me, standing opposite David, with a gun in one hand and his baby clasped tight with the other.

He looked so tired. As if he hadn't slept in days. I could smell the sourness of him.

'Casey, it's all right. I've taken care of it.'

'But she . . .'

'She would have stopped us, you know? Taken the house, all the money . . . it's better this way, Casey. We can start again, you and me. Just us.'

The way he said it sent chills down my spine. I could hear no other sounds in the house. No one living.

'Madison?' I said.

His face twisted. 'I – it's kinder for her. She won't feel anything now. She wasn't right, you know that. Abby had warped her. The bruises, the burns – what kind of mother does that to her child? Both of them, totally ruined. It's sad, but they're at peace now.'

I tried to move past him to get to her – maybe she was still alive, maybe it was a lie or I could reach her in time – but he blocked my way.

'There's no point,' he said, his voice flat. 'She's gone.'

'No . . . !'

'She's *gone*, Casey. She's in bed. She didn't suffer.'

I was terrified then. David had killed Abby and Madison. And I knew who was next.

'Come on,' he said, holding out his hands for Carson. 'Give him to me. It's better this way.'

Carson looked at his father and started to cry, dribbling down my top. I stood frozen. This couldn't be happening. My brain was a blank.

'Casey.' His voice hardened. 'Give me the baby. He's not even yours, what do you care? Let's put it all behind us. We'll go up the coast, just drive, we'll be happy. You can have a baby of your own.'

He was close enough now to reach out and stroke the sweaty hair back from my neck. I flinched. This couldn't be real. I could talk him round. I tried to reason with him.

'David, he's just a little baby. I love Carson! We can take him with us, it'll be fine.'

I just had to play along until I could get help. If Madison was dead, I had to at least save this little boy, his hands twining in my hair, fingers in his mouth. His satin skin and warm little head. I would do anything to save Carson. I would not let him die.

329

What would David have done to the baby? I wondered that later, in my darkest moments. The knife, like Abby, or a supposedly kinder death, the pillow? Or just his hands, his strong man's hands, crushing the little neck? No. I wouldn't let it happen.

'You can't have him,' I said, and I was surprised that my voice didn't shake. When you have something to protect, your own fear evaporates. I would literally die for this baby. I knew that.

David's face shifted, some tiny muscles adjusting, that was all, but I saw what was going on behind his eyes and I let out a yelp of fear, I couldn't help it.

'Why are you making it so hard! You stupid girl.'

That's when I ran. I dodged past him, baby and gun and all, and I ran into the hallway, slipping on the marble floors, my feet wet with Abby's blood. Hence the footprints the police found, but at the time I wasn't thinking about anything except the front door, that narrow portal to the outside world and to safety. Would anyone even have seen me? Would someone have come to help? I don't know, because I didn't make it that far.

Rachel

For the second time in my life, I was running from a man I was terrified of. First David, now Alex. I'd slammed the scissors into the wrong spot in his neck. Rhonda had been wiser than me.

Oh, help me, please, Rhonda!

I ran out the back door of the shelter, hearing Alex curse and slip behind me. The night air was fresh and cool. The moon glinted off the lake. I ran towards it. I don't know why – I wasn't even much of a swimmer, and the water was deep and cold. But what we do in such moments rarely makes sense. When someone is trying to kill you, you just run.

Soon I was at the stony lake shore, the cold water lapping at my jeans and soaking my shoes. Alex wasn't far behind, lumbering towards me. In the moonlight I could see his neck was a welter of blood, one hand clutched to it.

'You stupid bitch,' he panted. 'You're nothing. Everyone thinks you're guilty – and when they find you dead, they'll know for sure.'

I stepped back, and suddenly the lake shelved and I lost my footing. I was in the water, the fierce cold penetrating through to my skin in an instant. I gasped. Water filled my mouth, choking me.

Alex was splashing nearby, and then I felt his strong hands on my head, pushing me under the water. I fought to the surface again, only to hear his voice spewing bile, the same voice that had once spoken to me with such tenderness.

'You bitch! You murdering bitch! You're not getting out of this one!'

And then he pushed me down, harder this time, and I couldn't get any footing, the water was too deep, and I saw how it would look. I would drown here and they would find Alex with my scissors in his neck, my fingerprints all over them, and the story would write itself. Casey Adams was a killer. She had always been a killer. She had lured Alex Devine to the dog shelter and tried to murder him, as she'd murdered his wife, as she'd murdered that family, the poor little girl. She got away with it once, but justice caught up with her in the end. She drowned herself out of guilt.

Alex would get away with murder for the second time.

The lights of the town shone through the black water. I was under it. Over, gasping for air. Under again. Alex's hands pressed me down, his blood dripping into the water. My lungs bursting. *Just give up*, said a voice in my head. *You've fought so hard, but it wasn't enough in the end.*

Images flashed through me. Carson, his sweet baby laugh as I tickled him. Madison, spinning and spinning in her pink dress. Abby, coming downstairs with her hair piled up. David's tired face in the morning. Jenna, lighting a fag in her leopard-print coat. Jeremy, who'd only ever tried to love me. Rhonda, her head held high as they took her to her death. Brandy, leaping up to greet me. I had fought so hard for my life that day in Los Angeles, only to lose it to the state, regain it by some miracle, and now here I was again. I would die not in a lethal injection chamber, or shot or strangled or stabbed by David as I fought to save the baby, but here in this freezing black water. I sank down. Everything went black.

Then I was on the lake shore, gasping and choking out water, frozen to the bone. Air. It filled my lungs. Blinking the water out of my eyes, I saw Alex's body stretched out nearby. There was blood on his head, a rock beside him. I could see his staring eyes by the light of the moon. He was dead. I rolled over on to my back and saw a figure standing over me.

It was a teenager. Not Tom, but the other one, Callum. The boy whose CV I had been looking at when Alex arrived. He was breathing hard, wiping a hand over his face. He was soaked to the skin.

'Casey,' he said. 'It's all right, you're safe now.'

'Callum?' I said, and then I saw it in his eyes, the colour of agate framed in dark lashes. The eyes never change. My baby. 'Is it – Carson?'

'Hello, Casey,' he said.

And then it came to me. Callum's surname, Stevenson – that was the same as Abby's family name. The great-aunt he had gone to live with. Callum Stevenson was Carson Safran.

He prodded Alex with the tip of his Converse. The body – that's what it was now – shifted like a rag doll. He was dead. Alex no longer existed. I had done this. Killed a man for the second time in my life. Once, to save a baby. This time, to save myself. But I had not struck the final blow.

The boy looked at me, eyes wide with shock. 'He's dead.'

I started to hyperventilate. 'I'll go to prison. Life. This is it for me. You have to run, Carson, I'll say I did it. Maybe it'll be self-defence, he tried to drown me after all, and . . .'

His voice shook, but he said, 'No. I'm not leaving you. I'm here to help you.'

I stared at him. I didn't understand what was going on. 'But – why?'

'I remember you a bit, you know? Deep down somewhere. You protected me that day?'

I nodded.

'I've wanted to know for so long. Tell me what really happened. Please? It was my dad, right? He killed Mum and Madison?'

I sat up, with difficulty, still coughing out water. 'How did you – how did you know?'

He bent down to me. 'When Aunt Ruth died, she had all these boxes of evidence about the case. I don't know how she got hold of it, a private detective I think, but it was all there. Dad's weird behaviour beforehand, the strength it would take to . . . do that to Madison. You couldn't have done it. His DNA in Mum's nails and on the pillow. I saw the photos, you were only tiny.' *So were you*, I thought, *and look at you now*. 'I never thought you'd done it,' he said. 'When I think about you, somehow I just always felt . . . safe. Loved. Is that crazy?'

I was trembling. Carson didn't think I was a murderer. He believed me.

'How did you find me?' I said.

He shrugged. 'I looked online, asked people. You can find any-one if you pay enough.'

'The poster – BB2000 – that was you?' Of course. The year he had been born and . . . 'Butterball? You – remembered that?' He couldn't have.

'Aunt Ruth used to talk about you a lot, say how awful you were. She said what you called me, as if I was your own baby, but . . . it always sounded nice to me. When she died, all the evidence came to me, and I wanted to see you, and ask you what really happened that day. I just needed to know. When I started working at the shelter, I kept trying to find the right moment. But it never came, and then there was all this.' And now here I was, another dead man at my feet. 'You didn't do it, right? You were innocent?'

I sucked in a breath. I was tired of it, making up stories, alibis that no one believed, because the truth was too raw and bloody. This time I would say what really happened, and if I went back to prison I would just give up. Let myself die. Perhaps it would be a relief. I looked at his lovely face in the faint light, now grown up but his skin still smooth, his eyes the same. My baby.

'That's not entirely true,' I said, the truth rushing out of me like a collapsing balloon. 'But I did it for you, Carson. To save you.'

Casey

OCTOBER 2000

David caught me as I reached for the handle of the front door. His strong hands pulled me back. I shook him off, slick with sweat and blood, and still holding Carson and the gun I ran for the first door I could find, the walk-in cupboard in the hall. Inside was musty, the shelves stacked with tennis racquets and abandoned shoes. But there was no lock. I pushed myself against the door, bracing my whole body against it.

Carson was whimpering now, and I shushed him, mad with fear. I was weak. I was nineteen, five foot three. I had no strength. David was scrabbling at the door and I had my bare, bloodied foot against the wall, and now it slipped and he had the door open. He stood facing me and I raised the gun at him.

'No. Give me the gun. Give me the gun, Casey!'

I was facing him, my back to the cupboard. I could feel my sweat trickling down. Carson was on my hip still, and my arm ached from holding him. I held the gun in the other hand, pointing it at David, who backed away a few steps. How my hand shook. I had no idea how to fire a gun or if the safety was on or anything.

'What are you going to do with that?' he said. 'Come on, Casey, this is stupid. We can be together. I know you want that. I know you love—'

I shot him.

I'd like to think it was just to save the baby, to save myself, but part of it was because he thought I loved him. This pathetic man, who'd murdered his family, and he still thought I wanted to run away with him.

I had never fired a gun before and wasn't expecting the kickback, which spun me around and made Carson wail. David staggered back, blood spraying from his stomach. He fell on to the marble floor of the hallway, hitting his head with a crack.

You don't shoot yourself in the stomach if you want to die. No one would have believed that for a second. When he went down, a look of extreme surprise crossed his face, and he pulled himself a few inches across the floor, leaving a horrible trail of blood. Then suddenly the look on his face snuffed out.

The house was so quiet. Not a car outside, and not a bird singing. Only me and my panicked breathing, and the baby clinging to me. Carson had stopped crying in shock at the sound of the gunshot.

There were many things I could have done. Called the police and told them the truth, hoped they would believe me – perhaps there was some evidence to show that David had done this, that I had just been defending myself and the baby. Or I could have run, taken the car keys from the hall table and fled. Carson and I could have lived our lives somewhere quiet by the sea, and he would have been mine for ever. But that was crazy. That was kidnapping, on top of everything else.

Instead, I backed away, into the cupboard. I dropped the gun beside David, not even thinking to wipe my prints off it. My phone was in my pocket still, a heavy weight.

There was a spot of blood on the baby's head, so I rubbed it off and kissed him. His sweet baby smell. Very soon he would be taken from me and I would never see him again. But I didn't know any of that then. I didn't know I'd be sent to prison, sentenced to death. I didn't know that my life had completely and irrevocably changed. I just knew that I was alive and I had saved the baby. Holding Carson close against me, his every breath proof I had done the right thing, I dialled a number from my phone. It rang a few times, then was answered. 'Mum,' I said, gulping down terror and shock. 'Mum, it's me. Something terrible's happened.'

Rachel

When I'd finished telling Carson the truth about what went on that day, his face was stiff and pale.

'He wanted to kill me too? Dad?'

'It's how they – normally do it. These men.'

There was even a term for it, family destruction. Usually it was a murder-suicide, often triggered by a catastrophic work failure, but in this case David's crazed brain had told him I was the answer, the teenage nanny. That we could start a new life together. Maybe I was to blame for that, maybe I'd led him on, in my loneliness. Maybe that's why I never said what had really happened. Or maybe I was just too afraid to admit my own guilt, throw myself on the mercy of a foreign justice system.

'When I got back, they were already dead – your mum and Madison. I couldn't let him take you too.'

'You shot him. For me.'

'I – had to. And look at you!' I was crying. I was smiling too. He was alive, he was grown up, he was here. 'I'd do it again, Carson. If I had to.'

He shook himself, as if realising the situation anew. The two of us on the cold lake shore, soaking wet, a dead man at our feet. 'Come on. We'd better deal with this before someone comes.'

I looked again at Alex's body. He had murdered Stacey Donner and Anna, and he would have murdered me. Despite everything, I knew I had done what I had to and could not regret it, not really.

Carson was looking around. 'Are there cameras in the shelter?'

'Um, just at the front, not out here.' Dog thieves were a real risk in the area.

'Good. So we just need to weigh him down.'

Between us, we somehow worked it out, though we were both shaking with shock and cold. We filled Alex's jeans pockets with rocks. I piled them under his T-shirt too, on top of the chest where I'd once loved to rest my head. I tried not to think about it, the way his blank eyes reflected the moonlight, the wind whipping his lifeless hair. I just did the job. We dragged his body further out into the lake, and let him drift into the darkness. For a moment I was afraid he wouldn't go under, then his clothes filled up with water and he sank, slowly, out of sight. This lake was deep and dark. He might never be found.

We splashed back to the lake shore, puffing and panting, soaked through. We were both smeared in blood. There was even a faint trail of it back up to the shelter.

'Look,' I said. 'It's no use. There's too much evidence.'

But Carson never faltered. 'They won't suspect me. It's all about how it looks, Casey. Alex must have been a suspect too – they always look at the husband. So they'll think he was guilty, that he disappeared. We just need to clean up this blood. Bleach, that hides blood, I think. There's lots on the forums about it.'

Carson, with all his time surfing true-crime forums, had learned a lot of useful things. He thought of everything, while I stumbled behind, my brain soggy with shock. This is why it's so hard to cover up a murder. Most people are so shaken by what they've done, the act of taking a life, that they can't think straight.

They make mistakes. And I would have too, if not for Carson. I had saved him all those years ago, and now he saved me.

He wiped the last hour off the shelter CCTV, apparently quite easy to do if you knew how. He said he'd drive Alex's car to near Manchester airport and leave it there – he'd even thought to take the keys and phone from Alex's pocket before we sank him.

'They can track the phone,' he explained. 'I'll leave that in the car too.'

'They'll know,' I said. 'They'll see this was the last place he came.'

'Well, that makes sense – he might have been looking for you. To shut you up.'

'He was,' I said, a wave of shock hitting me again. 'He was going to kill me.'

'There you are then.' He squeezed my hand, and his was wet from the cloth he'd been wringing out, to remove any prints Alex might have left on the door coming in. 'We just have to get through the night, Casey, that's all. Just one night.'

Casey

October 2000

'You stupid cow,' said Jenna, down the phone. I flinched. Had she understood what I'd said?

'Mum, he was going to kill us. Me and the baby!'

'You didn't have to bloody go and shoot him, did you? What's going to happen now? You're in America – you'll go down for life!'

'But – it's self-defence!' I was shaking, struggling to hold the baby. He was grizzling and squirming against me. 'Isn't that a thing?'

'You really want to risk it? Don't they have the death penalty there?'

'Do they?' I had no idea. 'Mum, what do I do? Please help me!'

Jenna let out a long sigh. 'Don't tell them anything. You came home, they were all dead. They can't prove someone else didn't do it. Some stranger. It's America – there's all kind of loonies there.'

'But – are you sure I shouldn't just tell them the truth?'

'Don't be an idiot. You led him on, didn't you? Flashing your legs at him, batting your eyelashes. You think they won't blame you for that?'

She was right. Carson suddenly felt very heavy against me. 'So – just say I came back?'

'Right. Now you better get off this phone. And get rid of it – they can check to see what calls you made. Get rid of it now and ring the police. You've left it too long already, that's gonna look dead suspicious.'

I wondered afterwards why I had listened to Jenna, who had after all failed to steer me right in the rest of my life choices. But she was my mother, and I was little more than a child, and I had just killed a man. I would have done whatever I was told, in that moment. Still holding the baby, I ran out into the back yard, the grass prickling against my bare feet, and threw my mobile phone deep into the canyon behind the house. After a few seconds, I heard a faint crack. I was lucky the police had never found it – though, really, what was lucky about ending up on Death Row?

Then I went back inside and, stepping over David's body, part of me terrified he would rear up and grab my ankle, horror-movie style, I picked up the cordless landline. I called the police from the hall cupboard, and I didn't need to fake the shake in my voice.

'They're d-dead. The family I work for. I just came back and – I think they're dead.'

This same recording would be played over and over in court, on true-crime podcasts, on documentaries. Looking for evidence. Any tell-tale sign that I was a liar, a murderer.

The truth is, there are no signs, not always. Sometimes you can make yourself believe the lie, and I think I did, once I closed the cupboard door behind me. It was about ten minutes before the police arrived, entering the house, calling my name.

'In here!' I shouted, muffled. I stood up, smoothed my hair down with my free hand. Carson had looked around at the sound of the voices. He would need a change and feed soon. I'd used those ten minutes of waiting to prepare, as if for an audition. Jenna's lessons at last coming in handy. How I'd open the door. How I would cry, and maybe collapse into their arms. *Oh thank God.* The words I would say. *I took the baby for a walk and when I came back they were dead.* I had not seen Madison dead, something I'd always be thankful for, so I would say I didn't know where she was, that I would have searched but I was scared, so scared, and I'd seen David and Abby dead, and heard a noise and been so frightened I went into the cupboard. *The baby, Officer. I had to protect the baby.*

A rap on the door, a loud man's voice.

'Ma'am? It's the police. You're safe now.'

I let my breath out, and, on jelly legs, opened the door. A square of light, a uniformed man in shadow. Like stepping from the darkness of the wings on to a stage.

'Thank God,' I said. 'Oh, thank you, God. Carson, look, we're OK, we're OK, baby.'

'Can you tell us what happened?' said another officer, a woman. I felt her eyes on me. She was withholding judgement. She knew that how things looked were not always how they were, and she would later testify in court that my statements seemed rehearsed.

'I came home,' I said, the first time of many that I would speak those words. 'I came home and they were dead.'

Rachel – two days later

'So we've decided to drop the case against you. There's evidence that implicates Alex Devine and, well – the CPS don't think they can prosecute.' DS Hegarty squared off some papers, nudging them against the same old chipped table in Coldwater station.

I sat in the interview room, very quiet and still. This time I'd remembered to bring a cardigan against the chill of the place. There was no sign of Margaret Hope – she must have been furious I had, as she'd put it, got away with it yet again. I had made a formal complaint about her behaviour in the Barrow station, and I got the impression the police were trying to be as nice to me as possible now.

'So Alex did it – are you sure?'

'We had him on our radar at the start – he and Anna weren't getting on, and he stood to lose his family home in a divorce. Plus he has some history of violence. But he had an alibi, then the evidence against you . . .' He trailed off, sheepish.

'So he tried to frame me? You really think that?'

'It looks that way. We found he'd viewed a documentary online about your . . . case, and might have identified you from that. So when he killed her you probably seemed the perfect scapegoat.'

'But I didn't do it.'

He smiled. 'We believe you now, Rachel. You're free to go.'

The most beautiful words in the English language. The same words the judge had spoken to me all those years ago, when I walked from an American court. But I hadn't really been free, had I? Fear is a prison of its own. And back home I had been too afraid to tell anyone I was Casey Adams. Perhaps if I had, none of this would have happened in the first place. I stood up, scraping back the plastic chair. 'Thank you.' He had always been kind to me, even when I must have looked like a cold-blooded killer. That meant a lot.

'We'll let you know if he turns up, of course. There's no sign he's left the country, but of course he could have got a fake passport, or gone to Ireland on the ferry.'

He wouldn't turn up. Carson had covered our tracks so carefully, and it was unlikely the police would think to look around the shelter or dredge the lake. They would find Alex's car soon surely, and his phone, and hopefully conclude he had fled the country. Perhaps this time it would have been better to tell the truth about what I'd done, but I'd been too burned by the system before. Another lie to add to the one I'd been sitting on for years. And I couldn't, I just couldn't, be associated with another murder.

It was Carson, of course, who had brought the Disneyland photo over from America, hoping to make contact with me, explain who he was when the moment was right. He'd taken it in to work, left it in the drawer of his desk, where Tom had found it, snooping, and put two and two together. It was Tom and Katrin who had sold my story to the press, along with photos they'd taken of me on their phones. Katrin had tearfully confided this to me the day before, when I went into the shelter to clear out my desk, her mascara smeared prettily under her huge eyes.

'I'm, like, so sorry, Rachel – we just needed the money, you know for college, and Tom talked me into it. I didn't even want to.'

346

So that explained the photo. Carson said he hadn't spelt out Casey with my fridge letters, though, so that must have been Alex, trying to scare me into telling the police who I really was, which would make them suspect me more. Letting himself in with the key I'd so carelessly left out. I would never be stupid like that again, never allow myself to relax. Jeremy had also been in touch many times, begging for my forgiveness, but I thought I might let him go. I'd realised it was cruel, to keep him so close, giving him hope when really there was none. This time I had to start over without any crutches.

I wanted to say something to DS Hegarty before I went. I had already given up the lease on my cottage – in a few days' time, me and Brandy would be living somewhere else. I'd said goodbye to Marilyn, who had been tearfully apologetic for her role in what unfolded. I didn't blame her, but I knew our friendship was over now, like so much. Where I was going, I didn't know yet. Maybe Scotland. There seemed to be a lot of space up there, places to disappear and start over. At least I would never be too hot. The rain would fall on my face from the open sky and I would be thankful. And Carson – Callum – he would visit. I wouldn't lose him again, the baby I'd saved. He was an orphan, his great-aunt also dead, and I had no child of my own. Maybe it could work.

'DS Hegarty?' I said as I stood up. 'I just want to say – no hard feelings. I know you were only doing your job. And my past – the murders, the same way Abby and Anna were killed – well, I know how it looks. Anyone would have had the same suspicions.'

'It doesn't have to define you,' he said. He held out his hand – strong and warm – and I shook it. 'Take care, Rachel.'

'Thanks.' I didn't tell him it wouldn't be Rachel any more. When I moved on to my new life, I would take back the name Jenna had given me. Jenna, whose acting lessons had either saved

347

me from the execution chamber or perhaps sent me there in the first place. It didn't matter now.

I went out of the police station, pausing to appreciate it, the simple act of being able to open the door and step out into the fresh, rain-scented air.

Freedom. It was everything.

BOOK CLUB QUESTIONS

1. Rachel has changed her name by getting married and using her middle name, but as she points out it's not illegal to do this – would you find this suspicious all the same?

2. Rachel feels a lot of guilt for what happened to the Safrans – how much do you think she was to blame, if at all? Was she right to do what she did to protect Carson?

3. Casey is given the death penalty for murders she didn't commit. What are your views on capital punishment? Were you surprised that California has the death penalty?

4. Is Rachel wrong to trust Alex so easily, knowing so little about him?

5. How far would you go to hide your worst secret?

6. Rachel is terrified to go online because so many people on the internet still think she's guilty – what do you think about this aspect of the internet, that nothing is ever forgotten?

7. Casey is judged for her clothes and her behaviour around the time of the murders – can you think of real-life cases where this has happened?

8. Why do you think people are so fascinated by unsolved murders?

9. What should Casey have done when she came home and discovered the murders?
10. Both Alex and Rachel hide the truth of their pasts from each other – should you always be upfront with someone you're dating? What 'red flags' does Alex display that she misses?
11. At what point should Casey have realised something was very wrong in the Safran home, and sought outside help for the family?
12. Do you blame other characters for their actions as well as those who commit murder – Jeremy, Jenna, or Tom and Katrin, for example?

ACKNOWLEDGMENTS

Thank you to everyone at Amazon for the absolutely amazing job they do, and to Jack Butler, Ian Pindar, and Jenni Davis for the edit. Thank you to Graham Bartlett and Consulting Cops for help with UK and US police procedure. Thanks to Diana Beaumont and everyone at Marjacq for continued awesomeness. Thanks to Jochem Groeneveld for bidding to have his name included in aid of CLIC Sargent – I should say that, as far as I know, the fictional namesake is nothing like the real Jochem, who I have never met! And finally thanks to all my readers. I'd love to hear from you on Facebook at @ClaireMcGowanAuthor, or on Twitter at @inkstainsclaire, or Instagram at @evawoodsakaclairemcgowan.

ABOUT THE AUTHOR

Photo © 2021 Donna Ford

Claire McGowan was born in 1981 in a small Irish village where the most exciting thing that ever happened was some cows getting loose on the road. She is the author of *The Fall, What You Did, The Other Wife, The Push* and the acclaimed Paula Maguire crime series. She also writes women's fiction under the name Eva Woods.